Jill Mansell worked for many years at the Burden Neurological Hospital, Bristol, and now writes full time. Her novels PERFECT TIMING, MIXED DOUBLES, HEAD OVER HEELS, MIRANDA'S BIG MISTAKE, GOOD AT GAMES, MILLIE'S FLING, STAYING AT DAISY'S, NADIA KNOWS BEST, FAST FRIENDS, SOLO, KISS and SHEER MISCHIEF are also available from Headline.

Open House

Jill Mansell

headline

First published in 1995
by Bantam Books, a division of Transworld Publishers Ltd

This edition published in 2003
by HEADLINE BOOK PUBLISHING

10 9 8 7 6 5 4 3 2 1

ISBN 0 7472 6743 X

Typeset in Times by Avon DataSet Ltd,
Bidford-on-Avon, Warwickshire

Printed and bound in Great Britain by
Mackays of Chatham plc, Chatham, Kent

HEADLINE BOOK PUBLISHING
A division of Hodder Headline
338 Euston Road
London NW1 3BH

www.headline.co.uk
www.hodderheadline.com

For Lydia and Cino
with my love

Chapter 1

It might be Easter, but it certainly wasn't springlike. Marcus Kilburton, home from boarding-school for what was laughingly known as the spring break, lit a cigarette in order to practise his smoke-rings, tapped his foot in time with the Mini's windscreen wipers and broodily surveyed the miserable landscape as rain swept in waves across Kilburton Park. The lake was the colour of charcoal, the walls of the castle beyond it darker still. Even the deer, huddling together for shelter beneath the wind-blown chestnut trees, looked depressed.

Hell, he'd only been back a day and a half and already his father wasn't speaking to him. Other people, no doubt, would automatically envy him, assuming that because he was the heir to an earldom he had a brilliant life, no worries and everything a sixteen-year-old could ever want.

Hmm, thought Marcus, narrowing his eyes against the Marlboro's smoke and focusing on a figure approaching from a distance. Whoever it was, was going to get seriously wet. The trouble with being automatically envied as the boy who had everything was the fact that people conveniently forgot the flipside of all it entailed. There was nothing they liked better, furthermore, than hearing about the failings of so-called privileged families like his and gossiping about them.

1

Which was why he had been forced to tackle his father this morning, in an attempt to make him realize what a prat he was currently making of himself.

It was what had provoked this morning's huge argument and got the holiday off to such a thrilling start. Having to tell the ninth Earl of Kilburton that his supposedly discreet affair was, in fact, both common knowledge and the subject of much scornful derision, hadn't gone down at all well.

The lone figure battling through the rain was only a couple of hundred yards away now, and he was able to see who it was. Marcus's eyes narrowed further still as recognition slowly dawned. Just what he needed, he thought with bitter amusement. Yet another bloody O'Driscoll.

He'd never spoken so much as a single word to any of them, of course, but he knew *of* them only too well. Everyone did. The O'Driscolls were notorious, as talked-about in their own way as the Kilburtons themselves, and as common as they were colourful.

He even knew this one's name, simply because it was so outlandish. Petronella, he mouthed silently, his lip curling with disdain at the ludicrous, gypsyish sound of it. Petronella O'Driscoll, supposedly the smart one of the family. If she was that smart, thought Marcus, why wasn't she wearing a coat?

He hadn't formulated any particular plan as he put the Mini into gear and began to drive along the single-track road towards her. When it was raining this hard, it would be only natural – as a rule – to stop and offer a lift to the person on foot.

When the person on foot was an O'Driscoll, however, the overwhelming temptation was to push her into the lake.

Close enough now to see her properly, Marcus observed that she looked as if she'd just crawled out of the lake anyway. The black, waist-length hair was plastered to her head as if it had been painted on. Dark eyes deliberately ignored him. Her cheeks, bright red with cold, matched the thin scarf around her neck. Every single item of clothing she wore – from the navy school blazer and cheap-looking white shirt to the short, grey, box-pleated skirt and navy tights – was absolutely sodden.

Marcus had been driving slowly, still undecided whether or not to stop. The next moment, however, the girl's dark gaze had locked with his and the corners of her mouth lifted in a smile.

No, not a smile; a smirk. A condescending smirk at that. It was, he realized, a sly acknowledgement of the link between their two families, coupled with the merest hint of triumph.

Infuriated, he crashed his foot down on the accelerator. She was walking on the right-hand side of the road, skirting a large and muddy puddle. If he swerved just a fraction to the left, he would avoid it.

But why the bloody hell should he? The park was privately owned after all, Marcus reminded himself. She was trespassing, using it as a short cut home. Sod it, how *dare* she smirk at him like that?

He'd had to listen to Crispin Petersen-Vane in the sixth-form common-room drawling, 'I say, Kilburton, what's all this

I hear about your old man boffing some gyppo? The word is, he has to cross more than her palm with silver before she'll let him near her. Do tell, does he also have to wear one of her pegs on his nose when he's—?'

He had punched Petersen-Vane across the room. It had only helped a bit. Sending a great splattering wave of icy, muddy water over Petronella O'Driscoll, on the other hand, was much more satisfying.

The rock, flung with force and deadly accuracy, ricocheted off the boot of the Mini less than two seconds later. It sounded like a rock, anyway. Cursing, scarcely able to believe the nerve of the girl, Marcus slammed on the brakes and screeched to a diagonal halt.

'You threw that stone at my car,' he hissed, his face taut with rage as he pointed to the offending object which now lay on the narrow road between them. 'What the *hell* do you think you're playing at?'

To his even greater fury, as he leapt out of the car to inspect the damage he landed in another puddle. The girl, no longer smirking, still managed to look amused. At close quarters he was able to see the way the rain had spiked her eyelashes into clumps.

'Repaying a favour?' Nell, unafraid and not bothering to disguise the note of mockery in her voice, in turn studied Marcus Kilburton. Blond hair, flopping over his forehead in time-honoured Clark Gable fashion. Perfect profile. Very green eyes, straight dark eyebrows, and the kind of tan you didn't get in Grimsby. Nice body, thought Nell dispassionately; shame about the attitude.

It cheered her immensely to see how wet he was getting. Great droplets of rain, seeping into his ancient jeans, turned them a darker shade of blue-grey to match the sky.

'Look what you've done to my car,' he snapped, jabbing an accusing index finger at the boot. Disappointingly, the stone hadn't been as large as it had sounded, and there was no gaping hole to show for it, but at least the racing-green paintwork had been scratched. Only a small scratch, but still . . .

'Oh dear me,' mocked Nell. 'What is it, a complete write-off?'

Bloody bitch. In retaliation, Marcus gazed pointedly at the ladder in the left leg of her opaque navy-blue tights, and at the cheap shoes she wore.

'Why, do you seriously think you could afford to pay for it if it was?' He bent to run his fingers over the damaged paintwork, determined she wasn't going to get away with this. 'You'll receive a repair bill, you know.'

'Will I?' Apparently unconcerned, she shrugged. 'I won't pay it.'

'You caused the damage.'

'You deliberately drove your car at me.' The longer he stayed out of the car arguing, the wetter he got. Nell, hands on hips, took her time. 'You asked for it. I understand why you don't like me but it's still pretty ill-mannered, trying to run someone over just because you don't happen to approve of what their mother gets up to with your father. You should be careful,' she added, shaking her wet hair away from her face and slowly running a pink tongue over her upper lip. It was an oddly insolent gesture. 'Think how embarrassed you'd be if they decided to get married. You wouldn't be quite so superior then, would you? You couldn't, really. We'd be related.'

This time it was Marcus's turn to smirk. If this deluded girl seriously imagined such a scenario was even slightly on the cards, she was even more stupid than he'd first thought.

'Oh dear, I hate to be the one to dash your hopes,' he drawled, 'but there are certain facts of life you should understand. My father, you see, is a member of the aristocracy. To be precise, he's the ninth Earl of Kilburton. Kilburton Castle is our home. This is all ours . . .' His brief gesture encompassed the five hundred or so acres of visible parkland. The girl, her eyes never leaving his face, said nothing.

'People like us simply do not marry people like you,' Marcus concluded, shaking his head slightly for added emphasis and silently congratulating himself on having put it so well. He'd never made a deliberately snobbish remark in his life before now, but she'd goaded him beyond endurance. For a first attempt, he felt, it wasn't at all bad.

'Maybe,' the girl replied quietly, 'because people like us have more sense.'

It had been an undignified exchange, Marcus realized later, and pretty much out of character for him. What had he got out of it, anyway, apart from a soaking and the uncomfortable sensation that he might just have come off worse?

Ah, but he did have something else. Driving back through the park later in the afternoon when the rain had eased, he had spotted the raspberry-red scarf lying limply at the side of the road close to the main gates. Without even knowing why he was doing it he had stopped the car and picked up the scarf, which upon closer inspection was even more Bohemian than he'd first imagined. Made from panne velvet, silk fringed and tattered at the edges, it had been painstakingly hand-embroidered with deeper red beads and stars in what Marcus assumed to be typical gypsyish fashion.

He had no idea what prompted him to keep the thing. His conscience might have been pricking him but it didn't bother him that much. He certainly had no intention of delivering the scarf to the O'Driscolls' house, for God's sake. They lived in the High Street. He was damned if he'd give the residents of Kilburton the thrill of seeing him knock at the door of his father's frightful mistress. Now that *would* give them something to snigger about.

In the end, Marcus did nothing. Having shoved the scarf into the back of the Mini's glove compartment he put it equally firmly out of his mind and a fortnight later returned to boarding-school, leaving the car garaged in one of the converted stables behind the castle. One of the biggest pains about being sixteen – apart from having to put up with a hopeless, gambling-fixated father and a deeply tedious ten-year-old sister – was being limited to driving on private land. Roll on the summer when he hit seventeen, he thought impatiently. Then he'd really have some fun. Kilburton, with its sneering, smart-ass locals, wouldn't see him for dust.

If Marcus Kilburton had put the brief, stinging encounter with the uppity O'Driscoll girl almost entirely out of his mind, Nell O'Driscoll had not. Much to her irritation, as she walked through the park each day to catch the school bus, she found herself reliving their meeting. She didn't even know why – there were far more entertaining things to think about, after all – but every day it happened again, with such endless script revisions that the end result bore practically no relation at all to the original event.

Realizing that she was fantasizing, and furious with herself for being so idiotic, Nell took herself in hand and changed her route. No longer taking the short cut through the park meant adding three-quarters of a mile to the walk between home and the bus stop but at least she still had her dignity, she decided. Happily, as soon as she put the ruse into practice, the fantasies stopped.

Chapter 2

'I don't know why you bother with all that stuff.' Trish O'Driscoll, four years older than Nell, couldn't see the point of it. At nineteen, she had everything she'd ever wanted: dead-goodlooking boyfriend, nice little job behind the bar at the Hen and Chicken, baby on the way . . . and she'd managed it all without the help of boring old exams. Why Nell wanted to spend a heavenly afternoon in the garden hunched over the kind of textbooks you needed 'A' levels even to understand the titles was beyond Trish. All that stuff was *so* bad for your eyes. If Nell didn't watch out, she'd have to start wearing glasses. And then who'd bother to look at her twice?

'Just making sure I don't end up like my sisters.' Nell, unperturbed, prodded one of the books with her Biro. 'You should try reading occasionally. There's even a chapter in here on contraception.'

'Who needs it?' Trish wriggled comfortably on the rug, reaching for her tumbler of Coke. 'I'm going to have dozens of kids.'

'And I'm going to have dozens of GCSEs, though how I manage to get any work done around here is a bloody miracle,' grumbled Nell. 'Do you have to have that radio on *all* the time?'

'Yawn, yawn.' Trish, who had heard it all before, finished

off the Coke and adjusted the straining straps of her pink-and-white bikini top. Bosomy since the age of eleven, she was now overflowing the cups in truly spectacular fashion. 'Wait till me and Ricky get our own place. You'll miss me when I'm gone.'

'I won't miss that God-awful music.' Nell, flipping shut the book she'd been studying, rolled on to her side and chucked a crumpled-up sheet of A4 at her sister's stomach.

'Ouch!' lied Trish, cradling the sunburned bump and hurling the ball of paper back. 'I'll tell Mum.'

'Can't. She went out half an hour ago.' Nell ripped open a packet of peanuts which would have made ideal ammunition. Too greedy to waste them, however, she tipped the corner of the bag up against her mouth. 'Guess where.'

Since it had by this time been going on for years, Trish didn't even bother to reply. It only continued to entertain the villagers to such a degree because they didn't have anything else decent to gossip about. One of them, anonymously of course, had even submitted a message of mock congratulation to the announcements section of the *Cotswold Gazette*: To Miriam and James, five years and still going strong. Whoever said it wouldn't last?

Nell had come to the conclusion that the world was divided into two halves, those who wanted to be liked and those who didn't give a toss. Hetty Brewster, for whom she regularly babysat, had been compelled to say in flustered tones, 'What a sneaky, rotten thing to do . . . your *poor* family . . . how awful for them . . .'

Nell's mother, on the other hand, had thought it the funniest thing ever, shaking with laughter upon reading the announcement and gleefully embarking on a campaign of counter-gossip. The Earl of Kilburton, she hinted in the local shop, was boiling with rage and threatening to evict whichever traitorous coward had placed the ad.

Miriam O'Driscoll, the object of behind-the-hand whispering for the past forty-five years, positively revelled in the attention.

'They need someone to brighten their mundane little lives, bless 'em,' she declared, her dark eyes reflecting good-natured contempt for the villagers' small minds and passion for gossip. 'Can you imagine anything more depressing than always being the one doing the gossiping rather than being gossiped about? Good heavens, it isn't even as if I'm doing anything so terribly wrong. The colourless old bags are just jealous, that's all,' she concluded with a broad, careless smile, 'mad with envy because he chose me.'

Miriam's four children needed no further encouragement. As far as they were concerned, their devil-may-care mother was without fault. And since the simple fact that they were her children meant they were already thoroughly accustomed to being whispered about, it didn't bother them in the least.

They were individuals and they could do as they pleased.

In the case of Trish and Lottie, the two eldest daughters, doing as they pleased chiefly entailed getting a terrific name for themselves and producing babies out of wedlock at a rate of knots. Derry, the only boy, still only ten years old and already with the looks of an angel, seldom bothered to go to school and was widely suspected of having been the brains behind last year's great gnome escape, when poor Elsie Cutler's gnomes spent the entire summer decamping, turning up in other people's gardens, up their trees or on their roofs.

Fifteen-year-old Petronella, in contrast with the rest of them, at least attended school and appeared uninterested in the opposite sex. With her exotic looks and family background, however, it was generally acknowledged that it could only be a matter of time. Never mind the flashing smile and undoubted intelligence, they murmured. What about the quick temper, those eccentric clothes she sometimes wore, and that ferocious, unswerving loyalty to her mother? She was an O'Driscoll, wasn't she? They were half-gypsy, after all. It stood to reason, then. Getting into trouble was in the blood.

Trish, who was supposed to be reading Miriam Stoppard's *Pregnancy and Birth Book*, lent to her by an ever-hopeful health visitor, struggled through a couple of paragraphs about the second stage of labour before casting the battered paperback to one side and giving herself up to Radio 1 and mindless sunbathing instead. Anything she needed to know, she thought, she could learn from Lottie. Her big sister might be a bit of a dead loss when it came to hanging on to boyfriends but she was brilliant at having kids. Three already and still only twenty-two. What Lottie didn't know about gas, air and regular contraptions wasn't worth knowing.

'D'you know what I'd really love?' she said hopefully, above the blare of the radio. 'A chocolate milkshake.'

Nell carried on reading. 'Me too.'

'Oh go on, be an angel.' Trish heaved herself on to her side and looked plaintive. 'It's my big craving. And nobody makes milkshakes better than you do. Pleeease . . . ?'

Nell, who had been about to go inside and get herself a cold drink anyway, seized the opportunity. 'Only if you promise to turn off the radio.'

Trish pouted. 'How long for?'

'An hour.'

'Will you do me a sandwich too?'

'An hour and a half.'

Trish, tired of listening to music, grinned and said, 'Deal.'

When her eyes had adjusted to being indoors after the brightness of the sunlight outside, Nell studied her reflection in the mirror over the mantelpiece. Definitely browner, she saw with satisfaction, pulling aside the shoulder straps of her black bikini to double check. It made a nice start to the weekend.

The blue-and-white kitchen was blissfully cool. Humming to herself, leaning her hot legs against the fridge door as she set to work, she whisked vanilla ice-cream and chocolate sauce together in a glass jug. Trish, still only six months pregnant, had already exceeded her weight allowance for the whole nine months. Her love affair with chocolate milkshakes, however, continued to flourish. Nell chucked in plenty of ice-cubes in an attempt to dilute the mixture and save her sister a few unnecessary calories, then smiled to herself as she recalled Trish's hazy explanation of labour. The baby was unable to get out, she had solemnly informed Nell, until you were fully diluted.

The kitchen windows looked out on to the High Street, which was deserted. Everyone was enjoying the sun in their back gardens. Nell, cutting bread for the sandwiches, heard the sound of a lone car racing up the street and glanced up as it shot past.

All that really registered at first were the colours, dark green and a streak of red. When she had finished slicing the bread, curiosity rather than suspicion sent her across to the window.

Having screeched to a noisy halt outside the village shop, the driver had already leapt out of the car and disappeared inside. That it was Marcus Kilburton's Mini wouldn't have bothered Nell. Home from school for the weekend and seventeen at last, he was undoubtedly showing off the fact that forty-eight hours after his birthday he had passed his driving test. Tearing like a maniac along narrow country lanes, terrifying the wildlife, Nell thought with some scorn, was something all seventeen-year-old boys seemed to have to do in order to feel macho.

The streak of red, on the other hand, bothered her enormously. Nell had spent days searching for that scarf. Now, seeing it tied to the car's aerial like a trophy, she felt her fingers curl around the handle of the bread knife with almost murderous intent.

The bastard . . . how *could* he do such a thing? she thought wildly. It was as if he were openly taunting her. And what was worse – whether it had even occurred to him or not – was the fact that since it was such an instantly recognizable scarf, everyone in the village who saw it fluttering from his aerial was automatically going to leap to the wrong conclusions. Like mother like daughter, they'd crow with malicious delight. Well what else can you expect when it's in the blood?

Nell was out of the house and halfway down the dusty, deserted street before she even realized what she was doing. The pavement burnt the soles of her bare feet. The bread knife was still clutched tightly in her fist. She was also decidedly underdressed.

Nell, who wouldn't have cared if she'd been stark naked, wasted no time. Since she was never going to wear it again, she used the bread knife to slice the scarf in two, freeing it from the aerial in one go. The temptation to carve up a couple of tyres while she was about it was almost overwhelming. Taking a deep breath and exerting ferocious self-control, she turned instead and walked away.

Back at the cottage, however, and still buzzing with adrenalin, she knew she couldn't leave it at that. Simply removing her scarf hadn't been enough, not nearly enough. If she didn't do something more satisfyingly constructive she was likely to explode.

Minnie Hardwick, who ran the village shop, was a widow rumoured to have chattered her poor husband to death. Any customer even attempting to say they were in a hurry was immediately treated to one of Minnie's endless 'Now don't you talk to me about 'urry, why only the other mornin' I said to my son no wonder 'is ulcer's playin' 'im up when all 'e does is tire 'isself out rushin' 'ere, there and everywhere' diatribes.

Guessing that she had another minute at least before Marcus Kilburton could make good his escape, Nell gazed around for inspiration and found it on top of the fridge.

There was still no one else in sight. Covering the hundred or so yards quickly, she encountered no twitching curtains along the way. All the Mini's windows were open in an attempt to circulate the air. Choosing the rear window on the driver's side, she tweaked the carton's cardboard spout, took careful aim and tipped three-quarters of a pint of full-cream milk on to the dark-green carpeting behind the front seat. It sank in within seconds. In this stifling heat, it would start going off almost straight away. By nightfall, Nell thought happily, the terrible stench would be enough to make even strong men retch.

Feeling tons better, she sauntered back along the street swinging the empty carton between index finger and thumb. Now that she had used up the last of the milk – albeit in a thoroughly deserving cause – she would have to visit the shop herself before it closed. It amused Nell no end to think that Minnie Hardwick, pink-cheeked with pride, would undoubtedly boast about having had Marcus Kilburton in there. She could almost hear it now: '. . . what a charmin' boy 'e is, such lovely manners and *so* 'andsome . . .'

'How on earth long does it take to put together a sandwich?' Trish, shuffling into the kitchen, stared in dismay at the unbuttered slices of bread. 'You haven't even started,' she grumbled. 'What are you staring at, anyway?'

'Oh hell,' groaned Nell. Unable to resist peering through the window, she now wished she hadn't. Because the stocky, dark-haired boy climbing into the dark-green Mini definitely wasn't Marcus Kilburton.

* * *

16

Three weeks later, on the last day of term, she found him waiting for her as she stepped off the bus.

Marcus, having broken up for the summer holidays several days earlier, had parked in a gateway at the side of the road. His gold-blond hair glittered in the afternoon sunlight and his tan was deeper than ever. He wore very dark glasses, a loose, white cricket shirt and old, pale Levi's. Leaning casually against the gate, lighting a Marlboro in order to look extra-cool, he drew gasps of admiration from the other girls on the bus. The blackness of the sunglasses might make it impossible to tell in which direction he was looking but Nell didn't need to see his eyes. She knew anyway, with a sinking certainty, that he was waiting for her.

'Cor!' sighed Sharon Meldrew, emboldened by the fact that he was twenty feet away and she was safely ensconced on the bus. 'He can light my fags any time he likes. Coo-ee, gorgeous . . . over here! Go on, give us a smile.'

Maria Sharpe, sitting next to her, shoved her bony elbow into Sharon's spare tyre. 'Shuddup, he's talking to Nell O'Driscoll. D'you suppose he's her boyfriend?'

The bus driver, less enthralled by the idea than Nell's classmates, pulled away from the kerb, leaving Sharon and Maria craning their necks over the back seat.

'She doesn't have boyfriends.' Slumping back down, Sharon peeled the wrapper off a half-melted Mars bar. It was a source of some irritation to her that all the boys in their year lusted after Nell rather than herself, yet all Nell did was ignore them. 'Lanky cow,' she added in dismissive tones. 'I've heard her mother only does it for money.'

'I'd do it for money, if it was with that lad back there.' Maria, deeply envious of Nell, was still peering out of the window. 'Oh sod it,' she admitted finally. 'I'd do it for free.'

'. . . you see, something like that's OK when one's learning to drive.' Marcus's mouth twitched as he fought to contain his smile. 'But as soon as I'd passed my test I went for something with a bit more go in it. And sold the Mini to one of the stable lads,' he added unnecessarily. 'You'd probably have got away with it if you hadn't taken the scarf, you know. As soon as he mentioned it had gone I realized it had to be you. And as for the milk, poor Robbie . . . he still hasn't been able to get rid of the smell.'

He was loving every minute, Nell thought. As if she hadn't felt stupid enough at the time. Why the bloody hell had it not even seemed to occur to him that he was the reason she had done it in the first place?

'What are you saying, that it's OK for people like you to steal other people's property, but not OK for people like us to take it back?' Her dark eyes flashed with anger. 'It was my scarf.'

Marcus had the grace to look momentarily shame-faced. 'I know. I had meant to return it, as a matter of fact. When Robbie found it in the back of the glove compartment he didn't realize it was yours.'

'And that makes it all right?' Nell, beginning to despair, snapped. 'I tell you what, why don't I break into your house, rip one of those fifteenth-century Flemish tapestries off the wall, take it home and hide it in the back of my wardrobe? How do you suppose the police will react when I tell them I'd meant to return it?'

Irritated by her vicious mimicry, waving away a fat, lazy bumblebee, Marcus removed his dark glasses. 'Hardly the same thing,' he drawled. 'It was only a tatty scarf, after all.'

'My grandmother gave me that scarf.' Nell took a deep, shuddering breath. Her eyes glistened with tears. 'Just before she died.'

'Oh God.' This time genuinely appalled, Marcus said, 'I really am sorry. I didn't know.'

'Of course you didn't know.' Nell wiped her eyes and looked resigned. 'You didn't ask.'

'At least you got it back.' He half-smiled. 'If I hadn't found it, you might never have seen it again.'

The fact that she had bought the scarf for twenty pence in the school jumble sale was neither here nor there. Astounded by the sheer nerve of the boy, Nell said, 'Oh please! If you're expecting me to say thank you . . .'

Having come to gloat over her *faux pas* with the Mini, Marcus felt dangerously close to being out-manoeuvred. Yet again. What was it about this girl, he thought with rising annoyance, that made her think she was so superior to him? Anyone else would have been impressed by his new car, yet Petronella O'Driscoll hadn't so much as glanced at it. He'd have bet money she'd never even sat in a BMW before now.

'I don't expect you to say anything,' he replied, jangling his keys and moving towards the car. Dark blue, lovingly polished and a dream to drive, it was his pride and joy. The urge to show off overcame his irritation. 'Come on, I'll give you a lift home.'

'No thanks. I'd rather walk.'

So much for largesse. Enraged, Marcus demanded, 'Why?'

'Don't you remember?' Nell hoisted the bulging, end-of-term haversack containing far too many textbooks on to her shoulder. 'People like us shouldn't accept lifts from people like you. If we did,' she added sweetly, 'we might start getting ideas above our lowly station. And that would never do.'

Chapter 3

Curiously, Nell found herself able to recall almost every word of that tetchy, bickering roadside exchange. The details had stayed with her, even though she had neither seen nor spoken to Marcus Kilburton since that day.

Was it ten or eleven years ago? Putting her foot down as she left the Oxford traffic behind her and hit the dual carriageway at last, Nell idly figured it out. She'd been fifteen, now she was twenty-six. Marcus Kilburton had been seventeen then, so he must be twenty-eight. Goodness, what a lot had happened in eleven years. How things had changed.

And here I am, she thought with a grin, driving a BMW for my sins. Who knew what devious, subconscious workings of the mind had drawn her towards that particular make of car? If she drove up to the castle tomorrow morning, would he be reminded of his own dark-blue BMW, and of her refusal to accept a lift in it? Or had their brief, insignificant meetings faded entirely from his mind?

As she overtook a battered white Escort driven by a beautiful boy in his early twenties, Nell caught his eye and smiled. It would be interesting, she thought, to find out whether or not Marcus remembered her as clearly as she remembered him. And if he did, whether he would admit to remembering . . .

* * *

'Bloody young whippersnapper,' Miriam declared, scowling at the piece in the local paper and prodding the relevant photograph with her unlit cigarette. 'I'd go and see him myself and give him a piece of my mind, so I would—'

'Don't we know it.' Nell, who was still trying to read the article, gave her mother a dry smile. 'And wouldn't that go down wonderfully? Mrs Diplomatic O'Driscoll tearing round there and shaking the life out of him. I'm just glad you had the sense to phone and let me know what was going on.'

'Yes, well. You're so much better at making sense than I am.' Miriam, never one to back down from a skirmish, could nevertheless appreciate the fact that on this occasion her youngest daughter was undoubtedly the best man for the job. A fight might be fun, but not when there was this much at risk. Being booted out of The Pink House, her home for the past twenty-five years, wouldn't be fun at all.

'And if you do ever happen to bump into him,' Nell went on, 'it might be best not to call him a bloody young whippersnapper. He's the Earl of Kilburton now, Mum. He might not like it.'

'Hmm.' Shooting her daughter a dark look, Miriam fiddled with her many silver bracelets. 'Depends what he has to say tomorrow. If it's the wrong thing,' she added in warning tones, 'I'll say whatever I bloody well like. Better still, I'll knock the bugger's teeth out.'

Hetty Brewster, not having had the happiest of days, was delighted to see Nell making her way up the path. Hurrying to open the front door, wiping her wet hands on her housework-only track suit bottoms, she exclaimed, 'How lovely, what a perfect excuse to stop scrubbing the kitchen floor. I didn't even realize you were back.'

'It wasn't planned.' Nell threw herself into the deep, sagging patchwork sofa and kicked off her shoes. Reaching up to accept a tumbler of Hetty-strength gin and tonic, she nodded through the window towards The Pink House, two hundred yards away on the other side of the village green. 'I got a frantic phone call from Mum this morning. She's had a letter about the tenancy. Now that his father's dead, Marcus Kilburton wants her out.'

'But that's awful,' Hetty gasped, genuinely appalled. 'Can he do that?'

Nell wasn't sure. The agreement between Miriam and the last Earl had been delightfully informal. Nothing, it transpired, was ever committed to paper. In the beginning, of course, whilst Nell's father had been alive, it had all been entirely straight-forward. Donald O'Driscoll was employed by the estate as head gamekeeper which meant he and his family were entitled to occupy The Pink House. When he had died of pneumonia at the age of forty-two, nobody in authority had had either the heart or the nerve to turf Miriam and her four children out of their home. And by the time the other villagers had begun to complain amongst themselves about the unfairness of it all, Miriam and the Earl had already embarked upon their scandalous affair.

Estate cottages were occupied by those who worked for the estate, and in her own way that was what Miriam had done. All *I* have to do now, Nell thought wryly, is to persuade Marcus Kilburton to see it that way too.

'I don't know.' She shrugged, twiddling ice-cubes with her index finger. 'But we'll find out tomorrow morning. I'm seeing him at ten-thirty. Poor man, my heart bleeds for him; evidently times are hard and he's down to his last few million. That's why he needs to evict my mother.'

The friendship between Hetty and Nell, on the surface an unlikely one, had been founded over the years and remained firm. When Hetty, in a rare burst of defiance, had ignored the chuntering disapproval of busybody villagers and asked Nell O'Driscoll to be her regular babysitter, she had earned the young girl's eternal gratitude. And not only had Nell been brilliant with Rachel, she had become over the years a brilliant friend, too. Deeply loyal to her feckless family, she was irreverent, spirited and marvellous at cheering people up when they most needed it, yet she managed at the same time to exude an air of mystery that Hetty both envied and admired. It couldn't have been easy, being born an O'Driscoll, yet Nell had simply gone ahead and done her own thing, refusing to allow the gossips to get her down.

For Hetty, who was about as mysterious as a loaf of bread, and who had only recently discovered what it was like to be gossiped about, it was comforting to have Nell as a kind of role model and to know she didn't have to let it get to her either.

That wasn't to say the events of the past eighteen months had necessarily been easy. Using Nell as a role model was one thing, but keeping your spirits up when your husband swapped you for a younger, thinner and infinitely more glamorous woman was hard enough on its own. When he didn't even have the decency to move out of the village with her, moving himself instead into her immaculate, equally glamorous house within binocular-peering distance of his old home, Hetty had wondered quite what she'd done to deserve such public humiliation.

In some respects, of course, she knew she had been fortunate. The eventual death of the marriage hadn't been too bad at all, simply because the marriage itself hadn't been that great. Shaming though it was to have to admit it, no longer having to actually share a house with Tony had come as no hardship. After eighteen years of putting up with his pernickety ways, passion for golf and desperate attempts at social climbing, life without him was positively idyllic.

It was just a shame, Hetty felt, that he couldn't have moved further than two hundred yards away. Starting out all over again as a single woman was complicated enough on its own without the added handicap of feeling you were being watched over from a not-very-great distance. It was one of the famous drawbacks of village life anyway, having your every move monitored and commented upon. Hetty was used to that. But it really was a bit much, she felt, when the chief commentators were your ex-husband and his unbearably smug new mistress.

'How are love's young dreamers, by the way?' Nell, with her uncanny knack for reading people's minds, looked suitably serious. 'Still at it like rabbits?'

Hetty giggled. Tony, never one of life's more ardent lovers, had evidently been transformed by Vanessa into some kind of six-times-a-night stud. This was according to Vanessa, anyway, who was astonishingly open and above board when it came to sex, and who was forever boasting to Hetty how marvellous Tony was in bed. Personally, Hetty felt he must have undergone a willy transplant. Either that or Vanessa was telling vast, shameless fibs, fantasizing on overtime in a desperate attempt to convince herself he really was that good.

'Well, Tony dropped by yesterday to see Rachel, and all he could do the whole time was moan about his aching back.' Hetty tried not to laugh at the memory of her ex-husband hobbling across the kitchen. 'He says it's interfering with his golf swing. I asked him if he couldn't get one of the other players from the club to write him a sick note, excusing him from sex for a few days. Poor Tony, he must be in real pain. He was dreadfully cross with me.'

'Serves him right, silly prat.' Nell shook her head. It wasn't that she disliked Tony, she just despaired of him. Hetty was so lovely; sweet, funny and endearingly disorganized. With her rumpled hair the colour of Golden Shred, her short freckled nose and huge, trusting eyes she always reminded Nell of a friendly King Charles spaniel. How Tony could prefer power-dressed Vanessa with her Barbie doll make-up and overbleached hair, her ruthless, go-getting attitude and her alarming inability to keep her mouth shut was a mystery beyond belief.

But since Hetty didn't seem to mind, Nell didn't let it bother her either. As long as Hetty was enjoying her newfound freedom, who cared what kind of laughing-stock Tony made of himself? Men had no taste anyway; it was a known fact.

'So tell me about you.' Nell ran her fingers over the pink-and-yellow appliquéd cushions piled up on the sofa. The fact that Hetty had had the time to make so many wasn't promising, but she lived in hope on her friend's behalf. 'Any scintillating secrets you'd care to share? Anyone you'd like to introduce me to, maybe?' Her eyes narrowed in pseudo-speculation. 'What I mean is, any men?'

'Oh please,' Hetty protested, going pink beneath the freckles. 'I'm nearly forty, not to mention twenty-five pounds over-weight. Who'd be interested in me?'

That was another thing about Hetty; she had about as much self-esteem as an amoeba. The fact that she was on the dumpy side, Nell knew, had little to do with it. If Hetty woke up tomorrow looking like Joanna Lumley she would still auto-matically put herself down.

'Plenty of men would be interested,' Nell observed, adding drily, 'given the chance. If you ask me, it's those photocopied fly sheets you hand out headed "A List of My Faults and Failings, by Hetty Brewster" that puts them off.'

Sensing that she was about to undergo a damn good talking-to, Hetty refilled both their glasses to the brim. Nell, who was lithe, stunning looking and confident to boot, could have absolutely no idea what it was like to be . . . well, Hetty. Maybe chic divorcees in Oxford spent their days fending off heart-stoppingly handsome men but it wasn't like that in Kilburton. She was lucky if she saw one man a day, let alone a handsome one. More often than not, in Hetty's experience, it was seventy-four-year-old Abel Trippick walking his equally ancient dog past her front gate on his way to the Hen and Chicken.

'Look,' she said patiently, 'it doesn't matter. There really isn't any rush. I'm just enjoying getting used to the idea of being single . . . good heavens, it's just as well I'm not getting chatted up by men, because I wouldn't have any idea what to do with them . . . not the first inkling! I'm twenty years out of practice, Nell. The last time anyone showed any interest in me, Adam and the Ants were number one and my idea of sartorial elegance was a white stripe across my nose.'

'So you sit at home instead, making cushions.' Nell looked disapproving. 'Are you sure the excitement isn't too much for you?'

'I don't *want* excitement,' Hetty protested, not entirely convincingly. Of course it would be nice to fall in love again and go skipping hand in hand through the poppy fields . . . it was just the nerve-racking business of meeting men that she couldn't quite get to grips with.

'If you carry on like this, all you're going to end up with is a houseful of cushions,' said Nell, who knew only too well what Hetty was like. 'And before you know it, you'll be thirty years out of practice. There must be *some* spare men around here . . . what about the crowd you used to tell me about? Those endless dinner parties at each other's houses . . .'

Hetty pulled a face. 'You mean the ones Tony and Vanessa go to now?'

'Bastards! Can't you go too?'

'I'm a Spare Woman.' Hetty, far less outraged than Nell, drained her glass. 'We bugger up the numbers at dinner parties. All we're interested in is sex, because we don't have husbands. Oh, and other wives are terrified of us because we're a threat to their own marriages.' She shrugged and smiled. 'This is what I've heard anyway. Just as well I don't want to be invited to their boring old dinner parties. Tony and Vanessa are welcome to them.'

Nell, shaking her head in disbelief, said, 'Right, that's it. I've never heard anything so ridiculous in all my life.'

'What do you mean, that's it?' Torn between high anxiety and excitement, Hetty started biting her nails. 'I don't want you doing anything drastic.' Then, because there was really no knowing what might be going on in Nell's mind she wailed, 'I *especially* don't want Tony back.'

'I should hope not.' Nell broke into a grin. 'He's well and truly blotted his copybook. No, I have other plans . . .'

'What? What?'

Hetty couldn't help it; a tingle of anticipation shot down her spine. Nell had a way of making things happen. And she always kept her promises.

'Ah, wait and see.' Nell was openly teasing her now. 'Just keep your legs waxed and your diary free. Because I'm going to make sure you meet more men in the next year than you've ever met before in your life.' She winked. 'And I'm not talking about a season ticket to Old Trafford, either.'

Chapter 4

By ten-fifteen the following morning the temperature was already up into the seventies. The sun was blazing out of a cloudless sapphire sky and there wasn't a breath of wind anywhere.

Nell, making her way up the long, tree-lined driveway to the front entrance of the castle – in the end she'd decided against bringing the car – was reminded once more of her last meeting with Marcus Kilburton. The weather had been perfect then, too. And she had just stepped off a dirty, stiflingly hot bus in her cheap, second-hand school uniform, her body clammy with perspiration and her hair plastering itself in rat's tails against the back of her neck . . .

Nell smiled at the memory. At least this time she was prepared, having dressed with care in a yellow-and-white striped silk shirt and white Levi's. The shirt, the single most expensive item of clothing she'd ever owned, had been chosen to impress. The beloved denims on the other hand, close-fitting and absolutely ancient, were to show him she didn't need to. They might only be a pair of falling-apart jeans but they still looked great.

Kilburton Castle was looking pretty good too. Seeing it again at close quarters for the first time in several years, Nell was struck afresh by its majestic golden beauty. Six hundred years old, collapsing in places, extensively rebuilt and repaired in others, it seemed only to have improved with age. Built of bleached yellow Cotswold stone, sun-drenched and ancient, the castle walls were smothered in ivy. The gardens, laid out in the Tudor style, were lovingly maintained by Abel Trippick's son Adam, their geometric, manicured perfection at odds with the crumbling, asymmetrical battlements silhouetted against the deep blue sky. The scents of newly mown grass and honeysuckle hung in the air. From a gnarled holly tree, a lone blackbird sang.

Nell couldn't help wondering how it must feel to live here, surrounded by such beauty and historic splendour. She also wondered in which of the magnificent bedrooms her mother had carried on her happy, carefree, much frowned-upon affair with Marcus Kilburton's feckless father.

Hilda Garnet, who had worked as the Kilburtons' housekeeper for the last twenty years, opened the front door to Nell. Devoted to Sarah, Countess of Kilburton – whose tragic death in a riding accident it had taken her a good decade to get over – she had disapproved passionately of every one of the Earl's subsequent affairs, viewing them as a vile insult to his beautiful late wife. The bizarre relationship with Miriam O'Driscoll, however, had been the ultimate betrayal. The woman was a gypsy, a tramp and a shameless Jezebel. Hilda had made it her business never to so much as look at an O'Driscoll, let alone speak to one.

She had evidently been told to expect Nell this morning. Now, her Jimmy Hill chin quivering with disapproval, she managed to lead her through the Great Hall and along several echoing passages without uttering a single word.

The private quarters of the castle were situated in the south wing. Coming finally to a halt outside Marcus Kilburton's office, she tapped with reverence on the heavy oak door.

'Come in,' Nell heard him say.

'Your ten-thirty appointment to see you, my lord.'

'Really? And who would that be?'

Hilda's thin mouth had by this time all but disappeared. Rigid with distaste, scarcely able to spit out the syllables, she said, 'Petronella O'Driscoll, my lord.'

Nell grinned. He had almost certainly done it on purpose. Maybe he had a sense of humour after all.

'Oh, well in that case,' came the amused reply from the other side of the oak door, 'send her in.'

He was sitting on the edge of a massive, extremely untidy desk with a phone against his ear, a sheaf of papers in one hand and a brandy glass in the other.

In ten years he had lost the slight teenage tendency towards gawkiness but the changes were otherwise negligible. The light-and-dark-blond hair still flopped across his tanned forehead as it had always done. The thickly lashed green eyes were unchanged. That big, athletically proportioned body, filled out but not flabby, was evidently still kept in peak condition. And although he was only wearing a casual, dark-blue crew-neck sweater, a plain white shirt and beige cords, he exuded class.

He smelled nice too, Nell couldn't help noticing. Maybe Hilda Garnet was just jealous because she'd got her eye on him herself.

'Sorry about that.' Putting the phone down and chucking the handful of papers on to the desk, Marcus smiled slightly and inclined his head in the direction of the door. 'Couldn't resist it. You aren't exactly top of Hilda's Christmas card list, you know.'

Nell, shaking his outstretched hand before sitting down on one of the olive-green leather chairs he indicated, realized that it was in his interests to appear friendly, to charm her on to his side. All he needed her to do was agree that he wasn't being unreasonable and he was home and dry.

As if sensing her reservations, Marcus sat opposite her and unplugged the phone so they wouldn't be interrupted.

'OK,' he said, pushing his fingers through his hair. 'Well, it's nice to see you again after so many years but presumably this isn't a social visit.'

It was on the tip of Nell's tongue to launch into the old 'people like us' routine. Restraining herself, she got straight to the point instead.

'No, it isn't. Look, the letter you sent my mother has upset her dreadfully. It's hardly her fault that nothing was ever put in writing; as far as she's concerned, you're reneging on a gentleman's agreement. Your father told her she had a home for life.'

'Ah.' Marcus Kilburton's smile faded. 'The problem is, that may well have been the basic understanding . . . but then again it may not. We only have your mother's word for it, you see.'

The note of apology in his voice was not, Nell felt, entirely believable. He'd just put it in there to make himself seem more of a good guy and less of a shit.

'My mother doesn't lie,' she replied evenly, determined not to give him the satisfaction of losing her temper and squawking at him like a demented parrot. 'And I think you're being rather unfair.'

'OK.' Gesturing towards the mountain of papers on the desk, Marcus tried again. 'In that case, maybe you could try and appreciate my side of the situation here. When my father died he left serious debts. On top of those came the death duties. The amount of money needed just to keep this place standing is ... vast. Now I've considered all the options, listened to financial advisers and discussed our problems with endless so-called experts. Basically, if this estate is to continue running we have to sort ourselves out in a pretty major way. And that includes clamping down on rent-free occupation of a highly rentable cottage. Apart from anything else,' he added, still in ultra-reasonable tones, 'it's hardly fair on the other estate workers, is it? The Pink House is by far the largest of the estate houses, yet it's occupied by only two people, neither of whom even works for me.'

Clearly pleased with himself for having argued the point so succinctly, Marcus leaned back in his chair and began drumming his fingers lightly against the desk top. 'You think I'm being unfair?' he said with a brief, chilly smile. 'Well, snap. Your mother and brother are rattling around in a house far too big for them whilst families like the Carpenters and the Mitchells are crammed into much smaller cottages. Furthermore, since they work for me they are entitled to an estate cottage. As far as I'm concerned,' he concluded briskly, '*your* family are the ones who are being unfair.'

Damn, he was good, thought Nell.

'OK.' Uncrossing her legs and reaching into her bag, she withdrew a dark-blue folder. 'If that's the deal, fine. I've read the spiel in the paper about these big plans of yours. So I'll come and help you out. People who work for you live rent free, am I right? If I do that, and move back into The Pink House, then everyone will be happy.'

Ten minutes of arguing later, Marcus was beginning to wish he had something stronger to drink than flat Pepsi. The girl, hell-bent on becoming his personal assistant, was unstoppable. She wasn't taking No for an answer, either.

'No,' he repeated, emptying the lukewarm contents of the can into his glass. 'I've already given the job to someone else. Somebody with experience. Look, you weren't seriously expecting me to take you on as my assistant, just like that.'

'Why not?' Nell demanded. 'I can do it. I wouldn't have volunteered myself if I couldn't.'

'Maybe not.' Marcus sounded bored. 'But you don't appear to be listening to me. It's like saying, "I can be Queen, I can do that job." I'm sure you could, but since there's already a Queen, it's entirely academic.'

'OK.' She dismissed his argument with a flick of the wrist as if it were irrelevant. 'So that job's taken. There must be something else you can offer me.'

At that moment, in one of those unbalancing flashes of recognition, Marcus remembered that his sleep last night had been interrupted by a dream featuring Petronella O'Driscoll. A disturbingly intimate dream it had been too. The prospect of meeting her again for the first time in over a decade had clearly affected him more profoundly than he'd consciously admitted.

But this was no dream, this was reality. And instead of lying naked in his bed with her hair tied up in a red velvet scarf she was sitting opposite him, fully dressed and bolt upright, virtually demanding he gave her a job – any job – in order to keep The Pink House roof over her mother's head.

She had done her homework too. Having read the piece in yesterday's paper about his plans to open Kilburton Castle and its grounds to the public, he estimated she must have stayed up all night drawing up a deeply detailed plan of action. As his self-appointed personal assistant-cum-comptroller, the aim was evidently to get the business up and running within six months. Her ideas, furthermore, were expansive, including opera festivals, rock concerts and open-air theatre. Petronella O'Driscoll was serious. If he hadn't already hired someone else, Marcus might have found himself with a dilemma on his hands. As it was, he called her bluff instead.

'Any job,' he mused, idly flipping through the blue spiral-bound folder she had handed him earlier. 'Well, we'll be needing tour guides I suppose. How about that?'

'Fine.' Nell didn't flinch. 'But I'd still like to be considered for the other post. Just in case it should become available.'

'I'll bear it in mind,' said Marcus gravely.

'Good.' She rose to her feet and smiled as if she were in on some secret from which he was excluded. 'And in the meantime, I'll have my folder back. I wouldn't want you pinching my brilliant ideas, after all.'

Chapter 5

Derry O'Driscoll, recovering from a serious party the night before, was lying in bed wondering whether to live or die when he heard shouting in the street below. Where picturesque Cotswold villages were concerned, not a great deal of shouting went on in the street; the last occasion he could recall had been six months or so ago when one of his spurned girlfriends, in a fit of desolation, had turned up outside The Pink House wailing, 'Oh please don't do this to me, Derry . . . I can't bear it . . . I *love* you . . .'

This shouting, though, was different. It was male for a start. Prompted by curiosity, Derry emerged from beneath the emerald-green duvet and listened. If it turned out to be the body-building ex-husband of the blonde he had met at last night's party, he could always crawl under the covers and go back to sleep.

'Help, somebody please help,' came the voice again. It wasn't one he recognized but it sounded genuine enough. Clutching his aching head, Derry slid out of bed and crossed to the window. When he saw what had happened, his heart sank. He had a nasty feeling he was going to end up taking at least a bit of the blame.

'You poor man.' Miriam, who had also heard the shouts for help, spoke in soothing tones. Kneeling on the pavement next to the injured stranger, she mopped his perspiring forehead with a cool, damp cloth and patted his hand. 'There, there. My son's rung for the ambulance; they'll be here in no time at all. You just stay still and relax.'

Gritting his teeth, Archie Halifax suppressed a groan of pain mingled with despair. Of all the bloody stupid comments to make, he thought with impotent fury, 'stay still and relax' just about took the biscuit. He had to stay still because he couldn't bloody move. If he had been able to move he wouldn't be lying here making a spectacle of himself in the High Street. And as for 'relax' . . . how the bloody, *bloody* hell was he supposed to do that? First day in a new job, and something like this had to happen. What the Earl of Kilburton was going to say when he heard about it didn't bear thinking about.

By the time the ambulance arrived, quite a crowd had gathered around the prostrate figure on the pavement. The local doctor, also having been alerted by the emergency services, was attempting to take a coherent history from the unwitting star of the show, who was swearing like a sailor and becoming more irate by the minute. For some reason the GP had yet to fathom, the middle-aged man was clutching a fifty-pence piece in his left hand and hissing through gritted teeth that whoever had put it there was going to get sued.

'He was walking along the road when he spotted the fifty pee lying on the ground,' Miriam O'Driscoll explained. 'And when he bent down to pick it up, his back went ping. I expect it's one of those slipped discs; the poor fellow can't move so much as an inch.'

The doctor, opening his mouth to ask whether he might perform a brief examination, was interrupted by the poor fellow on the ground, by this time maroon with rage, yelling, 'The coin was not *lying* on the ground ... some bastard had *superglued* it to the ground. I only fell backwards because the glue gave way,' he stormed, 'and that makes whoever stuck it down there in the first place entirely responsible for this incident. By God, when I find out who did it,' he spluttered finally, 'I'll sue the pants off them.'

Derry, who had only stopped to sling on a pair of old jeans and a pale-pink T-shirt, wasn't wearing any pants. Happily, the sunglasses he'd put on to protect his aching, hungover eyes also hid any giveaway guilt. He had glued the fifty-pence piece to the ground weeks ago, in order to amuse his visiting nieces and nephews. Watching people's eyes light up as they spotted the coin, then their embarrassment when they realized they'd been caught out, provided hours of harmless entertainment. Well, he amended, it had been harmless up until now.

'Come on, calm down,' Miriam murmured, clasping the injured Archie's hand. 'You won't do yourself any good getting all hot and bothered ... I dare say it was just young children playing a prank, after all. Listen to me now, is there anyone you'd like me to contact whilst you're on your way to the hospital?' Her dark eyes glowed with compassion. 'A handsome man like yourself must surely have a wife waiting at home for him. If you tell me her phone number I'll give her a ring and let her know what's happening, shall I?'

Her voice had softened. Several of the watching villagers exchanged glances. The shameless trollop was actually flirting with the stranger on the ground. Well, what could you expect . . . ?

Archie Halifax, in turn so dazzled by the woman's gentle tone and wondrous smile that the pain was almost forgotten, replied awkwardly, 'Um . . . no, never been married. But if you could inform Lord Kilburton, I'd be most grateful. I was supposed to be starting work at the castle this morning, you see. He's expecting me. He'll be wondering by now where I've got to.'

'You're the new personal assistant,' cried Miriam, squeezing his hand so hard he winced. 'Oh, you poor thing . . . and now you've done this to yourself I suppose you'll be laid up for weeks. Now that's what I call *really* rotten luck . . .'

'How did you *do* that?'

Marcus, asking the question three days later, was only half-joking.

Not believing in gypsy curses was all very well, but what – in all seriousness – *were* the odds against something like this happening to his newly appointed assistant, the man he had personally head-hunted from world-famous Gresham Park because if you really wanted to turn a stately home into a top tourist attraction and seriously successful business, Archie Halifax was the man to help you do it?

Archie, however, was well and truly out of action for the foreseeable future. And Nell, this time wearing a geranium-red shirt with a long, black skirt which accentuated her long legs, was back in his office.

'You mean was I hiding in the bushes with a poison dart? Sorry, Officer,' she teased, 'I know it's all highly suspicious but I do have an alibi. I was fifty miles away in Oxford at the time.'

Marcus was still wondering if he was doing the right thing. The thought of those legs was an added distraction. Here he was, trying to concentrate . . .

'I can do the job,' Nell prompted, when several seconds had passed in silence. 'Look, I know I'm not what you wanted, and I'm really sorry about your Mr Halifax, but I won't let you down. I'm a bloody good businesswoman,' she reminded him urgently. 'I work hard. I want this thing to be a success just as much as you do.'

She spoke with such passion he believed her.

'Why?' Marcus frowned. 'Why should you care whether or not it's a success?'

'Because Kilburton isn't just a castle, it's a village. And it's my home too.' Nell, who had no intention of telling him the real reason, chose her words with care. The next moment, sensing victory, she broke into a smile. 'You won't regret it, you know. And you'll be making my mother happy, if nothing else.'

'Just as well,' he replied with feeling, 'because when Hilda Garnet finds out about this she's going to be as mad as hell.'

'Hmm,' said Jemima, who had arrived as Marcus was showing Nell out. 'No prizes for guessing why you hired her. More fun for you though,' she conceded, pausing on the top step to plant a kiss on her brother's cheek. 'At least more fun to work with than that geriatric sergeant-major type you dredged up from God knows where.'

As far as Jemima was concerned, anyone over forty-five was geriatric.

'Since the sergeant-major type is out of action for the next six months,' Marcus replied, 'I didn't have a lot of choice.' He shrugged. 'She seems efficient, anyway.'

'And you hadn't even noticed what she looks like,' his sister countered mockingly. 'It must be hell to be as old as you, darling, if that's what happens to your hormones. Actually,' she went on, glancing over her shoulder as the red BMW, kicking up dust, disappeared down the drive, 'do I recognize her from somewhere? Was she at Roedean by any chance? What's her name?'

'Shouldn't think so.' Marcus, amused by the idea, turned to go back inside. 'It's O'Driscoll. She grew up here in this village.'

At twenty-one, Jemima was possibly the only person even remotely connected with the village who had never been aware of her father's infamous relationship with Miriam. Six years younger than her brother, she had been shielded from gossip by a nanny even more fiercely protective of the family than Hilda Garnet herself. Subsequent prolonged spells away from home, first at boarding-school then finishing-school, meant it had entirely passed her by. The last four years had been spent largely in London, sharing an airy Knightsbridge flat with three girlfriends, socializing madly and indulging in the odd spot of work between holidays.

The name O'Driscoll, consequently, meant nothing to her. Now, having learned that Nell was a mere village girl, it mattered even less. Marcus could almost feel the interest evaporate.

Jemima was family and he loved her, but she could drive him to distraction. There was no getting away from it, she was definitely an airhead. Glancing across at his younger sister, Hermès scarf fluttering from the strap of her Chanel bag as she slung it over her Dolce & Gabbana-jacketed shoulder, he suppressed a grin. She meant well. She was, he reasoned, never deliberately malicious. And at least she was a designer airhead.

To prove it, Jemima interrupted him whilst he was outlining his plans for the castle over dinner.

'Are you absolutely sure about this, Marcus? I mean, hordes of gawping tourists traipsing around the place . . .' She wrinkled her nose in delicate distaste. 'Isn't it going to be a pain?'

Marcus exerted considerable control. It wasn't as if he was ideally suited to the task himself. Up until the time of their father's death six months earlier he had enjoyed a relatively free-and-easy lifestyle, dividing his time between London and New York, where the brokerage company for which he worked kept a sister office, and socializing happily in both cities. Returning to live at Kilburton was something he hadn't envisaged doing for some years yet. He was doing his best to cope with the awesome responsibilities associated with sudden succession to the title but it wasn't easy, and the appalling financial problems didn't help. According to the lawyers, he was lucky to have the castle at all. It had very nearly been lost in a poker game with a Texan trillionaire.

'Probably,' he conceded, realizing that in many ways his sister and father were terrifyingly alike. 'But we need to do something. We need the money. Unless you happen to have a spare ten million stashed away somewhere.'

Jemima, idly tracing patterns in Mrs Garnet's lovingly prepared mashed potato with a fork, decided this wasn't the perfect moment to talk to her brother about her bothersome overdraft.

'Of course I haven't. But why don't you do what everyone else does and marry someone who has? Surely that would be simpler?'

'Brilliant.' Marcus started to laugh. 'Now why didn't I think of that?'

Jemima, who was being serious, looked offended.

'It *is* brilliant,' she retaliated. 'And practical, too. For heaven's sake, Marcus, do you think half our ancestors didn't do exactly the same thing? They're called marriages of convenience.'

'Of course they are.' Still vastly amused, he said, 'I'm sorry, I've just never considered becoming a gigolo before.'

'Gigolos do it with women who are either ancient or grotesque.' Jemima dismissed his ignorance with an airy flick of the wrist. 'And they aren't earls. Honestly, Marcus, you aren't a gigolo, you're a catch. You could take your pick of suitable girls.'

'You mean Greek shipping heiresses with thighs like barrage balloons and full-blown moustaches?'

'I mean perfectly normal girls like Kiki Ross-Armitage. Now you can't tell me she isn't attractive. And she's wallowing in money . . .'

Kiki Ross-Armitage, needless to say, was Jemima's new best friend. Hence the heavy promotion, thought Marcus.

'You mean she's someone of whom you approve?' He looked innocent. 'As potential sister-in-law material, you wouldn't have any objections?'

'Oh, Marcus, it would be brilliant! I'd love it if you and Kiki were to—' Realizing she was being made fun of, she flung a bread roll at his head. 'Bastard. You can laugh, but marrying Kiki would be an awful lot easier than opening this place to the *hoi polloi.*'

Marcus had never met Kiki Ross-Armitage, though he did of course know of her, as did anyone who had ever picked up a paper and glanced at the gossip column. Her mother, a fabled beauty of the Seventies and the daughter of a duke, had caused a sensation at the time when she had jilted the Marquis of Stourton and eloped instead with billionaire newspaper and property tycoon Malcolm Ross-Armitage. The marriage, contrary to all expectations, had survived and Kiki – their adored only daughter – had been born six years later.

Marcus, who had seen innumerable photos, knew she had inherited not only an astonishing amount of money but a cheerful combination of her mother's dark good looks and her father's wide-boy smile.

Not at all unattractive, he conceded, and by all accounts perfectly good fun. A few less scruples and he might have been tempted to give Jemima's suggestion a serious go.

'So you think we should tie the knot. Go on then,' said Marcus, helping himself to more mashed potato. 'Book the church for next Saturday. No, hang on . . . give me her phone number first so I can introduce myself and get the proposing out of the way.'

'Ha ha.' Jemima pulled a face. 'It would jolly well serve you right if you did fall in love with her and ask her to marry you.

Kiki's pretty sought after, you know. She could always turn you down.'

Chapter 6

News travelled fast in the village, particularly when Hilda Garnet was at the helm. Outraged by Marcus Kilburton's decision to employ the O'Driscoll girl as his assistant, she wasted no time at all informing anyone who would listen that if Lord Kilburton himself hadn't practically gone down on his knees and begged her to stay, for two pins she would have handed in her notice. He hadn't actually begged, of course, but nobody else would ever know that, just as his actual words – 'Well, obviously we'd be sorry to see you go' – were between nobody but themselves. Disappointed though she'd been by such apparent lack of concern, Hilda had felt honour bound to stay. Men were weak and his lordship had been bewitched, just like his father before him. How could she possibly abandon him to the clutches of a wanton floozy, for heaven's sake? He was going to need her now more than ever before.

'I suppose you've 'eard?'

Hetty, puffing her fringe out of her eyes, had barely made it over the shop's threshold before Minnie Hardwick was off. Lighting an untipped cigarette, resting bosom and elbows on the counter for extra comfort and quite undeterred by Hetty's friendship with Nell, Minnie launched for the fifth time that morning into the latest word on the subject, the most riveting bit of news since old Ron Carpenter had cavorted through the churchyard on the night of his granddaughter's wedding, three sheets to the wind and buck-naked apart from his wellies.

'Nell O'Driscoll's goin' to be workin' for 'is lordship and she's movin' back into The Pink 'ouse.'

'Mmm.' Having dashed out in her oldest, droopiest sweater and without brushing her hair, Hetty was anxious to get back home without being seen. Nell had just phoned and was coming round in half an hour to give her the real low-down. 'I had heard. Just a bottle of Fairy Liquid please, Minnie. Oh, and a packet of those chocolate digestives.'

'You should 'ear what folks are sayin' about 'er, too.' Ignoring the fiver Hetty was frantically waving at her, Minnie shot her a meaningful look. 'What she's bin gettin' up to in Oxford. They reckons all sorts, I can tell you.'

It was no good; she was going to hear it anyway. Hetty, telling herself she might as well relax and enjoy it, said, 'Really? What do they reckon, then?'

'Ain't too difficult to work out. That posh car of 'ers didn't come cheap, did it? And what about that mobile phone she carries round with 'er wherever she goes? Every time it rings she makes an appointment and writes it down in a notebook,' Minnie continued darkly. 'Stands to reason then, don't it?'

Hetty frowned. 'What does?'

Stubbing out her cigarette, Minnie pushed the biscuits and the bottle of Fairy across the counter. Taking the proffered five-pound note and counting out change from the till, she prolonged the suspense like a professional. Only when she had dropped the coins into Hetty's palm did she reply with an air of triumph.

'Obvious, innit? Never mind that fancy Oxford education of 'ers. That girl's been earnin' her livin' on 'er back.'

As she left the village shop Hetty walked slap into Vanessa who had, in contrast, earned her living on her backside.

Vanessa had made quite a name for herself over the past few years as a churner-out of bodice-ripping historical novels, and if she was in no danger of being selected for the Booker short-list with her style of writing, she wasn't too bothered either. Her hot-historicals sold in eleven languages and the money just kept rolling in. Thanks to her ever-faithful legions of fans Vanessa wore designer suits, took three stupendous holidays a year and drove a soft-top ivory Mercedes.

She also took great pride in her appearance and never left the house looking less than immaculate. This was particularly unfortunate for Hetty, who hardly ever looked anything even vaguely approaching immaculate. Bumping into Vanessa when you hadn't even had time to wash your face that morning, let alone show it some make-up, wasn't exactly the ego-boost of the year.

'Just the person,' declared Vanessa, wafting DKNY as she opened her arms wide at the sight of her lover's abandoned wife. This new and expansive gesture was something she'd picked up during a recent trip to Hollywood to discuss a potential film deal. Hetty instinctively cringed away before she got kissed.

'I tried to ring you just two minutes ago,' Vanessa went on. 'Hetty, we must get together for a chat. There's something we really need to discuss . . .'

She was staring as she spoke at the drooping, canary-yellow sweater, one of Tony's golfing cast-offs. She probably thinks I'm one of those sad women who wear their ex-husband's clothes because it's the nearest thing they can get to them, thought Hetty. Either that or Vanessa was looking at the chocolate digestives and wondering how anyone so fat could possess so little self-control.

'Fine,' she said brightly, over-compensating as usual because theirs was a modern relationship. They were Tony's past and future wives and mere civility wasn't enough. They had to pretend to really like each other. 'Any time. You know where I am. Where are you off to now, somewhere nice?'

The Mercedes gleamed at the kerbside. Vanessa gleamed too, in a bronze Maxmara silk suit and matching high heels. Her extremely blond hair was smoothed into a chignon and her pouting apricot lips glistened in the morning sunlight.

'A rather smart "do" in London.' She swung her head from side to side, showing off intricate gold ear-rings. 'Look, miniature typewriters! Aren't they killing?'

Dutifully, Hetty smiled. 'Lovely. Um . . . I'd better get back now, but I'll see you soon. Have fun in London.'

'Don't worry.' Vanessa smirked. 'I always have fun. Just ask Tony.'

Back home at long last, Hetty gazed despondently at the Matterhorn of dirty crockery in the sink, even more than usual because she'd run out of washing-up liquid yesterday. She would have to make a start on it, even though Nell was due to arrive any minute now.

The kitchen looked every bit as hideous as she did, Hetty decided, inspecting a casserole dish with bits of mushroom and onion superglued to the sides. And she was going to need a new Brillo pad if she wanted to shift that little lot. Never mind fixing her hair and primping in front of a mirror with a mascara brush; if she didn't get down to some serious scrubbing there wouldn't be anything clean to drink out of when Nell turned up.

Hetty was kneeling on the kitchen floor with her head in the cupboard under the sink when she heard footsteps behind her.

'Hi,' she called, waving a soapy arm in the air behind her. 'Just looking for a Brillo pad. God, I bumped into you-know-who outside the shop this morning – couldn't you just take a Brillo to her? Never mind the hundredweight of foundation, all I want to do is scour that "I'm so wonderful" smile off her stupid smug face.'

'Oh dear.' Vanessa sounded amused. 'Prepare to be embarrassed. Maybe I should have knocked, after all.'

Blushing furiously, Hetty realized that this, more than almost anything else, was what really irritated her about Vanessa. She took everything in her stride. Where thick skin was concerned, she gave custard a run for its money. She was even rumoured to have asked Minnie Hardwick whether she kept coloured condoms in stock.

Hetty, still puce, slowly withdrew her head from the cupboard. 'Sorry. I was expecting someone else.'

'Of course you were.' Unperturbed, Vanessa sat down at the kitchen table. To Hetty's shamed eyes, the glance around the chaotic kitchen said it all. If she couldn't even keep a kitchen tidy, was it any wonder Tony had made his frantic bid for freedom? Vanessa, who employed one of the Mitchell girls to do those kinds of domestic chores, had conveniently forgotten what running out of Fairy Liquid was like.

Having struggled to her feet, and over-compensating madly once more, Hetty squirted another half pint of the stuff into the washing-up bowl and set to work with gusto. It was only nine-thirty in the morning, for heaven's sake. If she was supposed to offer Vanessa a drink of some sort, tough.

'Poor old you.' Vanessa, resting her chin on a manicured hand, was still smiling. 'Please don't feel embarrassed; I'm completely to blame. The thing is, you did say come over at any time.'

'I thought you were going to London,' Hetty mumbled. 'I didn't mean now.'

'Ah. But my reason for visiting the shop was to see whether the *Daily Mail* had printed their interview with me.'

For the first time, Hetty noticed the copy of the paper on the table.

'When I saw they had,' Vanessa continued smoothly, 'I thought it best to come over and explain right away before you read it yourself and took umbrage.'

Hetty, who didn't know what umbrage was, scraped day-old Weetabix off a pudding bowl.

'Oh yes?'

'Well, you know journalists.' Spreading the paper open at the relevant page, Vanessa crossed her long legs and leaned

52

forward to surreptitiously admire the photograph of herself. 'The thing is, it was my editor's idea to come up with something different. Make sex the selling point, he told me, and you're talking megabucks.' She paused and gave Hetty a meaningful look. 'You understand how it is; sex is such an *industry* these days. And the Press *do* so love an angle when it comes to publicizing this kind of thing. I knew you wouldn't mind but Tony insisted I have a quiet word,' she went on rapidly, 'just in case you heard about it from somebody else and thought I was going behind your back . . .'

Hetty, who had by this time stopped washing up, said, 'What exactly does this article say?'

'Oh, you know. How the new man in Vanessa Dexter's life put new life into her novels.' Fondly, she smoothed the page. 'We're just playing up the link between enjoying great sex and writing about it. This is a new departure for me, a contemporary novel with oodles of sex. I told the interviewer that I'd tried every move out on Tony before committing it to paper, and that the hero and heroine are based very much on ourselves . . . well, it's all there; you can read it later. I just felt I should let you know what was going on, in case anyone mentioned it to you and you felt you'd been left in the dark. We may be plugging the sex aspect as true-to-life but the fact that the plot revolves around an affair between an unhappily married man and a successful lady novelist is – as they say – purely coincidental.'

Vanessa beamed up at Hetty, who by this time had her back to the sink and was leaning against it looking thoughtful.

It didn't take a genius to work out what she was saying. It was only too easy to imagine the ghastly harridan of a wife the oh-so-fictitious hero was married to. Vanessa wasn't likely to have done her any favours there.

But something else was troubling Hetty.

'All this sex,' she ventured. 'Just how sexy is it?'

'Oh, sheer raunch!' Vanessa nodded so vigorously the typewriter ear-rings ricocheted off the sides of her neck. 'No holds barred! My agent says it makes Jackie Collins read like Enid Blyton.' She let out a girlish giggle. 'She also asked to be introduced to Tony.'

This was worse than Hetty had feared. The bodice-rippers had been pretty harmless, not too explicit and old-fashioned enough to be amusing. This new departure, on the other hand, was evidently in another league altogether.

'Look,' she said with an apprehensive frown, 'does Tony really not mind this publicity angle? Because I can't help wondering how it's going to affect Rachel. She's only fifteen and she's had a rough enough time coping with the split. Isn't all this business about her father's unstoppable sex drive likely to be a bit . . . well, unnerving?'

Vanessa bristled.

'You mean I should withdraw a wonderful book from publication and disappoint a quarter of a million avid readers, simply because I may offend the sensibilities of a single schoolgirl?' She shrugged and gave Hetty a pitying smile. 'I know she's your daughter, but even you have to admit that doesn't make sound economic sense. Of course, if you really think it might upset her, you could always tell her not to buy the book. Nobody's going to force her to read it, are they?'

'No, but—'

'Look, Rachel's a big girl now. I'm sure she's been taught about the birds and the bees, so even if she did take a secret peek at my novel it's not going to be teaching her anything she doesn't know already. And if you're concerned about the AIDS risk,' she concluded cheerfully, 'there's absolutely no need. All my characters practise safe sex.'

Vanessa beamed with pride. Now, more than ever, Hetty longed to either slap her silly face or – better still – strangle her with the wet dishcloth. The ease with which Vanessa had reeled off the list of arguments smacked of practice, and although Tony had horrendous taste in mistresses, he had never been a bad father. He had, Hetty concluded, already voiced his own concerns. The trouble was, not being the parent of a tricky adolescent, Vanessa had absolutely no idea what they could be like.

Even if she had, Hetty doubted whether it would have stopped her. The fact of the matter was that anybody could write just about anything these days and get away with it. All the ranting and raving in the world wasn't going to persuade Vanessa to change so much as a single syllable. The novel was billed as fiction and she could write whatever she damn well liked. If it upset her lover's daughter, so what?

'OK.' Biting her tongue – because there was still that ridiculous need to maintain a pretence at civility – Hetty turned back to the washing-up. 'If you'll excuse me now, I'm pretty busy. I'll read the article in the paper later, when I have time.'

Chapter 7

The poor old washing-up, destined never to get done, was still sitting miserably in the sink when Nell turned up ten minutes later. Hetty, who had pounced on the article with wet hands the moment Vanessa was out of the door, prodded the soggy page and let out a moan of despair.

'Ugh, I could throw up. The damn book isn't due to be published for another six months and already it's causing trouble. Will you just look at that sick-making photo . . .'

Tony had evidently taken to combing his hair up-and-over in the hope that it made him look younger. Vanessa, standing behind him in a very low-cut blouse, had her arms draped around him. Her chin rested lovingly on his shoulder. Her rather large teeth were on show. There was a definite touch of the Great White Shark about her. Tony, whose head was tilted up at an angle so that his double chin didn't show, looked unbearably smug.

'I keep thinking of all the people we know who are going to read this book,' Hetty sighed. 'I know it's stupid of me but I can't help wondering how poor Great-Aunt Myrna is going to react when she hears about it. She absolutely dotes on Tony, and all her friends in the old people's home with her take it in turns to read Vanessa's historical novels. Then there are the teachers at Rachel's school, not to mention all her school friends. Oh God, it makes me cringe to think about it.'

Nell read the piece in two minutes flat. Then, switching on the kettle, she shooed Hetty out into the sunny kitchen garden.

'Come on, don't worry about the washing-up. Vanessa's a brass-necked old trout, but we'll think of some way round it. Goodness, at this rate we're going to have to make you an honorary O'Driscoll. Nobody will even be interested in talking about us any more . . . they'll be far too busy getting the low-down on you and Tony, old marathon-man himself . . .'

As usual, Nell was making her feel better already. Blowing her nose and allowing Nell to make the tea, Hetty chucked a few cushions off the sun lounger and wriggled until she was comfortable.

'No chance of that. You should hear the latest in the shop.'

'About me?' Nell, who had managed to unearth a couple of clean mugs, carried them outside. 'How exciting. What have I done now?'

'Awfully well for yourself, considering.' Hetty nodded at the Nokia poking out of Nell's black leather bag. Mimicking Minnie Hardwick's gossipy, self-satisfied tones, she went on: 'What with that flash car o' yours and them secretive appointments you're always makin' on that fancy phone. Word is, you bin runnin' one o' them 'igh-class brothels, my girl. And now the coppers is on to you, you've closed it down and decided to move back 'ome sharpish, before you end up gettin' yourself slung in prison.'

'Sounds sensible to me.' Nell never failed to be amused by the speculation surrounding her undeniably successful sideline.

The fact that nobody in the village had ever dared to come out with it and simply ask her what she did made it funnier still. It was going to be interesting, she decided, to see how long it took this latest rumour to reach the ears of her new employer.

'You just don't care, do you?' Hetty gazed across at her with admiration.

'At least they think I'm a high-class whore.' Nell grinned, her teeth gleaming white in her suntanned face. 'If they'd said I was a tenner-a-trick girl I might not have been so thrilled.'

'Marcus Kilburton's bound to get to hear about it. You'd better warn him.'

'You mean tell him I'm not really a tart?' Closing her eyes and enjoying the heat of the sun, Nell said lazily, 'He'll be all right. I had to ask him yesterday to ignore my mother if she called him a bloody whippersnapper.'

Hetty almost choked on her tea. 'Goodness, what did he say?'

Nell opened her dark eyes and smiled. 'That he was too tall to be a whippersnapper.'

'I'm so glad you're coming back,' Hetty sighed two hours later. The washing-up still wasn't done, she had no idea what she and Rachel were going to eat this evening, and her pale, freckled arms were beginning to prickle with sunburn. 'This awful business with Vanessa and her bloody book is going to be a million times easier to bear with you around. And when you're not working,' she added hopefully, 'maybe we could go out sometimes . . . perhaps visit a few wine bars . . . ?'

It was a crashing great hint, none too subtly executed. Following Nell's promise to introduce her to lots of lovely new men, Hetty's daydreams had consisted of glorious weekends amidst the dreaming spires of Oxford, where people wouldn't automatically think of her as Tony Brewster's dumped wife and where she could re-invent herself as a glamorous – well, it *was* a daydream – divorcee.

Nell was looking suitably astonished. 'I say.'

'I know, I know.' Hetty hung her head in shame. 'There I was, spouting on about needing more time and now I sound like a desperate teenager. God, I can almost feel the acne erupting as I speak.'

'Hold your horses and listen to my plan.' Nell's tone was soothing, her eyes bright with laughter. 'When the castle opens to the public next spring, we're going to be holding major events in the park. We'll be opening a damn good restaurant. We'll have everything from antiques fairs to masked balls and firework fiestas . . . and we're aiming for one hundred thousand visitors in the first year. I said you were going to meet more men than you'd ever met before in your life,' she reminded Hetty. 'Come and work for us, and you will.'

'God, I'm selfish,' Hetty exclaimed suddenly. She had been so preoccupied with her own worries it had completely slipped her mind. 'Listen to me rabbiting on and I haven't even asked about Ben. How is he?'

You could get used to the question, thought Nell, but you somehow never got used to the answer. No matter how many times she said it, it invariably brought a lump to her throat.

'Oh, he's OK. Well . . . the same, I suppose. No better, no worse.'

In the brief silence that ensued, Hetty cast around for something helpful to say. Apart from Nell's own family, she was the only person in the village to know about Ben. It was, however, never easy for Nell to confide her true feelings on the subject. As far as Hetty was concerned it was an unbearably poignant situation; she didn't know how Nell coped. Finally deciding to make the move from Oxford, Hetty felt, must have been more heart-wrenching than she was letting on.

'I'm not abandoning him,' said Nell unexpectedly. She looked almost defensive. 'It's only forty miles. I'll still visit him every week.'

'Of course you will.' Hetty's nod was vigorous. 'For heaven's sake, you don't have to justify yourself to me. I'm on your side. And I'm sure you're doing the right thing,' she went on, willing Nell to believe her. 'For Ben's sake as well as your own.'

'I phoned his father last night, to let him know what was happening.' Nell's lips pressed together and she shook her head in silent resignation. 'Just as well I wasn't expecting some kind of miraculous response. He wasn't exactly galvanized into action . . . I think he'd have been more interested if I'd told him last week's racing results.'

'So he isn't going to do anything.' It had been five years; a change of heart was hardly likely now. The very thought of it, however, filled gentle, easygoing Hetty with a murderous rage and made her long to track him down and throttle the breath out of him with her bare hands.

Neither gentle nor easygoing, Nell's own views on the subject went beyond words.

'He has his image to consider,' she replied tonelessly. 'Not to mention his beloved other children. He's not interested in Ben . . .'

Chapter 8

It had never occurred to Nell to hanker for the anonymity of Oxford. Unlike Hetty, she had never dreamt of re-inventing herself.

In those first few weeks, however, it had made an undeniably refreshing change to be judged for the first time in her life not as an O'Driscoll but as just another undergraduate working towards a degree in economics.

It had been fun, too, living away from home for the first time. Everyone, it seemed, was in more or less the same boat, getting through their grant cheques at a rate of knots then grumbling about how much money they didn't have, racing to finish essays that should have been written days ago, complaining about the terrifying amount of work they were expected to do, going out to parties and struggling to stay awake during lectures the next day . . .

Nell enjoyed all of it. Halfway through the second year she moved, along with three girlfriends from St Hilda's, into a four-bedroomed flat, working as a croupier in an Oxford casino on Friday nights in order to pay her share of the rent. Her course work was going well and she still had the rest of the week in which to socialize. She was meeting new people all the time, enjoying her freedom, having the time of her life . . .

Returning home after a tutorial one icy November afternoon, Nell found she had an unexpected guest.

'Molly – there's a strange girl sleeping in my bed.'

Molly, finally emerging from her own room in a highly dishevelled state, rubbed her eyes and looked confused.

'What are you talking about? I don't know any strange girls.'

'Well, there's one in here.' To prove it, Nell pointed in the direction of the narrow bed. At that moment its occupant turned over and opened one eye.

'Oh hell,' murmured Ben Torrance, his lips curling with amusement. 'Don't tell me I've gone and had a sex change.'

He had hair like Byron. Nell, admiring the dark, glossy curls spilled across her less than glamorous pale-pink winceyette pillowcase, said, 'You don't seriously expect me to apologize. Why do you wear your hair so long anyway?'

'Because it gets me noticed, and I love it when that happens.' He winked at Molly, still hovering in the doorway. 'Because it impresses the girls. Oh, and because it really annoys my father.'

'This is Ben,' said Molly, relieved to have sorted out the confusion concerning the mystery girl. 'He's a friend of Stevie's. We all had a bit of a session in the Randolph at lunch-time and came back here to sleep it off.'

Stevie was Molly's latest lover. He, presumably, was lying in her bed next door.

It was a Friday. Nell, who was due to work an eight-hour shift at the casino that night, slowly unwound the white wool scarf from around her neck.

'Hi, Ben. At the risk of sounding selfish, I was quite hoping to grab a couple of hours' sleep myself.'

'No problem.' With a flourish he drew back the duvet and gave the pink winceyette pillowcase a pat. 'Always room for one more. Hop in.'

'At the risk of sounding bad-tempered,' said Nell, 'no thanks and why don't you just sling your hook instead?'

'Oh dear.' Ben tried to look apologetic. 'Now I've offended you.'

He had laughing, sapphire blue eyes and apart from a narrow gold chain around his neck was naked from the waist up. Since the temperature in the flat was arctic, it was an impressive and probably reckless gesture. Nell, praying he hadn't put his hands beneath the pillow and discovered the grandpa vest and long johns she used as pyjamas, said, 'You haven't offended me, you're just in my bed.'

Ben Torrance stood up, pushed his fingers through the tumbling, almost shoulder-length dark curls, and kissed Nell's hand. Then, taking Molly by the arm, he led her out of the room.

'Now I know how it feels to be hungry and homeless. Come on Moll, you must have a snowy stone doorstep I can curl up on . . . just put me out amongst the frozen milk bottles . . . I'll be OK . . .'

Nell was awoken from a sound sleep at eight-thirty by a light tap on her bedroom door. Since her alarm was set to go off at eight thirty-five she wasn't outraged by the intrusion.

'Come in.'

Having expected Molly, she was unable to conceal her dismay when Ben Torrance, carrying a loaded tray, pushed the door open with his knee.

'Oh please, don't *wince* like that.' He looked pained. 'I'm making amends. I don't boil eggs and burn toast for just anyone, you know. And you really should eat something before going off to work.'

'It's not that.' God, he was beautiful. And what a smoothie, thought Nell, smiling to herself; he'd even stuck a single yellow rose in a milk bottle. Since theirs wasn't a flat habitually awash with unseasonal fresh flowers, he must actually have gone out and bought it.

'What then?' Placing the tray across her lap, he perched on the end of the bed.

'If you must know, I was hoping not to be seen in my vest and long johns.' Nell glanced down at the offending garments. The neckline was fraying, the waistband fetchingly elasticated. The overall effect was not the stuff of red-blooded male fantasy. Just to make her feel worse, Ben was now fully dressed and wearing an apricot cashmere sweater that screamed money and good taste.

'I was prepared,' he replied, his expression solemn. 'I found them under your pillow earlier. Happily, Molly assured me you were a lot prettier than your pyjamas. I say, do you mind me sitting here like this or shall I leave you to eat in peace? Don't worry about having to catch the bus, by the way. My car's outside; I'll give you a lift to work.'

'Stay.' Nell spoke through a mouthful of toast. 'Are you always this obvious?'

'Oh dear.' His eyebrows rose. 'Am I being?'

'Oh yes.' She nodded.

'And is it working, do you think?' asked Ben Torrance hopefully.

65

Nell grinned. 'Oh yes.'

'Thank goodness for that,' sighed Ben. 'Those yellow roses always seem to do the trick.'

'I should think they'd have to.' She held up a buckled toast soldier. 'It's hardly likely to be the boiled eggs.'

At nine-thirty that evening, Ben drove Nell to the casino in his mud-spattered white Lancia. When she finished her shift at six o'clock the following morning he was waiting outside to take her home.

'How about breakfast at my place?' He spoke lightly. 'We have unimaginable luxuries . . . central heating . . . matching cups and saucers . . . double beds—'

'I'm not going to sleep with you.' Nell needed to shout in order to make herself heard above the roar of the car's powerful engine. 'I've never slept with anyone before. I'm a virgin.'

It was true. She was a source of considerable disappointment to her sisters, who had spent the last five years being baffled by Nell's lack of interest in the opposite sex. Talk about letting the side down.

'That's OK.' Enchanted by her honesty, Ben yelled back, 'We can have an old-fashioned courtship. I can woo you.'

'What?'

He braked as the traffic lights ahead turned red. 'I can woo you. Is your name really Petronella?'

Nell nodded. 'Why?'

Ben took her cold hand and kissed it again, only this time he kissed the palm. Nell squirmed with pleasure.

'I like it. It's a beautiful name,' he said, smiling. 'And it's going to annoy my parents even more than my hair.'

She was wooed for nine weeks. Ben called it extended foreplay and complained every now and again of feeling like some character out of a Jane Austen novel but Nell wasn't to be rushed. Being wooed was fabulous and she enjoyed every minute of it, and when they did finally sleep together for the first time that was fabulous too.

The smart money in Oxford at that stage – once the main hurdle had been overcome – was on Ben Torrance losing interest in Nell faster than you could say mission accomplished. Where girls were concerned, his boredom threshold was measurable in hours rather than weeks. It was a miracle, they observed, that he'd stayed interested this long.

Just this once, however, the smart money was wrong. Ben did stay interested. This was what *made* life so interesting, he decided; after years of endless easy conquests and precious little emotional involvement during which he had almost begun to wonder whether he would ever meet someone with whom he could fall properly in love, finding Nell had been the answer to a dream. He adored everything about her. She didn't bore him, either in bed or out of it. She was beautiful and intelligent, fiery, funny and brave. In return, and for the first time in his life, Ben remained steadfastly faithful because Nell didn't deserve to be cheated on and because there no longer seemed to be any point. He had the best. He neither wanted nor needed anyone else.

In choosing Nell, Ben had dashed the hopes of an awful lot of deeply interested female undergraduates, not to mention one or two tutors. With his stunning looks, infectious smile and irrepressible zest for life he was definitely one of Oxford's golden boys. He was also something of a catch financially, since his hugely wealthy parents, determined that their distractable son should achieve the kind of degree necessary for a brilliant and successful career in politics, made the kind of Mafia promises only an idiot would refuse. Bribery had got Ben through his school years and, since it continued to work, they continued to use it. Which was why he lived in a smart, professionally decorated Edwardian villa with landscaped gardens leading down to the Isis, drove around at breakneck speed in a Lancia, and always had plenty of money to spend on his friends.

'Come and live with me,' he urged, hating the way Nell had to scrimp, save and suffer the outbursts of the casino's bad-tempered losers in order to pay the rent on her own dump of a flat.

'How can I?' protested Nell. 'It isn't even your house. It belongs to your parents.'

She was making a particular point. When Miriam had come up to Oxford she had met and got on famously with Ben. Nell, close to her own family and unable to understand why she hadn't been introduced to Ben's, couldn't help recalling Marcus Kilburton's remarks about 'people like us'. Was Ben, she wondered uneasily, perhaps ashamed of her less than top-drawer background?

'Don't be so bloody stupid,' Ben countered robustly. 'If anyone's ashamed of their parents, it's me. OK,' he sighed, observing the glint of doubt and pride in Nell's luminous dark eyes, 'if that's what you've set your heart on, we'll go. But don't you dare say I didn't warn you.'

Forewarned and duly prepared – although for what she wasn't quite sure – Nell packed a small weekend case a fortnight later and set off with Ben up the motorway to York, where Thomas and Patricia Torrance lived in a vast, chilly Victorian mansion on the outskirts of the city.

What a pair.

It didn't take Nell long to figure them out, although the discovery was a startling one, and so incredibly sad she couldn't even bring herself to discuss it with Ben, just in case he didn't know.

The fact that Thomas and Patricia hadn't taken to her was no longer an issue, simply because they wouldn't have taken to anyone he brought home. But that paled into insignificance beside the altogether more chilling realization that they didn't even love their own son.

As far as she was able to make out, they didn't much like each other either. During the entire, excruciating weekend not so much as a single genuinely affectionate glance, smile or word passed between them. And their attitude towards Ben made Nell shudder.

They wanted someone to be proud of, to boast about, to fit their idea of how a successful son should live his life. But the list of necessary achievements seemed all-important. What Ben himself might want to do had little relevance. If he failed, Nell sensed, they would regard it as a personal betrayal and withdraw their support without a qualm. The normal bond of love was missing. It was downright sinister.

'Told you,' Ben said lightly, when they had escaped from the house for an hour on Sunday afternoon, ostensibly to see the sights of York through a veil of spring rain. 'That's what they're like. Buckets of fun. Come on, I'll buy you an ice-cream.'

He took his family in his stride, Nell realized, because he'd never known any different. They were his parents and what he'd never had he didn't miss.

'If you told them you were leaving Oxford,' she said carefully, 'and taking a job as . . . an ice-cream seller, what would they do?'

'God. Disown me, I expect.' Unconcerned, Ben stuck his foot down on the accelerator and negotiated a narrow bend. 'Talk about letting the side down!'

'But what if that was what you wanted to do?' Nell persisted. 'More than anything else in the world.'

'Sweetheart, that wouldn't make any difference. I'd be disappointing them, deliberately going against their wishes. And they wouldn't forgive me for that.'

Still staggered by his calm acceptance of the situation, she shook her head. 'Have you ever been tempted?'

'Happily for all concerned, no.' Ben grinned across at her. 'Could you really imagine me minus the car, the house, the allowance? Would you even be interested,' he added in mocking tones, 'if I were stripped of my assets?'

'Of course I would.' Amazed that he could even ask such a question – particularly of someone who had never had any financial assets of her own – Nell retorted, 'You'd still be you.'

'Would I? Well, we can relax anyway, because it isn't going to happen.' Ben winked. 'My assets, my darling, shall stay intact. And they're all yours.'

'Oh dear,' sighed Patricia Torrance over dinner that evening, when at Nell's insistence Ben raised the subject of their living together. She pursed her lips. 'I don't think that's a good idea at all. We didn't buy that house in order to provide free board and lodgings to heaven knows who, Benjamin. Think of the problems it could lead to with sitting tenants if we decided to sell.'

Beneath the dining table, Nell felt her fingernails digging helplessly into her thighs. The urge to stand on the chair and scream something obscene into the silence was almost overwhelming . . .

Ben half-smiled. 'I'm talking about Nell, Mother. I wasn't actually planning to invite the occupants of an entire Salvation Army hostel to set up home there.'

'Hmm.' Evidently unconvinced, Patricia exchanged a brief, you-say-something glance with her husband. He coughed and cleared his throat.

'Still not advisable, Benjamin. No offence, of course,' he added, turning to Nell. 'Nothing personal . . . um, Petronella.'

He had one of those Adam's apples, the kind that jiggled up and down like a table-tennis ball.

'Of course not,' Nell said cheerfully. 'And there's really no problem anyway. Ben can move in with all of us instead.'

The prospect was such a horrifying one, all objections to their son sharing his house with Nell were instantly forgotten.

71

If Ben was to gain the kind of degree they'd set their hearts on, he couldn't possibly be distracted by noise, poverty and the rowdy company of four other students.

If they only knew the kind of lifestyle he really leads, thought Nell, trying to decide which of the two she hated most, they would die on the spot.

But any doubts she might have had about living with Ben had now been swept away. To Molly she had confided her concerns that, much as she loved him, she couldn't help wondering whether she was too young to be taking such a major step.

Meeting his sour-faced, unloving parents, however, had made her mind up for her. Sod them. If moving in with their son was going to irritate them beyond belief, then fine. That was what she would do.

Chapter 9

It took seven months for Nell to realize she had managed to shoot herself metaphorically in the foot. Not for the first time either.

'It's that temper of yours,' Miriam declared cheerfully when Nell confided in her just before Christmas. 'You can't decide to live with someone just to spite his parents.'

It was all very well for her mother to dish out the I-told-you-so lecture, thought Nell, but Miriam hadn't met Thomas and Patricia Torrance.

'I didn't do it on purpose.' She frowned. 'It's not as if I hate Ben. It isn't even as if he's done anything terribly wrong.'

'If you aren't happy, get out,' said Miriam comfortably. 'If you are, then stay. I don't know, it seems to me you spend far too much time *thinking* about things. Whatever happened to instinct . . . ?'

It all erupted in a furious row less than a week after Christmas, when months of unspoken frustration on Nell's part finally boiled over. Ben, who was a demon skier, had his heart set on a fortnight in Kitzbühel before term started. Nell, who couldn't afford to go skiing, was, as far as he was concerned, being ridiculously stubborn.

'No problem,' he protested. 'I'll pay. Sweetheart, you'd love it.'

'Maybe I would.' Her heart was hammering in her chest. Sensing that this was the showdown her instincts had warned her to expect, she licked her lips and swallowed hard. 'But I can't possibly go. Ben, you wouldn't be paying for me. Your father would.'

'So?' Ben raised his eyebrows. That was simply the way things were. 'They pay me an allowance,' he said irritably. 'And I can spend it on anything I bloody well like. They should thank their lucky stars I'd rather spend it on you than a stash of coke.'

'But I don't *want* to go on a holiday paid for by them.'

He didn't understand at all, just as he was unable to comprehend her reasons for paying him rent. Nell, having refused to give up her part-time work at the casino, insisted on giving him the money each week. Thomas and Patricia might regard her as a freeloader but at least Nell's own conscience was clear.

'Don't be so bloody selfish.' Ben glared at her. 'If you won't go, I won't go. And why the hell should I have to miss out on a damn good holiday?'

'Go!' Nell yelled back at him. She knew she was over-reacting, but her period was due. She just hoped she didn't burst into floods of tears and spoil it all. 'I'm not asking you to stay at home! There are dozens of other so-called friends you could choose from to go with you – bunch of bloody freeloaders – I'm sure any one of them would be only too thrilled to take a skiing trip at your horrible parents' expense.'

Stung by her scathing demolition in one fell swoop of both his family and friends, Ben retaliated with an icy stare.

'Maybe they would. Maybe I will take someone else along with me.' Taunting her, he said sulkily, 'Maybe I'll ask Isabella Maxwell.'

From then on it went from bad to very much worse, developing into a huge, hideous slanging match and culminating several hours later not in rapturous love-making – as both of them would secretly have liked – but in Nell packing her belongings into two pitifully small suitcases and storming out of the house.

The split, just as the courtship had done, became the talk of Oxford. Nell, back at the flat she had shared with Molly and the others, slept on the sitting-room floor because there were no spare beds. Ben, who had never been walked out on before in his life, promptly flew off with glossy blonde Isabella Maxwell to Kitzbühl and sent back a great many postcards to all the friends most likely to show them to Nell, saying what a brilliant time he was having and how great Isabella was in bed.

It was heartbreaking but it was definitely over. Nell buried herself in her work and grimly remembered her mother's words about being happy. This wasn't happy, this was bloody hellish. But she knew that what she had done was right. If it hurt now, it would only hurt that much more in a few years' time.

She just hadn't realized it would hurt quite as much as this. The longing to see Ben again gnawed at her like a drug craving. Even though she hated herself for doing it, Nell found herself counting the days to his return. Three . . . two . . . one . . .

* * *

The accident occurred at midnight, at a roundabout on the outskirts of Oxford, and the irony of the situation was that Ben, breaker of a million speed limits, had been the passenger.

Isabella, at the wheel of the Lancia and equally blameless, was killed outright by the teenage driver of a Granada Ghia which smashed into them at over ninety miles an hour. The stolen Ghia, cartwheeling over the dome of the roundabout, crushed and killed the driver. It took the fire brigade over three hours to cut the bodies clear of the mangled wreckage.

By the time the second body had been freed – that of beautiful blonde Isabella, who hadn't been able to believe her luck when the divinely glamorous Ben Torrance had invited her to go skiing with him in Austria – Ben himself was already undergoing emergency surgery at the Radcliffe Infirmary.

With such massive head injuries, he was barely alive. His parents, contacted by the police, drove through the night to hear the surgeon's grim prognosis when he finally emerged from theatre. Ben was clinging to life by a thread. He could go at any time. Any recovery would be painfully slow, the surgeon warned them, and the extent of that recovery was at this stage impossible to gauge.

He talked at some length about intracerebral haemorrhages, subdural haematomas, craniotomies and tracheostomies and none of it made any sense whatsoever to Thomas and Patricia Torrance. All that mattered was that Benjamin was still alive. He was strong and he was intelligent, in his third year at Magdalen, they proudly informed their son's surgeon. He needn't worry about Ben's powers of recovery. As soon as he was on his feet again he would be bouncing back, making up for lost time. He had a glittering career ahead of him, his mother explained. Ben Torrance was going to *be* somebody . . .

'Oh my God, Nell . . .'

Molly, bursting into the sitting-room, was grey with shock. Coming properly awake with a start – she had dimly heard the purr of the phone a couple of minutes earlier – Nell said, 'Something's happened to Ben. He's had an accident.'

'You already *knew*?'

'No.' Nell felt sick. 'It's just the look on your face; it has to be something like that. Tell me everything, Molly. Now.'

'What do you mean, I can't see him?' Her knees were trembling so much she could barely stay upright. Nell, at the entrance to the hospital's intensive-care unit, gazed in horror at the kind but firm nursing sister barring her way. 'I *have* to see him.'

'Only relatives are allowed in, I'm afraid,' the nurse explained gently. 'Look, his parents are in the waiting-room. I'm sure they'll tell you how he is.'

'I'm a relative.' Nell stood her ground. 'We live together. That makes me his common-law wife.'

'I'm sorry.' The nurse, who had plenty of experience dealing with hysterical would-be visitors, pointed her in the direction of the waiting-room. 'Have a word with his mum and dad. If they agree, then fine. You can go in.'

Shock and exhaustion had taken their toll on Patricia Torrance.

'This is all your fault,' she said, when she saw Nell. 'Benjamin told us about your stupid argument.'

Nell willed herself to stay calm. If she lost her temper now, she wouldn't be allowed into the unit. But the accusation made her flinch.

'Why is it my fault?'

'That girl was driving. If you'd been with Ben, he would have driven.' For some reason Patricia had remembered that Nell didn't drive. 'And he wouldn't have been at that round-about at that moment, because he would have been going faster than she was . . .'

It was the painful 'if only' syndrome, guilt-inducing and endlessly futile. As if recognizing that what she was saying didn't make sense, Patricia shook her grey head and gazed instead out of the window.

Nell's dark eyes filled with tears. One of the shocking 'if onlys' which had already occurred to her was the thought that if she had been with Ben, she would now be lying in Isabella's place in the hospital morgue. This, in turn, meant she owed her life to Ben's parents because it was her dislike for them and their money which had been the reason she had refused to go skiing with him in the first place.

'Please . . . I'm so sorry . . . they won't let me in to see him unless you say it's OK . . .'

At that moment the nursing sister reappeared in the doorway. As Nell wiped her eyes on the sleeve of her baggy black sweater, Thomas Torrance nodded.

'Go on then.' His Adam's apple bobbed. 'I don't suppose it can do any harm.'

'Come along with me, dear.' Smiling at Nell, the nurse drew her back out into the corridor. 'But before we go in, let me just warn you what to expect . . .'

The dark, Byronic curls had gone. Beneath the heavy turban of pressure bandages Nell glimpsed white, ruthlessly shaved scalp. A trickle of blood had seeped from beneath the dressings on to his left temple. Both eyes were swollen shut and his slack mouth was wedged open by the tube through which a ventilator pumped air into his lungs.

There were drips and machines everywhere, and a faint, pervasive odour of disinfectant and dried blood. Nell found it hard to believe the figure lying motionless on the bed was really Ben. Her Ben. It was harder still to believe he could ever recover from what the nurse had admitted were desperate injuries.

Oh God, thought Nell helplessly, whatever has he done to deserve this?

Chapter 10

It was nothing like the movies, Nell realized six weeks later. Regaining consciousness simply wasn't a matter of opening the eyes and saying sleepily: 'Where am I?'

When Ben had first opened his eyes, he hadn't been conscious by any stretch of the imagination. When he finally opened his mouth to speak, the sound that came out was more of an animal's groan than any intelligible word. And whilst one day he might appear to squeeze Nell's hand in response to something she had said, for the next three days he would do nothing at all. His body was wasting before her eyes, his shaved head sprouted an inch of regrowth and the terrifying surgical scars, curved like purple scythes, made Nell squirm.

She was exhausted. Spending every spare minute at Ben's bedside, and at the same time struggling to keep up with her studies, was really taking it out of her, but finals were approaching and the work had to be done. If by some miracle Ben should recover, the last thing he would want to hear, she doggedly reminded herself, was that she had ploughed her exams because of him.

The mental and physical strains were catching up with Nell. Hardest of all to take, however, was the attitude of Ben's parents. Reluctant at first to believe what was actually happening, she had managed to persuade herself she was wrong.

But after six weeks, the signs were unmistakable. Ben wasn't making anything like the degree of recovery they had expected. It was as if in their eyes he was letting them down. They no longer had a super-bright, going-places son to boast about, and they didn't know how to handle the damaged invalid in his place.

The first two weeks they had spent in Oxford. After that, Patricia and Thomas had returned to York and driven down each weekend to sit beside his bed, but their visits had become measurably briefer. Last week Patricia had phoned the ward sister and explained that they were unable to make it. 'But do give Benjamin our best wishes. Tell him we're thinking of him.'

They were deliberately distancing themselves, unable to accept this new, less-than-dazzling version of a son who had once been capable of anything and who was now capable of nothing. Nell, filled with such rage that she had to make sure she was safely out of the hospital when they did condescend to visit, broke down and wept in the sister's office one night, unable to bear the wicked unfairness of it all.

'They're abandoning h-him,' she sobbed, scrabbling amongst her carrier bag of textbooks for a tissue. 'They've given up. I thought he might like to listen to some different tapes so I went round to the house this afternoon to pick them up . . . but when I got there the locks had been changed and the house was up for sale. I mean, what kind of people would *do* something like that? That woman gave birth to him . . . and now it's almost as if they're trying to forget he ever existed . . .'

'Some families can cope.' Sue, the auburn-haired nursing sister, handed Nell a cup of lukewarm hospital tea. 'Some can't.

I believe Dr Rashid spoke to Ben's parents the other day about the results of those tests he had last week. The thing is,' she explained carefully, 'they aren't promising. Of course it's impossible to be one hundred per cent sure, but the indications are that even if Ben does eventually make a reasonable recovery he isn't going to be able to move back into his old home, just like that, and carry on where he left off.'

'I know, I know.' Dr Rashid, perhaps sensing that Nell was at least as deeply involved as Ben's parents, had already broken with protocol and explained as much to her. 'But he can still make *some* kind of recovery. I just don't understand how they can be so uninterested . . . how they can abandon him like this . . .'

Sue, aware that she was being staggeringly indiscreet, said, 'I shouldn't tell you this, but Ben's mother also told me they were getting divorced. They're selling the house so they can divide up the proceeds. Like I said, people react differently when something like this happens.'

'Damn right they do.' Gamely swallowing the last mouthful of the terrible tea, Nell tried to imagine anyone being foolhardy enough to try and drag her own mother away from her bedside if she was ill.

But at least the Torrances were the exception rather than the rule. The neurosurgical ward was like Kilburton in that respect; everybody knew everybody else's business practically within hours of arrival, and on the whole families stuck together.

'Don't look like that.' Observing the rigid line of Nell's jaw, Sue gave her a sympathetic smile. 'They can't help the way they feel. It's their way of dealing with the tragedy. And you mustn't feel you have to shoulder the responsibility, either,' she went on, having heard Nell's explanation of her relationship with Ben. 'It isn't as if you're married to him. You don't have to sacrifice your own life, you know.'

Nell knew. Every single word of that hideous argument was indelibly imprinted on her mind. When Ben had shot off to Kitzbühel with Isabella, their thirteen-month love affair had been over. And no matter how many joyous reconciliations Nell's own imagination had been capable of conjuring up, it was all brutally irrelevant now. Because fate had intervened, the crash had happened between Heathrow and Oxford and the Ben who might have charmed her into reconciliation no longer existed. In his place lay someone who could do little more than blink, swallow and groan like a soul in torment.

And if his unloving parents had given up on him, thought Nell, all the more reason for her not to do so.

Someone, after all, had to have a little faith.

But there were, she discovered, unexpected comforts to be taken which helped to make it bearable. Many of the others on the ward were, like Ben, long-stay patients and the camaraderie that built up between regular visitors was tremendous. It helped to know they were going through the same torturous process, and to be able to talk to people who understood exactly how you felt. Every tiny triumph was celebrated. Nobody minded if the cheerful mask slipped when there was no progress at all. Fearing for the future was something with which they were all familiar because as Jenny, the tiny young wife of the man in the bed next to Ben's, pointed out: 'He can't walk, he can't talk and he can't feed himself. How could I look after him at home, Nell? It would be like trying to nurse a sixteen-stone baby.'

As the weeks passed, however, Ben began to show definite signs of improvement.

Slowly, the unintelligible grunts and wails became recognizable sounds. When he opened his eyes and found Nell at his bedside he would give her a lopsided smile and reach with agonizing slowness for her hand. Hearing one of his favourite tapes playing, he would nod approval. And when he was fed a spoonful of blackcurrant mousse one lunch-time – having hated blackcurrants since he was six – he promptly spat it out.

But although he remembered hating blackcurrants he had no memory at all of either the accident or the weeks preceding it. When Ben first placed his arm around Nell's neck, drawing her towards him and croaking, 'Love you,' she realized that, as far as he was aware, they had never broken up.

It was known as retrograde amnesia, Dr Rashid explained when she tentatively raised the matter with him, and the more severe the head injury the more prolonged it generally was.

Nell had until then drawn some comfort from the fact that at least she wasn't in the desperate situation of someone like Jenny, whose beloved husband Dan had been in a virtual coma for three years. When he had swerved to avoid an oncoming lorry, crashing instead into a ten-foot wall, Jenny's own life had ground to just as much of a halt. She hadn't the heart to divorce him, yet the man she loved had long ago ceased to exist. All that was left was the big, empty shell.

Even admitting to Nell that in her darkest moments she wished he could have died in the accident brought a flush of shame to Jenny's thin cheeks.

'He's only twenty-eight,' she said wearily. 'He could carry on like this for another fifty years. I'm twenty-six and all I ever wanted was a happy family; me, Dan, a couple of kids and a golden Labrador. What am I supposed to do now?' She blew her nose and stuffed the tissue back up her sleeve. 'If I'd been a widow I could have met somebody else by now. The bloke that caused Dan's accident got six months for dangerous driving. But how many years have I got, hmm? A bloody life sentence . . .'

The weight of responsibility was heartbreaking. Too late, Nell realized she was being sucked into the same emotional trap. Desperate to compensate for the lack of love and support shown by Ben's parents, she had all but moved into the hospital. And Ben, in return, had begun to rely on her just as much as if she had been his wife. Every day he looked forward to her arrival, listening for the sound of Nell's footsteps along the corridor outside the ward. Every day he held her, kissed her and told her in his strange, halting new voice how much he loved her.

If Jenny had described Dan as a baby, then Ben had the mind and emotions of a fractious three-year-old. His fixation upon Nell, furthermore, was unswerving. If she tried to back off, she would hurt him terribly, she realized. And as for living with her own conscience . . . well, it was out of the question. The ever-more-distant Torrances had clearly washed their hands of the entire business. Their son had proved to be unsatisfactory and that was that. Poor Ben, no longer the glamorous golden boy of Oxford, had precious little left as it was. There was absolutely no way, Nell decided with renewed determination, that she was going to abandon him too.

'When's the baby due?' She spoke without thinking to the woman in the caramel silk dress who was gazing out of the day-room window. Her husband, who had been admitted two days earlier for removal of a benign brain tumour, was currently being pummelled behind closed floral curtains by two physiotherapists.

'Good heavens.' Startled, the woman gazed down at her stomach. 'Is that a gentle way of telling me I should think about going on a diet? I'm not pregnant!'

Nell's cheeks reddened. 'Sorry, I don't know what made me say it. Of course you don't need to diet.'

'Chance would be a fine thing, anyway.' Smiling at Nell's embarrassment, the woman smoothed the silk folds of the dress and gave her waistline a rueful pat. 'Being pregnant, I mean. We've been trying for over two years. It's deeply shaming,' she went on, 'and I know I should concentrate on being grateful that Jeffrey's tumour isn't life-threatening, but I'm just so worried it might count against us with the adoption agencies.'

'I'm sure it won't.' To her intense relief, Nell saw through the open door of the day room that the physiotherapists had finished with the woman's husband. 'Look, they've pulled the curtains,' she said quickly. 'You can go back in again now.'

* * *

Eight days later, the woman – whose name, Nell had since learned, was Felicity – sought her out in the cafeteria. Sitting down opposite Nell and coming straight to the point, she said: 'How did you know?'

There was evidently no point in pretending to look confused. Nell simply smiled and shrugged.

'About you being pregnant? I've no idea. Every now and again it just . . . happens.'

Interested rather than astounded, Felicity fixed her with a bright, birdlike gaze. 'What are you, a form of psychic?'

Nell didn't know the answer to that either. As far as she was concerned it was all rather embarrassing. She didn't even know if she believed in all that stuff, which surely counted against her. How, after all, could a sceptic be a psychic?

'Well I think it's fascinating,' declared Felicity when Nell had shaken her head once more. 'I mean, I wasn't even overdue when you talked about the pregnancy . . . I couldn't even do the test until last night. So how on earth you were able to tell . . . well, that's anyone's guess. What happens, then? Tell me how it works. Do you hear voices?'

'No.' Feeling awkward and hopelessly fraudulent, Nell mumbled, 'There's nothing mystical about it. I just realize I know something that I haven't been told. Every now and again,' she added ruefully, 'I forget I haven't been told, and end up putting my foot in it.'

Deeply intrigued, Felicity leaned closer and lowered her voice. 'Is it always happening? Do you know everything in advance?'

'God, no.' Nell shuddered. 'And I wouldn't want to, either. I have enough trouble keeping it under control as it is.'

Felicity's hand fluttered over her flat stomach. After a moment's hesitation she said, 'Go on then. Can you tell what it's going to be?'

'Yes.' Nell, who had no idea at all, broke into a grin. 'Definitely a baby.'

Chapter 11

That was how the lucrative sideline had all started.

'You're joking. I can't do that!'

Nell had backed off in alarm at the very idea when Felicity had begged her to meet a group of her friends. 'What if I told them a lot of old rubbish? They'd be furious.'

'Look,' Felicity was brisk and to the point, 'that's all half these so-called clairvoyants trot out anyway. People never expect too much, and they always manage to twist whatever they're told into something significant. But I've already told them about you and they're *so* excited!'

'And they'd really pay that much money?' For a fifty per cent gypsy, Nell was shamefully out of touch with going rates. It might only be a one-off evening, but it promised to be a damn sight more profitable than working in the casino.

'Of course they would. Like a shot!' Delighted at having won her over, Felicity wrote down her address. 'That's settled then. Eight o'clock on Saturday at our house. Crystal balls optional.'

'Just promise not to call in the fraud squad,' Nell grinned, 'if I get it wrong.'

She had padded it out, of course, made up a fair amount of nonsense and promised an awful lot of tall, dark strangers, but this was what Felicity's circle of small, plump friends liked to hear. And when the intangible magic worked, so that Nell – much to her own relief – was able to tell a woman called Bunty that her widowed mother had broken both legs in a skiing accident the year before, her reputation was well and truly made.

The evening proved to be a wild success. The more Nell made up after that, the more she got right. Every guess was a good guess and she still didn't know whether some uncanny sixth sense was genuinely at work or if it was just plain luck of the draw.

Felicity's friends, on the other hand, thrilled to bits with their readings and excitedly exchanging notes, didn't doubt her for a second. They couldn't wait to rush out and tell everyone about Petronella O'Driscoll, the most brilliant discovery since oven chips.

Within forty-eight hours Felicity was back on the phone to her with a list of numbers to ring. Thirty-seven women, friends of her friends, were desperate to have their fortunes told. And word of Nell's talent was spreading like wildfire, Felicity warned her. She needn't think she could see that little lot and put it behind her. This was only the start.

Five years on, and to her own continuing amazement, Nell was in just as much demand as ever. The fact that she was totally trustworthy and discreet had worked in her favour, earning her the kind of dazzling client list the tabloids would have killed to get their hands on. Media celebrities, dowager duchesses, even – to Nell's secret delight – a pair of stuffily upright Tory MPs regularly consulted her. Supermodels and housewives, rock stars and barristers; they all knew she would never breathe a word about them to the Press.

And although she was still unable to tell with absolute certainty which of her predictions would turn out to be accurate and which were great big porky pies, Nell had finally stopped worrying about it. Either way, the punters were more than happy and she in turn was happy with the money they paid out, which enabled her to run the kind of car she could otherwise never have afforded and every now and again to splash out on nice clothes.

Most important of all, however, and the driving force behind the whole venture, it meant she could help to make Ben's life more bearable.

As recovered now as he ever would be, Ben was living in an Oxford nursing home for the chronically disabled. Following his parents' divorce – because pride in their son, it appeared, was all that had ever kept them together in the first place – his mother had moved to Andalucia and his father had promptly remarried. Kick-started into action by wife number two, who was only three years older than Ben, Thomas Torrance had fathered two more sons in quick succession. Almost four years had passed since his last visit to his eldest son.

And as his parents' interest had dried up to nothing, so had the flow of money. Although the nursing home was state-funded, facilities were limited and Ben wasn't used to doing without.

This was where Nell was able to help. Ben, confined to a wheelchair and only semi-aware of the seriousness of his injuries, complained that the other patients only ever wanted to watch 'oik' television and cartoons. Nell bought him a television and video recorder.

He read voraciously too, racing through a dozen or more newspapers and magazines daily as if his life depended on it. Books littered his room. Though his concentration wasn't up to maintaining the thread of a novel, their presence was obviously a comfort to him. And Ben's expensive tastes in food hadn't been curtailed by the accident. Any attempts to persuade him to eat the meals supplied by the kitchen staff met with flat refusal. Instead, he painstakingly wrote out lists of the kind of food he would most like and handed them to Nell at each visit.

Simply glad she was able to afford to do it, Nell took the lists and bought him his beloved Isle of Skye smoked salmon, fresh raspberries and Bendicks Bittermints. It never occurred to Ben to wonder where the money was coming from. As far as he was concerned it had always been there, an endless supply of the stuff, ready and waiting to be spent.

'You spoil that boy,' Daisy Barton, one of the nurses, remarked.

Nell, who had arrived laden down with carrier bags of food from Marks & Spencer, a midnight-blue silk dressing-gown, six new compact discs and every Sunday paper known to man, shuffled sideways through the double doors. 'I know.'

But as she bent to kiss Ben's thin, pale cheek, she thought: So bloody what if I spoil him? What else does he have to cheer him up?

Back in Kilburton in her purple, poster-infested bedroom, Rachel Brewster, who had been in love with Derry O'Driscoll since she was eight, turned sideways and sucked in her stomach, studying her reflection in the wardrobe mirror.

Big, definitely big.

Annoyed, she took a deep breath, stood on tiptoe and tried again. The bathroom scales might say nine but the mirror said twice that.

More importantly, earlier this afternoon whilst she'd been walking back from the shop enjoying a packet of salt-and-vinegar crisps, she had passed Nell and Derry, both looking breathtakingly glamorous as usual, climbing out of Nell's smart red car outside their house.

The excitement of seeing Derry so close to had been intense. Rachel, who had inherited her mother's red hair and hopelessly fair skin, had been enveloped in a ferocious blush. Twenty yards down the road, she had heard Derry murmur, 'Why do you suppose it's always the tubby ones who stuff themselves non-stop with crisps?'

Nell had smiled and said, 'Sshh.'

Rachel, who would have given anything to have died on the spot, somehow kept walking. The revulsion she felt towards her hideous, overweight body kept washing over her in great waves. As soon as she rounded the corner she hurled the rest of the crisps into Abel Trippick's yew hedge. She was grotesque. By the time she reached the house she had already decided to go on a diet.

She had made a start at tea-time, telling her mother she'd already had something at her friend Sarah's house and saving herself at least 600 calories by not eating Lancashire hot-pot and chocolate sponge pudding with custard.

The sensation of hunger gnawing at her stomach wasn't actually as bad as Rachel had feared, either. It was, she told herself, her body's way of letting her know things were going into action. The diet was starting to work. Why, at this very moment she was using up calories, losing weight. Maybe if she went jogging round the cricket field later on this evening, when nobody would be likely to see her, she could jolt her metabolism into overdrive and lose a bit more.

She would show Derry O'Driscoll, Rachel silently vowed. Glancing in the mirror once more, she sucked in her cheeks and assumed a hips-thrust-forward, head-thrown-back, Evangelista-type stance. It would have been more impressive without the sturdy white bra but she'd show him anyway. By next summer, he wouldn't be able to call her tubby. By next summer, she fantasized longingly, he wouldn't be able to keep his gorgeous hands off her.

Downstairs, Hetty was polishing off the last of the chocolate sponge pudding in the hope that it might give her the courage to get through the next hour.

Not that she had a lot of choice in the matter. Ever the wimp, she had spent far too long putting off the inevitable embarrassing talk with Rachel.

Now publication was only a fortnight away. Vanessa seemed to have spent the last couple of months doing nothing but talk to journalists, and any day now the magazines and newspapers were going to hit the news-stands.

At least Tony was coming over to help her through it. Scraping the pudding bowl clean, Hetty realized that she was going to miss *EastEnders* and wondered if she dared set the video. Her addiction to soap operas wasn't something Tony had ever approved of; she could just imagine the look of pained distaste on his face when halfway through their serious discussion the video recorder – at the awful giveaway time of seven-thirty – suddenly flashed its light and lurched into action like the Tardis.

But they were divorced, dammit! It wasn't even as if she was carrying a secret torch for him. Why, thought Hetty, was she always so pathetically bound by other people's opinions of her? Especially when the other person in question was as unimportant – no, *irrelevant* – as her snobbish old ex.

'What is it?' Sensing drama, because her mother was looking twitchy in the kitchen and her father was pouring himself an enormous Scotch, Rachel's mind was temporarily drawn away from thoughts of tubbiness.

Tony Brewster, who had revelled in all the pre-publicity surrounding the promotion of Vanessa's ground-breaking new novel, had in truth had a bit of a tussle with his conscience over the nature of the hype. To be publicly portrayed as the Rudolph Valentino of the nineties was on the one hand incredibly flattering, and had definitely aroused a fair amount of female interest. The downside, he now discovered, was having to face his innocent fifteen-year-old daughter, warn her about the gory details and maintain his composure in the face of the ensuing, mutual embarrassment.

'Come and sit down, sweetheart.'

With a genial smile, Tony put his hand on Rachel's shoulder as they made their way through to the living-room. Hetty, having evidently attempted a tidy-up before he arrived, had shovelled a great wodge of newspapers under the sofa; he could see them poking out from beneath the frilled loose covers. God knows what else was hidden under there, Tony thought; but if he bothered to look he wouldn't mind betting on last year's Christmas cards, several long-lost music cassettes and at least half a dozen pairs of shoes. And although the television was off, the video was surreptitiously running, he observed. *EastEnders*, no doubt. God help anyone fool-hardy enough to try and deprive Hetty of one of her appalling soaps.

Rachel, meanwhile, was still looking apprehensive. Hetty, who had told him that since Vanessa was his responsibility it was up to him to do the honours, was gazing unhelpfully through the window. Taking a deep breath, Tony said: 'Nothing to worry about, sweetheart. Your mother and I just felt we should have a bit of a chat about Vanessa's new book. Um . . . tell me, does the expression "media-hype" mean anything to you?'

Ugh, thought Rachel ten minutes later, how unbelievably gross. No wonder everyone had seemed to change the subject whenever she'd mentioned Vanessa's next novel. And how embarrassing, she decided miserably, when the girls at school got to hear about it. To her eternal shame she had done a fair amount of bragging when her father had first taken up with glamorous, bestselling author Vanessa Dexter. Several of the girls, whom she had never much liked before anyway, had retaliated out of sheer envy, jeering at Vanessa's novels, mimicking her film-star manner and mockingly begging Rachel for her autograph.

That awful clique, she now realized, were really going to think their boat had come in when they heard about this. She could just imagine their gleeful faces as they followed her around school, waving copies of the stupid book at her and quoting hideous bits of it aloud at every opportunity. Oh God, thought Rachel brokenly, if only I'd kept my mouth shut in the first place.

'It's horrid, darling, I know.' Hetty squeezed her daughter's hand and gave her a cheer-up smile. 'But it isn't the end of the world. And today's newspapers are tomorrow's fish-and-chip wrappers, after all. People will soon forget the whole silly business.'

Rachel, who was finding it hard to meet her father's gaze, glanced sideways at her mother instead.

'Have you read it?'

Hetty, who had been given a personally inscribed advance copy by Vanessa ten days earlier, was forcing herself through a lurid chapter a night. And if she'd thought having to listen to Vanessa burbling on about her no-holds-barred sex-life was bad, seeing it in actual print, in an actual *book*, was much, much worse.

She had been right, too, about the fictional ex-wife whom Vanessa had been careful to describe as tall, gangly and with lank dark hair but who otherwise bore a humiliating resemblance to Hetty, right down to the kind of cruel personal details she could only have learned about from Tony. How else, after all, could Vanessa possibly have known about her beloved Snoopy bedsocks, her inability ever to remember the punchlines of jokes, or the disinterest in sex that bordered on frigidity, eventually driving her long-suffering, totally heroic husband into the arms of a younger, more perfect, altogether more *deserving* woman?

'Yes.' Hetty nodded, wrinkling her nose. 'Well, bits of it, anyway. It's rather poorly written. Not my kind of thing at all.'

It had been a cheap jibe but allowable, she felt, under the circumstances. Pleased with herself for having had the courage to say it, she added with a bit of a smirk, 'I hope Vanessa hasn't set her heart on winning the Booker this year.'

The trouble with making cheap jibes, of course, was the risk you took of having them thrown straight back in your face. Tony, springing instantly to the defence of Vanessa's literary style, looked po-faced and said, 'She brings happiness to millions.' Then, making a point of his own, he shot a withering glance in the direction of the video, still busily recording. 'Of course, you have such intellectual tastes yourself,' he murmured. 'Don't tell me, you couldn't bear to miss *Panorama*.'

'Don't.' Rachel, realizing that her parents were on the verge of slipping into bicker-mode, stared at Hetty. 'So when do I get a chance to read the book?'

'Oh, sweetheart, I really don't think you'd enjoy this one. No, no. I'm sure you wouldn't want to read it . . .'

Hetty felt slightly sick. If Vanessa's novel with its wildly explicit sex scenes had been made into a film, it would be X rated without a doubt. Nobody under the age of eighteen would be allowed to see it. But because it was a book, marketed as romantic fiction, it could be bought by anyone at all. Anyone, that is, with money to waste and no taste.

Rachel, however, was looking horribly determined. 'I wouldn't expect to enjoy it,' she said tightly. 'I'd just look even more of a prat at school than I do already, if I didn't know what it was all about. At least this way I'll be able to recognize when I'm being made fun of.'

Oh *hell*, thought Hetty, a massive lump rising in her throat. Awash with maternal instincts, she was seized with longing to seek out and systematically beat to a pulp anyone who had ever even dreamed of making fun of her adored only daughter.

'I'll speak to your form teacher,' she blurted out. 'She can keep an eye on you, make sure the other girls don't—'

'Mum, *no*!' Genuinely alarmed, Rachel leapt to her feet. 'You mustn't say anything to Miss Wall. Promise you won't. I couldn't bear it!'

'There won't be any trouble,' Tony declared, when Rachel had slunk back upstairs. Covering his own sense of guilt, he attempted to reassure his agitated ex-wife. 'No need to get into a flap about it. She'll be fine.'

'Bloody Vanessa.' Hetty was less convinced. Nell, who had promised to come up with a solution to this dilemma, had been up to her eyes instead with the imminent opening of Kilburton Castle. Apart from a vague: 'Don't get mad, get even,' she hadn't come up with anything at all, thought Hetty with a touch of indignation. And much as she would like to, the one thing in the world Hetty knew she was completely incapable of doing was dashing off a mega-selling bitch-and-tell blockbuster about a shameless, husband-stealing novelist with galloping cellulite and great big teeth. Except Vanessa didn't even have cellulite. Life, thought Hetty, was cruel.

'Come on, cheer up.' Tony, who hated to see her looking so upset, gave her an awkward smile. 'She'll come through it.'

'Oh, what do you care? Just so long as the royalties roll in and you get your stupid face in the papers.'

'That's not true,' he protested. 'Now you're being unfair.'

Hetty bit her lower lip. 'I don't feel fair. Why does everybody always expect me to be fair, anyway? I'm fed up with being bloody fair.'

She sat and sulked whilst Tony made them both a pot of coffee. Vanessa was up in London again, so he didn't need to rush off.

'I hope you don't mind. I found this in the blue tin.'

Hetty looked up. He was carrying in the walnut cake she had made yesterday, a multi-layered masterpiece sandwiched together with buttercream. She might be a disaster in every other department but she'd always had a way with cakes, probably because she was so interested in eating them.

Tony, on the other hand, was certainly not supposed to be eating them. Only last week Vanessa had been boasting in the village that thanks to her influence and watchful eye, Tony's month-long diet had resulted in him losing a good stone and a half.

Hetty had to admit that it suited him, too. His stomach was flatter, long-lost cheekbones were reappearing and there was definitely one less chin.

'Sure you can spare the calories?' Having embarked in her time on a thousand diets and only too well aware of what a miserable occupation it was, her tone was teasing rather than censorious. Tony had always adored his food. Some of their very best evenings together had been spent pigging out at home on all their favourite things.

'Sod the calories.' Tony picked up the biggest slice of cake and sank his teeth into it, guilty but defiant. Sighing, spraying crumbs, he said, 'This is heaven. Don't tell Vanessa, whatever you do: she'd hit the roof if she could see this.'

Hetty nearly laughed aloud. Of course, she thought with delight, that was it. This was what Nell had meant when she'd said don't get mad, get even. Vanessa, who set such tremendous store by appearances, wanted the man in her life to be someone of whom she could be publicly proud. Tony, handsome but on the heavy side, was the man in her life and Vanessa was counting his calories. How blissful, Hetty decided, to think that by encouraging Tony to stuff himself with her very own layered walnut cake, she could undermine Vanessa's best efforts. If he ate enough of the stuff he might even gain weight. Triple bliss!

'I won't breathe a word,' she said happily. 'Help yourself. And there are some caramel biscuits in the other tin, if you're still hungry. You always used to say they were your favourites.'

Chapter 12

Over at the castle at about the same time, Marcus Kilburton was returning from a drinks party in nearby Tedbury. He hadn't intended leaving so early but the only too obvious attentions of a bosomy, scarlet-sequinned redhead called Mavis Elson-Smyth had resulted in a hasty change of plan. Having extricated himself with the excuse that he was due to meet his comptroller at nine o'clock – it might not be true, but it sounded impressive – the sight of a light burning in Nell's office took him aback. It had only been a spur of the moment fib but it seemed as if he was going to meet her anyway.

'Oh my God!' Nell jumped a mile when she glanced up and saw him in the open doorway. She clutched her heart. 'I thought you were the Kilburton ghost.'

Spread out across her desk were timetables, plans and an awful lot of scribbled-on lists. Evidently engrossed in her work, she had dropped her felt-tipped pen when he had taken her by surprise. As she leaned sideways, bending to retrieve it from beneath the desk, Marcus found himself admiring her long, elegant legs. Not too many comptrollers, he wouldn't mind betting, could get away with wearing a black sweater, beige leather skirt, black opaque tights and high-heeled ankle boots. Her long black hair was tied with a beige ribbon. He couldn't decide which she most reminded him of; a younger, thinner, whiter Tina Turner or a Liquorice Allsort.

There was no doubt about it, though; no matter what unlikely outfits Nell appeared in, she knew how to work. The opening of the castle was a fortnight away and as far as Marcus was concerned she had exceeded all expectations. He did sometimes wonder, however, if he knew her any better now than on the day he had taken her on.

'We don't have a Kilburton ghost.'

Nell, having finally located the pen, resurfaced. She grinned and waved one of the scribbled-on pieces of paper at him.

'You should. It's just what a place like this needs to thrill the punters, especially the kids. If we move fast we could even include it in the guidebook. I thought maybe a wailing young servant girl in a white nightie wandering barefoot through the dungeon tower, endlessly searching for her lost love. What do you think?'

'Are you sure it's a servant girl? Sounds more like Jemima.' Where men were concerned, his sister had been going through something of a rough patch recently and he was having to bear the brunt of it. 'This wailing ghost,' Marcus drawled. 'She wouldn't happen to have a rich best friend called Kiki?'

In the five months since Nell had come to work at the castle she had only met Marcus's sister on a handful of occasions, simply because Jemima still spent the majority of her time either in London or abroad. When she did descend on Kilburton for a recuperative few days, she didn't bother herself with the boring work-in-progress so inconveniently going on all over the estate as it prepared to open to the public. She was, however, bringing Kiki down with her for the opening weekend, in order that Marcus could meet her for the first time.

Since Jemima was about as subtle as a steamroller, Marcus was dreading it. The trouble was, this was one event he wasn't going to be able to walk out of.

'Here, take a look at these.' Nell handed him the chart to which she had just put the finishing touches. 'The staff rota for the restaurant, gift shop and guided tours. Those along the bottom are the cleaners, here are the car-parking attendants, and over here are the security chaps. Anyone needing to switch shifts has to OK it with me. Oh, and there's been a good response from the mailshots . . . I've taken a dozen or so coach party bookings this afternoon, and we've had a few calls about the banqueting facilities. Also, a location agent is interested in hiring the castle next October for some movie location work.' She paused for a second, deep in thought. 'Ah yes, and the boys putting the new roof on the stable workshops are complaining that Hilda Garnet gives the gardeners chocolate Hobnobs with their tea and all they get are ordinary digestives. They say it's favouritism. I did try and mention it to Mrs Garnet,' Nell added with a glimmer of a smile, 'but you know how it is. She didn't seem to hear me. It might be easier if you have a go.'

The amount of work she had accomplished over the past months was phenomenal. Marcus was deeply impressed. Whilst he had been out organizing the financial side, Nell had taken charge of everything else. She had visited an awful lot of stately homes too, observing the different ways in which they were run, deciding what worked and what didn't, chatting anonymously with members of staff and other visitors and taking careful note of what they said. What they most often said was 'more toilets', since queuing hours for the loo was nobody's favourite pastime. Nell promptly trebled the number they had originally planned to build, and quadrupled the budget. Scrupulously clean, beautifully decorated rest-rooms, it appeared, were going to make a far more lasting impression on the ticket-buying public than that weeny, grubby old painting of Kilburton Park hanging in the darkest reaches of the drawing-room.

The seventeenth-century painting, which was by Henry Danckerts, was duly despatched to Sotheby's and sold at auction in order to pay for the elegant new lavatories. Marcus shouldn't think of it as selling off family heirlooms, Nell had airily informed him; he must think of it instead as investing in the future of the castle.

In the future of the village, too, he reminded himself now, gazing down at the chart she had so painstakingly filled out. Altogether, including a number of part-timers and the odd 'casual', they had taken on fifty-seven new members of staff, almost all of whom were local. The very nature of the village was about to undergo a tremendous change from quietly picturesque to overrun – in the summer months at least – with camera-snapping tourists. Those who would soon be working up at the castle were delighted by it all, even if it had meant enduring the indignity of being interviewed for their jobs by Nell O'Driscoll. But there had been detractors, too. Several of the smarter houses in Kilburton – in particular the glamorous 'weekend' cottages – had been purchased by highly stressed city dwellers in order to allow them somewhere to relax and unwind. They had been less than amused by the proposed developments to the estate. Marcus had received letters of complaint. 'Sod 'em,' Nell had declared, cheerfully unconcerned by their plight. 'Them and their clean green wellies. Go on, I dare you. Tell them to sell up and bugger off back to London. Nobody ever wanted them here in the first place.'

Marcus found this partisan attitude highly amusing. Nell might be regarded as something of an outsider herself, he realized, but she and her family were nevertheless an integral part of the village. They belonged to it. At least other people *bothered* to talk about them behind their backs. The flashy, Volvo-driving weekenders, it seemed, weren't even deemed worthy of gossip.

Marcus was just glad he'd threatened Miriam O'Driscoll with eviction. If he hadn't, he would never have been railroaded – somehow or other – into giving Nell the job. He knew now that he could never have managed without her.

'The priest hole in the west wing,' she said suddenly. Her dark eyes lit up in triumph. Reaching for a fresh piece of paper, she scribbled down a few words and underlined them with vigour.

'What about it?' Marcus's mind had been on Nell rather than priest holes. The narrow hidden passageway which ran between the main corridor and the dungeon tower wasn't the kind of thing one daydreamed about. Nell's leather skirt and elegantly crossed legs, on the other hand, were endlessly distracting.

'I've just thought of it.' She beamed. 'Gosh, I'm brilliant. We tape the sound of chains rattling – not all the time, just every now and again – and add on a few wails and whispers.

Then we leave it playing inside the priest hole. It can be the ghost of the handsome young priest who had a doomed affair with the servant girl in the white nightie . . .'

'Tapes run out after an hour.'

'No problem.' Nell was unperturbed. 'I've got plenty of nephews. I'll just chuck a couple in there to do the honours instead.'

He wouldn't put it past her. He wasn't sure he'd put anything past her. They had worked together for almost six months and Nell intrigued him more than ever. For one so given to plain speaking when the occasion demanded it, she still exuded that tantalizing air of mystery. He couldn't decide, either, whether she found him even remotely attractive.

Not that he had any intention of getting involved with her, Marcus reminded himself, watching the glossy swathe of her hair fall across her shoulder as she bent her head to scribble down yet another reminder. That was definitely the kind of complication he didn't need.

But it would still be nice, he felt, to know where he stood in her private estimations. Nell didn't flirt. If she did, Marcus realized, he would only wonder whether she was making fun of him, doing it purely for her own amusement. In that respect, he didn't trust her an inch.

The villagers' initial belief that she was some kind of executive tart had been understandable. Having asked her if it was true, and believed her when she'd smiled and said it wasn't, he could still sympathize with the locals on this one.

What Nell did in her spare time remained a mystery, but it apparently involved leaving the village at around seven in the evening and returning in the very small hours. This happened, according to the ever-disapproving Hilda Garnet, three or four times a week. On occasions, Nell didn't come home until the following morning. It was almost as if she led a double life. What was she then, if not a shameless whore? Hilda had demanded with a sneer. Either that, or some rich man's mistress.

As soon as the bitter words had spilled out, she had regretted them. Remembering Marcus's father and his own affair with Miriam O'Driscoll, she clamped her mouth over her false teeth and flushed an unbecoming shade of beetroot.

'Now, now.' Marcus still found her disapproval hugely entertaining. 'Why does it have to be something like that? You don't know, Nell could be working for the Samaritans on the quiet . . . fundraising for some charity . . . helping the homeless—'

'In those skirts?' Hilda had by this time recovered her colour. 'The only person that girl helps,' she retorted with a loud, you-mark-my-words sniff of disapproval, 'is herself.'

But Nell hadn't disappeared this evening. She had been at her desk working non-stop. With a swift glance at his watch, Marcus saw that it was nine-twenty. Apart from a few melon-and-prosciutto canapés the size of your average marble, he'd eaten nothing since breakfast.

'Look, are you hungry?' Even as he said it, he wondered what he thought he was playing at. 'It's not too late to drive over to Nailsworth. We could have dinner at Flynn's.'

This was plain stupid, Marcus told himself. Was he mad?

Working together was one thing; driving to a restaurant to share what would undoubtedly be interpreted as a romantic, candle-lit dinner *à deux* was in another league altogether. It wasn't even as if he wanted to drive to a restaurant, for God's sake. Nor did he need to. The faithful Mrs Garnet would undoubtedly have left something just as fabulous in the fridge.

But curiosity had got the better of him. He needed to ask because he had to know whether or not Nell would accept. Not that it mattered either way, as far as he was concerned; he was just interested in finding out.

Nell, continuing to write, replied absently, 'No thanks. I had a Twix earlier.'

Bloody bitch. Marcus felt his jaw muscles tighten in silent outrage. What the bloody hell did she think *she* was playing at? Of all the damn cheek.

His mouth, evidently unable to believe what his ears had heard – Marcus wasn't used to being turned down – said, 'Oh come on, have you ever been to Flynn's before? They do the most amazing stroganoff . . .'

This time he *really* couldn't believe his ears. For heaven's sake, he was practically begging.

'I know they do.' Nell stopped writing. She looked up and smiled. 'But I'm not really hungry tonight. Sorry.'

He had known she would say that. If there was one thing he did know about Nell O'Driscoll, Marcus irritably recalled, it was that once she'd made a decision, she stuck with it. She didn't change her mind.

Chapter 13

Alicia Pemberton lived in a five-storey Georgian mansion overlooking Regent's Park. Kiki Ross-Armitage and Jemima, pulling up outside the house in Kiki's Porsche – powder blue to match her favourite Ferragamo shoes – were forty minutes late.

'It doesn't matter, it takes ages anyway,' said Kiki breezily. 'We'll be last in the queue, that's all. More time to have a good old girlie gossip with the others first.'

Kiki, who had been twice before, knew the routine and was bright-eyed with anticipation. It was only to stop her going on and on about it that Jemima had finally agreed to come along with her. Jemima thought all this fortune-telling business was claptrap. She was just astonished so many other perfectly sensible people appeared to believe in it. She had been even more astounded when Kiki had casually thrown in the names of some of this particular fortune-teller's starrier clients.

'Don't knock it 'til you've tried it,' Kiki had declared, when she'd dared to mock. 'I'm telling you, this girl is good. I can't wait,' she added with a lascivious wink. 'I'm going to ask her what my chances are of getting off with your desperately dishy big brother.'

Jemima, who still didn't believe in any of it, nevertheless felt her heart do a quick skip and a jump. If this clairvoyant was so great, maybe she could just ask about her own chances with Timmy Struther. Just for fun. Fortune-telling was like religion, after all; believing in it wasn't going to do you any actual damage. And if it gave you the courage of your convictions, to go ahead and do something you desperately wanted to do anyway, well, where was the harm in that?

'It's still claptrap,' she complained now, as Alicia Pemberton's terminally ugly butler opened the door to them. 'Oh God, I'm going to be the only unbeliever. What happens if I get the giggles, will she put some kind of spell on me?'

'She's a clairvoyant.' Kiki's tone was brisk. 'Not a witch.'

'What did you say she was called?'

'Petronella.'

'Of course. Petronella.' Mimicking the word with relish, Jemima pulled a face. 'Made-up name.'

They had crossed the black-and-white marbled entrance hall. Ahead of them, in the drawing-room, the others were already gathered.

'Go on then, smirk.' Kiki, who liked to know that her fringe was level, paused to check her hair in a vastly ornate Venetian mirror. 'I don't care what you think. You're the one,' she added carelessly, 'who's going to end up looking stupid.'

The system had evolved quite naturally, almost of its own accord, and since it suited everyone there had never been any reason to change it. Lots of Nell's regulars lived in London. She had been living in Oxford. It made perfect sense, therefore, to organize small-but-select parties of up to ten people, each of whom paid forty pounds for a reading. This made it worth

Nell's while to travel up to London, and more fun, too, for her regular clients. Alicia Pemberton's long-suffering husband, who shared Jemima's views on the subject of fortune-telling, called them her Mystic-Tupperware parties. Whenever his home was invaded he promptly decamped to his club, winking at Nell if she happened to arrive before he left the house. 'Evening, my dear. I hope you have plenty of mumbo-jumbo up your sleeve tonight, for the gullible girlies.'

Nell always grinned, nodded and said nothing at all, because Michael Pemberton was the Vice-President of a vast petro-chemical consortium. And unbeknown to him, its ruthless, all-powerful President was one of her most devoted clients.

'Hi,' said Kiki, poking her head around the door of the pale-green sitting-room an hour and a half later. 'Me next.'

'Make yourself comfortable.' Nell, who had kicked off her shoes, occupied a sage-green, silk upholstered chair. 'It's nice to see you again. How did that holiday in Antigua go? Was I completely wrong about the yellow jacket?'

Kiki thought Petronella was wonderful. For one thing, no matter how many people she saw, she remembered the stuff she'd told you last time. Also, a trait Kiki found endearing, she always seemed amazed when her own predictions came true.

'You were exactly right.'

Beaming, Kiki lit a cigarette. Nell had told her to watch out for a foreigner with a yellow jacket whilst she was away; he wouldn't be all he seemed. Upon discovering that one of their fellow hotel guests was a German TV host attempting to holiday incognito, Kiki had cried delightedly, 'Tell me, do you own a yellow jacket?' The TV host, who had once borrowed a raincoat from his father-in-law and never returned it, had looked bemused. 'Well, yes. But why?'

'I knew it,' screeched Kiki, tipping her white wine spritzer all over his expensive trousers. 'I just *knew* you'd have one! I swear, every word that girl says comes true!'

'Exactly right,' she repeated now, almost missing the marble ashtray with her cigarette. 'And the holiday was great, apart from not meeting anyone gorgeous.'

'Ah,' said Nell, 'but it won't be long now.'

Kiki's carefully plucked eyebrows shot up. This time, in her excitement, she missed the ashtray completely.

'Really? How long . . . less than a fortnight?'

'Well . . .' Nell was cautious.

'The thing is, a good friend of mine is going to be introducing me to her brother next weekend.' Kiki giggled and blushed. 'Maybe I shouldn't be telling you this, but as far as I'm concerned the more you know about the situation, the more likely you are to be able to help. Besides,' she went on breathlessly, 'you're so brilliant you probably already know about it anyway.'

Nell, looking suitably modest, sidestepped the extravagant compliment. 'So you have a definite feeling about this chap?' she persisted. 'You really think he could be the one you've been waiting for?'

'Golly!' Struck by her careful choice of words, Kiki gazed in awe at Nell. 'You don't suppose I could be psychic too, do you? Oh I say, what a scream, but yes, I *do* have some kind of weird feeling about meeting him . . .'

'That's it then.' Nell grinned. 'You don't need me any more. You can tell your own fortunes.'

'Do you see it too, though?' Kiki was desperate to hear it from someone she trusted. 'I mean, I've always gone for dark-haired men before, but . . .'

'This one is blond. And tall.' Nell grinned. 'Not to mention fabulously good-looking.'

With a sigh, Kiki said, 'You are brilliant. And do you really think we might . . . ?'

Nell, who was getting nothing, didn't have the heart to say so. Kiki was practically begging to be given the go-ahead.

'Look, I can't say one hundred per cent. But it's a definite maybe. Just don't scare him off,' she warned, feeling the need to interject a note of caution. The proverbial bull at the gate, she guessed, had nothing on Kiki when she got into full flow. 'Be casual. Be cool. And,' she threw in for good measure, 'wear pink.'

'That was great,' said Kiki happily twenty minutes later when her time was up. Then she bit her lip and looked apologetic. 'Look, I'd better warn you. This friend of mine, the one with the brother, is coming in next. I'm almost embarrassed to say it, but she doesn't believe in this kind of thing. I do hope she isn't too difficult.'

'That's OK.' Nell was amused by her concern. 'If she isn't happy, she doesn't have to pay.'

It was what she always told them; all they had to do was ask for a refund. So far – and to her continuing amazement – nobody ever had.

'If she isn't happy, she's out of her mind.' Kiki rose to her feet, her own mind already occupied elsewhere. Frantically visualizing her walk-in wardrobes, with their colour co-ordinated racks of Miyake, Hempel and Joseph must-haves, Roberto Cavalli spectaculars and Conran classics, she turned to Nell for help.

'This pink I'm going to be wearing. Exactly what shade do you think would work best?'

When the unbeliever sidled into the sitting-room thirty seconds later, her jaw actually *physically* dropped open.

Oops, thought Nell, trying not to laugh at the ludicrous expression on Jemima's face. She must be slipping. Here was something she definitely hadn't foreseen! And, oh dear, that meant the gorgeous man Kiki was so keen to impress was, of all people, Marcus Kilburton himself.

'What's going on?' Dumbfoundedness having given way to suspicion, Jemima's eyebrows drew together. The rather small, blue-green eyes narrowed. 'Is this some kind of a joke? Is my brother here?'

'No.' Nell shook her head and smiled. 'Marcus isn't here. It isn't a joke. It's not *This Is Your Life*, either.'

'I don't get it.' Leaning back against the door, clearly unhappy about this, Jemima folded her arms. 'There's some-thing odd going on. So what are you going to tell me, that by day you work for Marcus as some kind of super-efficient PA and by night you transform yourself into Gypsy Petronella, fortune-teller to the rich and famous?'

There was nothing else for it. At moments like these, Nell

decided, you discovered whether or not someone possessed a sense of humour. Although in this case she didn't hold out a great deal of hope.

'Well, if you want to put it like that,' she said, 'um, yes.'

Chapter 14

Good Friday, the day of the gala opening of Kilburton Castle to the public, dawned clear and warm. Since it was only mid-April, and since Nell had never had the slightest bit of success when it came to predicting the weather, relief that such a gamble had paid off was tremendous. It could, after all, have been a lot worse, as one of the young apprentice electricians helping to set up the television outside broadcast unit cheerfully pointed out to Nell.

'Could've been a howlin' blizzard,' he reminded her, with an appreciative glance at her bare brown legs. She was wearing a long, extremely fitted, fuchsia-pink jacket, a brief white skirt and pink-and-white striped shoes. When he had been dragged by his parents around mouldy old stately homes as a kid, there had never been anyone like this working in any of them. If there had, he thought now, he might not have found them so bleedin' borin'. 'Could've been pourin' wiv rain, freezin' cold and howlin' a gale,' he went on. 'Or thunder and lightnin', electrocutin' everyone left, right and centre. You just don't know, love, how lucky you are.'

Nell was too scared to feel lucky. She had barely slept. Somehow, when she had made her cavalier offer to come and work for Marcus, she had imagined getting the place *ready* to be opened, and she had imagined running it once it *was* open.

But this bit, the actual nerve-racking opening day itself with all its attendant traumas and scope for disaster, was the bit that had somehow managed to skulk past unnoticed.

The sun is shining, Nell told herself, repeating the words like a mantra in the hope that they might sink in and do some good. The sun is shining, it's a bank holiday, the signposts are up, the advertising has gone out, absolutely everyone knows we're opening today, there's no reason on earth to suppose that nobody will turn up.

'Hi.' Hetty, who had come up behind her, beamed. When she saw Nell's expression, her own face fell. 'Oh dear, whatever's the matter?'

'Nobody's going to turn up.'

'Yes they will.'

'No they won't.'

Hetty started to laugh. 'OK, have it your way. Nobody's going to turn up. It's going to be an out-and-out disaster. You'll be so humiliated—'

'Bitch,' wailed Nell. She felt better, but only fractionally so.

'Thank you.' Hetty was delighted. 'I'm getting into practice. Apparently Vanessa told Minnie Hardwick she didn't think it was very wise, me working in the Castle restaurant, because I clearly have no self-control whatsoever when it comes to food.'

'She said that? Bitch!'

This time Nell meant it.

'She also said no wonder I was so lonely,' Hetty went on. 'Men aren't interested in little dumplings, according to Vanessa. And they certainly don't respect the kind of woman who can't be bothered to take care of her own body.'

'You could always hire a hit man.' Bloody Vanessa and her big mouth, thought Nell. And bloody Minnie Hardwick, too, for not being able to resist making sure the hurtful message was passed on.

Hetty, who had been gleefully wreaking her own revenge for over a fortnight now, couldn't care less. Tony had taken to dropping in 'for a chat' more and more often and she was only too delighted to give him what he clearly wasn't getting from Vanessa. By pretending to be on another boring diet herself, too, she had been able to join him in the naughty subterfuge, sharing her home-made cakes with him and saying guiltily, 'I really shouldn't . . . oh, go on then, I'll have another slice if you will.'

As far as Hetty was concerned, every kilo Tony didn't lose was another thrilling slap in the face for Vanessa and her raw-carrot roulade. He was being gastronomically unfaithful to her, cheating on her with someone who truly understood his craving for extra-curricular excitement, a bit on the side, forbidden fruit, not to mention rum-and-chocolate torte . . .

And he's being unfaithful to her with me, Hetty reminded herself a dozen times a day, because just thinking about it cheered her up. Vanessa would kill him if she ever found out. That was, she thought with a brief flicker of guilt, if the cholesterol-induced heart attack didn't get him first.

Nell and Hetty made their way around the castle grounds, enabling Nell to oversee the last-minute preparations and ensure they were proceeding smoothly. In honour of the occasion, Abel Trippick was wearing his best flat cap, the one normally reserved for Sundays. The outside broadcast unit, who were going to be linking up live with 'What's on in the West', as well as local news programmes, were getting ready to roll. The last of the five hundred Kilburton Castle balloons were being pumped up and stuffed into a vast, bulging net. The Butterfly House was alive with heat, humidity, tropical foliage and butterflies. The gift shop and garden shops were on standby. The restaurant gleamed. The Tedbury brass band was tuning up. The freshly painted Victorian horses on the fairground roundabout waited to be ridden. The south stable block, converted into a dozen or so workshops where sculptors, painters, woodworkers and potters both demonstrated and sold their work, buzzed with excitement. One of the artists, a caricaturist, was skilfully capturing the profile of one of the television reporters whose vanity was notorious, to the undisguised delight of the camera crew.

'It seems weird, watching it come to life like this.' Outside the second stable block, now an antiques market, the fire-eaters, stilt walkers, mime artists and jugglers, hired for the day by Nell, were lounging together on the emerald lawn, chatting animatedly, enjoying the warmth of the sun and drinking Coke. Peacocks strutted past, their iridescent tails sweeping the clipped grass like bridal trains. One of the entertainers, a magician, winked at Hetty and with a flick of the wrist pulled a stream of coloured silk scarves from his left ear.

'How brilliant!' She clapped her hands with delight. 'Wherever did you get them from?'

'Circus school.' With her head bent, Nell was going obsessively over her list once more. 'Loo paper,' she murmured beneath her breath. 'Waste bins. Ice-cream sellers. Damn.'

'What?'

'We're supposed to be having an Easter egg hunt at midday. I've hidden two hundred chocolate eggs in the adventure playground . . .'

'And?' said Hetty when Nell's voice had trailed away. 'What?'

'It's too sunny,' Nell wailed. 'Too sunny and too hot. The stupid things are going to bloody well melt.'

The gates opened at ten o'clock. By eleven-thirty the car-park was full and the treeless swathe of parkland next to it had been pressed into service. It seemed that everyone living within a fifty-mile radius had woken up that morning, seen the sun, wondered what to do on a fine Easter holiday – in itself, enough of a rarity to confound them – and had decided to do as all the advertising had urged them to do, which was come to Kilburton.

Marcus found Nell in her second-floor office. Having come upstairs to pick up bags of change from the safe, she now stood with her back to him, gazing out of the turret window at the scenes below. In the far distance, glittering sunlight bounced off a thousand windscreens as yet more cars snaked their way along the narrow lane leading up to the castle. Once inside the grounds, people milled like multicoloured ants, enjoying the gardens, picnicking on the lawns surrounding the hugely popular adventure playground and feeding the ducks on the lake.

As he moved closer to Nell, Marcus was able to see more from the window. There were the entertainers, surrounded by admirers, stilt-walking and juggling their way across the courtyard. People were queuing for ice-creams. Others, happily emerging from the craft and antiques markets in the stable blocks, carried their purchases in matte, dark-blue carrier bags which discreetly bore the Kilburton crest. Nell had insisted on top-quality carriers, the kind of prestige bag which could be used again and looked good enough to make you want to do so.

It was a point over which they had argued, he recalled, but Nell, as usual, had stuck rigidly to her guns. As usual, too, she had been right.

'Well.' Having heard him come into the office and recognized the sound of his footsteps, she didn't need to turn round. 'They turned up.'

'They certainly did.' Marcus smiled, watching over her shoulder as a horde of children clowned for the TV cameras in front of the merry-go-round. Nell's dark hair, braided into a plump, glossy plait and tied at the bottom with a fuchsia ribbon, smelled of Pears shampoo. At such close quarters he could see that her complexion really was flawless, as fine and velvety as a peach. Her cheeks were slightly flushed, too, from having raced around all day like a maniac. The fuchsia pink lipstick was practically worn off.

'That photographer from the *Express* is looking for you.' As she turned to speak to him, Nell glanced at her watch. 'And the TV people want to film the balloon launch at three. You're supposed to be down there, not up here.'

'I was looking for you. All this,' Marcus nodded in the direction of the window, 'is thanks to your hard work. I thought you might like to do the honours with me.'

TV cameras, thought Nell. And press photographers. Pictures of the two of them together in all the papers.

'No thanks.'

'No thanks,' Marcus mimicked with an air of exasperation. 'You're making a bit of a habit of this, aren't you? Is it just me, or do you turn down every offer as a matter of principle?'

She flashed him a grin. 'I'm strictly a back-room girl. Go on, it's your castle. You're the one they want to see.'

God, she was infuriating. He still didn't know why she had come to work for him in the first place. As far as Marcus was concerned, people fell into categories. The mystifying thing about Nell O'Driscoll, however, was the fact that she didn't appear to fall into *any* recognizable category. And how the hell was he supposed to get to know her better in order to be *able* to categorize her, when every time he asked her to do anything she said no?

'What are you looking at now?' he demanded, following her intent gaze. The sky, a cloudless cornflower blue, was as empty as sky could get. There was nothing at all to see.

'Helicopter.'

This signalled the arrival of Kiki and Jemima. The day after their meeting at Alicia Pemberton's house, Jemima had flown to Nice for a brief holiday with friends. It was going to be interesting, Nell thought, to see what she was going to say about it to Marcus. Although Kiki was very definitely on Nell's side, Jemima hadn't taken the unexpected discovery nearly so well. Her suspicions clearly aroused, she felt there had to be some kind of ulterior motive. The chances of her not mentioning it, Nell felt, were slim. Maybe she should have got in first and done it herself – confessed her shameful secret – after all. The trouble was, she thought with secret amusement as the helicopter finally came into view, it sounded so bloody *daft*.

Chapter 15

Hetty's shoes were too tight. Her feet were killing her. After five hours in the restaurant she felt she deserved her break. Taking a squishy, home-made coffee éclair and a big pot of tea out on to the sunlit terrace, she searched in vain for an empty table and stood there hovering, undecided whether to give in and limp back inside.

'You can sit here,' a young voice offered behind her. 'We'll be going in a minute as soon as Beryl's finished her scone.'

Turning with relief – because these helpless where-can-I-sit scenarios always made her flustered – Hetty identified the voice as belonging to a girl she had served twenty minutes earlier. Beryl, crouching at her owner's feet with half a wholemeal scone balanced delicately between her front paws, was a panting, pale-yellow Labrador.

'Thank you. Goodness, it's bliss to sit down.' Sinking gratefully on to her chair, Hetty smiled across at the girl. 'Actually, I think I recognize you. Haven't you just moved into Swan Cottage?'

'Fame at last,' sighed the girl, who had wavy, light-brown hair, small but sparkling blue-grey eyes and a sweet, rounded face. She looked intrigued. 'Gosh, I'd heard it was impossible to keep secrets in the country. Do you really know everything about us already?'

'We taught MI5 all they know.' Hetty took the first heavenly lick of coffee icing. Beneath the table, Beryl thumped her plumy tail. 'You moved in two days ago. Your father's going to be our new GP taking over from Dr Carling when he retires next month. Your mother is incredibly glamorous, with long blond hair and red lipstick. She's also rather sporty because there are squash and tennis rackets on the back seat of her car, together with a hang-gliding manual. You have a dark-red leather Chesterfield settee, you only use skimmed milk and your dad's middle name starts with a W, so it's probably William. I'm afraid we don't know yet which brand of toothpaste you use, but it's only a matter of time.'

'I'm impressed.'

The girl was laughing. With a jolt, Hetty realized how long it had been since Rachel had laughed out loud like that. They must be pretty much the same age, she estimated; maybe they would become friends.

'My name's Hetty Brewster,' she said happily. 'I have a daughter who's fifteen. Rachel. We live at The Gables, on the corner of the High Street and Woods Lane.'

'I'm Clemency Munro.' The girl, who had effortless manners, stuck out her hand. 'I'm fifteen too. My mum and dad are divorced, Mum lives in Spain, the glamorous blonde is my dad's sister Kate, and she isn't the least bit sporty, she just leaves that stuff in her car to show off. She doesn't live with us,' Clemency explained, 'she helped us move in, that's all. And my dad's middle name isn't William.' She hesitated, then lowered her voice to a conspiratorial whisper. 'He'll kill me for this. It's Walter.'

* * *

By the time her fifteen-minute tea-break was over, Hetty felt as if she had known Clemency Munro for years. Entranced by the girl's unaffected manner – it made such a change to meet a cheerful teenager – she was already wondering if her father was anywhere near as nice.

Oh dear, thought Hetty, inwardly appalled at the depths to which she had sunk. Talk about clutching at straws. How desperate could a divorcee get? At this rate, the next thing would be checking out the sound of Hetty Munro and doodling it all over her order pad to see how it looked.

'Oh look, there's Rachel now!' To cover her own embarrassment, Hetty leapt up and frantically waved her arms in order to grab her dawdling daughter's attention. 'I can introduce you.'

If Rachel was impressed by the gala opening of Kilburton Castle, she would have died rather than admit it. Looking studiously bored, wearing a black Slipknot hoody over black jeans, she appeared to have forgotten how to smile, let alone laugh. In one so pale, such a fixation with black wasn't flattering. This, together with the permanently sullen expression, meant that even Hetty had to concede her daughter was a bit of a daunting prospect just now.

'Darling, this is Clemency Munro.' Hetty, trying not to gush, was already out of her seat. It wouldn't do to be late back from her very first tea-break. 'She's the daughter of the new doctor I was telling you about; they've just moved into Swan Cottage. Oh dear, I really must get back to work. Why don't you sit down, sweetheart, and fill Clemency in on all the local gossip? I'm sure you'll have lots in common.'

It wasn't the first time her mother had done this to her. Rachel, an only child, had grown up hearing such cringe-making lines as: 'Do you think your little boy would like to play on the swings with my little girl?' It might have been bearable when she was five years old, but at fifteen it was downright embarrassing.

With a brief, unfriendly glance in the direction of Clemency Munro, Rachel saw a plump, extremely ordinary-looking girl of about her own age who was wearing the kind of deeply un-fashionable clothes no sane fifteen-year-old would have been seen dead in. A blue-and-white candy-striped shirt. Totally gross, for starters. Clean blue jeans with – ugh, ugh – neatly ironed creases down the front. As for the blue-and-white plimsolls, Rachel decided, it was a miracle the girl's feet hadn't died of shame.

But it was no good, her mother had disappeared and the girl was smiling up at her, clearly determined to be friendly. At her feet lay a dopey-looking dog.

Hell's bells, thought Rachel. Why does this always have to happen to me?

'Hi!' Clemency didn't appear in the least put out by the forcible introduction. 'Isn't your mum terrific? Mine lives in Majorca; she's great, but I only get to see her a couple of times a year. You're really lucky, what with that *and* the hair.'

'What?' Rachel stared. Had she missed something? Was this girl actually daring to poke fun at her?

'Your hair.' Clemency, dimples going in both cheeks, reached across the table and touched it. She sighed. 'I'm so jealous. The thing I'd like more than anything else in the world is to have hair the same colour as yours.'

She wasn't making fun of her, Rachel realized. She meant it. Caught off-guard by the compliment, she put her own hand up to her head, as if to make sure they were talking about the same stuff.

'It's red.' Her voice sounded gruff and awkward. 'I hate it. You wouldn't like red hair if it was what you'd been born with.'

'You can't call it red,' Clemency protested. 'That's what traffic lights are. I'd call your hair burnished copper.'

'Oh.' It sounded . . . nice. Unable to help herself, Rachel wondered whether Derry O'Driscoll would be likely to take more notice of a girl whose hair was burnished copper rather than plain old red.

'And I would love to have been born with hair your colour, let me tell you.' Clemency was laughing now, leaning towards her as if they were already best friends. 'Or for that matter hair any colour at all. I was as bald as an egg until I was two,' she confided. 'When that happens, you get kind of desperate.'

'Bloody hell, haven't they gone yet?'

Moodily, Jemima gazed out of her bedroom window in the south wing. It was now six-fifteen. The gates were supposed to have been closed at six and there were still plebs scattered like obstinate confetti across the lawns. Didn't they have homes of their own to go to? And why the bloody hell was Marcus still out there *talking* to people? He was just encouraging them to stay on, thought Jemima, and make even more of a nuisance of themselves than they already had.

'I knew it was going to be vile.' With a fretful glance over her shoulder at Kiki, who was stretched out across the bed engrossed in *Hello!*, she heaved an elaborate sigh. 'But I had no idea it was going to be this bad. I feel like some kind of exhibit in a zoo . . .'

'You'll get used to it.' Kiki kept her head down. She was on the verge of losing her patience with Jemima, who could whinge for England when she put her mind to it. All Kiki cared about right now was slithering into something pink and meeting Marcus Kilburton for the first time at tonight's party. Getting wound up about the paying public, as far as Kiki was concerned, was a shameful waste of adrenalin. It was so necessary to conserve one's energy, she felt, in order to seriously smoulder.

'Mrs Garnet, what is Nell O'Driscoll *like*?'

The subject had continued to bother Jemima and it was something else about which Kiki hadn't been the least bit sympathetic. Now, finding Hilda Garnet in the kitchen putting the finishing touches to tomorrow morning's breakfast trays, she decided to ask the housekeeper for her opinion. She'd never paid much attention before, but if she thought back, there had almost certainly been signs of tension between the two of them.

To prove it, Hilda Garnet's spine visibly stiffened at the very mention of Nell's name. Gratified to have been asked, she was nevertheless torn between protecting her beloved Jemima from the sordidness of the truth and letting her know what the O'Driscolls were *really* like.

Jemima, sensing weakness, said cosily, 'Oh go on, do tell. I'm only asking because I'm not at all sure I trust her.' With a sly glance across at the housekeeper's pursed mouth she went on, 'I'm so afraid Marcus may be taken in. The thing is, who knows where that could lead? She's hardly what you'd call plain.'

'I really shouldn't.' Hilda, who was dying to, made a feeble last stab at discretion.

'Of course you should. If you don't,' Jemima gave her a Cheshire cat smile, 'I'll only ask somebody else.'

Chapter 16

Marcus hadn't originally planned a party to celebrate the opening of the castle. When Jemima had announced that she was bringing Kiki down with her for the Easter weekend, however, it had seemed easier than facing the pair of them alone. There was a lot to be said for safety in numbers. Having found himself on the receiving end of less-than-subtle female attentions before now, Marcus had promptly invited a couple of dozen guests, a combination of people whose hospitality he had enjoyed in the past and must now return, and those he actually liked. He had also asked Nell. It was a toss-up which of the two of them had been more astonished when she had said yes.

'My little girl,' crowed Miriam. Her dark eyes burned with pride as Nell made her entrance into the kitchen, rifled through the bread bin and dropped a couple of slices of malt loaf into the toaster.

The bottle-green dress clung to every inch, wrapping itself around her like wet seaweed. The off-the-shoulder neckline was edged with gold braid. The green-and-gold high heels were a perfect match. With her hair up and those elongated ear-rings accentuating her slender neck she looked, Miriam decided, just about perfect. 'Like mother, like daughter.' She winked. 'He won't be able to resist you, sweetheart, mark my words. And another Kilburton succumbs to the charms of an O'Driscoll!'

'Shut up, Mother.'

Miriam loved it when Nell gave her that long-suffering look.

'What's the matter? Can you help it if you look like a goddess? Of *course* he's going to want to—'

'I mean it,' warned Nell.

'No sense of humour,' Miriam murmured, still smiling to herself. 'Body of a temptress, brain of a nun.'

The toast popped up. Nell, who was more nervous than she was letting on, needed something to stop her stomach gurgling like a drain.

'Meddling old bag of a mother,' she said, turning her back on Miriam as she piled butter and apricot jam on to the toasted malt loaf. 'Has it ever occurred to you that I might not even be interested in Marcus Kilburton?'

'Don't be silly, darling.' Lighting a cigarette, Miriam began to laugh. 'Of course it hasn't.'

Once Mrs Garnet had got going there had been absolutely no stopping her. Now, every time Jemima thought of it, she felt sick.

Ugh, it was all so disgusting . . . darling Daddy, whom she had hero-worshipped, carrying on for years with some ghastly gypsy from the village, evidently making a complete fool of himself and at the same time bringing shame on his entire family.

And the ghastly common gypsy, to add insult to injury, was Petronella O'Driscoll's mother.

As the whole repulsive story had spilled out, Jemima had felt herself going hot and cold all over. This was so much worse than she had ever imagined. When she had told Mrs Garnet she didn't trust Nell with Marcus, she hadn't actually meant it, it had simply been a device to get the gossip on Nell. She hadn't bargained on hearing nauseating details of her own father's sex life.

Kiki, breathless with the effort of wriggling into the first of the three pink dresses she had brought down with her, gasped, 'Bloody thing's shrunk. Come on, Jem, zip me up. What do you think, any chance it'll stand the strain?'

Wordlessly, Jemima tugged at the zip of the strapless, jewel-studded Lacroix. Since it didn't have a hope in hell of doing up, she shook her head. Kiki, who was forever dieting, was also forever secretly raiding food from the fridge. Getting fat, she appeared to believe, was like getting pregnant; so long as you did it standing up, it didn't count.

Disappointed by the lack of effort, Kiki had twisted round. She heaved an impatient sigh.

'Look, I'm the one who can't squeeze into her sodding frock. I don't know why you have to look so tragic. Whatever's the matter now?'

'Nothing.'

It was all so desperately shaming. Kiki might be her best friend but Jemima didn't trust her not to blab. Besides, she'd got her make-up in place. If she did start talking about it, she wasn't at all sure she trusted herself not to burst into tears of rage. She shook her head, unable to speak.

'Suit yourself, then.'

Kiki, who wasn't that interested anyway, had other matters to preoccupy her. How stupid she'd been to bring down only three cocktail dresses. Having already mentally discarded the peony pink Karl Lagerfeld, because it was even tighter across the hips than the Lacroix, she cast a regretful glance down at her slightly protruding stomach. This meant she was going to have to settle for the floating, figure-skimming multi-layered Valentino after all. It was ravishing, of course, but patterned with ivory roses. It wasn't *just* pink. Biting her lower lip, Kiki only hoped it would still do the trick.

By eight o'clock, Jemima's spirits had lifted a fraction. She would deal with Nell O'Driscoll when the time was right. For now, she decided, she would allow herself to be distracted by Timmy Struther, Marquis of Barham, eldest son of the Duke of Caveley. Secretly smitten with Timmy for over five years – during which time he had cut quite a swathe through London society, falling effortlessly from one bed to the next and leaving a trail of dumped débutantes in his wake – Jemima had been thrilled when at a charity ball at the Grosvenor six weeks ago he had seized upon her, whirling her out on to the floor for a slow dance.

'I've had my eye on you for quite a while,' he had murmured into Jemima's hair as his fingers lightly explored the super-sensitive skin between her shoulder blades. 'You aren't like the rest of them, are you? Something tells me you're rather special.'

That was all, but it had been more than enough. Jemima, her stomach flip-flopping with delight, had at last dared to hope he could seriously be interested in her. Timmy Struther might be what the older generation referred to as a bit of a cad, but as far as her girlfriends were concerned he was deeply desirable. After all, how many dishy, heterosexual heirs to a dukedom under the age of forty were there? If Timmy Struther hadn't taken advantage of his enviable situation he wouldn't be human, it was generally agreed by those still desperate to be taken advantage of. The thing was, sooner or later even a womanizer as inexhaustible as Timmy had to settle down, make a suitable marriage and produce heirs of his own.

This, Jemima felt, was where she came in. She could do that. She was suitable. She would make a brilliant Duchess of Caveley.

And Timmy already thought she was special. All she had to do now was persuade him to keep thinking it.

'Introduce me to your brother,' Kiki murmured breathlessly, because if Marcus Kilburton was extra-special in theory, he was even more stupendous in the flesh. 'Oh my God, I've spent my entire life waiting for this moment. Introduce me this minute, Jem. Quick, before that pain-in-the-neck Clarissa Cardew-Tate gets her claws into him.'

It was already eight-thirty. It had been Kiki's idea that they should be the last guests to arrive. Eager to make maximum impact, she had insisted on keeping Jemima upstairs with her, unearthing a bottle of Gilbey's from her case to get them both in party mood and speculating endlessly about what fate might have in store. Now, as they paused at the top of the grand staircase in order to give everyone the opportunity to notice them making their dazzling entrance, Jemima wondered if she might not have overdone the gin a bit. For a fraction of a second, the ground appeared to shift beneath her feet. Take it steady, she told herself. One step at a time. Losing her footing, cartwheeling down the staircase and no doubt flashing her knickers in the process definitely wasn't the kind of maximum impact Kiki had had in mind.

She could feel Kiki, next to her, doing her beauty-queen beam, a surefire sign that she meant business. Once the stairs had been safely negotiated, Jemima found herself being propelled, by a firm hand in the small of her back, in Marcus's direction.

'Ah. There you are.'

He had been listening to a balding, phenomenally wealthy rock star lament the fact that his groupies nowadays were too ancient to chase him.

As he turned to greet his sister and her friend, Marcus glimpsed Nell at the far end of the hall, deep in conversation with a rival stately home owner who also ran a wildlife park. Lighted candles flickered in sconces on the wall behind her, illuminating the centuries-old stained-glass windows and the priceless Oudenaarde tapestries hung on either side of the massive stone fireplace. Nell's green-and-gold dress shimmered in the dim reflected light and her teeth flashed white as she laughed at something she had just heard. One of Marcus's old school friends, now a high-goal polo player, was hovering behind her waiting for an opportunity to join the conversation. Timmy Struther was on his way over as well, by the look of it. So much, thought Marcus, for worrying that Nell, not knowing anyone, might feel ill at ease.

'We're over here, actually.' Jiggling impatient fingers in front of his face, because she too had spotted the flicker of interest on Timmy's narrow, handsome face, Jemima recaptured her brother's attention. 'Marcus, say hello to Kiki Ross-Armitage. Kiki, this is my brother Marcus.' As if Kiki didn't know, she added, 'The Right Honourable the Earl of Kilburton.'

'Nice to meet you at last.' Marcus smiled slightly, because Kiki was staring at him. He felt very much on parade. He also wished Jemima hadn't given him that marry-the-girl-for-her-money lecture. It didn't help.

'Thank you for inviting me down here.' Kiki had practised this bit. Good manners were important in a future wife.

Marcus, who had had nothing to do with the invitation, nodded. 'My pleasure.'

'Um . . . I love your home.' Casting desperately around for something to say, because for the first time in her life she appeared to have lost the knack of coherent speech, Kiki gazed up at the seventeenth-century vaulted ceiling. 'It's so, you know . . . *old*.'

This was too painful to watch. Having done her duty, Jemima slipped away and left them to get on with it. Kiki was so screamingly obvious, she might just as well have hung a placard around her neck announcing her infatuation to the world. OK, so she was smitten, but didn't she realize how off-putting that was to the man on the receiving end? Hadn't she understood that you had to use a bit of subtlety if you really wanted to capture their interest?

* * *

Across the hall, Nell was thinking much the same. She might not be able to hear what was going on but the visible signs were only too apparent. She cringed in sympathy as Kiki laughed too loudly at something Marcus had said. He was beginning to look bored. Knowing him as she did, Nell knew too that he was perfectly capable of glancing at his watch, making not-very-convincing excuses and moving off at a rate of knots. Unlimited patience wasn't one of Marcus's virtues.

Timmy Struther, meanwhile, carried on regardless.

'. . . so I bet Buzzer a monkey he couldn't ski down the black run with a bottle of shampoo in one hand and a glass in the other.' His brown eyes glittered as he relayed the story of his adventures in Gstaad.

Nell, who had already worked out what she thought of Timmy, turned politely back to him.

'I'm sorry, I was distracted. So why did he need to wash his hair?'

He laughed, revealing dazzling, slightly pointed teeth. Definitely good-looking, she thought with a tinge of regret because it seemed such a waste. Definitely a prat.

'Not that kind of shampoo, sweetheart. We're talking Moët. Bottle of fizz, you know. Rather like lemonade, except sooner or later you fall over.'

A condescending prat, at that. Nell kept a straight face.

'Oh, right. So what happened when he skied down the black run? Let me guess, he fell over.'

'Damn right he did! Broke both legs!' Smirking, Timmy drained his own glass. 'I won my bet fair and square. Made him pay up before the blood-wagon carted him off to hospital.

Let me tell you, I went out that evening and got absolutely smashed.'

Nell said, 'You mean you broke *your* legs?'

'No! Oh, I see. Ha ha.'

For the first time he appeared to drop the hooray front. Taking her hand and raising it to his lips, Timmy drawled, 'I do believe you're making fun of me.'

Too right, thought Nell. Front or no front, she had heard enough for one night.

It was just as well. The next moment she found herself being elbowed abruptly to one side as Jemima joined them.

Ignoring Nell, she handed Timmy a fresh glass and pulled a face. 'Hi, this is such a bore, don't you think? Marcus does invite the most peculiar people to his parties.'

The duke who ran the incredibly successful wildlife park, and who had never much cared for Marcus's young sister, gave Nell an engaging smile. 'As one peculiar person to another, would you care to show me that Van Dyck in the library? I may be able to help you date it.'

'No need to do that now,' Timmy protested. He was rather enjoying being made fun of by Marcus's enigmatic but strikingly attractive PA. The quiet, outwardly unimpressed ones were always more of a challenge. 'Don't leave me,' he added with a persuasive grin. 'Anything you need to know about Van Dycks, I'm your man. We have heaps of his stuff at our place. I tell you what, I'll show you mine if you show me yours.'

Terrific, thought Nell. What an offer.

Jemima thought so too. Fury bubbled up inside her. This, she decided, was simply too much. Having determined not to breathe so much as a word in public about what was, after all, a private matter of the utmost humiliation, she now realized she was going to have to say it anyway.

'I shouldn't bother.' She spoke in a loud voice, addressing Timmy but making sure everyone in the hall could hear. 'I imagine the only thing my brother's brilliant assistant keeps at her place is a crate load of condoms and a worn-out bed. She's nothing but a con-artist and a tart.' Bitterly, Jemima added, 'It must run in the family. Her mother's a tart too.'

The hideous ensuing silence was broken by Timmy. Still smiling, seemingly unperturbed, he murmured, 'Great. I've always been attracted to tarts.'

Nobody, after that, appeared to know what to do next. Nell, whom Jemima had expected to either scream back at her, slap her face or storm out of the room, was saying nothing at all. Unnerved by the lack of reaction, since it effectively robbed her of an excuse to justify the outrageous slur, Jemima gazed down at the empty glass in her hand and felt her eyes fill with tears of self-pity. Nobody else understood why she'd been compelled to say it. They were all staring at her. Kiki, in particular, was looking shell-shocked. And Timmy, whose only too evident interest in Nell O'Driscoll had prompted her to lose her stupid temper in the first place, was at this moment sliding his arm around the tart's waist. Now, dammit to hell, he had a genuine reason to placate her.

Nell, who was used to being talked about behind her back, knew she had to stay calm. No matter how fiercely she longed to retaliate – oh, the temptation to seize a tray of caviare and quail's egg canapés from a passing waitress and tip the lot over

Jemima's gleaming blond hair – she mustn't allow herself the luxury. Because *not* reacting, remaining in control and riding the situation out with grace and style, was so much more effective. She would be admired for her restraint. Jemima, on the other hand, would be derided. The utter shame of it would return to haunt her for years to come.

And if I really wanted to put the boot in, Nell thought with a flicker of a smile, I could always sleep with Timmy Struther.

But no, that was definitely going too far. Annoying Jemima was all very well, but Timmy was still a prat.

'What the hell do you think you're playing at?'

Marcus, with a face like thunder, had crossed the room and taken a ferocious hold on Jemima's bare brown arm. Following behind, looking as if she was attached with elastic, Kiki hovered wide-eyed at his shoulder.

'Ouch.' Jemima winced and looked sulky. The duke with the wildlife park had diplomatically moved away. Other guests were resuming their conversations and pretending not to be fascinated. The caterers rushed round proffering fresh trays of canapés, as if hopeful of diverting attention from the taut little group at the far end of the hall.

'You're drunk,' stormed Marcus. 'You only came downstairs fifteen minutes ago. How can you possibly be drunk?'

Kiki, who looked even more miserable than Jemima, hung her head. Her heavy blond hair, which was blunt-cut in a shoulder-length bob, swung forward like a close-of-play curtain. 'I'm sorry, it was my idea. We had a couple of drinks upstairs. For Dutch courage . . .'

So much, she thought with a stab of despair, for playing it

cool and wearing pink. The look Marcus shot her was nothing short of contemptuous.

'Terrific.' He turned back to Jemima. 'Although I don't suppose she poured the stuff down your throat. You'd better apologize.'

What the hell, thought Nell. In for a penny, in for a pound.

'It's all right.' She smiled at Marcus. 'Jemima was upset. From the sound of it, she's just heard a bit of very old village gossip.'

Nell purposely didn't elaborate. If neither Kiki nor Timmy were aware of this fascinating snippet, there was no reason why they should know now. Timmy's lingering hand around her waist, however, was starting to get on her nerves. Taking a sideways step in order to free herself, she said in an undertone, 'You aren't helping, you know.'

He looked innocent. 'I tell you what, why don't I go and say hello to Clarissa?'

And then he winked, because saying hello to Clarissa was guaranteed to irritate Jemima.

'Fabulous idea,' said Nell.

When he had left them, Marcus gave his sister a grim look. 'Jemima. I'm waiting.'

It was exactly the wrong attitude to take. At the prospect of being treated like a naughty schoolgirl, her temper flared.

'OK. Maybe I shouldn't have said it so loudly, but I don't see why I should apologize. I still can't believe you were stupid enough to hire her.' She glared back at her brother, her plucked eyebrows arching in irritation as she rattled on. 'Has it not even occurred to you that there's something pretty damn peculiar about this whole business? She's spying on us, Marcus, stirring up trouble . . . what's she *really* after, do you suppose? Money or revenge? Frankly, I wouldn't be surprised if it wasn't all a massive scam. Before long you're going to find yourself calling the police to report half our art collection stolen.'

'For God's sake—'

'Right, that's enough,' Nell interjected smoothly. 'If you want to get this out of your system then fine, but you aren't going to do it here. You can come upstairs with me. And don't even think of it,' she warned as Jemima, white faced, opened her mouth to protest, 'because if you do, I shall slap you. Very hard indeed.'

Chapter 17

Upstairs in the safety of the private wing, Nell made a couple of cups of strong coffee and carried them through to the drawing-room. Jemima, still looking mutinous, had thrown herself down on the most comfortable sofa and was picking at the pale-pink nail polish on her thumbs.

'Here,' said Nell.

Jemima took the cup with ill grace. 'What's in it, deadly nightshade?'

This time Nell didn't bother to reply.

Goaded by the silence, Jemima went on, 'So why *exactly* are you here? I'd love to know.'

'For a start, it has nothing to do with your father's relation-ship with my mother.'

'Huh.'

'Look, it obviously bothers you,' Nell flashed back, 'but as far as I'm concerned there was never anything to be bothered about. If you must know, I needed an excuse to move away from Oxford. Taking this job seemed a good enough reason to me. There's really nothing sinister about it,' she went on. 'I like the work. I'm good at it. Everything seems to be going well so far. Why *shouldn't* I do something I enjoy?'

'Like working with Marcus, you mean? I suppose you enjoy that too.'

The more ultra-reasonable Nell was, the more irritated Jemima became. 'It's him you're really after, isn't it? Look at you.' She waved a negligent hand at Nell. 'All dressed up in that tacky dress, introducing yourself to *our* guests and trying desperately to pass yourself off as one of us. It's so *obvious*, for God's sake, it really doesn't fool anyone for a second. And if you seriously think you stand a cat in hell's chance with my brother, well . . .'

It was the bit about the dress that did it. It wasn't a designer original. It wasn't a designer copy. Nell had even wondered herself if it wasn't just a teeny bit tacky. But she had been noisily overruled by her mother and sisters, who had adored it.

Now she knew they had been wrong, and Jemima Kilburton was right. The thing was, there were still some home truths you'd prefer not to hear. And having your dress sneered at was one of them.

'Oh please,' she said wearily, 'you can't be that stupid. Men are men, whatever their class. However do you suppose I landed the job in the first place?'

It had been ten-thirty before the last of the guests had left. Now, at almost eleven o'clock at night, Marcus made his way down the High Street and wondered whether it was too late to be knocking on strange doors.

When he reached the house in question, however, he saw with some relief that there were a lot of lights still on. Practically every ground-floor window was ablaze.

As he approached, Marcus spotted a middle-aged man in

the shadows on the opposite side of the road, walking his dog and in turn watching the Earl of Kilburton, with a bottle of Krug tucked under one arm, make his way up the overgrown path to the front door of The Pink House.

It was a while since Marcus had last seen Miriam O'Driscoll at close quarters but she remained as he remembered her. Dark hair, greying slightly, was pulled back into a loose bun. The dark, knowing eyes surveyed him with mock amusement. She wore a loose, white, cotton shirt worn open over a dark-green T-shirt and matching skirt, and silver bracelets jangled on both wrists. She had put on a bit of weight in the past few years, Marcus decided, but it rather suited her. She was still attractive in an earthy, couldn't-care-less way, despite the fact that she was also wearing rather too much dark-green eyeshadow and a cigarette lighter in a pouch slung on a leather thong around her neck.

She didn't appear particularly surprised, either, to see him.

Behind her, there seemed to be some kind of noisy party in progress. Through the open door leading into the living-room came music and screams of laughter. There had to be more than a dozen people in there. From the sound of it, Marcus decided, they were having a far better time than his own guests had done earlier.

'Well, well,' declared Nell's mother. 'It's the whipper-snapper.'

'Hello.' He smiled slightly. 'Is she here?'

Miriam stepped aside, indicating that he should follow her. 'Nell's having a bath,' she explained over her shoulder. 'You can wait in here; she'll be down in a tick.'

By the time Nell arrived downstairs fifteen minutes later, unsuspecting and unfetchingly enveloped in an ancient, tatty, pale-pink bathrobe, Marcus had been introduced to her family, had guessed the name of the song being acted out in a boisterous charade by Lottie O'Driscoll and had seen the Krug borne unceremoniously away by Miriam, to be opened and poured into eleven glasses in the kitchen. There was, happily, enough to go round because Miriam, having tasted a mouthful and rolled her eyes in disgust, had diluted it fifty-fifty with Seven-Up.

Nell, acutely reminded of her first meeting with Ben in Oxford, wondered why it was that nobody ever turned up to catch her unawares when she was wearing anything remotely glamorous.

She wondered, too, what Marcus Kilburton was making of it all, sitting there amid the chaos of Trish and Lottie and five over-excited children, several of whom were fighting over a bowl of popcorn. Derry, in the old, dark-blue armchair, held his two-year-old niece in his arms as they slept peacefully together through the racket. Lottie's boyfriend Tom was teaching Miriam card tricks. Davy and Declan, Trish's two boys, were singing. Lottie's daughter Maeve was dancing to the music belting from the radio. A black-and-white cat Nell had never seen before in her life was crouched in front of the fire devouring a plate of fish fingers.

Nell was used to it; this was the way her family lived. But what was Marcus thinking? There was no getting away from the fact that it was nothing like the cocktail parties at Kilburton Castle.

'Here she is,' Miriam announced, before Nell had a chance to escape back upstairs and change into something less awful. Marcus, who had been leaning forward watching the card tricks, hadn't even noticed her standing in the doorway.

With evident reluctance, he dragged his attention back to the reason for his visit. 'Hi. Sorry to turn up unannounced. I did try phoning but I couldn't get through. I thought maybe you'd unplugged the phone.'

'I explained it was one of Derry's girlfriends,' Miriam put in. 'How many times has she called tonight? Fifteen at least. That poor girl's going to end up with a phone bill the size of a mortgage, and as for Derry, just look at him. Thinking up all those excuses for not seeing her has worn him right out. Give him a nudge, Lottie. He asked to be woken at quarter past. He's meeting Megan at midnight.'

'Mother.' Nell spoke in warning tones. Megan Dotrice was the latest unwise love of Derry's life. She was also married to Joe Dotrice, one of the carpenters who worked up at the castle and whose proprietorial attitude towards his pretty young wife was legendary. Megan worked behind the bar of a pub in nearby Sherringham. The name of the pub was The Hatchet. Since Derry was clearly dicing with death, Nell felt it appropriate.

'It's "Three Days of the Condor",' Trish giggled as Declan finished his charade. 'Not condom.'

At the mention of the word, Derry opened his dark eyes. 'What's the time?'

'Go on then, maybe you're right.' Lottie handed the glass of Krug and lemonade back to Maeve and pointed her in the direction of the kitchen. 'Add some Ribena and see if that helps.'

One of Declan's all-time favourite songs was playing on the radio now. Letting out a yell of recognition he hurled himself across the sofa, zipping the volume up to maximum.

'This is silly.' Nell shook her head. 'I don't know why you're here. If anyone should be apologizing, it's Jemima.'

'Too right,' Miriam briskly interceded. 'Telling my daughter her dress was cheap! You can tell your sister from me, young man, that she has no taste at all. That dress cost sixty-three pounds ninety-nine, and as for the shoes—'

'Come on.' Nell had to get him away before her mother dug out the catalogue and started rifling through the pages to prove it. 'We can talk in the dining-room. It'll be more peaceful in there.'

He had at least changed out of his dinner jacket and into a denim shirt and jeans. Not that it made her feel any better about her own appearance, thought Nell with a rueful smile. Taking a sip from the glass Marcus had handed her, she stopped smiling and stared down at the drink in dismay.

'Don't tell me. This has to have something to do with my mother.'

'You missed out,' Marcus explained. 'I thought you deserved something to thank you for all your hard work.'

Krug and warm lemonade. Jemima, Nell decided, would have an absolute field-day with this one.

'And I am sorry about Jemima,' he went on. The famous green eyes were fixed upon her, searching her face for clues. 'She'll apologize eventually, but I wanted to come and make sure you were OK. When she told me you'd walked out, I realized she must have said something unspeakable.' He hesitated. 'That is, even more unspeakable than the remarks she'd made earlier.'

The reason Nell hadn't minded being called a tart was because she knew it wasn't true. She had minded the jibe about the dress, on the other hand, because it was.

But she had kept her temper. Jemima was the one who had made an idiot of herself in front of everyone else.

'It doesn't matter.' Pulling the lapels of the dressing-gown more securely together, Nell shook her wet hair from her neck. Remembering her own parting shot, she broke into a grin. 'I suppose I owe you an apology too, for telling her I'd slept my way into the job. I know it was stupid but I couldn't think of anything else on the spur of the moment that would annoy her as much.' She paused, then continued casually, 'Out of interest, did she happen to mention anything else about me?'

Jemima had mentioned plenty. Marcus, however, guessed what Nell was hinting at. That she was approaching the subject with some caution didn't surprise him; he'd have been embarrassed to just come out and say it, too.

'You mean the business about the fortune-telling?' He tried to keep a straight face. 'As a matter of fact, she did have a word or two to say about that.'

'I can imagine the words she used.'

'Mmm.'

Nell, who was curious, said, 'So now you know what I've been doing in my spare time. It isn't a problem, is it?'

'I don't have any objections, if that's what you mean.' Marcus gazed across the dining-room, clearly saved for best and seldom used. A gilt-framed mirror hung above the empty fireplace and he could see Nell reflected in profile, decidedly un-mystic in her dressing-gown and with tendrils of wet black hair plastered to her neck just as they had been that first time he had met her, in the middle of a thunderstorm in Kilburton Park.

'If people want to believe in that kind of thing, it's up to them.' He recalled with amusement the note of fervour in Kiki Ross-Armitage's voice as she had leapt to Nell's defence earlier. 'My sister might not have too high an opinion of what you do but Kiki's evidently a fan.'

Nell nodded. 'Good.'

Without bothering to sound apologetic, Marcus said, 'I'm afraid I don't believe in that kind of thing myself.'

'That's OK. I'm not even sure I do.' Her smile broadened. Glancing in turn at his reflection in the mirror, she said, 'As long as you don't feel it interferes with the work I do for you.'

Marcus, who still thought it was funny, rose to leave. 'Not at all. No problem.'

She was still watching him in the mirror. For a brief second, their eyes locked. Nell, putting her hand up to her head, touched the damp tendrils of hair.

'That day in the park,' she said idly. 'Do you remember it?'

Marcus experienced a mild jolt of surprise. That was a coincidence, just when he'd been thinking of it too. He nodded.

'When I threw that stone at your car,' Nell continued, 'weren't you amazed at the time by my lightning reflexes?'

He had been amazed. He clearly recalled having been amazed. He nodded again.

'Go on.'

'I'm just saying, out of interest, that I knew you were going to drive deliberately through that puddle.' Nell winked at his reflection in the mirror, her good humour restored. 'I was waiting for you to do it, you see. The stone was already there in my hand.'

Marcus was slightly surprised when he got back to find Kiki, in the voluminous pink-and-cream-flowered dress which reminded him so much of a tablecloth, still draped across one of the sofas in the drawing-room. She was sipping white wine, heroically resisting a nearby tray of canapés left over from the party, and tapping her feet out of time with the music wafting from the CD player. It was Genesis, singing 'I can't dance'.

'Still up?' said Marcus. There was no sign of his sister.

Of course I'm still up, thought Kiki. I'm waiting for you, stupid. This is my big chance to be alone with you, without interruptions, so we can be cosy and intimate and really get to know each other.

'Jemima's gone to bed. I wasn't tired.' Her efforts to be cosy and intimate instantly backfired. She had meant to pat the seat next to her. Forgetting the glass of wine still in her hand, she spilt quite a bit of it over a frayed tapestry cushion instead.

But it didn't seem to matter, Kiki realized, scarcely able to believe her luck. Because he wasn't looking irritated and he wasn't ordering her to clean up the mess.

The magic must be working, she thought with rising excitement. For the first time, Marcus actually seemed keen.

Now he was pouring himself a Remy, making himself comfortable on the sofa opposite, regarding her with that heavenly brooding intensity.

I'm in a centuries-old castle, thought Kiki ecstatically. It's midnight. I'm with Marcus Kilburton. There's even a fire burning in the fireplace. Is this romantic, or what?

'So tell me everything you know about Nell and this clairvoyant business,' said Marcus, not very romantically at all. Leaning back and resting one arm along the back of the sofa, he gave her an encouraging smile. 'Tell me what she's said about your future.'

Not bloody likely, thought Kiki, crushed. What do you think I am, stupid?

Chapter 18

The good weather held the next day, the car-park overflowed once more, and Nell, studying the visitors' book at five o'clock, saw that amongst the long list of signatures, far-flung addresses and polite remarks, Elvis Presley had paid them a visit. In the space left free for comments, Elvis had written in a surprisingly immature hand: Not so good as Graceland. Beneath this, Dracula of Transalvaneer had added: I like children, I just couldn't eat a whole one.

Nell had a discreet word with Stan, the security officer. A visitors' book didn't warrant the installation of yet another security camera but a convincing replica, prominently displayed, might do the trick. Younger children were on the whole fairly easily deterred. Besides, Trish and her new beau had brought the boys along this afternoon. Nell wouldn't give much for Davy's or Declan's chances, were she to dust for fingerprints.

Rowan House, on the outskirts of Oxford, was set back from the road, shielded from both passing traffic and prying eyes by massed banks of pink and mauve rhododendrons, flowering chestnut trees and elegantly sculpted cedars.

Nell, making her way up the narrow, winding drive overhung with knitted branches, wondered if Ben had remembered she was coming to see him tonight. With little comprehension of time he had recently taken to accusing her of not having visited him for months. Her twice-weekly visits were gone from his mind, it seemed, the moment she left the room. Yet at other times he would seize a fragment of memory and cling to it, asking her why she wasn't wearing the blue shirt she had worn on a visit six months earlier, or why she hadn't brought him the Jaeger grey-and-white striped silk dressing-gown he had pointed out to her in February's edition of *GQ*.

'It costs three hundred pounds,' Nell had protested at the time. Ben, giving her his lopsided smile as he attempted the joke, had said slowly, 'But I'm worth it.'

And when eight weeks later the dressing-gown still hadn't arrived he had looked bewildered and said, 'Aren't I worth it, then?'

The remnants of memory were what made it so heart-breaking. Ashamed of herself for having even hoped he might forget about the dressing-gown, Nell had rushed out and bought it. By the time she gave it to Ben, of course, he had forgotten he'd ever wanted the damn thing in the first place.

'He's waiting for you.' Oscar, the charge nurse who took care of Ben, met up with her in the corridor as she made her way towards Ben's room.

Big, black and endlessly cheerful, Oscar was married to another nurse, the father of three cherubic children and, by his own admission, the second-best-looking man at Rowan House. He dealt brilliantly with Ben, who was not the easiest of patients, and was always capable of cheering Nell up.

Now, taking the carrier bags she was struggling with, Oscar walked with her.

'He's read all about the opening of the castle in the papers, watched it on TV and boasted about you to everyone who's gone near him.' His deep voice dropped another octave. 'Although I think you may have a spot of bother explaining this Lord Kilburton away. Ben seemed to think he was just some ancient, doddering old guy. Now he's seen what he looks like,' he waggled his eyebrows at Nell and gave a discreet cough, 'well, I guess he's feeling a bit insecure.'

Nell pulled a face. This wasn't totally unexpected. Aware that he was living apart from the outside world, Ben had often voiced his concerns, wondering aloud whether Nell was ever tempted to see other men and begging her not to leave him. It was why she had glossed so briefly over the subject of Marcus Kilburton in the first place.

He was sitting in his wheelchair next to the window when she entered the room. Strewn all around him across the floor were sheets of newspaper, some torn, others crumpled.

'Ben.' Nell wondered what on earth had happened. But when he turned his head at the sound of her voice, his thin face lit up. When he smiled it was almost as if the accident had never happened. He was, as he frequently informed Oscar, still the undisputed best-looking man at Rowan House.

'Nell.' Holding his arms towards her, he let the remains of the ripped-up newspaper on his lap slide to the floor to join the others. 'I haven't seen you for weeks.'

'Look.' She pointed to the calendar on the wall, where she signed herself in at each visit. 'Three days ago. I was here on

Wednesday. And now it's Saturday.'

But Ben chose to ignore the calendar. It *felt* like weeks since he had last seen her. That was what counted.

'You're here now.' He kissed her cheek, twice. 'I missed you. I love you.'

Nell gave him a hug in return. One of the auxiliary nurses had washed Ben's hair for him and the glossy black curls, smelling of almonds, were still damp against her cheek. He was wearing her favourite cobalt-blue silk shirt. And Calvin Klein cologne.

'You smell nice. Expecting someone special?'

Ben gave her his slow, lopsided smile. 'Only you. It's Eternity.'

Damn, of course it was. Sensing that he might be in danger of becoming maudlin, Nell changed the subject.

'Not a rabbit?' She glanced at the piles of shredded newspaper surrounding them and raised an eyebrow. 'OK, so what's it in aid of?'

'The Earl of Kilburton.'

Ben's speech would always remain slow and desperately slurred. The therapists had done their best but the words would never come fluently again. He struggled to say Earl, stumbling over the difficult vowel sound. There was, however, no mistaking the look of pain in the flawless, sapphire-blue eyes.

'He's my boss, Ben. The man I work for. That's all.'

Attempting to jolly him out of it, Nell stroked his arm and said, 'And a stroppy, bad-tempered bastard he is too. He might look cheerful in those newspaper photos but you should see him when things start going wrong. He is *mean*—'

'Bullshit.' As Ben mumbled the word beneath his breath, he kicked a crumpled ball of newspaper in the direction of the TV. 'He's not old. He's good-looking. And I bet he's after you.'

'No he isn't.'

'Of course he is. Why wouldn't he be?' Ben glared at her. 'Is he gay?'

There was a thought. Nell wondered if she could get away with it.

But Ben, who wasn't stupid, shook his head. 'Don't bother. Of course he isn't.'

I'm the one who's being stupid, thought Nell. All I have to do is tell him the truth.

'Look, remember how your parents disapproved of me?'

Ben shrugged and nodded. Those parts of his memory hadn't been affected.

'Well, there you go. Multiply that much disapproval by five hundred.' Nell broke into a smile, to show how silly it all was, and to prove how little it concerned her. 'It's simple enough; my blood's the wrong colour. They stick to their own kind. And if you've ever read the gossip columns you'll have heard of Kiki Ross-Armitage.'

Ben nodded once more. That name was definitely familiar.

'There you are then.' Nell sensed he was on the way to being convinced. With some relief she said, 'A bit of off-the-record gossip. Kiki's staying at the castle this weekend. Marcus invited her down. I really think it's true love. He's wild about her, Ben. Absolutely head over heels.'

* * *

Thunderthighs, thought Rachel, staring down at them in disgust. Thumping great thighs. She had been dieting for nearly two whole weeks and her thighs were still there, bigger than two thin people's waists and bruised into the bargain where she'd scrubbed frantically with a cellulite brush.

Why was losing weight such hard work, anyway? Why did it have to be so slow?

Desperate for answers, Rachel rifled through her diary once more. It was pathetic; thirteen days now and all she'd lost was eight and a half lousy pounds. Seven hundred calories a day were still too many, that much was obvious. She had to reduce it, get it down to five.

But she was hungry, and the emptiness was beginning to feel as if it was gnawing away at her brain as well as her stomach. All she really wanted to think about, too, was food. She liked counting up how much she hadn't eaten, envisaging the great mound of cakes, crisps, Mars bars and sticky-toffee puddings piled up in the middle of her bedroom floor. The thought of all those thousands of unconsumed calories stretching across the carpet filled her with elation.

The only disappointing part was the discrepancy between the weight of all the food she hadn't eaten and the amount she'd actually lost. If only it corresponded, Rachel felt, it would be so much simpler. Quicker, too. She hadn't much fancied the idea of laxatives before now, but as time went on and her thighs remained as stubbornly thunderous as ever, she was beginning to think they were what she needed. No need to get addicted to them, Rachel reminded herself – not like Katy Platt from 4B, who'd ended up doing fifty a day. Nothing stupid like that; just a few to get herself kick-started, to show her body she meant business.

And she did mean business. The trick, Rachel had decided, was to alter your attitude towards food. If you told yourself you didn't want it, you would beat the craving and win. If, on the other hand, you did what your mother did, which was endlessly torture herself, bleating on and on about how she could murder an éclair, the whole thing was doomed to failure from the word go. The reason Hetty had never managed to last more than a week on any diet was because she adored food.

This was completely the wrong attitude to take, Rachel now realized. In order to win, you had to despise food. And the way you did that was by looking in the mirror and despising your body. Food made you fat, so it was simple.

Rachel studied her reflection. 'If you don't want to be fat,' she told herself, 'don't eat.'

Hetty, who was carrying a pile of ironing upstairs, paused on the landing outside Rachel's room.

'Did you say something, darling?'

'No.' Rachel kicked the bathroom scales under the bed. Through the closed door she called out, 'I was just revising. Geography.'

Highly unlikely. Smiling to herself, Hetty tapped on the door.

'I've got your grey shirt here, if you want to hang it up.'

The purple bedroom walls were covered with posters of bands Hetty had never even heard of. In my day, she thought with a giddy rush of nostalgia, it was David Bowie and Dire

Straits. My father used to sit there reading his paper whilst I watched *Top of the Pops*, and every now and then he'd look up and say, 'Flaming Nora, another nancy boy wearing make-up.'

Rachel's pop heroes, in contrast, were decidedly unglamorous. They seemed very ordinary. Everyone these days had to look glum and wear black. Not a sequin in sight. How sad.

'Excuse me,' Hetty said brightly, 'while I wade through this sea of geography books.'

'Ha ha.'

Rachel, half-sitting, half-lying on her bed, was flicking through an old copy of *Mizz*. She was looking pale, Hetty decided. That awful black sweater didn't help.

A moment later Hetty spotted a familiar figure in the street below.

'There's Clemency,' she exclaimed, moving closer to the window. 'Look, going into the shop. Now that's a pretty sweater, don't you think? It's the colour of sherbet lemons! Something like that would suit you, you know.'

To humour her mother, Rachel looked up. She already knew what to expect. Anything Hetty liked was bound to be putrid.

'She looks gross, Mum. Ugh, it's even got lace round the collar.' Rachel shuddered. 'I wouldn't be seen dead in something like that.'

'I know,' said Hetty sadly.

'And I wish you'd stop going on about it. I don't criticize your clothes, do I?'

'Sometimes you do.'

Despite herself, Rachel grinned. 'Only when they really deserve it.'

'There's Clemency again. Goodness, she got away from Minnie Hardwick in record time. Oh look, she's seen us. She's waving.'

Hetty waved back like a windmill and said with longing, 'She seems such a nice girl. Wouldn't it be super if you two became friends?'

Rachel, with less enthusiasm, went, 'Hmm.' Clemency Munro was the Girl Guide type, the head prefect type, the kind who volunteered for things any normal person would run a mile from. *And* she wore totally icky clothes. Not wanting to be friends with someone like that was almost instinctive.

These were the minuses.

On the plus side, she had found herself succumbing to Clemency's easy chatter and gift for flattery. Being told you had hair like burnished copper was an ego-boost, after all. And Clemency, Rachel guessed, weighed a good stone more than she did. This fact, together with the icky clothes – now handily turning themselves to her advantage – meant that if the two of them were to go around together, she would look good by comparison.

Hetty had by this time flung open the bedroom window. From the street below, Clemency called up, 'Is Rachel there? D'you think she'd be interested in a game of tennis?'

Hetty doubted it very much indeed. Rachel, who had never been sporty, was more likely to be interested in jumping into the village pond naked. Turning, she gave her daughter a not-very-hopeful look.

But Rachel was bored, and tennis would burn up calories. To her mother's utter amazement she sat up and reached for her black trainers.

'OK. Tell her I'll be down in two minutes.'

'You can't wear that.' Horrified, Hetty realized she wasn't planning to change her clothes. The black sweater and baggy jeans were apparently it.

But Rachel knew how to handle her mother. She stopped tying her laces. 'Mum, do you want me to go or not?'

Hetty hung her head. 'I want you to go.'

'Well then. Don't fuss.'

'I'll make a steak-and-kidney pie for tea, shall I?' Hetty cheered up. 'Your favourite. All that exercise will give you an appetite.'

'Clemency might invite me to have something at her place.' Rachel's response was deliberately vague. 'I'll be fine, Mum. Don't do anything special just for me.'

Chapter 19

One thing about Clemency Munro, she certainly had bounce. Rachel, who hadn't done this much running around since primary school, soon found herself on the receiving end of a whitewash.

'Game, set and match,' cried Clemency. Rachel almost expected her to go *boinng*, like Zebedee, over the net.

'Sorry. Out of practice.'

'You probably aren't used to that kind of racket.' Clemency gave her an apologetic grin. 'It's a bit highly strung. Mine's like an old shrimping net, but at least it means I can control the ball. I should have asked, really, which one you'd prefer.'

At 6–0, 6–0, thought Rachel, Clemency could afford to be generous. She looked ready to go again, too. No bloody chance.

But Clemency, picking up the hint, zipped her ancient Slazenger into its cover. 'That's enough, don't you think? I'm gasping! Come inside and have something to drink.'

Downstairs, Swan Cottage was still awash with packing cases. Moving in and getting everything straight was evidently a gradual process for Dr Munro and his daughter.

'It's mainly Dad's junk.' Having poured warm, rather flat Pepsi from a giant bottle into two glasses, Clemency gestured towards the mess in the sitting-room and headed towards the stairs. 'All his precious medical journals and stuff. I daren't touch it. Come on, let's go up to my room instead.'

To Rachel's eyes it was as impersonal as an hotel room. There were no posters on the walls, no clothes on the floor. It was unbelievably neat. Clemency, she realized, had no intention of painting these walls purple and black; she actually *liked* pale pink flowers on a dainty yellow-and-white striped background, just as she apparently liked pukey china ornaments, even pukier musical boxes and endless photos in polished silver frames showing a beaming Clemency with her arms around an assortment of friends and relatives. She had even made her bed, Rachel was fascinated to observe. Weird.

The next moment a shudder went through her as something familiar caught her eye. It was upside down on the bedside table but she recognized it anyway.

'Oh dear, I suppose I should have hidden it under my pillow!' Having spotted what she was looking at, Clemency picked up the book and giggled. 'Here I am, supposed to be studying Chaucer, and what do I secretly read instead? The latest Vanessa Dexter. I know I should be ashamed of myself, but she's one of my favourite authors. Have you read any of her books, Rachel? I tell you, she's really gone for something different with this one. It's an absolute eye-opener.'

'Mmm.' Rachel gazed out of the diamond-leaded windows, at the overgrown back garden and the tatty tennis court beyond, but being non-committal wasn't going to deter Clemency.

'Of course, you probably know her.' She looked eager. Her eyes were bright with curiosity. 'I've been reading all about this fabulous love affair of hers in the papers. Do you know the man she lives with, too? It's weird, isn't it, to think that when you read this book you're getting all the nitty-gritty on their love life. I admire her for being able to write it all down but I have to admit it made me feel a bit voyeuristic.'

Rachel didn't know what voyeuristic meant but if it was another word for sick, that was how she'd felt too.

The book, *One and Only*, had already managed to make her life more miserable than she'd thought possible. Each new piece of publicity was like another shovelful of salt being heaped into the open wound. And because there had been such a terrific amount of hype, press interest had been correspondingly high-level. The book had only appeared on the shelves eight days ago, but to Rachel it seemed more like eight months.

Everybody at school seemed to have bought it. They took delight in parading it in front of her, sniggering at the more blatant sex scenes and reading them aloud for added effect.

Vanessa, endlessly interviewed on television and in the papers, only made things much, much worse. In order to keep herself in the public eye she had taken to coming out with quotes to make even the strongest toes curl. 'I call him my Big Growly Bear', 'Fifty uses for melted chocolate', 'Doing IT the Dexter way!' and 'In the bath with Vanessa and Tony', had been only some of the headlines.

School, for Rachel, was hell. Her classmates, as she had guessed they would, were revelling in her humiliation. Their latest nickname for Tony was The Studfather. Everyone seemed to be going around with a copy of *One and Only* sticking out of their satchels. Linda Childerley, for a bet, had put up her hand in drama class and asked if they couldn't do it as their end-of-term play. Vanessa, who had no shame, had even offered to turn up one day and do a book signing right there in the playground. If this wasn't a situation straight from hell, Rachel thought bitterly, she didn't know what was.

'Well?' Clemency was by this time sitting cross-legged on the perfectly made bed. 'Come on, I've only seen her on TV. You must know her in real life. So what's she like, brilliant fun?'

Having finished her horrible lukewarm Pepsi, Rachel balanced the empty glass on the window-sill next to a photograph of Clemency and Beryl, her Labrador. Of the two of them, the dog was undoubtedly the more attractive.

'Of course I know her, and she isn't brilliant fun at all. She's pushy, loud and a wall-to-wall liar. If you must know, I hate her guts.'

'Oh.'

Ha, thought Rachel, pleased with herself. That wiped the stupid, eager smile off your face.

Downstairs, the front door banged and a dog barked. 'Dad's back, with Beryl.' Clemency frowned, bewildered. 'Why, then? Why do you hate her guts?'

'Because she's an old slag,' Rachel drawled. 'And she's probably going to marry my father.'

Vanessa, wallowing in the bath at home, was in a good mood.

She was approaching the end of the next novel and knowing she was on the last leg always cheered her up. The storyline flowed more easily, too, which meant she got more done. This afternoon she had rattled off another three thousand words and tonight she was being driven down to Bristol to pre-record an interview with one of her favourite TV chat-show hosts. More lovely publicity for *One and Only*, she thought smugly. Sales were rocketing and there was even talk of a mini-series. She wondered if Amanda Holden would be interested in playing the character she had so closely based on herself. And how fabulous if they could get Nigel Havers for the Tony-based role. Now there was a man with looks and oodles of charm.

The phone rang at six o'clock, whilst she was up to her elbows in cinnamon-scented moisturizer. Stretching naked across the bed, Vanessa switched on the state-of-the-art ghetto-blaster. She kept some opera or other by Puccini in there, always mid-way through the tape. Despite finding music irritating, she adored the idea of adoring opera. It was, she felt, so good for the image, so chic. Consequently, whenever the phone rang she liked to switch on the tape at full blast, yell above it for a few seconds then say: 'Hang on a sec, let me go and turn the music down. Don't you *adore* Puccini?'

But it was only Tony, she found when she finally picked up the receiver. And every time he caught her doing the trick with the ghetto-blaster he said, 'Is that you, Hyacinth?'

'Oh darling, I was expecting you home by now.' Hastily Vanessa switched the tape off again. Damn, now she'd managed to smear moisturizer across the pillows. 'There's a yummy beansprout-and-cucumber salad in the fridge. I thought we'd be able to have a nice meal together before my driver comes for me. This is too bad; at this rate we're going to miss each other completely. Where are you, still on the motorway?'

'Um, yes.' Tony, who had forgotten about the Bristol trip, and who had left the motorway twenty minutes ago, did a rapid rethink. 'Sorry, darling. Problems at the office. I can't see me getting home before six-thirty.'

'And I'm being picked up at six forty-five,' Vanessa fretted. 'Oh well, you'll just have to help yourself to salad. I'll be back at around midnight. You'll wait up for me, sweetie, won't you?'

'Of course I will. Maybe I'll drop in on Rachel, in that case.' Three miles from Kilburton, Tony felt his stomach rumble. 'I haven't seen her for a couple of days.'

He was such a good father. Vanessa thought it an admirable quality in a man. When the daughter in question was as sulky and difficult to get along with as Rachel, she privately felt, he deserved an extra gold star for devotion above and beyond the call of duty.

'It doesn't seem fair; you're always doing the dropping in. She never comes to see us nowadays.' Vanessa made the effort, for form's sake. It sounded good, and she was on pretty safe ground. 'Tell her she's welcome to pop over at any time. And do send her my love,' she added for the hell of it. 'Darling Rachel, give her a great big kiss from me.'

It had been a confusing afternoon, thought Rachel. All the unaccustomed exercise had made her so hungry that when ever-competent Clemency had rolled up her sleeves and made a huge pot of chilli and rice, she had been unable to prevent herself guzzling two whole bowls of it. After that, of course, the diet was so totally blown that there hadn't been a lot of point refusing the ice-cream. It was another zillion calories, but at the same time it was such bliss to feel full again, instead of hollow with hunger. As Josette Wilson who sat next to her in maths had whispered, there was definitely something to be said for bulimia. If only she didn't have such a phobia about being sick, Rachel thought, she could have been tempted to give it a bit of a whirl herself.

But it was such a gross idea. And it made your teeth drop out. No, Rachel decided she would restart the diet tomorrow and just enjoy this meal while it lasted. If Clemency was unconcerned enough about her own weight problem to be merrily helping herself to yet more banana ice-cream and raspberry sauce, why should she worry?

Dr Munro, Clemency's father, emerged from his study at six-forty looking harassed.

'Run down to the pub and get me twenty Benson and Hedges.' He rummaged through his trouser pockets, finally unearthing a fiver.

'No.' Clemency was washing up. Rachel, much to her own surprise, had found herself doing the drying. If her mother could see her, she thought, she would have fainted.

'Go on,' Alistair Munro pleaded. 'I'm desperate.'

'You shouldn't smoke. It's bad for you.'

'I know. I'm giving up soon. Please, Clem? I'd get them myself but I'm expecting a call from the hospital about Mrs Murphy. I can't leave the phone.'

'You mean Mrs Murphy and the quadruple by-pass operation she has to have because of all those cigarettes she's smoked?'

Alistair Munro had short, tousled, light-brown hair and rather nice grey eyes. He was thin, of medium height, and dressed in a creased check shirt and what looked like a pair of gardening trousers. He wore an air of harassment and a pair of apparently forgotten spectacles on top of his head. When he tried to glare at his daughter, it didn't quite come off.

'Clemmy, you know how irritable I get when I'm deprived of nicotine.'

She grinned over her shoulder at him. 'I'm not scared.'

Rachel, slowly drying a plate, felt sorry for Clemency's father. To be bullied by your own daughter was pretty humiliating. He was taking it awfully well.

'How about you, then?' He turned his attention hopefully to Rachel. 'Clemency's friend. Would you run down and get them for me?'

'No she wouldn't.' Clemency's tone was brisk.

He waved the five-pound note at her. 'How about if I said keep the change and buy yourselves some crisps?'

'Sold.' With an air of triumph, Clemency whisked the fiver from his fingers. 'To the girl in the Marigold gloves. We'll go as soon as we've done the washing-up.'

Vanessa, sitting in the back of the courtesy car, spotted Rachel together with a girl she hadn't seen before. They were crossing the road, apparently leaving the Hen and Chicken and heading away from Rachel's house.

Tony wouldn't be seeing his daughter after all, she thought. He wouldn't be missing much, either. How Hetty could let that girl walk the streets in those terrible clothes was beyond her. On the other hand, of course, you only had to look at Hetty to see where Rachel got it from.

But the next moment, as they rounded the corner, Vanessa saw that Tony's car was parked outside Hetty's house anyway. He was back, it seemed, and had gone straight there rather than calling in at home first.

And Rachel wasn't even there, Vanessa thought with some indignation. He had evidently been trapped by Hetty, bending his ear as usual, whinging about her miserable life as a hopeless housewife and mother. It was hardly surprising she hadn't been able to hang on to her marriage. Poor Tony, what he had to put up with. The trouble with him, Vanessa decided, was he was just too easygoing. Too *nice*.

Chapter 20

Tony hadn't minded in the least when he had turned up to find Rachel out. Hetty, her red-gold hair flopping over her forehead as she bent to study the battered Delia Smith paperback propped on the kitchen table, was there instead. She had already baked a steak-and-kidney pie – he couldn't see it, but the smell was sublime – and was now busily layering sliced apples into a flan case. He watched her small, capable fingers arrange the slices in ever-decreasing circles. Her absorption was complete. When she had finished the task, and was reaching for the cinnamon, she looked up and saw him standing there in the doorway.

'One day,' said Hetty, 'you're going to let yourself into the house and get a shock. I'll be naked, making wild love to some heavenly young man on the kitchen floor, and then what will you do?'

Her tone was only mildly reproving. It was such an unlikely prospect, it had never seemed necessary to ask Tony to stop using his key. Eventually, she supposed, she would have to. Give it another decade or so and she might actually have a love life to want to keep private.

Tony, jolted to realize that his initial reaction would be anger, maybe even jealousy, felt his blood pressure rise a notch and rapidly changed the subject.

'Where's Rachel, upstairs?'

'Out with a new friend.' Hetty sprinkled a generous layer of Muscovado sugar over the apple flan. 'Clemency Munro. Her father's taking over from Dr Carling,' she explained. 'They've just moved into Swan Cottage. Clemency's a really nice girl.'

'That steak-and-kidney pie smells pretty good too.' Tony glanced longingly in the direction of the oven. His stomach had been gurgling for the past three hours.

Hetty looked up and grinned. 'It'll be ready in twenty minutes. I've almost finished here. Why don't you pour us both a nice gin and tonic, if you're staying to dinner?'

What bliss, thought Tony as he unscrewed the lid on the bottle of Schweppes. Tonic with calories. Somehow gin was never the same with slimline.

Dinner was leisurely and fun. Rachel's phone call at eight o'clock to let her mother know she was still at Clemency's house but would be home by eleven had put Hetty in a holiday mood. Tony was being good company, the steak-and-kidney pie had been even more heavenly than usual and the apple flan had been gooey and gorgeous. She was even wearing trousers with a drawstring waist, so she was spared the indignity of having to sit with her zip undone and her tummy hanging out.

Best of all though, Hetty decided with a frisson of triumph, was the simple fact that she was yet again getting one over on Vanessa. So much for beansprout-and-cucumber salad, she thought as she licked the last morsel of cream from her pudding spoon. The thing was, would Tony risk dumping it in the kitchen bin when he got home or would he have to ensure the evidence was well and truly disposed of and flush it down the toilet instead?

175

'What are you thinking?' Tony had loosened his collar and tie and was swilling Sauternes around in his glass, enjoying the bouquet.

'I'm thinking surely Vanessa must wonder why you still haven't lost any weight.'

'I told her it was a problem with my metabolism.' He looked shamefaced. 'The trouble is, now she's trying to persuade me to see some Harley Street quack about it.'

Hetty, envisaging endless painful and humiliating tests, hooted with laughter. 'Be sure your sins will find you out.'

By the time they had finished eating and moved on into the sitting-room, Hetty had begun to realize there was something different about Tony tonight. She didn't even know what it was, she was just aware of some indefinable change in him, in the way he was looking at her and the way he appeared to be paying more attention to whatever she said.

Minutes later, it clicked. She realized with a start that the reason Tony's manner seemed so distantly familiar was because it was. This was how he had been when they had first started seeing each other over twenty years ago. It had been known in those far-off days as courtship, she fondly remembered. They had been young, innocent and in love, spending all their free time together and never running out of things to say, because one of the happy side-effects of being in love was the fact that you *could* talk non-stop without having to worry that you were being either boring or plain silly. Your partner wanted to hear what you had to say. He was interested. Entranced. As far as he was concerned, you had no faults, only lovable foibles . . .

Hetty smiled at the memory. How naïve she had been, to think it would always be that way. It had never even occurred to her that the day might come when Tony, no longer fascinated by her opinions, would heave great sighs of irritation instead and accuse her of wittering on like a demented canary.

Not that she had been much better, Hetty dreamily recalled. She used to yell back that at least she wasn't a boring, pompous, social-climbing git.

'What?' said Tony, because his ex-wife had drifted off into one of her reveries.

But he wasn't sounding irritated. Hetty shifted on the sofa until her legs were tucked comfortably beneath her. Sitting like this made her poor thighs look huge, but since she wasn't out to impress, she reminded herself, so what?

'I was thinking about us, when we were first married.'

'Strange. So was I.'

'How we've both changed since then.' Hetty cupped her chin in her hand. 'It seems so long ago, doesn't it? Like looking back at somebody else's life.'

'Some things don't change.' Tony was running his fingers through his hair. Moments later, as if remembering that the amount of hair on his head was something that had definitely changed, he put his hand back down smartish. 'Go on then,' he continued idly, 'tell me what you miss most about being married.'

'Gosh.' Hetty laughed. 'I don't know. You losing your temper with me because I never managed to iron the collars right on your shirts. You getting up at six o'clock on a Sunday morning to play golf and not coming back until six o'clock at night. Your unspeakable socks.'

'Sex?'

'What!'

'Sex,' Tony repeated calmly. 'Oh come on, no need to look so stunned. We were together for nearly twenty years, Hetty. You must miss it. There'd be something wrong with you if you didn't.'

When Hetty was feeling defensive, a muscle beneath her left eye invariably began to twitch. She tilted her head slightly so her hair fell forward and that side of her face was concealed from him.

'Who says I need to miss it? You don't know, I could be seeing someone. I might have a fabulous sex life!'

But all Tony did was give her one of his are-you-kidding looks.

'Sweetheart, this is Kilburton. Of course I know you aren't seeing someone.'

'I might be seeing him on the quiet,' she protested, adding pointedly, 'Some people prefer their affairs to be discreet.'

'So they might, but they don't get away with it if they're living in a village like this.' Tony, speaking as one who had tried and failed, realized he was drifting away from the point. 'And there's no need to look so indignant.' He spoke in soothing tones, adoring the way her big spaniel eyes fixed upon him. In those far-off days of early marriage he had teased her about it, calling her het-up Hetty and threatening to put her out in her kennel until she'd calmed down. 'It isn't a criticism. There's nothing wrong with a spot of celibacy. I was just interested to know if you did miss . . . well, the whole bed thing.'

As if Tony would have the first idea about celibacy, thought Hetty, teetering between laughter and clocking him one with her shoe. In the end, because she couldn't be bothered to start telling elaborate lies and because Tony always saw through them in a flash anyway, she gave up and just nodded instead.

'Of course I do.'

'You don't have to.' He cleared his throat. 'Miss it, I mean.'

Hetty, who wasn't quite sure what he did mean, said, 'You're recommending bromide?'

'I'm recommending sex.' Tony broke into a grin. 'With someone you know and trust. No strings, of course. Just for fun. So what do you say?'

Goodness, a proposition! At last! What rotten luck, thought Hetty, for it to have come from the man who had left her, putting her in need of a proposition in the first place.

But oh, she thought with longing a moment later, wouldn't it be heavenly to fall into bed with someone and just go for it? And with someone you knew, so there was no pressure to hold your stomach in the whole time and pretend to be perfect. She thought it amusing that Tony imagined himself as someone she could trust, but she knew what he meant. Since he had more to lose than she did, she could guarantee his discretion.

Best of all, Hetty realized, was the fact that saying yes would mean finally getting her own back on Vanessa. Never mind all those sneaky diet-breaking dinners; they paled into insignificance compared with actual sex . . .

Now this, she thought happily, is what I really call sweet revenge.

* * *

'You've just been unfaithful to Vanessa.' Not even bothering to wipe the smug, self-satisfied grin off her face, Hetty stretched luxuriously and glanced at her watch. 'Do you feel guilty?'

'Some things are too nice to feel guilty about.'

It was ten-thirty. Rachel would be home soon. Tony watched Hetty slither out of bed, pick her grey-and-white sweater off the floor and pull it over her head.

Next came turquoise knickers then finally the loose-fitting white trousers with their user-friendly drawstring waist.

It made a change to watch someone complete the business of getting dressed in thirty seconds flat. Lying back against the pillows, as relieved as Hetty had been not to feel he had to keep his stomach muscles pulled in the whole time, Tony wiggled his toes pleasurably against the duvet and decided that it had all gone rather well. He may have been seduced by Vanessa's confidence, energy and fame but he still liked Hetty; he was still fond of her. To want to sleep with one's ex-wife wasn't such an odd idea anyway, he felt. And Hetty had cooked him some marvellous meals during the course of the past few weeks. If she needed cheering up in return, why on earth shouldn't he oblige? If he'd known it was going to be this nice, in fact, he would have done it a lot sooner.

'Nice or not,' Hetty said briskly, 'you aren't lying there like a wet lettuce. Rachel will be home any minute. Come on, shift.'

So much for romance, thought Tony.

'Not even time for a quick cuddle?' he protested. She *had* changed. When they'd been married Hetty was forever complaining about the miserable amount of *après-sex* attention he paid her. Yet now she was actually holding the door open, making hurried little shooing movements with her arm. She could hardly get rid of him fast enough, he realized with a touch of pique.

The irony hadn't been lost on Hetty either. At the mention of the word cuddle, her cheeks dimpled with amusement.

'Don't be daft, Tony. This is platonic sex, not an affair.'

Later, as she was seeing him to the front door, he touched her arm.

'When can we do this again?'

Hetty, who had been pondering the same question, said, 'When Rachel isn't here. When I'm not working up at the castle. When you aren't working. When you're able to sneak away from Vanessa without arousing her suspicions.' She shook her head in dismay. 'Oh dear, it isn't going to be easy.'

Tony risked a brief hug. As the familiar adrenalin-rush zipped through him, he dropped a kiss on to her warm, freckled forehead.

'That just makes it all the more exciting,' he told her, eager to initiate Hetty into the delights of extra-curricular subterfuge. 'Don't worry, we'll manage to arrange something. This is going to be great,' he added happily. 'I promise you, sweetheart. You'll love it.'

Too much of a good thing, however, was enough to give the fittest of men a headache.

'I'm sorry, sweetheart, it's been one of those days,' Tony murmured much later that night when Vanessa sidled across the bed and began rubbing herself against him. 'Can I take a rain check? I'll feel better in the morning, I promise.'

Vanessa, buoyed up by the obvious interest of the handsome TV interviewer who had monopolized her in the Green Room after the show – he had paid far more attention to her than to the other guests – took immediate umbrage. 'Oh brilliant. That's great,' she said crossly. 'Really great. Don't think I don't know who to blame for this.'

In the darkness, Tony's eyes snapped open.

'Who?'

'Bloody Hetty.' Grabbing an extra foot of duvet for good measure, Vanessa rolled away from Tony in a furious huff.

Not for the first time that day, adrenalin thundered through his veins.

'What?'

'You remember. Your precious ex-wife. *That* Hetty.'

'I know which Hetty. I'm just wondering what you're talking about.' Deny, deny, thought Tony. Always deny everything. But how the hell had Vanessa leapt to such a conclusion so soon?

'Oh shit,' Vanessa wailed suddenly. 'I'm sorry!'

The next moment, to his utter bewilderment, she had rolled back across the bed. Her arms slid around him. She began nuzzling his shoulder.

'It isn't your fault. I'm only annoyed because she takes such advantage of you.'

More flummoxed than ever, Tony said with extreme caution, 'Ah.'

'I saw your car outside the house,' Vanessa explained. 'And I know Rachel wasn't even there. You're such a good man, my darling, but life is just too short to waste precious time listening to a hopeless ex-wife who doesn't have the guts to go out and build some kind of new life for herself. I mean, look at you! Hetty does her level best to make you feel guilty and you end up worn out with the strain of it all. You must be *firm* with her, Tony . . .' I was, he thought, stifling a smile. '. . . and she must learn not to be feeble,' Vanessa concluded, her expression forceful. 'She can't lean on you for ever, relying on your good nature and understanding. You're just going to have to tell her to pull her socks up, darling. Tell her that playing the helpless housewife is *passé*.'

Chapter 21

'It's Kiki's last day down here and all you've done so far is ignore her.'

Jemima, who was sitting on the edge of a seventeenth-century carved-oak chest, drummed her manicured fingers ominously against the dark polished wood. 'Apart from anything else it's bloody rude. Kiki's embarrassed. I'm embarrassed. You're the one who *should* be embarrassed, and you don't even bloody care.'

The eighteen-hour days, coupled with the weight of responsibility for the entire launch, had caught up with Marcus. All he needed right now was a couple of hours' uninterrupted sleep. He could barely open his eyes. He was stretched out comfortably on the best sofa for the job. But now he was being subjected to a verbal battering by Jemima.

Without even bothering to look at her, he murmured, 'Correct.'

'Well, it's too bad! The very least you could do is say "yes" to dinner.'

'Why?' This time Marcus briefly opened his eyes. 'I didn't invite her down here.'

Jemima longed to hit him, but it was hardly likely to help. She tried pouting instead.

'Marcus, *please*. Poor old Kiki, you're spoiling her weekend.

She was so looking forward to coming down here—'

'Give it a rest,' drawled Marcus. 'What were you seriously expecting me to do, throw her over my shoulder, carry her up to bed and screw her senseless? Would that make her happy?'

Jemima visibly bristled. 'A damn sight happier than being ignored.'

'Well forget it. I don't fancy Kiki Ross-Armitage and I don't screw to order. So why don't you do the decent thing and leave me in peace? I'd quite like to get some sleep.'

Jemima wailed, 'I *did* the decent thing! Bringing Kiki down here so you could meet her *was* doing the decent thing! If you married Kiki, you wouldn't need to keep this place open to the stupid public, you wouldn't have to work all the time and you wouldn't *be* so bloody knackered . . .'

Despite everything, Marcus smiled. 'Know what you are?' This time he kept his eyes closed. 'A pimp.'

'The Manor House at Castle Combe,' said Jemima quickly, because it was one of his favourite places to eat. 'I'll book a table for eight o'clock, shall I?'

'Go on then.' Marcus heaved a sigh. 'What is it, just the three of us?'

'May as well make up the numbers.' Glad he wasn't watching her, she said ultra-casually, 'I thought I might invite Timmy Struther along.'

'Great idea. He's keen on girls with a bit of money behind them, isn't he?' Marcus was unable to resist the dig. 'Maybe he wouldn't mind giving Kiki the quick once-over.'

'You are such a pig,' Jemima hissed as she flounced past

him, heading for the door. 'I don't know what I ever did to deserve a brother like you.'

'Just lucky, I guess,' drawled Marcus.

'You haven't been to see me for weeks.'

'Oh Ben, that's not true.' Nell was glad she was on her own in the office. At the sound of Ben in yet another of his picky moods she found herself doodling a desolate face in the margin of her notebook.

'Months, then.' Ben would never admit to being wrong.

'It's been two days.' She knew what was coming and suppressed a sigh. So much for a lazy evening enjoying a long, scented bath, doing her nails and catching up on whatever was showing these days on television.

'Please, Nell. I can hardly remember what you look like.'

'Short, fat and ugly. No teeth. Hardly any hair.'

'Lots of hair,' said Ben wistfully. 'I remember that much. Say you'll come over.'

'OK.' Nell smiled. 'Eight o'clock, think you can hold out 'til then?'

'Just about.' He perked up at once. 'See you later. Oh, and Nell?'

'Mmm?'

'I need cigarettes, a couple of Charentais melons – make sure they're ripe – and another bottle of that Calvin Klein aftershave. Buy the biggest size they've got this time. Don't forget anything and don't be late. See you at seven, OK?'

* * *

Nell spotted the helicopter coming in to land while she was clearing her desk ready to leave for the night. Glancing out of the window as it hovered briefly above the treetops, she wondered what it must be like to have Kiki's kind of money, to charter a helicopter as effortlessly as normal people jumped on a bus.

This one, she supposed, having already heard from Marcus about Jemima's plans for the evening, had been sent to pick up Timmy Struther from his own family seat in Northamptonshire. In an hour or so, the pilot would no doubt ferry them across country to Castle Combe and bring them back again much later. It wouldn't occur to any of those making the trip, either to exclaim delightedly over the view, or to appreciate the sheer thrill of the ride.

What a waste, thought Nell. Why can't they just take a taxi instead? Hetty and I could take off on a jaunt in the helicopter. Now we really *would* appreciate it . . .

She bumped into Timmy five minutes later. As she was crossing the outer courtyard he strolled into view, having made his way from the helipad in the park. Now, rounding the old stables, he grinned in recognition at Nell and quickened his pace towards her. Before she could juggle the carrier bags of ring binders in her arms and free a hand in order to manoeuvre the key ring from between her teeth and unlock the car door, he had done the deed for her.

'Thanks.' Nell threw the bags into the back and prepared to climb into the driver's seat. Timmy put his hand on her arm. This time, instead of a dinner jacket, he was wearing an altogether more crumpled and casual off-white Armani-ish suit with a peacock-blue polo shirt. Only the cologne – once smelled, never forgotten – remained unchanged.

'Homework?' He lifted his eyebrows in the direction of the bags. 'Does this mean you haven't been invited to join us for dinner this evening?'

'My invitation must have got lost in the post,' Nell replied equably. Narrowing her eyes against the sun above the west tower, she pretended not to notice Jemima's cross, white face peering down at them from one of the second-floor windows. 'I think you're wanted.'

'Of course I am.' Timmy winked. 'The real trick, though, is to keep them wanting. And right now I'd prefer to talk to you. Unless you'd really rather I didn't?'

Nell hesitated. She didn't particularly want to talk to him because he was a prat. Jemima, on the other hand, practically had her nose pressed against the window . . .

'Oh dear. Not such an easy decision,' Timmy drawled. 'If it helps, maybe I should tell you that I'm actually much nicer than you think. If I made a bit of a wrong impression the other night, all I can say is it's a kind of bad habit I somehow just find myself falling into every now and again.' He grinned. 'Comes of socializing with too many Jemimas, no doubt. One tends to forget there are other, far nicer types of girl around. Then, when you meet one, you don't realize until too late that you've blown it.'

'You poor, poor thing.'

'There I was, you see, waiting with bated breath for you to come back downstairs.' Timmy gave her a sorrowful look. 'Although goodness knows why, since all you'd done was take the piss out of me.'

'Hang on,' said Nell. 'Where's me hanky? I think I'm going to cry.'

'And now you're doing it again. Give me a break,' Timmy protested good-naturedly. 'I'm truly not that much of an idiot. Look, why don't you let me take you out to dinner? Then I can prove to you how sweet, shy and altogether wonderful I really am.'

Nell was almost tempted. Happily, good sense prevailed.

'Thanks, but I don't think so.'

Timmy broke into a grin. 'Coward. What's the problem, scared of upsetting Jemima?'

'Not at all,' Nell replied demurely, because nothing could have given her more pleasure.

'Marcus, then?'

'What?'

'You don't want to upset Marcus.' His grin broadened. 'Keen, is he? Showing a bit of interest?'

'Don't be silly. I'm far too common.' Feeling it was high time she made her getaway, Nell slid into the driver's seat. She glanced mockingly up at Timmy. 'Weren't you listening to what Jemima had to say the other night?'

Nell would have left it at that, too. But as Timmy opened his mouth to protest, he was interrupted by a piercing yell. Behind him, Jemima had actually puffed her way up the west tower's seventy-six spiral stairs and clambered out on to the battlements. For reasons best known to herself, she had evidently decided this would have more impact than stomping jealously across the courtyard to stake her claim.

'Coo-eee, Timmy!' Jemima waved gaily down at him. The

next moment she stopped waving and hurriedly clamped her skirt to her thighs as an unexpected gust of wind threatened to send it billowing up round her ears. 'Come on inside,' she called. 'We're having drinks in the drawing-room.'

'Silly cow,' Timmy murmured. His eyes locked with Nell's. 'Oh, go on. If I don't have anything worthwhile to live for, I could end up hurling myself from the battlements. Say you'll have dinner with me on Thursday.'

'Timm-EEE!'

The shriek this time was bordering on the frantic. Jemima, Nell decided, was afraid that if he moved any closer he might catch something.

That did it. Suddenly the decision had been made for her. 'Now I come to think of it,' she said, 'I am free on Thursday evening.'

'Brilliant.' To really infuriate Jemima, who was still screeching away on top of the tower, Timmy bent and gave Nell a none-too-fleeting kiss on the cheek. 'And such a relief, too,' he murmured, enjoying the physical contact. 'Kiki said you charged forty pounds.'

The nice thing about not wanting to attend some boring, bound-to-be-disastrous social event was that there was always a chance it might exceed expectations and turn out not to be so bad after all.

Not this time though, Marcus realized with a surreptitious glance at his watch. Tonight, sadly, was one bound-to-be-disastrous evening that had turned out worse than even he had anticipated. What a waste of time.

But it was almost midnight, nearly over now. He had done his duty and they were on their way home. At least the food had been dazzling.

What he had imagined couldn't get any worse, however, promptly did so the moment their helicopter landed in Kilburton Park. Timmy Struther, who had tanked himself up on Dom Pérignon and apparently decided to stay overnight after all, grabbed a delighted Jemima by the hand and ran off with her into the darkness. This left Marcus and Kiki to make their own way back to the castle together.

Kiki, who had spent four and a half rigidly self-conscious hours feeling about as desirable as a grub-infested Granny Smith, gave up and started to cry.

For Marcus, boredom turned to dismay. If he was actively annoyed with anyone, it was with his sister, who had organized the so-called blind date. Kiki hadn't done anything wrong and it wasn't as if he disliked the girl. He just wasn't . . . *attracted* to her.

Now his indifference had reduced her to tears. With a stab of guilt, he put his arm around her plump, heaving shoulders. This had the effect of quadrupling the volume of Kiki's crying; what had until that moment been subdued sniffles were promptly replaced by huge, heart-rending, gulping great sobs. Marcus wondered briefly if taking his arm away again would turn the noise back down to sniffle-level . . .

'I'm s-s-sorry,' hiccuped Kiki, ashamed of herself but at the same time feeling so much better for the outburst. 'Oh hell, my face. What a m-mess. Do you have a handkerchief I could b-b-borrow?'

'Here. I'm sorry too, if I've upset you.' Marcus handed her the handkerchief from his breast pocket. 'Look, I know I haven't been on great form, but opening the castle has pretty much taken it out of me. To tell you the truth, I'm knackered. But that's no excuse for being a lousy host.' He gave her arm a squeeze. 'I am sorry. It hasn't been fair on you.'

If Kiki's hopes for this long-awaited visit to Kilburton had not been so sky high, the disappointment wouldn't have been so great. That, she acknowledged, was really what had prompted the tears. The fact that Marcus was so breathtakingly desirable hadn't helped much either. If only *he* could have turned out to be a bit of a disappointment after all the advance publicity, it would have made it that much easier to bear.

As it was, Kiki felt a complete failure and miserable to boot. She felt badly let down by Nell, too. It was enough to make even the staunchest believer lose faith.

'Better now?' said Marcus, when she had finished mopping up mascara and blowing her nose. They were approaching the main entrance to the castle. Kiki, a bit bleary-eyed but not bad considering, managed a fragile smile.

'So much for fortune-tellers.'

'Oh dear.' So Nell could get it wrong, too. Marcus, who was extremely glad to hear it, said, 'What did she tell you, that you were going to meet someone halfway decent this weekend?'

'Something like that.' Kiki heaved a gusty sigh. 'I don't understand it; she's never usually wrong. Maybe she got my fortune muddled up with Jemima's.'

'And Jemima's seriously interested in Timmy Struther?' Talk about poor taste, thought Marcus. God help her.

Chapter 22

By the following Thursday Nell was deeply regretting her decision to have dinner with Timmy Struther. She had only said 'yes' to get back at Jemima, and now Jemima was in London. It rather spoiled the effect.

Crossing her fingers and hoping Timmy might have forgotten about it didn't work either; he had called on Wednesday to let her know he hadn't and to arrange a time to pick her up. Marcus, answering the phone and passing it to Nell, had said nothing at all. He had, though, given her a long and extremely pointed look.

But as Marcus had recently reminded himself, when you didn't want to go somewhere it sometimes turned out not to be so bad after all. And this time, happily for Nell, it wasn't. Timmy, whisking her off in his dark-grey Maserati, was enormous fun. He told a lot of jokes very well, regaled her with wonderfully indiscreet gossip about his hordes of ex-girlfriends and their frightful families and took her to Le Manoir for dinner, which impressed Nell no end.

He was shameless, charming, slightly immature and clearly a veteran sweeper of girls off their feet. The initial prattishness, she now realized, had indeed been something of a front. Either that or the result of way too much to drink. Tonight's version of Timmy Struther was far more bearable. For the first time Nell was able to understand what all these hopelessly besotted females saw in him. Goodness, she could almost have been tempted herself.

Almost but not quite, Nell amended with a fleeting smile. She wasn't that naïve. She dreaded to think how many of those smitten women he must have slept with. Whole lorry loads, probably.

'OK, your turn.' Timmy recaptured her attention with a click of the fingers. Nell was gazing out of the window at the sculptured, floodlit gardens beyond. The dark-blue velvet dress she wore was completely plain and looked expensive. Personally, he preferred the skin-tight glittery job she'd poured herself into last week.

'My turn to what?' Idly, Nell stirred sugar into her coffee. If Timmy was expecting her to bitch about Jemima, he was going to be disappointed.

But Timmy already knew pretty much all he needed to know about Jemima, who, desperate to get him into bed on Monday night, had almost had to carry him upstairs to her room. Too much Dom Pérignon and brisk night air had hit him like a brick following the brief flight back to Kilburton. Timmy, who had forgotten to bring any coke along with him, had only a hazy memory of lying full stretch across a lace-draped Jacobean four-poster whilst Jemima struggled desperately to get out of her clothes before he passed out. She hadn't been quick enough. There were times in one's life when sleep didn't so much beckon as come tearing typhoon-style towards you, both arms outstretched. Timmy had given himself gratefully up to it even as Jemima, ever-hopeful, rummaged frantically in her dressing-table drawer for condoms. The next morning there hadn't been time to rectify the situation because he had to be in London by noon to attend an ex-girlfriend's wedding.

Jemima was therefore unfinished business, her ardour undimmed. She was mad about him, too. What else, Timmy concluded, could he possibly need to know?

This whole Nell O'Driscoll business, on the other hand, interested him intensely. She was unstarted business. His favourite kind.

'Your turn to tell me about you,' said Timmy. 'And Marcus. I wonder if there isn't something quietly going on between the two of you. Don't worry,' he added with a reassuring wink. 'I wouldn't say anything to Jemima.'

'Just as well. Since there's nothing to say.'

'Oh come on. I pride myself on being a bit of an expert on these matters.' Timmy lowered his voice to prove how trustworthy he was. 'Marcus didn't do that great a job of pretending there was nothing to hide. He could hardly keep his eyes off you the other night.'

This wasn't simply untrue; it was a thumping great lie. Nell burst out laughing.

'Is this because of something Jemima said? Look, I'm afraid I'm going to have to disappoint you. I wanted to upset her, so I told her I'd slept my way into the job. But it wasn't true. Sorry,' she concluded, because Timmy looked so let down. 'Obviously not what you wanted to hear.'

She was sitting back in her chair, disentangling a stray tendril of hair that had got caught up in her ear-ring. The dress might be demure but the gold hooped ear-rings, as big as bangles, provided an intriguing contrast.

'Never mind.' He ran a playful finger up her slender forearm, because it was always a good sign if the little hairs on the back of the arm stood on end. Sadly, Nell's didn't. 'More fool Marcus, I say.'

'More coffee?' Nell offered to pour.

Timmy allowed her to change the subject, because it wasn't in his best interests to tell her what he really thought. The bit about Marcus not being able to keep his eyes off her the other night might have been an exaggeration but Timmy wouldn't mind betting he wasn't thrilled about Nell having dinner here with him tonight. Marcus hadn't made his move yet, but whatever else he might be, it certainly wasn't disinterested.

The bill had been settled. Nell was surreptitiously sliding the after-dinner chocolates into her handbag when Timmy strolled back from the loo.

Snapping the bag shut, she said, 'Ready.'

He stood with his hands in his pockets, grinning down at her.

'We don't have to leave. I've just checked; the hotel isn't fully booked.'

'Gosh.' Nell blinked. 'Are you always this subtle?'

'Life's too short,' said Timmy, who had never found much use for subtlety. Then, because Nell was starting to laugh, he puckered his eyebrows in boyish concern. 'You aren't going to turn me down, are you?'

Taking his arm, she pointed him in the direction of the exit.

'Don't tell me,' Nell murmured, 'you hate it when that happens.'

'This is the first time it *has* happened.' Still looking charmingly perplexed, Timmy said, 'To me, anyway. And damn right I hate it. Frankly, I think you have a nerve. That meal cost an absolute fortune.'

'Ah, but think of the money you've saved on the price of the room.' Nell gave him a consoling smile. For someone so unaccustomed to rejection he was taking it extremely well.

'Sure you won't change your mind?' Timmy breathed hopefully into her ear. 'It would annoy Jemima no end . . .'

The *maître d'* helped Nell into her jacket. Forty minutes later they were back in Kilburton. As the Maserati roared down the High Street before coming to a graceful halt outside The Pink House, curtains twitched in all directions.

Making a last-ditch effort, Timmy said, 'You could always invite me in for a coffee. See if I can't persuade you to change your mind about annoying Jemima.'

'You're more than welcome to come in.' Nell looked amused. 'But I feel it's only fair to warn you, I live with my mother.'

'Ah!' Timmy grinned and nodded, remembering what he had heard. 'The famous mother. Or should that be infamous? Now there's a thought. If you won't sleep with me, maybe she'd be interested.' He gave Nell a look of innocent enquiry. 'What do you think, worth a try?'

Chapter 23

Now that the castle had been open for three weeks things were beginning to settle down. A routine of sorts had begun to emerge as those working became more used to doing so and more proficient at their jobs.

Hetty was thoroughly enjoying her own part-time work in the café-cum-restaurant. Since Rachel, in typical teenagerish fashion, had become so monosyllabic it was lovely to be able to chatter away to people who actually chatted back. All Rachel seemed to do nowadays was groan 'yeah, yeah' and 'Mu-um, don't go on.' For Hetty, who had to pretend not to be hurt by each fresh rebuff, it had come almost as a relief when her daughter began spending more and more of her free time over at Swan Cottage.

At least whilst she was working she could fuss to her heart's content over the old dears who came in for tea and flapjack, gossip with co-workers over the sandwich making and exchange pleasantries with the customers whilst they recharged their batteries over lunch.

But whilst the work was fun, Hetty's initial hopes of meeting countless desirable new men had been sadly dashed. The castle wasn't going to win any prizes as pick-up joint of the year, as far as men of her age group were concerned. There were loads of old age pensioners, and at the other end of the scale plenty of youngsters. There were also, particularly at weekends, a fair number of divorced fathers taking their young children out for the day, spoiling them rotten and buying them far too many sweets. These fathers were too young for her, Hetty sadly realized. And the only decent middle-aged men who visited Kilburton invariably came along with their wives.

Ah well, you couldn't have everything. Hetty, pausing in the middle of wiping down one of the tables, managed a brief, halfhearted wave as Nolan Ferguson burst through the doors.

Nolan, a silversmith who made and sold jewellery from his studio in the old stables, was as brash as his avant-garde designs. He was single, he was available, he was even the right age. If it weren't for those tufts of dark hair on his toes, sprouting offputtingly through the leather straps of his enormous open-weave sandals, Hetty might have been able to look at him without thinking of a werewolf.

But Nolan didn't appear to own any socks. Desperate though she was, Hetty couldn't persuade herself to fancy a sockless, hairy-toed vegetarian. Glancing out of the window and spotting Clemency Munro heading across the courtyard towards the restaurant, she raced shamelessly to the door leaving Nolan to order his cheese-and-broccoli quiche with salad from one of the other waitresses on duty.

Nolan, who definitely fancied Hetty Brewster, was most put out when he realized he was being ignored, unceremoniously dumped in favour of a chirpy, podgy little pudding of a teenager with a thin, older man in tow.

Hetty couldn't care less what Nolan thought. She was far too busy murmuring 'thank you, oh thank you, God' under her breath. Because this was it. This was the answer to all her prayers. This was . . .

'My dad,' Clemency announced with the kind of pride it would never have occurred to Rachel to use when introducing her own mother to a stranger. 'Dr Alistair Munro.'

'I guessed you must be.' Beaming, Hetty shook his hand. It was a very nice hand, too. Slender and strong looking, like the rest of him. Good, firm handshake. Clever, blue eyes that crinkled at the corners when he smiled. Not over-tall, but tall enough. No hint of paunch either, beneath the grey-and-white Fair Isle sweater and worn corduroys.

My word, thought Hetty, momentarily lost in admiration. This exceeded all expectations. The man was right up her street.

Sadly, it was a one-way street. As Marcus had shied instinctively away from being paired up with Kiki, so Alistair Munro now found himself on the receiving end of a similarly pre-arranged spot of matchmaking.

All Clemency's idea, no doubt, but embarrassing none the less. Particularly when you had to submit to this kind of none-too-subtle once-over, he thought with weary resignation. These eager divorcees were all the bloody same.

'Dad had a couple of hours to spare, so I dragged him along to have a look at the castle,' Clemency cheerfully explained. 'Otherwise he'd never get round to seeing it. When it comes to doing anything that isn't connected with medicine, he's hopeless.'

'Thank you so much.' Alistair rifled through his pockets in order to avoid Hetty Brewster's bright gaze. The look of devotion in those big brown eyes of hers was making him feel more uncomfortable by the minute.

'Are you having lunch or just a snack?' asked Hetty, reaching for a menu and thrusting it at him. 'The day's specials are chalked up on the board over there, and I can really recommend the seafood tagliatelle. I'm afraid we've sold out of the beef casserole, though.'

Much to Alistair Munro's relief, he spotted the sign on the wall.

'Just coffee, thanks. Oh dear, I see you're a no-smoking restaurant.' He waved his packet of Bensons like an alibi. 'We'll have to sit outside.'

'You said you were starving,' Clemency protested. 'I thought we were going to have something to eat. *I'm* starving . . .'

'Just coffee,' he repeated firmly. 'And then I really must be getting back.'

'Just coffee,' Hetty echoed. He wasn't even looking at her. She'd blown it. She had been well and truly rebuffed.

'Dad, you were terrible! I don't know how you could *be* so rude.'

Away from the castle, in the privacy and comfort of his own home, Alistair was able to speak his mind. His mood wasn't improved, either, by the fact that he was still hungry and Clemency was flatly refusing to cook lunch.

'I wasn't rude, I just didn't play the game you wanted me to play. Clem, couldn't you see the way she was looking at me, like a lovesick spaniel? Have you any idea how nerve-racking it is, being stared at like that?' Having finally managed to prise the cellophane wrapping off a packet of frozen pork chops, Alistair slung them into the frying pan. 'I'm sorry, but just because we're both divorced doesn't automatically mean we have to like each other. I've told you before, I don't even *want* to get involved with anyone right now. Taking over a new practice is quite enough to be going on with. How long am I supposed to cook these bloody things for anyway?'

'I wasn't trying to set you up.' Clemency, who had been watching the charade with the pork chops, heaved a sigh and pushed her father out of the way. He knew perfectly well how to cook; he would just do anything to avoid having to. Tipping the chops on to a plate, she put them into the microwave to defrost. 'Hetty's really nice, that's all. I like her. It would have been rude not to introduce you. As for the way she was looking at you,' Clemency added with a touch of impatience, 'she always looks like that. So don't flatter yourself, Dad; it's her natural expression. After the miserable way you treated her, anyway, I'd be amazed if Hetty ever wanted to speak to you again.'

When the bedside phone rang, Hetty jumped. When she picked up the receiver and realized who was on the other end, she felt the little hairs at the back of her neck prickle in alarm.

'Hetty? Vanessa. Caught you at last.'

The phone was jammed against her ear but Vanessa's brisk clear voice managed to spill out anyway. Beneath the bedclothes, Tony froze.

Hetty said faintly, 'Caught me?'

'I expect it's that funny little job of yours. I tried ringing you twice yesterday, but no joy.'

'I'm sorry. What was it you wanted?' Struggling into a sitting position, Hetty shook her head at Tony as he emerged, tortoiselike, from the depths of the duvet. They hadn't been discovered. Their secret was still safe. Caught, but not caught out.

'This party of ours,' Vanessa explained. 'You've probably heard about it. Now, I know this is a bit short notice, but the Newmans have had to drop out. Jerry's gone down with pneumonia, apparently. Well, it seems a shame to muck up the numbers so we wondered if perhaps you wouldn't like to come along instead. We thought you might enjoy a night out for a change.'

This was old news. Hetty had already heard about it from Tony. Vanessa, casting around for a couple of suitable last-minute substitutes, had hit on the perfect pairing. As she had patiently explained to Tony, the sooner Hetty found herself a new man, the sooner she would stop relying on him to do all those endless little tasks around the house for her. And since Hetty clearly wasn't making much headway in that department herself, Vanessa continued, it was up to them to give her a helping hand. She knew just the man for the job, too . . .

'Oh,' said Hetty, squirming with pleasure as Tony kissed her shoulder. 'How kind of you. Um . . . is it just me?'

In arch, deeply patronizing tones, Vanessa replied, 'My dear, we have a *super* chap for you! That nice looking new doctor who's just moved into the village. His name is Alistair. I bumped into him a couple of days ago and introduced myself. My goodness, he is charming! I don't think you'll be disappointed, Hetty, when you meet him.'

'How exciting.' Hetty didn't dare glance across at Tony,

lying next to her. 'Friday at seven-thirty it is, then. Thanks, Vanessa . . . dear.'

'What the bloody hell did you do that for?' Tony demanded, when she had replaced the receiver. 'When I told you about it, you said you wouldn't come to the party if she paid you.' He was outraged. 'You said you'd rather eat dog food than accept an invitation from Vanessa. Now you've done a complete U-turn. What's happened to make you change your mind?'

Tony wasn't outraged, Hetty realized. He was nervous; suddenly afraid, she guessed, that perhaps he couldn't trust her quite as much as he'd first thought. What does he think, she wondered, that I'm going to trot along to Vanessa's party and spill the beans in an attempt to win him back?

'Keep your hair on.' Smiling, she smoothed her fingers affectionately over his head. With her bare toes, she tickled his legs. 'I enjoy this as much as you do, don't I? I'm not going to do anything to spoil it. I'm certainly not planning anything sinister, if that's what's getting you twitchy.'

Tony relaxed. He didn't want the *status quo* disturbed. He still couldn't understand why sex with his ex-wife should be so much more fun than doing it with Hetty when they had been married. But it was, and he would hate to lose what they had now.

He gave her a hug.

'OK. Good. But I still don't know why you're coming to the party. Unless,' he added slyly, 'you really are desperate to meet dashing Dr Kildare . . . ?'

'Been there, done that.' Hetty had already put the rebuff down to experience. Some you won, some you didn't, she reasoned, and this one had been a monumental non-starter. It certainly wasn't something to get churned up about. She was going to the party despite the fact that Alistair Munro would be there, not because of it. 'And I don't know that I'd call him dashing,' she added as an afterthought. 'In a Fair Isle pullover? Not very James Bond.'

'Why, then?'

'It might be fun.' She shrugged. 'As Vanessa so kindly pointed out, I never go anywhere; a party might do me good.'

'Crap,' said Tony.

'But mainly,' Hetty admitted with a grin, 'I'm going to enjoy listening to Vanessa bragging, telling everyone what a perfect couple you are and all the time knowing that you aren't quite as faithful to her as she thinks you are.' She heaved a sigh of contentment. 'How could I turn down an opportunity like this? I wouldn't miss it for the world.'

Chapter 24

'Boy, was I glad I listened to you,' exclaimed Meg Tarrant, her glamorous eyebrows rising above her Wayfarers as she relayed the saga of the house move to Nell. 'So there we were, gazumped. The home of our dreams, lost for ever. Andy was doing his nut, which was fairly understandable, and every time I told him not to worry because you'd said it would be all right, he nearly strangled me.' Reaching across, she poured more inky-red Barolo into Nell's glass. 'So when the estate agent phoned and told him the gazumper had gone swimming off the Great Barrier Reef and been eaten by a shark, poor Andy thought it was one of our friends playing a trick on him. It was a week before he believed we could actually buy the house after all. And now we've moved in.' She rolled her eyes in appreciation. 'It's a dream come true. Thanks to you, of course. Andy doesn't believe in psychics, so he hates to admit you were right, but I'm telling everyone what you said. They all think you're incredible.'

'I didn't get it *that* right,' Nell protested. 'All I knew was that it would seem as if you'd lost the house, but at the last minute everything would work out. I just said you shouldn't give up hope, because—'

'Because someone with big teeth would come to the rescue,' Meg chanted, reminding her. Raising her own glass in triumph,

206

she clinked it against Nell's. 'There I was, silly me, pinning my hopes on Esther Rantzen . . . and all the time it was a darling Great White. Cheers!'

Nell grinned. 'Happy to help. So why are you buying me lunch? I have to say, I'm not great when it comes to choosing kitchen units.'

They had known each other for quite a while. Meg had shared a flat in the same house as Nell during their student years. They had crammed into the same parties, cycled the same narrow Oxford streets, shared the same pizza when neither was able to afford a whole one, and sunbathed together in their tiny, bedraggled back garden, drinking lager, pretending to write brilliant essays and getting a tan and a headache instead.

'I want to do a piece on you.'

Meg had gone into journalism. Now working for one of the major dailies, with her quirky, popular features she was considered very much a rising star.

It wasn't the first time she had raised this particular subject. Her fascination with Nell's apparent gift for second sight showed no sign of fading. To prove it, she took off her sunglasses.

'Come on, Nell, I don't know why you won't let me. It'll be great for both of us. Think of the extra business it would put your way.'

Meg was cajoling. Nell shook her head. Having shied away from publicity for years, she wasn't about to start now.

'I really can't do it. Too many people would think I was round the bend. If I read a piece in the paper about me,' she went on, 'I'd *definitely* think I was round the bend! I'd be labelled a crank. Besides, I'm working for Marcus Kilburton; he's hardly going to be thrilled with this kind of publicity, is he? Nobody would ever take me seriously again.'

There was Ben, too. Nell had never told him. At first, she had been embarrassed by the silliness of the whole thing. As time went by, it had simply been easier not to mention it. And now she had left it too late. Discovering the truth at this stage, Nell sensed, would only fuel Ben's anxieties and paranoia. Because if she had kept a secret like this from him for so many years, he would argue, how many other secrets might there be? What else was she hiding from him? And how could he trust anything she said ever again?

'No,' Nell repeated firmly. 'I couldn't handle going public. Knowing my luck I'd end up with scientists wanting to pin me down and carry out experiments on me, like ET. And what would it do to the business if they proved I was a big fraud?'

'But you aren't!' wailed Meg.

Nell looked doubtful. 'I might be.'

'God, I hate it when you do that. How can you have so little faith?' Resigned to failure, Meg gave up and signalled the waiter to bring more wine instead. In true journalistic style, she had demolished the first bottle herself. 'And now I'm really stuck,' she grumbled. 'If I can't do you, what the bloody hell *am* I going to write about?'

'Ah, well.' Nell's dark eyes glittered with mischief. 'I may have a bit of an idea for you there.'

Intrigued, hardly daring to hope that it might be some deliciously dirty piece of gossip concerning Marcus Kilburton

– now *there* was a man worth pinning down and experimenting on – Meg leaned forward. 'Go on.'

'Vanessa Dexter.'

'Oh please! I've had it up to here with Vanessa bloody-gorgeous Dexter,' Meg cried. 'She's been splattered across the news-stands for weeks. Everyone's sick to death of her. The stupid bitch thinks she's England's answer to Erica Jong; if you ask me, she can't even write!'

'Calm down.' Nell smiled, because this was the reaction she'd been hoping for. 'I'm not suggesting an interview with Vanessa. You might be interested in talking to my best friend, though,' she continued idly. 'You see, Hetty just happens to be Tony Brewster's dumped wife.'

'Stop it,' commanded Nell, because Hetty's teeth were chattering with terror.

Hetty, who had never mastered the art of applying make-up, tried not to fidget as Nell set to work with a rose-pink lipliner. She still couldn't believe she was actually going through with this.

'What's the time?'

'Don't talk.' Nell filled in the rest with a lighter shade of pink, blotted Hetty's mouth with a tissue and gave her a second, finishing coat. 'It's two-thirty. Meg and the photographer will be here at three. And for goodness' sake stop panicking,' she chided. 'They're on your side. Vanessa made you out to be a pathetic mess, didn't she? Well, now's your big chance to prove you aren't.' Nell broke into a grin. 'And to show the rest of the world what Tony's missing.'

'Except he isn't missing it.' Nell was the only one who knew about Tony's clandestine visits. Hetty studied her glossy, immaculately outlined mouth in the mirror. That lipstick would be lucky if it lasted ten minutes on her. With a stab of renewed fear she said, 'And I am a pathetic mess, anyway. Let's face it, I'm never going to be chic.'

'This afternoon you are.' Nell's tone was brisk as she reached for the blusher brush. 'For the photographer, anyway. You're going to be drop-dead perfect. And there's no need to look at me like that,' she added cheerfully, 'I'll be here too, won't I? Like I said, we're all on your side. You'll be fine.'

'Aren't you supposed to be working?' It was Friday. Hetty's conker-brown eyes narrowed in suspicion.

'I asked Marcus for a few hours off.' Nell waggled the blusher brush like Harpo Marx. 'He's on your side too. Seems Vanessa collared him a couple of days ago and asked him if he wouldn't like to stock a few dozen signed copies of *One and Only* in the castle gift shop.'

Hetty giggled. 'What did Marcus do?'

'He asked her who she was. Then, when Vanessa finally finished telling him, he said, No thanks, he didn't need any old dears keeling over and having heart attacks in his flower-beds.'

'Hooray.'

'*And* Vanessa invited him to the party tonight.' Nell assumed an expression of mock-horror. 'Poor Marcus had to come up with an excuse, sharpish. He thought she was awful; called her a pushy, social-climbing old trout. I said Vanessa gave old trout a bad name. That was when I told him why I needed this afternoon off,' she explained, looking pleased with herself. 'It was great, worked like a charm. He said yes straight away.'

By three o'clock Hetty was dressed and ready. Nell, in charge of the clothes, had chosen a big white cotton shirt and well-cut black trousers. These were Hetty's own. To complete the outfit, Nell produced a rose-pink silk waistcoat with pink bugle beading. The beads, shimmering in the light, created a waterfall effect. Hetty almost fainted when she saw the label.

'Valentino! You have to be joking.'

'Courtesy of Kiki Ross-Armitage,' Nell explained. 'She was wearing it the other week. When I admired it, she gave it to me. Poor Kiki, she said it hadn't brought her much luck with Marcus.'

Hetty felt nervous just looking at such a glorious, hugely expensive item of clothing. She was a naturally messy person. Keeping the waistcoat on for twenty minutes whilst the photographs were being taken was bad enough, but Nell was insisting she wore it to the party tonight, too.

'What if I spill something on it?' She looked fearful.

'I'll say it couldn't matter less,' said Nell with relish. 'Especially if what's getting spilled is Vanessa's blood.'

Despatched by the boss to interview Hetty Brewster, I braced myself for the ordeal ahead. Because I'd read the book, hadn't I? And I knew what to expect, didn't I? A cross between Cruella De Vil-hits-the-menopause and Nora Batty in bedsocks, that's what.

Yes, Hetty Brewster is *that* ex-wife, dumped by husband Tony in favour of Vanessa Dexter and so hideously portrayed in *One and Only* that I was tempted to go armed with a string of garlic and a crucifix. Needless to say, no threat there. No need for lovely *me* to wear mascara!

Well, now I've met her and all I can say is, serves me right for believing what I read in the tatty tabloids. (The other tatty tabloids, I mean. Not this one!)

Because Hetty is heavenly, and if you ask me, Tony Brewster was either paid a fortune to defect or he needs his handsome head read.

Don't take my word for it, though. Study the photos below and make up your own mind. All I can say is, the one and only Hetty Brewster made even me feel a frump. Damn, I wish I'd worn that mascara.

As she reached the end of what had been written so far, Hetty started to laugh.

'What d'you think, not bad?' Meg looked pleased with herself. Preening, she tossed back her golden hair. 'To be going on with, at least. It's just a guideline, see, a bit of an intro before we really stick the boot in.'

'Golly.' Hetty swallowed, enthralled by the deceit. 'You actually wrote all that before you'd even met me? Won't you get done for trade descriptions or something?'

'This is journalism, I can write whatever I like.' Meg beamed. 'Even if you were totally doggish – which you aren't, by the way – I'd make you out to be fab!'

It was like listening to a schoolgirl casually confess to having cheated in her GCSEs. Meg Tarrant, blonde, sleek and gleaming, couldn't have the least idea how it felt to be frumpy. Hetty couldn't help noticing, too, that she was wearing a ton of mascara.

But this, she realized, was what it was all about.

Meg wasn't doing this piece because she was on Hetty's side, but because it made a great tit-for-tat story for her faithful female readership. This was Meg's job. It was all in an afternoon's work. Never mind that it was also fairy-tale time, thought Hetty recklessly. It didn't matter. She was just going to relax, stop panicking and have fun.

It helped, too, that Gareth, the photographer, was so sweet. By four o'clock, buoyed up by the difference a beaded silk waistcoat and a faceful of unaccustomed make-up can make, Hetty was out in the sunny garden posing like a pro.

Her photograph was going to be published alongside a chronically unflattering one of Vanessa. Meg, who had already chosen it, assured them it was a beaut.

'We are talking mistress-from-hell,' she declared happily. 'We're talking an uncooked boiler chicken *way* past its sell-by date.'

By six o'clock the gin had been cracked open, two whole walnut cakes had been demolished and between the four of them the interview had been all but written. Nell and Gareth, sprawled out on the lawn, chipped in with their suggestions. Hetty, still in her Sunday-best in readiness for the party later on, sat on a wicker chair and worked at keeping herself pristine. Meg, drink in one hand, pen in the other, occupied the hammock slung between two apple trees. She was chewing the arm of her sunglasses, scribbling shorthand in a notebook, reading bits back and laughing uproariously at her own jokes. Hetty had had a terrible job persuading her not to turn up at the party in disguise, in order to see for herself how appallingly Vanessa treated her.

Meg had been riveted, too, to hear of Hetty's ongoing affair.

'Don't panic, you can trust me,' she said as Hetty winced and wished she'd kept her mouth shut. 'If for no other reason than that Nell would cut off all my fingers if I let slip. But even if we can't mention Tony's name, we can still use it.' Pausing, thinking hard for a few moments, she recited: 'Hetty's social life nowadays would make a dervish dizzy. Too graceful to name-drop, she admits, nevertheless, to being happily involved with a certain special someone. You lot out there can only guess and drool. I know who it is and I'm not blabbing . . . but take it from me, girls; he's fab and I'm jealous.'

'I'm loving every minute of this,' sighed Hetty.

'I know who's really going to wonder about this stunning mystery lover of yours,' Nell said with a grin.

Hetty could think of lots of people. The entire population of Kilburton for a start.

'Who?'

Above the rim of her gin and tonic, Nell's dark eyes glittered with fun. 'Tony.'

They left, finally, an hour later. Hetty was alone upstairs applying a cautious fresh dusting of powder to her flushed cheeks when Rachel arrived home. She must have gone straight from school to Clemency's house. Hetty waited until the sound of clumping footsteps reached the landing before popping her head around the bedroom door.

'Look at this, darling. Nell's done my face . . . what d'you think?'

The contrast between them couldn't have been more marked. Rachel's hair, in need of a wash, hung like string around her pale, naked face. She could see herself reflected in her mother's dressing-table mirror. There were smudgy grey-green shadows beneath her eyes and her skin had a yellowish tinge. Lucky she wasn't planning to enter any beauty contests, she thought morosely. What with all that fat *and* a yellow face. She'd seen better looking sea slugs.

Her mother, on the other hand, hardly looked like her mother at all. Rachel wasn't sure if she approved, either. Such an abrupt transformation made her feel uneasy. First her father had run off with a complete slag; now Hetty was doing herself up to the nines in the hope, no doubt, of catching a new husband. Nothing, Rachel realized with a lurch of fear, was the same any more. And it never seemed to occur to anyone to ask her what she thought of it all. They just went ahead and bloody did it anyway.

Hetty, meanwhile, was still waiting for her to say something nice.

'It's OK I suppose.' Rachel knew she sounded grumpy but she couldn't help it.

'Just OK?' Hetty looked hurt. 'Do you like the waistcoat, at least?'

'It looks like something Miriam O'Driscoll would wear.'

'Thanks.'

'You asked for my opinion,' snapped Rachel, suddenly wanting to cry. 'I gave it to you. What are you wearing all that make-up for, anyway? To try and impress Clemency's father at the stupid party tonight?'

'Maybe I'm wearing it to impress *your* father.' Hetty, who could see she was upset, tried again. 'Look, sweetheart, people do get dressed up for parties! I just want to look nice in front of Tony and Vanessa—'

'And everyone will think you're trying to look like Vanessa.' Biting her bottom lip until it hurt, Rachel began to turn away. 'Well it won't work. It's a waste of time. All the make-up in the world can't change Dad's mind and make him want to come back.' Bitterly, she said, 'You're too old, Mum. That's why he left you in the first place.'

Chapter 25

Alistair Munro, having been dealt a fearsome pep talk by his daughter prior to setting out, found himself looking at his watch and almost looking forward to Hetty Brewster's arrival at the party. She was late, and he was in the awkward situation of not actually knowing anyone at all. Vanessa, far too busy to introduce him to the other guests, was throwing all her energies into welcoming a Texan in a stetson, evidently some movie mogul by the sound of it, with whom she was on the brink of doing big business.

After being served a drink at the bar by an extremely good-looking young man, Alistair moved over to a quiet corner of the sitting-room. Vanessa's home, The Old Schoolhouse, had been ritzily converted into the kind of property found more often in *House and Garden* than in real life. No expense had been spared, every detail bore the stamp of professional interior design and the overall effect was every Texan millionaire's idea of a typical English country cottage, glossy, over co-ordinated and ever so slightly unreal. Who needed authentic ceiling beams, after all, when a top quality imitation complete with precision-drilled woodworm was available? Who could possibly prefer Colefax and Fowler curtains which you had to draw across yourself, when there was an electronic thingumajig to do the tedious task for you?

It was nothing like the clutter and chaos of Swan Cottage, Alistair ruefully acknowledged. Between them, he and Clemency had done their best but their efforts had been half-hearted to say the least. Their home definitely lacked the woman's touch.

The trouble was, asking a woman's advice was a tricky business. Women tended to get the wrong idea and launch themselves at Alistair like trains. It had happened before and it made him nervous. It was on the whole simpler to leave things as they were.

A moment later Hetty Brewster came into the room and Alistair found himself seized with remorse. Because he had been wrong and Clemency had been right; that look of Hetty's was not, after all, a sign of adoration. It was, he realized, the way she always looked.

She was doing it now as she glanced around the room. Reminded of Bambi in the forest, wide-eyed and wary, shy but at the same time eager to please, Alistair Munro thought too how much more attractive she looked this evening. The difference was astonishing although he couldn't quite figure out why. Face paint had never appealed to him. Clothes were simply clothes as far as Alistair was concerned. No, there was something else about Hetty Brewster tonight. And whatever it was, he liked it.

He put up his hand and waved as the Bambi-ish gaze swung finally in his direction. It would be nice to have someone to talk to, as well. All the other thirty or so guests appeared to know each other and he was beginning to feel left out.

There was Alistair Munro, no doubt heaving an inward sigh of boredom, gritting his teeth and preparing to do his duty as spare man. Hetty blinked and turned away before he could think she was going to rush over like a lovesick teenager and bore him to death before dinner. She had learned her lesson already, thanks. Some men – well, most men, in her experience – just weren't interested and it was a waste of time even trying to change their minds. She would be polite to Alistair Munro but that was absolutely all. No way was he going to regard her as some kind of fawning groupie. At least, no more than he did already.

'Well, well, look at you!'

Hetty spun round, not immediately recognizing the rather sexy-sounding voice in her ear.

'Derry!' Her face lit up. 'What are you doing here?'

It was a typical dopey question. He was holding a bottle of Moët in one hand and a silver tray in the other.

Understanding what she meant, though, Derry O'Driscoll broke into a dazzling grin.

'I know, isn't it great?' He spoke in a conspiratorial whisper. 'A lady friend of mine was supposed to be doing the job but she went down with flu at the last minute. I offered to step into the breach and Vanessa was so desperate she said yes. I'm sure she's keeping an eagle eye on me, terrified that at any minute I'm going to start stuffing bits of silver cutlery and other people's watches into my pockets.'

As far as preserving the O'Driscoll mystique was concerned, Derry was in no danger at all of letting the side down. At twenty-one his romantic gypsyish good looks meant he could have just about any girl he chose. Being Derry, the girls he chose were almost always engaged or married to other men.

His life, as a result, was endlessly complicated. Derry treated it all as a terrific game.

Nobody was ever quite sure where his money came from, either. He seemed to have plenty of it, but no regular job. Buying and selling smart cars appeared to be more of a hobby than real work. He gambled too, and was frequently lucky, but surely couldn't be making a career out of it.

When Minnie Hardwick – egged on by her friends and bursting to know – had dared to ask in the shop one day what he actually did for a living, Derry had replied, 'Didn't you know, Minnie? I'm a drugs baron.' Then he'd given her a friendly nudge. 'So if you think you might be interested in a little something to make the next church fête go with a swing . . .'

The truth, far less enthralling, was that Derry scraped by. Between betting on the horses, keeping a level head in the casino, and odd jobs here and there when the going was particularly tough, he survived. Living at home was easy and cheap. Buying and selling-on the occasional classic sports car was easy and profitable. As far as Derry was concerned, he might as well enjoy himself whilst he was still young and single. At the moment, what with four and a half regular girlfriends, he simply didn't have time for a proper job.

Hetty had always got on well with Derry, even if he did make her feel ancient. Gosh, she could remember him at the age of ten, angelic and incurably mischievous, on one occasion eating an entire harvest festival display for a bet and then throwing it up in spectacular fashion in the middle of the service. The congregation had been singing 'All Things Bright and Beautiful' at the time, Hetty remembered, and the organist had promptly fainted.

But not many people, she thought, could get themselves expelled from the church choir, then manage the following year to persuade the vicar to give them the coveted role of Joseph in the nativity play. What Derry lacked in serious application, one had to admit he had always more than made up for in charm.

'What?' he demanded now, as Hetty's mouth began to twitch.

'Just thinking how old you make me feel. Nell used to cart you along to our house when she was babysitting. Do you remember that?'

'She was always scared I'd break some priceless ornament.' Derry nodded, smiling down at her. 'Or else teach your baby terrible swear words behind her back. You really mustn't feel old,' he chided. 'I think you're looking brilliant. And I love that waistcoat.'

'Now I know you're having me on.'

'OK, so Nell told me to say that.' Cheerfully he added, 'But it's true, so I probably would have said it anyway.'

From the other side of the room, Alistair Munro watched Hetty being chatted up by the good-looking young barman. Behind Hetty another, older man was also keeping a covert eye on her. As a doctor, Alistair missed nothing. So much, he thought with a rueful glance at his empty glass, for thinking he was going to be stuck all night with the village wallflower.

'Come along, come along. You're supposed to be topping people up.' Vanessa, employing her I-sound-jokey-but-I-mean-it voice, had materialized at Derry's side. Bony, bejewelled fingers fastened around the neck of the Moët bottle in his hand. She tut-tutted. 'Empty. Oh dear.'

'It's OK,' Derry looked innocent. 'I didn't drink it.'

If he weren't so stunning, Vanessa thought, he wouldn't be able to get away with making flip remarks. She still wasn't completely sure she trusted him, either. She'd heard some extraordinary tales about the O'Driscoll family since moving to Kilburton.

But it was too late to worry about that now. Briskly, she took control.

'That's hardly the point, dear. There are guests with empty glasses. Hello, Hetty, I thought it was probably you from the back. Good gracious, whatever have you done to yourself? New hair cut?'

'No,' said Hetty, 'new lover.'

Not strictly true, of course. Just the same old one, recycled. But she enjoyed saying it.

Vanessa gurgled with laughter, throwing her head back to reveal strong white teeth and several amalgam fillings.

'Good for you, good for you! Keeping a sense of humour is so important, I always feel. Tony, darling, don't you think Hetty looks sweet in that funny little waistcoat of hers. Like a Greek waiter or something! Actually, sweetheart, if you could keep an eye on the O'Driscoll boy and make sure he keeps circulating with the drinks, I'll steer Hetty across the room.'

As she was seized by the arm, Hetty murmured, 'Help, I'm being kidnapped.'

'Come along now,' Vanessa chided. 'We didn't invite you here so you could spend the evening flirting with young boys.

I know he's pretty but you're old enough to be his mother. Look, that nice Alistair Munro's over there, all on his own. He's the one you're supposed to be getting to know.' Catching a glimpse of the expression on Hetty's face, she lowered her voice and added with exaggerated patience, 'We're doing this for your benefit, dear. You're the one always moaning you don't have a social life.'

'Sorry, Vanessa. Thank you, Vanessa. I appreciate it, really I do.'

What *was* the matter with Hetty tonight? Vanessa, too hyped-up by the party to give the matter her full attention, steered her briskly towards Alistair Munro.

'Here we are then. Hetty . . . Alistair . . . if you'll excuse me, I see my editor's arrived. Dinner will be in thirty minutes. I'm sure you two must have lots to talk about.'

'Does she always treat people like that?' said Alistair, when Vanessa was safely out of earshot. She reminded him of a terrifying headmistress he had once known.

'Good grief no. She's usually far more bossy and insulting.' Undeterred, Hetty smiled across at Tony, now trapped at the far end of the room between the big Texan and a beaky woman with legs like a flamingo.

'She's like a bulldozer with ear-rings.' Alistair still couldn't get over Vanessa. He shook his head in amazement. 'She calls everyone dear, even people twice her age. Is that your ex-husband over there with the cravat?'

'Mmm.' Cravat, thought Hetty with amusement. Honestly.

'He keeps looking over at you.'

'Maybe he recognizes me from somewhere.'

223

'Why did you come here?' He couldn't help it. He was intrigued. 'Why do you let Vanessa talk to you like that? Doesn't it bother you?'

The fact that Hetty wasn't even looking at him was beginning to bother Alistair. Perversely, he found himself wondering what made her think he wasn't worthy of her full attention. Now he knew that dewy, doe-eyed look of hers didn't signal deadly marital intent, he would have been more than happy to be on the receiving end. Sadly, it was being directed elsewhere.

'I'm sorry, what was that?' Hetty murmured. Derry, having caught her eye, was uncorking another bottle, pretending to aim it at Vanessa's backside. 'Oh, you mean the insults. She does it to everyone, not just me.'

'But you're the one whose husband she ran off with.' Stung by her indifference, Alistair Munro said more sharply than he had intended, 'And she's deliberately rubbing your nose in it. I would have thought you might have more pride than to let her humiliate you in public.'

The luminous, conker-brown gaze swung round, locking on to him at last. Having prepared to be indifferent to Alistair Munro this evening, Hetty now found herself beginning to actively dislike him. So much for that lightning flash of attraction she had felt upon first setting eyes on him, she thought, marvelling at her own abysmal judgement. He really wasn't very nice at all.

'You're assuming I wanted to keep my husband in the first place,' she replied, 'when, in fact, I was quite glad to see the back of him. Not that it's any of your business, either way.'

Hardly able to believe she'd been so daring, Hetty excused herself and rushed upstairs. Hot on her heels in a streak of scarlet satin came Vanessa.

'I say, I couldn't help overhearing that last remark of yours. And there I was, just wondering how you two were getting on.'

If Hetty had been hoping for a bit of privacy, she was out of luck. Vanessa examined her face in the bathroom mirror, in order to check her teeth. 'I know I'm a bit of an old clodhopper when it comes to treading on toes, but that doctor chappie must have really hit a nerve.' The look she gave Hetty was almost one of admiration. 'I didn't know you could snap like that.'

This was the difference between Vanessa and Alistair, Hetty realized. Vanessa's talent for unfortunate remarks was entirely without malice. It would never occur to her for a second that what she said might be hurtful. She had been snubbed dozens, if not hundreds of times by tactless, thoughtless Vanessa and it was par for the course.

Whereas although Alistair Munro had only done it twice, each snub had been quite deliberate.

It was a different ball game altogether. Besides, Alistair Munro had no right to deliver personal snubs. He didn't even know her.

'Oh, I can snap when I want to.' For something to do, Hetty opened her bag and uncapped a phial of perfume, one of those trial sizes that came superglued to the front of glossy magazines. She had only meant to dab a bit on her neck. Somehow, though, the whole lot slid out in one go. 'Shit.'

'Such a shame.' Vanessa pushed scarlet-tipped fingers

through her artfully disarranged hair. 'We were so hoping you two might hit it off.'

'Sorry.' Not sorry at all, Hetty gazed down in dismay at the spreading perfume stain on the rose-pink silk front of Nell's waistcoat. She had a horrible feeling it was there to stay.

'Oh well, I dare say it was mutual. You probably wouldn't have been his type anyway.' Evidently satisfied with her appearance, Vanessa prepared to head back downstairs. 'Never mind, maybe we'll have better luck next time. Can I say something personal, Hetty?'

Astonished that she should have asked, Hetty said, 'I expect so.'

'That perfume.' Vanessa wrinkled her nose. 'It's very sexy, very . . . sensual, isn't it? I can't help feeling, dear, it isn't quite *you*.'

Chapter 26

They were twenty-eight at dinner. Vanessa had had an enormous table shipped in for the occasion. As they made their way to their places, Tony caught up with his ex-wife.

'What were you saying to Vanessa?'

'Nothing much.' Hetty, by this time beginning to enjoy saying whatever came to mind, added blithely, 'I told her I was pregnant, but that I wasn't sure who the father might be. Could be you, could be Abel Trippick—'

'I don't know what's the matter with you tonight.' Tony cast a hasty glance over his shoulder, terrified that someone might have overheard her. 'Are you drunk?'

'Don't panic, we weren't discussing you!' Hetty gave his forearm a brief, consoling pat. 'We weren't comparing technique and giving you marks out of ten, if that's what you're worried about.'

She found herself seated next to the Texan film producer. Over a first course of designer pigeon and orange salad, they made casual small talk. It was his wife, the woman with legs like a flamingo, who finally made the connection.

'So you're the ex!' Her mascaraed eyes widened. 'You were married to Tony Dexter.'

'Brewster.' Hetty nodded. 'That's right.'

'Ma Ga-ad!' Evidently stunned, the woman nudged her own

227

husband and pointed a forkful of lollo rosso at Hetty. 'Check this out, Irving, she's the one in Vanni's naarvel, the moaning one with the bedsocks. Oh honey, you British are so *civilized* . . . if someone had done a number like that on me I'd have been mad as *hell*.'

'Don't get mad, get even.' Hetty risked an innocent smile. 'Isn't that the expression?'

The Texan producer rumbled with laughter. 'That's what I like about you Brits. You never are quite as civilized as you look.'

Over steamed mullet with a saffron-and-tomato sauce, Alistair Munro attempted to make amends.

'I'm sorry if I offended you earlier.'

'No "if" about it.' Hetty speared a wild mushroom and trawled it through the delectable tomato sauce.

'Well, I'm still sorry.' He gave her a rueful look. 'Maybe I can blame it on the job. We poor overworked doctors have to ask a lot of strangers a lot of personal questions. There isn't always time to observe the social niceties, I'm afraid.'

But Hetty was still giddy with that sense of newfound power. Having decided she didn't like Alistair Munro, she had no intention of forgiving him for being an ill-mannered pig.

'All the more reason, I would have thought, to think before you speak.'

'Oh dear. We aren't doing very well, are we?'

And he was a patronizing shit. 'Speak for yourself,' said Hetty, thinking that Nell would be proud of her. 'I'm doing fine.'

'What rotten luck,' Vanessa's clear voice carried down the table, 'darling Marcus not being able to make it this evening.

The Earl of Kilburton, you know.' She nodded at the Texan pair with pride. 'Lives up at the castle. Now he's a *great* friend of ours – such a shame you couldn't meet him.'

Hetty stared at Tony. Tony looked embarrassed. From the kitchen, where Derry had been eavesdropping, came a hastily muffled shout of laughter.

It had been a good evening. Reassured that Hetty was not after all out to spoil the fun, Tony murmured, 'Next Tuesday, elevenish,' as he helped her into her coat.

Hetty thought for a moment. She looked regretful. 'Can't. I've got a doctor's appointment on Tuesday.'

'Really?' Alistair Munro, waiting by the front door, looked interested. From Monday, he was taking over morning surgery. 'With me?'

'I'm not registered with the Kilburton practice.' Hetty barely glanced at him. 'I go to Dr Mather in Tedbury. She's lovely, so sympathetic. Not at all brisk, like some doctors.'

'*Touché.*' Alistair Munro nodded and half smiled. 'OK, is that it? Have I been punished enough? If you've finished turning the thumbscrews, maybe I could be permitted to walk you home.'

Everyone was leaving at once. The oak-panelled hall was crowded with people locating coats and car keys and with the caterers loading boxes of equipment into their blue-and-white van. As Hetty hesitated, Derry materialized at her side. Tall, elegant and in the amber light more effortlessly beautiful than ever, he rested his hand briefly on Hetty's shoulder.

'Or we could walk together.' He smiled down at her, as if she alone was capable of sharing the joke. 'If you'd like to.'

'I say, what a turn-up for the books,' crowed Vanessa. 'It must be quite a while since anything like this last happened, eh, Hetty? Two men, practically fighting over you . . . well, one man and a boy, anyway. It's enough to turn anyone's head!'

'She really is a silly bitch.' Amused, shaking his head, Derry glanced back over his shoulder at the lit-up Old Schoolhouse. They were crossing the village green rather than keeping to the road, since Hetty's home was diagonally opposite Vanessa and Tony's. The sky was inky, the moon a sliver of white. Stars glistened like mica. They really do twinkle, he thought, gazing up at them. How kitsch!

Hetty, listening to the rhythmic clink of glass as he strode easily along beside her, said, 'How many bottles have you got stashed under that jacket, by the way?'

'Two red, one white. A rather nice-looking Australian Chardonnay.' His teeth gleamed in the darkness. 'Well, the stingy cow only paid me a tenner for the entire evening. What does she expect? You should have seen how much booze those caterers spirited away into their van.'

Hetty, who whole-heartedly approved, said, 'Thanks, anyway, for walking me home. And for cheering me up.'

They had reached the back gate. All the lights were out, which meant Rachel was in bed asleep. Now that she had stopped walking, Hetty felt her thin heels begin to sink into the soft ground.

'My pleasure,' said Derry. 'You're shrinking.'

With great efficiency, he took hold of her arms and pulled her back into an upright position. Giggling, Hetty said impulsively, 'Why don't you come in for a drink?'

'That's the best offer I've had all night.' He lifted the bottles from their hiding-place inside his jacket. 'And what a co-incidence. I just happen to have about my person a rather nice-looking Australian Chardonnay.'

'Don't get too excited.' Hetty, glancing at the label, was revelling in her newfound bitchiness. 'If it's the same as the stuff we had to force down at dinner, it tastes like platypus piss.'

Upstairs, Rachel was far too hungry to sleep. Lying in bed, tensing her stomach muscles with all her might and realizing to her disgust that she could still pinch an inch – if she was honest, it was more like two – she tried to force her mind away from the contents of the fridge downstairs. From the cold sausages on the top shelf, the Marks & Spencer cheesecake below, the half-full tub of blackcurrant ice-cream in the freezer . . .

Before she could give in and sneak downstairs, Rachel heard the sound of the back door being unlocked. When she heard semi-whispered voices and a brief burst of laughter she realized her mother had brought a man home.

Listening intently but unable to identify the voice at this distance, she wondered if Hetty had done it on purpose, just to prove she still could. Maybe that jibe earlier about being too old had hit home. Rachel, half-reluctant and half-dying to know who was downstairs, envisaged some hideous old wrinkly of about forty-five with even less hair than her dad. It was almost impossible, she felt, to imagine going out on dates and stuff with men of that age. As for actually having to kiss them . . . yeugh, gross.

After several minutes in the kitchen and more tantalizing laughter interspersed with the sound of glasses being recklessly taken down from the cupboard, bottles being uncorked and the fridge door opening and closing half a dozen times – Hetty was a great one for late-night cheese and biscuits – Rachel heard them move into the sitting-room. The door closed behind them. Within a couple of minutes, music was drifting up through the house. Hetty had put on one of her beloved Rod Stewart tapes, which was bad news as far as Rachel was concerned. *Now* how was she supposed to be able to eavesdrop on whatever was going on downstairs?

Half an hour later, barefoot and wearing only a black, drooping-to-the-knee T-shirt and taking care to avoid the creaky stairs, Rachel crept down into the hall. The plan was to listen at the sitting-room door, take a quick peek through the keyhole, satisfy her curiosity on that score then sneak into the kitchen, raid the fridge and satisfy the gnawing pangs of hunger. In this way she would be killing two birds with one stone, which she felt justified the expedition. Then, no longer starving and curious, maybe she would be able to get to sleep.

In order to be able to make a quick getaway should the need arise, however, Rachel changed her mind at the foot of the stairs. Fridge first, checking-up-on-Mother second. And just pray Hetty hadn't pinched all the cold sausages.

No, thank God, there were still four left. Scooping three into her left hand, stuffing the fourth into her mouth like a cigar, she reached for the cheesecake with her right hand and nudged the fridge door shut with her hip. Since she wasn't about to start jangling around in the cutlery drawer for a spoon, she'd just have to eat the crumbling cheesecake with her fingers and give the blackcurrant ice-cream a miss. Oh, these sausages were the best thing *ever*.

If you couldn't trust Derry, Hetty had decided, then who the hell could you trust? He was an O'Driscoll, after all, as well as a philanderer experienced beyond his years.

He was perfectly used to being discreet, she concluded. And he had been so sweet, telling her Tony must be out of his mind to leave her for someone as brassy and pretentious as Vanessa. Hetty, feeling deliciously naughty, had in turn told Derry all about her own clandestine affair.

'Well, good for you,' Derry declared, when she had finished. He was lying on his side on the carpet, with his head propped on one elbow. He looked very handsome and very young. He was also demonstrating a remarkable capacity for stolen claret. It was going down like Ribena.

Hetty refilled both their glasses.

'Yes, but am I cutting off my nose to spite my thingamy?'

'Why? Do you want him back?'

'No!' She shook her head with vigour. 'No, really not. I'm beginning to wonder, though, if I'm using this fling with Tony as an excuse, a kind of shield. As long as I'm sleeping with him, I don't need to worry about finding a proper man . . .' Breaking off, Hetty giggled. 'Well, you know what I'm trying to say. I'm happy to carry on like this, but basically I suppose it's a bit of a cop-out.'

'So what?' Derry shrugged and flashed her a grin. 'Maybe that's what I'm doing, too. I think I love my girlfriends but, as far as my mother's concerned, what I love most about them is the fact that they're already married. *Safely* married. She says one of these days I'm going to get the fright of my life, because one of them's going to actually up and leave her husband. And then I'll have to emigrate.'

Rod Stewart, damn him, was still drowning out the murmured conversation on the other side of the door. And was there anything on earth more frustrating, seethed Rachel, than a keyhole-sized view of a room almost entirely blocked by the back of the bloody sofa? All she could see, over to the right, was a corner of the TV set, a swathe of beige curtain, the hopelessly over-stuffed magazine rack and one of Hetty's upturned black suede shoes.

Typical, Rachel fumed, taking another bite of cold sausage and shifting from one knee to the other in a hopeless attempt to see round the edge of the sofa. The voices were low but it definitely didn't sound like Clemency's father, Dr Munro. Maybe when this side of the tape came to an end she would be able to hear what was going on.

'Excuse me a sec.' Levering himself up from the carpet, Derry placed his glass on the coffee-table. 'Now, can I remember where the loo is? Second left at the top of the stairs?'

'You'd get a shock.' Hetty, who was stretched across the sofa, grinned. 'That's Rachel's room. The bathroom's first left.'

But Derry got a shock anyway. So did Rachel, on her knees in the hall with one eye pressed against the keyhole and half a sausage sticking out of her mouth. The door opened inwards far too suddenly for her to be able to do anything about it. She only just managed to avoid toppling forward like a skittle. As it was, she found herself groping blindly at a black-trousered knee in order to keep her balance. When she was finally able to look up and see who the knee belonged to, her heart almost stopped beating there and then. She wanted to die of shame.

'Ouch.' Derry winced as Rachel's fingernails dug into his leg. He took a step back, his mouth curling with amusement at the stunned expression on her face. If anyone should be stunned, he thought reasonably, it was him. It wasn't every day, after all, that you opened a door in all innocence to find a girl on the other side with a sausage in her mouth like Groucho Marx, three more in her hand and an upturned bowl of cheesecake in her lap.

It crossed his mind to make a mildly *risqué* joke about bangers, but Hetty's daughter, whose bare white legs beneath the T-shirt were so at odds with her shiny red face, didn't look in the mood for jokes. Besides, he didn't want to offend Hetty.

'Rachel? What in heaven's name are you doing down there?'

Hetty had appeared behind Derry. Glancing over his shoulder at her, he remarked, 'Making sure my intentions don't get too dishonourable, by the look of it. Does she lie in wait like this every time you invite someone back for a drink, or am I just more of a threat than the rest?' His eyes glittered as he stepped past Rachel then made his way towards the staircase. Mimicking Minnie Hardwick's voice with wicked accuracy he murmured, 'That O'Driscoll boy, can't trust 'im y'know, 'specially not when there's innocent divorcees around . . .'

Rachel gazed numbly down at her fat white knees. Raspberry cheesecake was smeared all over them. She still had a mouthful of sausage that wouldn't go down and her hair was an uncombed mess. She didn't need a mirror to tell her she looked a fright.

She didn't need a mother, either, asking stupid bloody questions.

Oh God, thought Rachel, mortified. If he thought I was fat before, what's he going to think now? How can I ever look him in the face again?

'You daft thing.'

The brief spat earlier was forgotten. Hetty, who could never hold a grudge for long, gave her an indulgent smile. 'Who did you think was in here with me, Clemency's dad? Come on, sweetheart, up you get. Why don't you pop upstairs and change into something else?' As she spoke, Hetty was mopping ineffectually at the cheesecake with a tissue. 'Then you can come back down for a cup of cocoa or something, and we'll tell you all about Vanessa's party. Oh cheer up, sweetheart,' she begged, gesturing towards the sitting-room. 'You can join us, we're having a lovely time. And it isn't as if I've invited some awful stranger back. It's only Derry.'

Chapter 27

It promised to be another fine, sunny day. Vestiges of mist still hung in the air but the sky was already an intense shade of blue. There wasn't so much as a hint of breeze.

In the secluded, high-walled garden beyond the castle's east wing, the still air was blissfully warm. Marcus, wearing only a khaki shirt and Levi's, made his way along the narrow path leading to the summer house and watched from a distance as Nell, unaware of his presence, stretched across one of the flower-beds to reach the delphiniums.

She was wearing a backless, lemon-yellow sundress. Her dark hair was tied back with a yellow bow. Her feet were bare, Marcus observed. Well, apart from the nail polish on her toes. And her arms were filled with flowers, which she would carry into the kitchen and arrange in terracotta bowls. Visitors to the castle enjoyed seeing flowers around the place; they smelled wonderful and brightened up innumerable gloomy corners.

Rather like Nell herself, thought Marcus, who had now reached the summer house. In that dress she looked like a daffodil.

Nell, who had by this time spotted him, smiled and carried on picking flowers until her arms could hold no more. When she came towards him he saw the faint sheen of perspiration on her chest. Bending carefully, resting the delphiniums,

237

foxgloves, cornflowers and lavender in the wicker basket along with the flowers already gathered, she then straightened up, reached across and with one fluid movement ripped open Marcus's khaki cotton shirt. Buttons sailed through the air in all directions.

Nell smiled. 'I can't tell you how long I've waited to do that.'

'I can't tell you how long I've waited for you to do it.'

'You aren't scared?' As she murmured the words, her warm hand was snaking around his neck.

'You don't scare me,' said Marcus. The pale-yellow straps of her dress were sliding from her tanned shoulders. 'I'm your employer. Your boss. You have to do whatever I say.'

Nell, who was by this time lying on the sun-warmed stone floor of the summer house, had somehow brought him down with her.

'I say make love to me,' she whispered, which wasn't what Marcus had said at all. 'Who cares if people laugh? Who gives a stuff if I'm just a common gypsy and you're the eligible Earl? There's more to life than perfectly matched couples, courtesy of Debrett's. See? You've taken my dress off. I may not have blue blood, but you still want me, don't you? My mother told me all about it, of course. You aristocrats think you can get away with anything just because of who you are, and hush it up. But this time you aren't going to get away with it, because I've got witnesses. All these people are watching you now, and they're on my side. They'll back me up . . . they won't *let* you deny it—'

'What people?' yelled Marcus, and Nell burst out laughing.

'These people.' She gestured lazily behind her. To his absolute horror, he saw hundreds of them, visitors to the castle, surrounding the summer house and applauding with enthusiasm.

'Oh don't worry, they've paid their entrance fee,' Nell consoled him. 'They didn't believe you'd actually go this far, but I told them you would.' She smiled up at him. 'I promised them you'd be good, too. Miles better than Abel Trippick. So come on, Marcus. Don't let them down. Show them what you can do.'

'Jesus!' Marcus awoke with a start. The dream, so real he could taste it, was the most lifelike he had ever experienced. Even as he rolled over on to his side, taking in the reassuring familiarity of the bedroom, he found himself checking the pillows next to his, needing to make sure he really was alone.

Then, having double-checked, he said, 'Damn,' because although the bit about being cheered on by an enthusiastic audience was something he could do without, the actual seduction itself rather appealed.

Shit, it more than appealed. Waking up and realizing that it wasn't about to happen after all, if he was honest, was a downright utter let-down. For a mad moment, Marcus wondered if Nell was out in the walled garden at this moment, gathering flowers for the displays.

Then he glanced across at the window. So much for fantasy, thought Marcus with a rueful half-smile. It was bucketing down with rain. *Damn.*

In the event Marcus didn't set eyes on Nell until gone eight in the evening, following a day of tedious but necessary wall-to-wall meetings in London.

When he walked into his office he found her sitting with her feet stuck up on the desk, speaking into the phone. Outside, it continued to pour with rain. It definitely wasn't a day for yellow backless sundresses. Nell was wearing a black sweatshirt, white denims and trainers. The only exposed bits of her were her slender forearms and brown ankles. The only summer flowers in sight, furthermore, were the big green-and-white enamelled daisy ear-rings dangling from her ears.

The last time he'd seen her – or so it felt, to Marcus – had been that morning outside in the walled garden, when Nell had torn off his shirt and he had been about to make love to her on the floor of the summer house. It had seemed so natural, too. And incredibly real. Watching her now as she listened to the voice on the other end of the phone and waved a red ballpoint at him in casual greeting, it was almost impossible to believe that nothing had happened, that Nell had no knowledge of what had gone on. Or of what had so nearly gone on . . .

'Better watch out,' Nell grinned as she replaced the receiver. 'You could wake up tonight to find someone creeping into your bed.'

'Oh yes?' Shit, he hated it when she did that. Was she reading his mind, thought Marcus, or what?

'That was Tedbury children's home.' Nell nodded at the phone. 'One of their boys did a bunk this morning. The police are out looking for him but one of the care workers thinks there's an outside chance he may have come here. She supervised a visit to the castle a few weeks ago and this lad was apparently quite smitten with it. The care worker wondered if we could take a quick look around, just in case. The poor little chap's only ten. He could be cowering behind some firescreen by now, scared out of his wits.'

'He could be shredding tapestries, slashing paintings and chucking bricks through mirrors,' Marcus pointed out. He gave her a look. For someone supposedly so streetwise, Nell could be unbelievably naïve at times. 'He could be unlocking doors and flashing his torch out of the window, signalling to a lorry load of thieves that the coast's clear for them to come on in and help themselves . . .'

'You know, for a nicely brought-up aristocrat,' she mocked, 'you have an awfully suspicious mind.'

'That's because I know how much stuff gets lifted from the gift shop each week.'

'Personally,' said Nell, 'I blame those coach trips from the WI.'

'This is a waste of time,' sighed Marcus an hour later. It was almost nine-thirty, he was hungry and he hadn't even had a chance yet to change out of his suit. Nell, accustomed to playing hide-and-seek with innumerable nephews and nieces, was carrying out an ultra-thorough search of each room in turn, checking even the most unlikely hiding-places. Marcus, by this time past caring about thieves and vandals, was bored. 'There's nobody here. Come on, let's go.'

They had almost finished working their way through the bedrooms of the west wing. Nell, who had moved ahead, pushed open the last but one heavily panelled door. Hoping to speed her up, Marcus hung back in the corridor.

When she withdrew from the room seconds later she had a finger to her lips and was grinning.

'Take a look at this.'

'He's in there?'

'Sshh.'

Marcus looked. Why Nell had said 'sshh' he didn't know, because from the look of him the boy wouldn't have heard the massed band of the Coldstream Guards if it had marched into the room.

A grubby-looking red anorak had been thrown across the eighteenth-century marquetry table, along with an even grubbier khaki haversack. The boy, wearing a black-and-white Incubus T-shirt, was sitting up in the centre of the four-poster bed reading a comic and clutching a carton of Ribena. From his Walkman belted the tinny sound of mega-decibel hard rock. As he slurped the Ribena up through a straw, his fair head dipped rhythmically in time with the beat.

At the foot of the bed, Marcus observed a pair of well-worn mud-caked trainers. Ironically they were the same make as Nell's.

'I don't believe this! Does he have any idea what he's doing?' Astounded by the boy's nerve, Marcus gestured towards the faded, crimson velvet canopy, the ancient carved wooden supports, the hand-stitched linen sheets. 'Henry the fucking Eighth slept in that bed.'

His first instinct was to grab the boy by the scruff of his neck and haul him out of there so fast his dirty little feet didn't touch the ground. Nell, however, was blocking his path. She turned and smiled up at him.

'Oh come on, don't be cross. I think he looks sweet.'

'Sweet?' Dear God, thought Marcus. He sometimes wondered if Nell said these things deliberately, just to gee him up.

'You could try being pleased,' she chided. 'He hasn't caused any damage to anything, has he?'

'We don't know that yet. He may have wet the bed.'

'If it coped with Henry the Eighth,' said Nell, 'it can cope with anything. Don't be such a grumpy sod.'

'I'm not a grumpy sod,' Marcus protested. 'Just a pessimist.'

'Allow me to know,' said Nell.

Just then, the tape in the Walkman ran out. The boy in the bed, glancing up to find two people arguing in the doorway, let out a shriek of dismay and cried, 'Bloody 'ell!' The next moment, having pulled off his Walkman and dropped the Ribena carton on to the silk embroidered bedcover, he started to cry.

Great bawling sobs reverberated around the room. Marcus, feeling uncomfortably to blame for the lad's distress, heaved a sigh and glanced across at Nell. This was what she was good at. It was the kind of thing she did best.

'That's not very convincing,' said Nell.

The boy, who was thin and blond, took his hands away from his face. 'Oh dear,' Nell sighed. 'Not a tear in sight. Now listen to me. First, tell me you haven't wet the bed.'

Outraged, the boy said, 'Of course I haven't wet the bed! I'm eleven, aren't I?'

'Ten, actually.' Marcus, correcting him, had picked up the Ribena carton. Mercifully, it was empty.

'Well, I still wouldn't wet the bed.' The boy looked indignant. 'This is where 'Enry the Eighth slept, innit? It's 'istory, this bed.'

To prove it, he pulled a tattered, rolled-up copy of the castle guidebook from the back pocket of his jeans. With a dirty finger, he pointed to the appropriate section.

'See? Told you. 'Enry was 'ere. And Charles the First. *And* Prince Rupert . . . not all at the same time, mind.' He held the cover of the guidebook up to show Marcus. 'You should try reading this. It's dead good, 'specially the stuff about the Civil War—'

'Flattery will get you everywhere,' interrupted Nell, who had written the guide herself. 'But you still can't stay here. The police are looking for you, for a start. I'm going to have to ring your care worker.' Tilting her head in Marcus's direction, she added, 'This is the Earl of Kilburton, by the way. It's his castle.'

'Oh shit.' This time the boy did look scared. 'I thought you was a caretaker or sumfing. Look, you can't do me for breaking and entering. I didn't break nothing.' His eyes widened. 'I paid me entrance fee an' all.'

'That's right.' Nell, grinning, backed him up. 'He entered. He just forgot to leave. It's a mistake anyone could make.'

'So why *are* you here?' Marcus frowned, because this was all very well, but somebody had to make the boy realize he couldn't spend the rest of his life stowing away in other people's homes.

The boy shrugged, thought for a moment and looked embarrassed.

'I just wanted to sleep in the same bed as a king,' he said finally. 'I like it 'ere. It's great. No other kids yelling and fighting. And everything's dead old.'

Living in the children's home, Marcus supposed, was no picnic. Warming slightly to the small boy with a passion for history, he nodded. 'Quiet, too.'

'Yeah.' Dreamily, the boy gazed around the room at the centuries-old oil paintings, the carved-oak furniture and the painstakingly preserved lace bedhangings. 'Love it. If you 'ad a big telly in 'ere an' all, it'd be perfect.'

Chapter 28

By the time a harassed social worker had arrived, apologized profusely, picked the boy up and driven him back to Tedbury, it was gone eleven.

'Now I'm really hungry,' said Marcus. Removing his jacket and tie, he ran an index finger around the inside of his shirt collar. He wanted a shower. And food. 'Do you want to stay for something to eat, or is it too late for that? I suppose you'd rather be getting home.'

But Nell, as she so often did, surprised him.

'It's OK,' she said unexpectedly. 'I'm hungry too. You could have a bath and change, if you like, while I start cooking something. By the time you've done that, with any luck the food will be ready.'

Unable to help himself, Marcus said, 'Good God.'

'What?' Nell looked alarmed. 'Did I call your bluff or something? If you'd rather I didn't stay—'

'I'd much rather you did.' He broke into a grin. 'Sorry, I'm just not used to you saying "yes".'

She gave a good-natured shrug. 'I must be getting soft in my old age.'

Oh dear, thought Marcus, who could feel stirrings. Not like me . . .

As she moved about the kitchen putting together a meal of

sorts, Nell wondered if she knew what she was doing. It wasn't something she had properly thought out. If the boy, Danno, hadn't hidden in the castle she would have left for home before Marcus had returned from London.

But Danno had hidden, she hadn't left and now, at almost midnight, she was still here mashing potatoes, frying mushrooms and microwaving a Marks & Spencer readymeal. There were candles on the table, together with an opened bottle of red wine. It was all very cosy and deeply suspicious. Nell didn't trust herself one bit.

But what the hell, she thought with a stab of longing as Marcus reappeared. The city suit was gone, replaced by a navy cashmere jersey and those heavenly denims. Oscar Wilde was able to resist anything but temptation, thought Nell. I can resist anything but Marcus in his Levi's. What a body. She felt a rush of sympathy for Kiki Ross-Armitage, too. No wonder poor Kiki had hurled herself at him with all the subtlety of a charging rhino – albeit a rhino in a fabulous pink frock.

Never mind poor Kiki, Nell hurriedly amended, poor me if this backfires. Maybe I'm reading the signals all wrong and he isn't interested after all.

The thing was, she was pretty certain she hadn't misread the signals. And that was where the other risky bit came in. A delightful night of lust in bed with Marcus was most definitely what she wanted, but at what cost? If they did do it, would Marcus be mortified afterwards, appalled by his own idiotic mistake and horrified at the prospect of having to continue working with her? So overcome with horror, in fact, that he would be forced to come up with some excuse to sack her?

Nell, who wanted Marcus but quite wanted to keep her job too, only wished she knew the answers. She could be about to make a huge and truly horrible mistake, yet was she getting the tiniest bit of help? No. That elusive sixth sense remained stubbornly incommunicado. Now, when it mattered, it had gone to ground. The harder she tried to summon it up, the more deafening the silence became. She really felt as if her batteries had been taken out.

Damn, thought Nell, frustrated by the lack of help she was getting. If Marcus had been fat and flabby with three chins and a face like a wart-hog there wouldn't be this dilemma. It was his fault for being so bloody good-looking, for having such a stupendous smile and for wearing such *completely unfair* Levi's.

After months of waiting and wondering, it felt extraordinary to be just minutes away from blast-off. Nell, overcome by an attack of nerves, found herself suddenly unable to eat a thing. Luckily for her, Marcus hadn't made an issue of it. His own appetite undimmed, he had polished off his own dinner then helped himself to most of Nell's. He talked non-stop, too, about Danno, about ten-year-old boys in general, about the latest outbreak of graffiti in the stable-block loos and about the plans so far for September's rock concert in the park. He kept on talking until all the food had gone and there was no wine left in either of their glasses.

In the end, because she could stand it no longer, Nell said, 'Well, it's a comfort to know you're nervous as well. I tell you what, why don't we pretend we've already got the preliminaries out of the way? Why don't we just . . . go to bed?'

At least it stopped him talking. Hardly able to believe she'd said it, Nell felt herself holding her breath. She began to feel light-headed. It took an almighty effort of will to keep on looking at him, not allowing her gaze to slide away from those unnerving, expressionless, heavily lashed, dark-green eyes. What seemed like six or seven hours later, Marcus replied.

'I take it,' he said slowly, 'you mean just the one bed.'

Beneath the table, out of view, Nell's legs were wound tightly around each other, every single muscle as tense as steel. It was the only way she could keep the rest of her looking relaxed. But although her elbows rested casually upon the table and the fingers of her left hand twiddled a strand of hair as if it hadn't a care in the world, Nell could feel herself begin to tremble.

'Believe it or not,' she said, 'I find it helps.'

'I see.' A ghost of a smile touched the corners of Marcus's mouth. 'Anybody's in particular? I mean, Danno wanted to sleep in Henry the Eighth's bed. So what are you trying to tell me here, that it's always been your ambition to . . . er . . . *not* sleep in it?'

'Not at all.' Nell rose to her feet, thinking that this was it; if Marcus stayed sitting now, she was going to look a complete nit. 'Any bed will do. Even yours.'

It was the same, yet not the same, Marcus decided. To dream that he and Nell were consummating their relationship at last was one thing. To find himself in exactly that situation, so soon after dreaming it, was bizarre.

But if the circumstances were different, the reality of being in bed with Nell exceeded all expectations. Naked, she was more beautiful than he could have imagined. Making love to her was everything he had ever imagined and more.

At long last, after months of wondering if he would ever know how Nell felt about him, Marcus had the answer he most wanted. He felt as if he'd been waiting all his life for this night.

'Oops,' said Nell afterwards. 'We did it.' Raising herself up on one elbow, she gave him a mischievous look. 'I meant to make you promise me something first.'

Her gleaming black hair spilled over her shoulder, spreading across the jade-green pillowcase. Marcus, inhaling the faint remnants of her perfume – Eternity, which was promising – ran his fingers along the curve of her collarbone.

'Sounds ominous. Go on then. What was I supposed to promise?'

Nell bit her lip, then smiled. It was OK now. There wasn't going to be any awkwardness between them. It would only have been awkward, she belatedly realized, if the sex hadn't been great.

But it had. It had been more than great. It had, Nell amended with a shiver of remembered pleasure, been downright miraculous.

'Not to sack me,' she admitted. 'I had a horrible thought, earlier, that you might feel a bit of a need to boot me out of the castle and never darken your doorstep again.'

The only need currently troubling Marcus was the urgent one to pull her back into his arms. He wanted to kiss her, to breathe in that wonderful scent of hers and to make love to Nell once more.

Glancing at his watch he saw that it was, by this time, two-thirty. Time, however, had become irrelevant. Right now, sleep was the last thing on his mind.

'OK. I promise not to sack you.' Grinning, giving in to temptation, he reached for her. 'You can carry on darkening my doorstep as long as you like.'

'Hooray,' said Nell. Her legs, no longer wrapped around each other, wrapped happily around his legs instead.

'There is one thing.' Too intrigued not to ask, he pushed a damp tendril of hair away from Nell's face. The light, silvery sheen of perspiration at her temples had reminded him once again of that extraordinary dream. Feeling faintly ridiculous Marcus said, 'Did you *make* this happen?'

'Of course I did.' Breaking into a grin, Nell chided, 'Just as well, too. If we'd hung around waiting for you to get around to saying something we'd probably have been too ancient and decrepit ever to make it up the stairs.'

'That's not what I meant.' Marcus paused. 'Look, I've told you before; I don't believe in this second-sight rubbish. But I've never properly understood how you managed to see off Archie Halifax just as he was about to start working for me. I've tried, but I can't figure it out. How the hell *did* you pull that trick with the fifty-pence piece?'

'It wasn't a trick.' Nell, busy admiring his broad, tanned shoulders and wonderfully flat stomach, said absently, 'I didn't know it was going to happen like that. I just knew that something *would* happen to stop him coming to work here. So it wasn't anything specific,' she concluded with an almost apologetic shrug. 'I just kind of realized I'd take over his job.'

'Hmmm.' With a thoughtful nod, Marcus wondered if he could at least believe that much. 'And this? Did you kind-of-realize we'd end up in bed together, too?'

'Maybe.' But Nell's eyes had lit up. She was teasing him now. 'It has its uses, this second-sight rubbish. You don't think I'd have made a move in the first place, do you, if I'd known you'd be a lousy lay?'

'I'll take that as a compliment.' Gently, Marcus pinned her down. 'I think.'

Nell gave a sigh of pleasure as he moved on top of her, his warm mouth exploring the hollow at the base of her throat. 'Although maybe I shouldn't make up my mind that fast,' she murmured. 'It isn't really fair, is it? Just to be on the safe side, you'd better do it again. Prove it wasn't a fluke.'

Chapter 29

'Gosh, decadent or what?' Nell, wearing one of Marcus's white shirts, stood at the window gazing out at the gardens below. 'Five-thirty in the morning, and here we are drinking cognac. It's going to be an absolutely gorgeous day, you know. Look at the sun, and the way the mist hovers above the ground. Listen to those birds, too . . . Marcus, you can't go to sleep now, there's no point! Come on, what you need is some good fresh air.'

'You mean you want to go for a walk outside?' Yesterday's rain had cleared. The sky was already a cloudless lavender blue. If Nell suggested a visit to the walled garden, thought Marcus, he would find it creepy beyond belief.

'A walk outside?' Echoing his words in disbelief, Nell laughed. 'Don't be daft! All I want you to do is open this window. I can't do it,' she explained. 'I can't reach.'

'It's only just occurred to me,' said Marcus when they were both back in bed. He looked amused. 'Jemima's going to love this.'

'Love what?'

'This. Us.' With exaggerated emphasis, he pointed first to Nell, then to himself. 'She may even spontaneously combust.'

Now there was a thought. A tempting one, too. Reluctantly, Nell abandoned it.

'How about,' she suggested instead, 'we don't tell her?'

'What do you mean?'

'Well, why should we have to? She doesn't need to know.'

Nell was sitting cross-legged in the bed, still nursing her brandy glass. Seeing that Marcus was giving her a decidedly odd look, she protested, 'But she doesn't! It's nothing to *do* with her, is it? Look, if anyone's going to be a problem it's Hilda Garnet. She's the one we're really going to have to watch out for.' Leaning forward, Nell planted a kiss on Marcus's unamused mouth. 'Oh, don't panic. We'll manage somehow. You know I'll be discreet.' Smiling, she added, 'A damn sight more discreet than my mother was anyway. Although I suppose that's hardly reassuring. Compared with my mother, the *News of the World* is discreet.'

'What?'

Oh dear, now Marcus was seriously worried. Hurrying to reassure him, Nell said, 'It really *is* OK, you know. I'm just as keen as you are to keep it quiet. I swear to you, it's completely different this time around. Not like it was with them at all.'

Finally, having overcome his initial amazement, Marcus started to laugh.

They had managed to spend an entire night together, completely misunderstanding each other's motives.

'I'm sorry,' he said at last. 'I'm not sure how to put this but we appear to have been bonking at cross purposes. I'm not doing this because I want some hush-hush, on-the-side mistress. I want *you*.' Marcus hesitated, searching for words which didn't come naturally to him. He was more used to fending off the over-eager attentions of Sloaney girls like Kiki Ross-Armitage.

He had certainly never needed to say anything like this before. 'It feels right, you being here. I think we're well matched . . . I mean, we make a pretty decent team . . .'

He floundered, realizing that what was coming out didn't sound fantastically romantic. Shit, making the running was harder than he'd thought. 'Look, we could stand a good chance of making a go of it.'

'No we couldn't.' It was Nell's turn to be astounded. Not that it wasn't nice to hear, of course, but she found it hard to believe Marcus actually meant what he said. Now who was being naïve to the point of stupidity?

'Why not?' Marcus was challenging her, his green eyes narrowed in concentration as he prepared to shoot any argument down in flames. 'And don't try to tell me this hasn't meant anything to you, or that you haven't enjoyed yourself every bit as much as I have, because that just is not true.'

Nell, acknowledging that much, shook her head.

'So what, then?' He looked cross. 'You don't want to upset Jemima? Even more unlikely.'

'Oh come on, this is silly,' Nell protested. 'We're on the same side, aren't we? There's absolutely no need for us to get into an argument about it.'

'I'm not arguing,' Marcus replied irritably. 'You are.'

'And I am . . .?' Nell pressed a hand to her chest. Her dark eyes blazed. '*Who* am I, exactly? Oh dear, I seem to have forgotten. Never mind, let's just look me up in Debrett's.' Mimicking the actions, she leafed through an imaginary copy. 'Ah, here we are, listed under Gypsy. The glamorous, ever-popular, brilliantly connected O'Driscolls—'

'Now you're being ridiculous,' snapped Marcus. 'That's inverted snobbery.'

'It's common sense.' Abruptly, Nell's anger subsided. It wasn't his fault, after all. It wasn't hers either. It was just the way things were.

'Look, all I'm doing is being realistic,' she said patiently. 'You know that as well as I do. This isn't a fairy story, it isn't *Cinderella on Ice*. It's real life. And Jemima isn't the only one who'd be horrified,' Nell went on, before he could try and deny it. 'This class business *matters*, for heaven's sake! Can you begin to imagine how your lot would react if they thought you were taking up with someone from my background, someone descended from a long line of caravans? They'd laugh at you, Marcus. In their eyes, I'd be your bit of rough. And they'd laugh at me, too,' she said in matter-of-fact tones, though her fingers, fiddling with the over-long cuff of her borrowed shirt, betrayed her agitation. 'As Jemima so kindly pointed out the other week, I wear the wrong kind of clothes. I say the wrong things in the wrong kind of voice. And,' Nell concluded heavily, 'I have about as much breeding as Roland Rat.'

Marcus hesitated for a second. This wasn't how he had been expecting things to turn out. And as if being rejected out of hand wasn't bad enough, there was the added discomfort of having to acknowledge that what Nell said wasn't altogether untrue.

'There, you see?' demanded Nell, because that momentary silence told her all she needed to know. Then she smiled and gave his knee a reassuring squeeze. 'But it's OK, it's not your fault. And like I said, I can do without the hassle, too. Can you imagine what the rest of the village would have to say about it if we went public?'

'That's crap.' Marcus's expression hardened. 'Now you're inventing excuses. Since when have you cared what the rest of the village has to say?'

Nell shrugged. 'I don't. They can say what the hell they like about me. But not you.'

Infuriated beyond belief by her calm acceptance of the situation, he snapped, 'And what do you mean, anyway, when you say you have the wrong kind of voice? You don't even have an accent!'

'Just because I don't go "Ooh-aaarr, ooh-arr"?' A faint smile lifted the corners of Nell's mouth. 'Come on, Marcus, admit it. I don't have your kind of accent either.'

He looked outraged. 'I don't give a stuff about accents.'

'Maybe you don't, but there are plenty who do. Right, that's enough arguing for one night.' Turning his arm briskly towards her, Nell glanced at his watch. 'Time to get up. And I'll have a bath now, if that's OK with you.' She pulled a face. 'The last thing we need is half the High Street watching me leave here at seven in the morning. I'll pop home later and grab a change of clothes.'

Having uncrossed her legs, she was already sliding off the bed, heading for the bathroom. As she reached the doorway she paused, turning to survey the casual splendour of the ancient, south tower bedroom and the view of endless rolling parkland through the window. It was a very far cry from The Pink House, and from her own bedroom window overlooking Miriam's beloved vegetable patch.

'Nell, listen to me—' began Marcus.

'No, you listen. I don't know if you remember any of this but I wanted to kill you once, because you sneered at something I said. You told me then that people like us didn't marry people like you.'

She raised her eyebrows, waiting for Marcus to react. Finally, and with reluctance, he nodded. 'OK, I remember. But come on,' he protested, 'I was seventeen years old! What are you planning to do, spend the next fifty years taunting me with it?'

Nell shook her head. 'Quite the opposite. I hated you for saying it, and I was convinced you were wrong. Now I know you were right.' She broke into a slow smile. 'I don't hate you any more, either.'

Marcus relaxed. He had already made up his mind about Nell. All he needed to do now was persuade Nell to change hers.

'Well, good.' He nodded thoughtfully. 'That's a start.'

'So that's it.' Nell looked relieved. 'We'll keep this to ourselves. I think it'll be fun, don't you?'

'You're the clairvoyant. You tell me.' Marcus's stomach rumbled. His attention drawn to food, he said, 'How about dinner at Harvey's tonight? Don't worry,' he added, humouring her, 'we can be discreet. I'll book a private room.'

'Sorry.' Nell, who had to see Ben, shook her head. 'I'm busy tonight. Visiting a friend.'

Not that Ben, when Nell finally arrived at Rowan House that evening, was the least bit appreciative of the sacrifice she had made.

'You don't care about me.'

'Of course I do.' Nell, who had had this conversation a million times before, busied herself unpacking the half-dozen boxes of Bendicks Bittermints he had ordered and tried not to let her impatience show.

'I hate it here. I hate bloody Oscar,' Ben said fretfully. 'How dare he lecture me about smoking?'

'It's for your own good. He's thinking about your lungs.'

'Sod my lungs. He's a tub of lard.' Ben could be spiteful when he wanted. 'I told him I'd stop smoking if he stopped eating. Where are my cigarettes anyway?' He gazed at the packets Nell produced in horror. 'Oh God, not those! They're the wrong kind.'

'I've been busy.' Nell, who could have been enjoying a spectacular dinner at Harvey's, gritted her teeth. 'These were the only ones I could get.'

Ben looked at her. Seconds later, his eyes filled with tears.

'I'm sorry. Oh Nell, I'm sorry. Please don't hate me.'

'I don't hate you.' As he clutched in desperation at her hand, a lump rose in Nell's own throat.

'But I love you so much. I mean it, Nell. I'm so sorry.'

'Good.' Smiling, forgiving him instantly, Nell stroked his hair away from his pale forehead. 'And tomorrow morning maybe you could try apologizing to Oscar too.'

Chapter 30

It wasn't taking Hetty long to realize that being written about by Meg Tarrant in ultra-glowing terms was a zillion times more embarrassing than being referred to in print by Vanessa as a hopeless frump.

She had blushed earlier, just reading Meg's article, entitled 'The One and Only Ex-Wife', and that was in the privacy of her own home. Meg, as good as her word, had been outrageously biased. The photo of Vanessa, too, had been as frightful as promised. All Hetty had to do now, she realized, was try and live up to the tremendous hype.

Terrified that complete strangers might race up to her, shaking copies of the paper under her nose and yelling scornfully 'But you're ugly!' Hetty had spent a frantic forty minutes upstairs, flinging clothes off and on in search of something decent to wear and struggling to do her face just as Nell had done it last Friday. This was such a dismal failure she had ended up cleaning it all off again with baby lotion and settling for mascara and lipstick instead.

Clinging to the hope that if she looked completely different nobody would recognize her, Hetty arrived at work at ten o'clock and went slap into a coach load of fascinated OAPs from Cheltenham, one of whom had been reading the paper on the way to Kilburton and had noted the mention of Hetty's job up at the castle. Since they all felt Vanessa had turned into a brassy, sex-crazed, husband-stealing trollop, the old dears were determinedly on Hetty's side.

'I used to read her historical novels,' confided one. 'Things were so much nicer in olden days. People knew how to behave then, didn't they, love? Never mind all this modern stuff, sex and suchlike.'

'Give me a Catherine Cookson any day,' chirped another with rakishly dyed tomato-red hair and grey roots. 'You always know where you are, don't you, with a nice Catherine Cookson?'

'That Vanessa Dexter, she's let 'erself right down. You're well shot of your old man, I reckon, if that's the type of woman 'e goes for. More fool 'im, I say.' This from a third woman with a Cockney accent and a throaty smoker's laugh. Cackling, she patted Hetty's arm. 'Come on then, ducks, you can tell us! 'Oo's this secret lover in your life? Is 'e 'andsome?'

Hetty was entranced to realize that despite her lack of make-up these dear old ladies were still on her side. She smiled and looked modest.

'Oh, wonderfully handsome. Like a Greek god.'

'And rich?' The one with the tomato-red hair leaned forward and looked hopeful. 'Got plenty of money, has he?'

'Heaps,' Hetty fantasized cheerfully. 'Loads.'

'I expect he lives in a nice house, too,' the first woman prompted.

'Huge,' sighed Hetty.

'Got it!' The one with the Cockney accent let out a squeal of delighted recognition. 'It's the Earl of Kilburton, right? Tall, blond 'air, touch o' the Errol Flynns about 'im ... oooh, you're a lucky girl, you are!' She rolled her currant eyes in appreciation. ' 'e's gorgeous, that Marcus Kilburton. I'd give my false teeth for a night of passion wiv 'im.'

'Actually,' Hetty tried to say, 'you're making—'

'Doris Cartwright, you hussy,' the redhead exclaimed. 'Married to Albert for forty-seven years and here you are lusting after somebody else's young man. I swear you're no better than that dreadful Dexter woman herself. Just wait 'til your Albert gets to hear about this.'

'But it's not—' began Hetty.

'I say, fancy that! You and the Earl of Kilburton,' marvelled the first woman, gazing at her with new respect. 'That's why you're working here, of course. Well, good for you, dear. Now that's *really* one in the eye for that silly old ex-husband of yours!'

'But it isn't the Earl of Kilburton,' Hetty protested, the words spilling out in a rush before any more wrong conclusions could be leapt to. That was the trouble with old dears, they weren't afraid to say what they thought in public. In very loud voices, too.

The three women stopped talking all at once. Finally, the redhead said, 'What, dear?'

'Marcus Kilburton. He isn't the one,' Hetty insisted, anxious to make herself crystal clear. 'I'm definitely, absolutely not having an affair with him. Goodness, the very idea!'

Behind her, Marcus had come into the restaurant. Listening to Hetty's protestations, he raised his eyebrows.

'Ah, but you'd have to say that.' The redhead, not a bit convinced, gave Hetty a knowing nod and a wink.

'Don't worry, pet, your secret's safe with us. We won't breathe a word.'

'Please!' wailed Hetty. 'You must believe me . . . there is nothing going on between myself and Lord Kilburton. He's too young, too good-looking . . . for heaven's sake, he's way out of my league!'

The women were by this time covering their mouths and nudging each other in the ribs. Lord Kilburton himself was standing less than two feet behind Hetty Brewster and the more she protested her innocence the more vigorously her head shook from side to side. More than likely, from the way his lordship was grinning, her bottom was wiggling too.

'You 'ave to be careful,' the Cockney one explained knowingly, 'in case them gossip column people get on to you. Spill the beans, like.'

This was ridiculous. Hetty, going hot and cold, felt perspiration begin to prickle her forehead. It was all she could do not to stamp her foot.

'Listen,' she pleaded, 'this is silly. I'm *not* having an affair with Lord Kilburton—'

'Sad but true, I'm afraid.'

Behind her, looking regretful, Marcus shook his head.

'Oh help!' All colour promptly drained from Hetty's face. No wonder the old dears had been sniggering. 'This is awful,' she wailed. 'Now I'm really embarrassed.'

'No need to be.' Vastly entertained by Hetty's abject horror, Marcus added, 'It would only be embarrassing the other way around, if you said we were having an affair and I denied it.'

'Told you 'e was 'andsome.' The Cockney woman, nodding vigorously at her companions, turned to Hetty. 'I reckon you're missin' out, my girl. Can't tell me this mystery lover of yours is better lookin' than 'is lordship 'ere. You want to give 'im the push, I reckon, and 'ave a go at this 'un instead.'

Some old dears, Hetty decided, weren't dear at all. They were wicked old mischief-makers, bent on having fun at completely innocent younger people's expense, and they deserved to be put down. Marcus Kilburton was no better either, she thought darkly. What did he have to be so bloody cheerful about anyway?

'Sorry.' Marcus was still grinning. 'I'm putting you off your work. I only came over to let you know the *Tedbury Gazette* phoned earlier. They're sending someone along at eleven to take a few photos and have a chat.'

'Photos of what?'

'You.'

Hetty looked appalled. 'I can't do that. I'm working.'

'Doesn't matter; it's all good publicity.' To reassure her, Marcus said, 'You don't need to worry. You look absolutely fine.'

'Where's Nell?'

Nell had sloped off home to change out of last night's clothes. Marcus shrugged.

'Not sure. She had an appointment somewhere. I'm sure she won't be long.'

'Oh help,' said Hetty for the second time.

The Cockney old dear tugged at her sleeve.

' 'ow about 'aving us in these photos with you, my love? I've wanted me picture in the paper all me life.'

'Scuse me, miss. Give us yer autograph.'

Hetty could have cried with relief when she turned to find Nell behind her, looking fresh and summery in a sea-green silk shirt and a short white linen skirt.

'Not funny,' Hetty wailed, because visitors to the castle had been coming into the restaurant all morning to gawp and pass comment. 'This is getting out of hand . . . I'm never going to be able to carry it off.'

'Course you will. You're getting back at Vanessa, aren't you?' Nell realized she needed a bit of encouragement. 'Somebody must have phoned and told her,' she went on. 'As I was leaving the house just now she almost ran me down in her Merc. She screeched to a halt, *thundered* into the shop and shot back out again with a copy of the paper under her arm.' Nell, who wasn't afraid of anyone, smiled gleefully at the memory. 'Derry thought she looked like a bulldog chewing a wasp.'

Hetty was afraid of very nearly everyone. Last week's brief burst of self-confidence had dwindled to nothing; she had reverted to feeble-mode. The daunting prospect of having to explain her wicked actions to a hopping-mad Vanessa made her feel quite faint.

It happened less than half an hour later, and Vanessa more than lived up to Hetty's unhappy expectations. The trouble was, whilst she might just have been able to cope with mere outrage, there proved to be more to it than that.

'How could you do this to me? How *could* you?' begged Vanessa. The whites of her eyes were pink and rabbity-looking, and there were little pouches beneath them. Black eyeliner and lots of bronze eyeshadow couldn't conceal the fact that she had been crying.

'I don't understand why you should have wanted to do something like this,' she went on. 'Do you *hate* me, Hetty? Is that it? Do you really think this is the kind of treatment I deserve?'

Hetty's defences crumbled in an instant. She almost didn't mind being upset herself because she was so used to it happening, but the thought of deliberately upsetting someone else was awful. Horrible. And much, much worse.

Awash with guilt, she realized belatedly what a spiteful, vindictive trick they had played on Vanessa, who might be awful but who didn't mean to be. Whereas she, Hetty, had joyfully colluded with Meg Tarrant with the sole intention of hitting back where it hurt. It had been a premeditated act. And it had done the trick, too. Vanessa was deeply hurt. She, Hetty, had actually made her cry.

God, thought Hetty, hating herself, I'm such a bitch.

'I'm so sorry.' She hung her head. The words came out in a miserable whisper and she couldn't for the life of her think what to say next. Typical; she was even managing to make a pig's ear of a simple apology.

'Yes, well.' Vanessa glanced briefly around the courtyard. Hetty had been cleaning empty tables outside the restaurant when she had arrived, but it was verging on lunch-time. Visitors were milling around, enjoying the June sunshine, studying the menus and deciding what to eat. It was hardly the occasion for an out-and-out shouting match.

'I must say, Hetty, I was surprised to say the least when I read the article. Surprised and disappointed. I didn't expect it of you.' She heaved a sigh. 'I thought you liked me.'

Hetty was by this time close to tears herself. Only thankful that Nell wasn't there to hear her say it, she murmured fervently, 'I *do* like you. Of course I do. It was just . . .' She half-expected to be struck down for telling such a whopping lie. Unable to carry on, she gave a helpless shrug. 'I didn't think, that's all.'

'Tony isn't happy about this, either.' Vanessa glared at two small children, daring to approach with a boisterous looking border collie. Sharp-clawed dogs and 7-denier stockings didn't go together.

Fortunately her attention had been diverted at the right moment. At the mention of Tony's name, Hetty flinched and turned puce. Hastily she recovered her composure. 'No, well, he wouldn't be happy.'

'No man likes a spiteful woman.' Vanessa, beginning to get into her stride, pronounced the words like the opening of a public debate. 'It's not an admirable quality, you know, Hetty. Something like this is hardly likely to impress him, if that's what you were pinning your hopes on. And Tony's so very protective of me . . . heavens, when I phoned him at the office just now to tell him about this dreadful thing in the paper he was practically beside himself with rage. Poor darling, he can't *bear* to see me upset.'

Chapter 31

Kiki didn't read newspapers as such, she just whizzed through on her way to the gossip columns. Since Jemima was off table-hopping, however, and it didn't do any harm to look brainy every once in a while, even in Quaglino's, she turned the pages in a thoughtful, intelligent manner. To the casual observer, she would appear to be studying the financial pages, checking out off-shore thingamies and gilt-edged whatsits. Dead impressive.

In reality, she was checking her horoscope which promised her a gloomy day money-wise.

Definitely not true, Kiki thought with a flash of impatience, because she'd never had one of those in her life. Reading on, though, she found a bit that made perfect sense. 'How annoying,' went the astrologer chummily, 'to have to sit and watch a friend do something stupid. You know it's going to end in tears, don't you? But don't give in to temptation; don't butt in! You can't live another person's life for them. Speak out too strongly and they'll only want to prove you wrong.'

Smirking, Kiki raised her gaze from the paper. Because there, eight tables away and exactly on cue, was a friend doing something very stupid indeed.

Jemima, silently congratulating herself on playing it so casually, had managed to work her way across the noisy, packed-to-the-rafters restaurant, all the time moving closer and closer to Timmy's table. Now, having arrived beside it, what could be more natural than to look surprised, greet him with a kiss, exclaim over his tan and ask how his holiday had been?

And stuff Kiki, who was only bitter because Marcus had been so spectacularly uninterested in her. This, thought Jemima, was how it should be done, with a bit of subtlety and finesse. She wasn't going to ask Timmy why he hadn't phoned her, for God's sake. The trick was to make him wish he had. What did Kiki think she was, anyway? *Completely* dim?

'The bastard. That *bitch*. God, you are not going to believe this.'

Kiki, who had actually got quite engrossed in a feature, put the paper down. Jemima was back, speaking through gritted teeth so the words shot out like pips, and twisting the chain of her Chanel bag round and round her fingers like a garrotte.

'Go on then, amaze me. On second thoughts, let me guess. Timmy's given all the other girls in his life the push and he wants to marry you. Or, or . . . he's taken a vow of celibacy. No, hang on, I know, he's gone gay.'

'Worse.' Jemima glared at a waiter, daring to approach with lunch menus. 'I can't possibly eat now. We'll have to leave.'

'Don't take any notice of her.' Briskly, Kiki seized the menus. 'She's been crossed in love, that's all. I'm starving.'

Jemima sometimes wondered why she bothered to be friends with Kiki Ross-bloody-Armitage. How unsympathetic could one person get? And how dare Kiki not even ask her what the problem was?

'Ooh, yum! Chilli mushrooms to start, I think. Then the tournedos with polenta. How about you, Jem? Come on, don't be such a drama queen. At least look at the menu.'

'Just vodka,' Jemima instructed the waiter. Having helped herself to one of Kiki's cigarettes, she lit up and started flicking the tip furiously against the side of the ashtray. 'My God, wait until Marcus hears about this.'

Kiki sighed. 'Go on then. Tell me.'

'That cow, Nell O'Driscoll. She's only been throwing herself at Timmy. He took her out to dinner and could hardly prise her off him. I *said* she was just like her mother, didn't I?' Jemima shuddered in her seat. 'I suppose she did it on purpose to get back at me. Timmy says she's unstoppable in bed . . . ugh, it's *so* unfair. She couldn't wait to get her claws into him, could she? Spiteful, social-climbing bitch.'

'And poor sweet innocent Timmy,' Kiki mused. 'How completely dreadful for him, having to lie back and take it. All that nasty old sex—'

'Don't be vile,' stormed Jemima. 'Huh, I might have guessed you'd be on her side.'

'I'm just saying it doesn't seem very fair. You were dead against the idea of Nell and Marcus,' Kiki protested. 'Now you're saying she isn't allowed to have a crack at Timmy either. So who on earth *can* she have a bit of fun with?'

'Somebody of her own class.' Viciously, Jemima stubbed out her cigarette. 'Some clodhopping yokel. Some disgusting, long-haired gypsy . . . I don't care, so long as she keeps her hands off my chap.'

Kiki's eyebrows sky-rocketed. '*Your* chap? Oh, come on!

You're making Nell out to be the big baddie here, but let's face it, I'm just about the only person we know who *hasn't* been to bed with Timmy Struther. He's hardly the selective type. If I stood on this table now and said hands up everyone who's ever had a tussle with Timmy, you'd see an awful lot of hands, darling. Not all of them female, either.'

Jemima, who didn't appreciate the joke, gulped down her vodka. 'I asked him what he thought he was doing messing around with a common village girl and he said that was what village girls were there for, surely; to be messed around with. It isn't as if he really fancies her. She just threw herself at him. If it's offered up on a plate like that, what man *would* turn it – for God's sake, Kiki, are you even listening to me?'

'Mmm? Oh, sorry.' Kiki, bored with Jemima's obsessive ranting, had allowed her attention to drift back to the article in the paper. Pointing to the photograph, she exclaimed, 'How about this for a coincidence? Look, this woman's wearing a pink waistcoat exactly like that one of mine. There I was, just thinking how nice it looked and wishing I still had it, and I've just realized . . . this waistcoat *is* mine.'

'You mean it was stolen?' Peering across at the paper, Jemima abruptly snatched it up and scanned the first few lines. 'I don't believe it! This Brewster woman lives in Kilburton. I've seen her working up at the castle . . . she's Nell O'Driscoll's friend! That means Nell stole your waistcoat. Oh, Kiki, now we've really got the bitch! This is so *great.*'

Poor thing, thought Kiki. What it was to be bitter and twisted.

'Actually,' she said, 'not as great as you think. Nell didn't steal that waistcoat. I gave it to her.'

'For fuck's sake, what *is* it with everyone?' Jemima, foiled again, let out a wail of sheer anguish. 'Even you're turning against me now!'

By the time she got home from work Hetty was emotionally wrung out. Too whacked to even think about dinner, she collapsed on the sofa with a mug of tea and the biscuit tin instead.

Thirteen Garibaldis later, she heard a key turning in the front door. Without even giving her a chance to brush the avalanche of crumbs from their nestling place on the front of her shirt, Tony marched into the untidy sitting-room with a face like . . . well, like an outraged man whose infinitely lovely mistress has been humiliated in public by his stupid fat ex-wife.

'I know, I know.' Hetty leapt in before he could start raging in earnest. 'Poor Vanessa, I'm sorry sorry sorry, it was a terrible thing to do, I didn't think, I definitely didn't mean it and I'll never speak to another journalist as long as I live.'

'Sod that,' said Tony grimly. 'Sod Vanessa. What I want to know is who's this secret sodding lover of yours?'

Stunned, Hetty gazed up at him. It took a couple of seconds to click, to sink in. But there it was, she realized, Nell had been spot on after all. And here was Tony, standing before her all macho and masterful like Rhett Butler with chins, boiling not with rage but with jealousy.

'Tony, it's you.'

'Don't give me that,' he roared. 'Jesus, I *knew* you'd try and wriggle out of it. I just knew that's how you'd do it, too, by pinning it on me.' He shook his head like a bear in the zoo. 'I trusted you, Hetty. *Trusted* you. I didn't think you were capable of this kind of behaviour, but you've changed. You're two-timing me,' he concluded heavily, 'and I want to know who with.'

This was going too far.

Hetty, whose patience and capacity for forgiveness was the bane of Nell's life, sat up straight and decided that enough was enough.

'You have a nerve.' She pointed an accusing finger at him. 'I'm your bit on the side, aren't I? Yet you're telling me I can't have my *own* bit on the side . . . talk about double standards, Tony.' Mockingly, she added, 'Better watch out; I may have to report you to the Equal Opportunities Commission.'

'I didn't mean it like that,' Tony spluttered, back-pedalling fast. It wasn't true, of course; he had meant it exactly like that, but he hadn't expected Hetty to retaliate. 'I'm just saying we shouldn't keep those kind of secrets from each other.' He was beginning to sweat. 'It's a matter of being responsible. You know who I'm sleeping with. I think I should know who you're . . . seeing, in return.'

'No need to worry about AIDS.' Hetty, who hadn't slept with anyone but Tony for the past twenty-odd years, was damned if she was going to admit as much now. Coolly, she said, 'I know all about safe sex.'

Tony gritted his teeth. 'I still need to know who he is. It's only fair.'

'It doesn't matter, anyway.' Glancing up at the clock on the mantelpiece, Hetty saw with some relief that Rachel would soon be home from school. 'I've decided I don't want us to carry on like this any more.'

'What?'

She smiled briefly. 'I don't want to be your bit on the side. It was fun while it lasted, but now it's over. This might be a good moment,' Hetty added as an afterthought, 'to ask if I could have that front-door key back. Don't you think?'

It was Tony's turn to look stunned.

'Why?'

Hetty gave him a look.

'Not the key.' He shook his head in dismay. 'I'm not talking about the key. Why don't you want us to see each other any more? Why should it have to be over? There's no reason on earth—'

'Don't say that.' Hetty shuddered, at that moment despising him. 'Of course there are reasons. Vanessa, for one.'

'But she needn't know,' Tony protested.

This was old ground.

'She'd find out sooner or later,' said Hetty. 'These things always come out in the end. Besides,' she added matter-of-factly, 'I only did it because I wanted to pay her back for pinching you in the first place. I thought it would boost my self-confidence.' She paused, then smiled. 'And it did. So now I don't need you any more. My self-confidence has been boosted quite far enough, thanks, and I've finished paying Vanessa back. I don't need you any more, and I don't want to hurt Vanessa. She loves you, Tony. You should try being faithful to her. You never know, you might even like it.'

Tony gazed down at his ex-wife. She was sitting, holding

out her hand. Wordlessly, he dropped the front-door key into her upturned palm. He knew there was no point arguing. Hetty had made up her mind.

'OK, I get it. You mean you've got yourself involved with this other man, this "fab guy",' – he mimicked Meg Tarrant's words with derision – 'and you think *you* should be faithful.'

I hate him, thought Hetty in amazement. I really hate him.

'You know what's sad?' she said quietly. 'The fact that you think being faithful is weird. It isn't weird, Tony. It's normal.'

Tony was by this time almost beside himself with jealousy. His brain was working overtime. He had his suspicions about this mystery lover, whom Meg Tarrant had met and drooled over. Now, with nothing to lose, he voiced them.

'Who is it, then? Are you going to tell me, or are you too embarrassed?'

He was jeering at her. So angry she no longer cared what he thought, Hetty said in cutting tones, 'Funny, that. You're the one combing your hair up and over your bald patch, yet I'm the one you think should be embarrassed.'

The dig about the thinning hair – a veiled reference to his age – finally convinced him he was right.

'It's the O'Driscoll boy.' Tony looked disgusted. 'Jesus Christ. You're having an affair with Derry O'Driscoll, aren't you?'

Hetty wondered briefly what would infuriate Tony more than anything in the world. Then she smiled.

'No comment,' she said.

Chapter 32

'I say, your dad looks mad,' Clemency murmured.

The cricket team were having a practice game on the village green and she had persuaded Rachel to sit on the wall with her instead of going straight home, in order to drool surreptitiously over their star bowler, sexy blond Phil Dotrice.

Rachel shielded her eyes against the sun and watched her father storm out of his old home, climb into his black Volvo and drive furiously down the lane to The Old School-house.

'It must be that thing in the paper. He hasn't taken it too well,' Clemency went on, nodding sagely and offering Rachel half a semi-melted Mars bar. 'I thought your mum looked great. Good for her, I say. Oh, wow . . . what a brilliant catch! Don't you think Phil has stupendous shoulders? I swear, I *dreamt* last night about those shoulders.'

For someone with such a goody-goody Girl Guide image, Clemency never failed to astound Rachel with her frankness. She was as intensely interested in boys as she was in doing her homework, endlessly volunteering for things and organizing the school summer play. When Rachel had remarked upon this, Clemency had shrugged and said happily, 'I'm nearly sixteen years old. My hormones are on a roll. Of course I'm interested in boys . . . it's normal!'

'Mum's been a bit odd lately.' For the first time, Rachel heard herself admit it. 'She's always asking me what time I'm going out and when I'll be home. Then, when I get home, she's in her dressing-gown acting all strange. And sometimes when the phone goes, she has one of those stupid, one-sided, yes-no conversations. I'm sure she's seeing someone,' Rachel concluded fretfully, 'but I can't figure out why she's keeping so quiet about it. I mean, it isn't as if I wouldn't understand.'

'Maybe he's married.' Clemency, ever-practical, hugged her pale, dimpled knees and gazed dreamily across at Phil Dotrice's perfect posterior as he began his run-up. 'Maybe he's wildly unsuitable. Maybe he's ancient and ugly.' Her eyes widened with pleasurable intrigue. 'Or gorgeous and young.'

Phil Dotrice, thankfully, chose that moment to bowl someone out. Stumps cartwheeled in all directions and Clemency leapt ecstatically to her feet.

'Oh, well done! Forty-three for six . . . yeee-haaa!'

Rachel, who hadn't breathed a word to anyone about the traumatic events of last Friday when she had found herself unexpectedly nose-to-crotch with Derry O'Driscoll, said, 'But why should anyone gorgeous and young be interested in my mother?'

'You only think that because she *is* your mum.' Clemency's gaze remained fixed on the game but she spoke with confidence. 'I was the same with mine. I love her, but it's still hard to think of her as sexually attractive . . . actually *fanciable* to the opposite sex. It was quite an eye-opener, I can tell you, going over to Spain last summer and seeing how many men she's got chasing after her over there. It just goes to show, I suppose,' she added dreamily, 'life's still worth living even when you're that old. I say, look at the way Phil rubs that cricket ball on his trousers. Do you know if he's still going out with that barmaid from the Hen and Chicken, the one with the flat chest?'

'Dumped her last Sunday. Hello girls, good game?'

Lottie O'Driscoll had come up behind them. She was trundling a pushchair and licking a chocolate Cornetto. Her daughter Maeve, who was two, clutched a handful of bedraggled dandelions and an empty crisp packet.

'Very good game.' Clemency waggled her fingers at Maeve, who had inherited the trademark black O'Driscoll eyes. 'Except for your Tom. He was caught out for three, I'm afraid.'

'Caught out? Why, what's he been up to?' Lottie grinned and hauled a whimpering Maeve into her arms. 'Only kidding. Listen, would either of you two be interested in a spot of babysitting tonight? It's Tom's birthday and we were planning a quiet evening out. Mum was going to do it but she thinks she's going down with flu.'

Lottie and her boyfriend Tom lived in one of the small terraces of council houses on the outskirts of the village. Buxom and with an affinity for tight skirts and high heels, she was the original good-time girl. Nell might have the glamour and mystique but Lottie exuded more than her fair share of down-to-earth sensuality. She was also alarmingly extrovert. Her idea of a quiet evening out, thought Rachel, invariably involved dancing on tables.

Lottie's dark eyes, meanwhile, were upon her. Rachel, who

had never actually been inside Lottie's house but who could only too easily picture the state of it, shook her head.

'Sorry, I can't.'

Volunteering as usual, Clemency said brightly, 'I will. No problem. What time would you like me there?'

Brilliant, thought Lottie. A babysitter who hasn't even asked how much an hour. She beamed at Clemency. 'Seven o'clock?'

'You must be mad,' said Rachel, when Lottie and Maeve had trundled out of earshot. Only the distant squeak of irritatingly unoiled pushchair wheels hung in the air. 'She's common as muck. They've probably got flying plaster ducks going up their living-room wall.'

'Oh no, you should have *told* me,' Clemency mocked. Sometimes she despaired of Rachel, who was her own worst enemy. 'I'd never have agreed to do it if I'd known that. Now, where's the rest of that Mars bar? Don't tell me you've eaten my half too . . .'

It was extraordinary, thought Nell, that Ben could be so incapacitated in some ways yet so intuitive in others.

It was ridiculous, too, feeling guilty.

'Must be this dress,' she said helplessly, brushing the amethyst silk. 'It's new.'

But Ben was scowling so hard his eyebrows almost met in the middle.

'There's something else different.' His once-beautiful mouth contorted with the effort of pronouncing the words, but he wasn't about to give up. 'You *look* different. Your eyes . . .'

Earlier that day, Hettie had made much the same observation. Long-awaited sex, it appeared, definitely had an effect.

Wishing it wasn't quite so visible, yet at the same time having to remind herself that she hadn't done anything wrong, Nell leaned forward to brush away a wasp that was hovering inches from his face.

'I bought some eye drops.' This time she spoke with an air of finality. 'Now, what's all this about you having a run-in with the bank? Oscar tells me you threatened to have the bank manager arrested.'

Ben heaved a sigh. In the old days his lack of patience with those he considered less intelligent than himself had been tempered with wit and good-natured resignation. Now he just flew into a rage instead.

'The manager's a prat. Told me I couldn't have the money. I told him he was an incompetent wanker.'

Nell couldn't help smiling. 'And that's an arrestable offence?'

But Ben wasn't amused. With a snort of irritation, he said, 'Bloody should be. Bloody Oscar wasn't any better either. Took the phone away. Sweetheart, you'll have to sort it out.'

Nell kept his bank account in the black, though it was at times an uphill struggle. Ben, accustomed to money simply being there, endlessly available, could spend it like nobody's business and had never once asked where it came from. It was simply *his* money; with it, he retained a tiny measure of independence. As far as he was concerned, this afternoon's tussle represented nothing more than a hiccup, a temporary cash-flow problem. All Nell had to do was transfer more money from some deposit account to the current one. To free some cash.

'How much?' asked Nell, who had put in a couple of hundred only last week. 'And what's it for, anyway?'

'Couple of grand.' Ben gave her a lopsided smile. 'And how I spend my money is none of your business. It's a secret.'

'Hmm. Just so long as it isn't the three-thirty at Epsom.'

Inwardly, Nell was wincing. Having to magic up an extra two thousand was going to have a horrible effect on her own bank balance. She would have to step up the fortune-telling, she realized, in a big way. Just as she had been hoping to take it easy, too, and have a bit more time free for . . . other things.

It was just as well, Nell thought ruefully, that 'other things' were free.

She smiled at Ben, who was stroking her hand.

'OK. You're sure it needs to be that much?'

'Of course I'm sure.' Ben looked offended. 'If I didn't need it, I wouldn't ask.'

Chapter 33

Hetty's fib had been bothering her all evening. Letting Tony storm out of the house believing she was embroiled in a torrid affair with Derry O'Driscoll had been a spur-of-the-moment thing, which was all very well until you stopped to consider how awful it would be if news of the affair should actually get out.

The idea was positively shudder-making. When, at eight-thirty, Hetty glanced out of the sitting-room window and caught sight of Derry sauntering up the High Street she knew she had to act. The least she could do, after all, was warn the person most intimately concerned. Poor Derry, too . . . as if he didn't have a wicked enough reputation already.

Derry's face lit up when he saw her hurrying down the garden path. Just to make matters worse, Hetty realized, he was looking embarrassingly young in a cropped, cyclamen-pink T-shirt and white jeans. His long, dark hair was still wet from the shower and he was wearing Armani cologne.

'Hi! I saw that piece in the paper. You looked terrific. Bet Vanessa was wild—'

'She wasn't the only one.' Three gardens away, with her ears on stalks, Elsie Cutler pottered amongst her regimented herbaceous borders. Hetty lowered her voice. 'Tony had an absolute head-fit. Now he's convinced I'm seeing someone else. Look, I can't tell you how sorry I am about this, but he thinks it's you.'

'Me?' Grinning, Derry raised his eyebrows.

'Because you walked me home from the party, I suppose.' Breathless with embarrassment, Hetty rushed on. 'We were in the middle of this huge showdown, you see, and he just came out with it.'

'I'm flattered.'

'Well,' she admitted, 'I let him think it. I should have said it wasn't you, I know, but I was so *mad* . . .'

'No problem.' Derry, unconcerned, leaned against the front wall, idly stripping the needle-like leaves from a frond of Hetty's overgrown rosemary bush. 'It's too late to name me in the divorce.' He shrugged and said easily, 'He's not going to run me over in his nice clean Volvo . . . or is he?'

Vigorously Hetty shook her head.

'God no, nothing like that. I just thought you should know what's going on, rather than get to hear about it third-hand in the pub or something. And I hope it doesn't mean you landing in hot water with your real girlfriends.'

Derry winked. 'Don't look so worried. Sauna's my middle name. And speaking of nice clean Volvos . . .'

Was it immaculate timing or had he been lying in wait? They both turned to watch the car's approach. Tony, doing a stately thirty miles an hour, drove past without so much as a sideways glance and continued on to the end of the High Street. Then, having signalled left, he turned into Woods Lane and disappeared from view.

'Oops,' said Hetty.

'Well, he's jealous.' Derry nodded his approval. 'That's always a good sign.' His dark eyes softened. 'Don't worry, he'll be back.'

'I don't want him back. I gave it some thought ... you know, what we were talking about last week. It's the best way.' Hetty smiled. 'Time to make the break. And don't laugh, but I started feeling sorry for Vanessa.'

'You are ...' in search of the right word, Derry spread his arms in admiration, '... gorgeous.'

'Stupid,' said Hetty, 'more like.'

Above them, safely out of the way this time, Rachel rested her elbows on the bedroom window-sill and watched. Derry's arms were outstretched. He and Hetty were both laughing and Hetty's yellow-and-white striped shirt was undone two buttons too many. From this position, Rachel could see her emerald bra.

After years of nursing a delicious, clandestine crush on Derry O'Driscoll, it was all being spoiled. Her mother was muscling in, instead, on a boy practically young enough to be her son.

This was her punishment, Rachel miserably concluded, for calling Hetty old.

Lottie and Tom were due back at midnight. When the back door creaked at ten-thirty, Clemency picked up a bottle of Diet-Coke and hid behind the sitting-room door, ready to bring it down on the head of whoever was about to try and burgle the house.

'Don't shoot!' Derry's dark eyes widened at the sight of her poised to attack. He broke into a grin. 'Don't make me drink Diet-Coke either.'

'Phew, you gave me a fright.' Clemency puffed her mousy fringe out of her eyes and moved away from the wall.

'Sorry.' He recognized her now. It was the doctor's dumpy but sweet-looking daughter from Swan Cottage who hung around with Hetty's sulky kid. 'I'm in hiding, you see. Spot of girlfriend trouble . . . there's one on the warpath, on her way over from Sherringham. I know she'll head straight for our house so I thought I'd come over here instead, lie low for a bit until she runs out of steam.' He gave Clemency an apologetic look. 'That is, if it's OK with you. If *you* don't mind . . .'

'Of course I don't mind.' Clemency was overjoyed. 'I've finished my homework and there's nothing decent on television. We can keep each other company. You can tell me,' she said eagerly, 'all about this girlfriend you're hiding from. I just *love* sorting out other people's problems. I'd make a terrific agony aunt.'

'Better still,' as he stretched out on the sofa, Derry flashed her an irresistible smile, 'I bet you make a terrific cup of tea.'

This was stupid, Marcus concluded as he stepped out of the shower and fastened a dark-blue towel around his waist. Since spending Tuesday night with him, Nell had come up with one excuse after another for not doing so again. On Wednesday she had needed to travel to Oxford to visit some mystery friend. On Thursday it had been a fortune-telling evening in Bath. And now it was Friday morning, and Jemima was due home for the weekend. This, thanks to Nell's determination that their affair should remain a secret, meant she wouldn't be staying here before Monday night at the very earliest.

So much for togetherness, he thought irritably, frustrated more than anything else by the fact that this wasn't a situation he had ever had to face before. It came to something, too, when your ultra-efficient method of contraception was your own sister.

Chapter 34

'You shouldn't be here,' said Nell when she walked into the office an hour later. Marcus, looking delectable in a dark-grey suit, was sitting on the edge of the desk leafing through his diary. 'You're supposed to be on the motorway by now. Heritage meeting, remember?'

'Plenty of time yet.' He stood up, came towards Nell and kissed her on the mouth. She smelled deliciously of Pears soap and toothpaste. 'I wanted to see you before I left. I've had an idea.'

'Mmm?' Nell smiled, thinking how nice it would be to be greeted this way in the office every morning. Maybe the Government should pass a law, make it compulsory.

'Tonight. If we can't stay here, how about an hotel? I could book us in somewhere.' Mocking her insistence on secrecy, Marcus said, 'We can register as Mr and Mrs Smith . . . you can wear dark glasses . . . I'll put a bag over my head . . .'

'I can't.' Nell heaved a sigh. 'I'm working. A party of ten in Cheltenham. They're regulars, too,' she said with genuine regret. 'I know what they're like . . . I wouldn't even be able to get away before midnight. Sorry.'

'Brilliant.'

'Don't look at me like that. I can't cancel them.'

'Why not?' Marcus, knowing he was being unfair, couldn't care less. 'Why can't you bloody cancel them?'

Nell, briefly tempted to make the feeble joke about the fortune-teller cancelling because of unforeseen circumstances, glanced at the expression in his eyes and decided not to after all.

'It wouldn't be businesslike,' she said instead. 'And I need the money.'

'Two excuses where only one would do?' Marcus's earlier good mood had taken a massive dive. His mouth narrowed. 'Isn't that a tiny bit suspicious? I always thought it was a sign of a guilty conscience. And talk about feeble—'

'You're too used to getting your own way,' said Nell. 'And they aren't excuses, they're reasons. Perfectly good ones. So don't even bother trying to make me change my mind.'

'Why do you need the money?' Marcus was damned if he'd give up that easily. 'You don't *need* the money—'

'I do.'

'OK, how much? Tell me how much you would have made tonight and I'll write out a fucking cheque.' Reaching inside his jacket, he pulled out his cheque-book. From the other inner pocket he took a pen. His green eyes fixed on Nell, waiting for her to speak, daring her to protest.

'Four hundred pounds,' said Nell. She smiled slightly. 'Plus VAT. That makes it four hundred and seventy. I tell you what, as a gesture of goodwill why don't you round it up to five?'

Here, thought Marcus as he wrote out the cheque, was a prime example of a mild disagreement spiralling ludicrously out of control.

'Thanks.' When he had handed it to her, Nell studied the spiky signature for a second. She beamed. 'Isn't this romantic?'

'Highly,' said Marcus. 'What are you doing?'

Nell had torn the cheque into quarters. She dropped the pieces on to the floor.

'Did you really think I'd take it?'

'Of course.' He shrugged, his good humour restored, and beckoned her towards him. 'Come here, I've had another idea.'

Moments later it was Nell's turn to say, 'What are you doing?'

Marcus's mouth brushed hers. His fingers, having carefully unfastened each pearl button in turn on the bodice of her black cotton sundress, slid the thin straps from her shoulders.

'Guess.'

'What about London? The meeting with English Heritage. You'll be horribly late,' gasped Nell. Goodness, this was even nicer than a good-morning kiss . . .

'Don't worry.' He smiled and pushed her gently back against the desk. 'They'll understand. I'll explain to them that this was a particularly urgent meeting . . .'

'Oh yes?' Nell, who was busy undoing buttons of her own, reached across the desk and switched on the answering machine.

Marcus, meanwhile, ran his fingers along the flawless smooth curves of her bare brown shoulders.

'I'll tell them,' he drawled, 'that now was the only time you could fit me in.'

* * *

'Heavens,' said Nell, twenty minutes later. Pink-cheeked and breathless, she lay back in Marcus's arms and wondered if she had the energy to climb back into her clothes. The little black dress lay in a heap over by the window. One of her shoes was dangling by its heel from the wastepaper basket. Her black-and-white polka-dot bra was draped across the fax machine on the desk. 'Oh dear, now you're really going to be late for that meeting.'

'I'm heartbroken.' Marcus ran his tongue along the groove at the nape of her neck. 'Bloody Heritage meetings. This is a much nicer way to start the day.'

'Lucky we haven't had Hilda Garnet tapping on the door with your coffee tray.' Nell grinned, too lazy to move. 'Or a herd of American tourists, dying to meet a genuine British earl and desperate to discover what he gets up to at twenty past nine on a Friday morning.'

'Do you really have to do the Cheltenham trip tonight?' Marcus kissed her ear lobe. 'I like this. I want us to spend *real* time together. I've been thinking about a holiday, too . . . maybe a quick fortnight in St Lucia.'

'I'm going to Cheltenham,' said Nell languorously. 'I'm not letting these people down. And if this is a joint holiday you're talking about, who were you planning to leave in charge here? Jemima?'

'More excuses,' grumbled Marcus, though as excuses went it was perfectly valid. He and Nell were the only ones capable of ensuring the business ran smoothly. 'OK, so we'll wait until October when the castle closes.'

Nell hesitated, thinking of Ben.

'What?'

Determined this time to get a 'yes' out of her, he threatened to slide on top of her again. 'More reasons why we shouldn't enjoy ourselves? And don't even *think* of telling me you can't afford it, because you won't be paying. It won't cost you a bean.'

'Well—'

Just then, the fax burst into life. Nell jumped, then burst out laughing as her polka-dot bra slithered off the machine and dropped into the wastepaper basket along with her shoe. A moment later, before she had a chance to say anything more, the heavy iron handle on the door went clunk-clunk as someone on the other side tried to wrench it open.

'Hilda Garnet,' Nell squeaked, stifling her giggles against Marcus's tanned chest. 'She's brought your coffee. Tell her to leave it outside and—'

'Marcus, open this bloody door,' shouted Jemima. Nell's muffled laughter shuddered to a halt.

'*Shit* . . .'

'It's OK, it's locked,' Marcus murmured. 'She can't get in.'

But Nell had already slithered out of reach. Within seconds the crumpled black dress was on. One high-heeled shoe was on. Knickers were on. The other shoe had vanished from sight . . .

'Marcus, let me in!' Jemima sounded irritated beyond belief. Frantically, Nell threw Marcus's shirt at him. Desperate to keep Jemima's suspicions to a minimum, she ran her fingers through her hair, found her other shoe behind the filing cabinet and helped Marcus into his jacket.

'I can't imagine what she's doing here so early,' he complained good-naturedly, because as far as he was concerned there was no reason on earth why Jemima shouldn't find out about Nell and himself. 'Amazing. I've never known her to get out of bed this side of midday before.'

'Let her in,' hissed Nell, grabbing a pencil and the fax that had just spilled out of the machine. She dodged smartly out of the way as Marcus, still grinning, slid his arms around her waist and brushed her mouth with a final, teasing kiss. 'Stop it. Say you were on the phone. And for God's sake do up your belt . . .'

Chapter 35

Jemima shot into the room like a rocket when Marcus had unlocked the door. Her straight blond hair, held away from her forehead by a dark-blue, velvet headband, swung from side to side as she glanced first at Marcus then, sharply, at Nell.

'You.' Jemima uttered the word with a snort of derision. Too distracted, however, to notice Nell's flushed cheeks and faint air of dishevelment, she turned her attention back to Marcus.

'I was on the phone,' he offered, not totally convincingly.

'And I'm in a hurry,' Jemima snapped. 'Kiki's waiting in the helicopter. Rufus and Sarah Gardiner-Finch have invited us down to their place in Truro for the day; they're having a beach barbecue. I just dropped by to pick up some clothes.' She paused, pointedly ignoring Nell. 'And to pass on a message to that assistant of yours. Because I don't know what she thinks she's playing at, but sleeping with other people's boyfriends isn't clever and it isn't sensible. What she needs to realize,' Jemima rattled on, 'is that as far as men like Timmy are concerned, village girls are what you screw when there's nothing decent around. They're a way of passing the time, that's all. If she thinks for a moment he's interested in *her*, she must be off her head.'

Marcus, cold-eyed, said, 'What?'

'Yes.' Nell's shoulders went back. She stared in disbelief at Jemima. 'What exactly *are* you talking about?'

'What am I talking about?' Jemima, continuing to address Marcus as if they were the only two people in the room, began to count the answers off on her fingers. 'Your lousy choice in assistants,' she said in mocking tones. 'That common, jumped-up little cow giving herself all kinds of airs and graces . . . not to mention sloping off behind my back with *my* boyfriend. She threw herself at him, Marcus . . . poor Timmy didn't even have a chance to say no! That's the kind of person you've employed—'

'I don't believe I'm hearing this.' Nell's first impulse, to laugh, was rapidly replaced by an overwhelming urge to hurl something heavy at Jemima's shiny, blond head. 'I don't know where you picked up this fairy-tale but it's a complete lie. I wouldn't sleep with Timmy Struther if you paid me.'

It was an unfortunate choice of words. Jemima, sneering, pounced at once.

'From what I hear, you'll sleep with anyone if they pay you.'

'Shut up, Jemima.' Marcus looked furious. 'You're only trying to stir up more trouble. Now where did this come from?'

'Timmy told me.'

Nell's eyes blazed. 'It's not *true*—'

'Bingo,' said Jemima contemptuously. 'He said she'd deny it, too. That's because he gave her the brush-off afterwards,' she explained to Marcus. 'She begged to see him again and he told her she'd served her purpose. Stupid bitch, thought she was on to a good thing there. She really thought she had him—'

'OK, fine, you've said what you came here to say.' There was a razor-sharp edge to Marcus's voice. He stood very still between them. 'Now get out.'

'Just in time.' Nell breathed a sigh of relief when Jemima had stalked out. 'I nearly brained her with a box file. Can you believe she *said* that?'

The next second her heart did a sickening slow somersault. From the expression on Marcus's face it was only too obvious that whilst he wanted to believe her, he wasn't out-and-out convinced. He couldn't even bring himself to speak. Now, suddenly, she no longer knew who she wanted to murder most.

'So it's my word against theirs.' Nell, inwardly fuming, rose stiffly to her feet. 'And you aren't sure, are you? Because you know I went out to dinner with Timmy Struther and there's just that chance I might have been tempted to see if he really lived up to all the hype. The fact that I'm telling you I didn't sleep with him isn't quite good enough, because you probably think I have more reason to lie about it than he does. Thanks, Marcus. Your faith in me is touching. I'll always remember this.'

Miriam, sitting with her feet up on the sofa, was ploughing pleasurably through a box of Black Magic and trying to watch *The Weakest Link* in peace. It wasn't easy, what with the persistent crash-thump, crash-thump of Nell behind her, taking her temper out on a defenceless pile of ironing.

'Come on then.' Stretching voluptuously, she chose another chocolate and held the half-empty box out to Nell. 'Are you going to tell me what the problem is or are you just going to batter that poor shirt to death?'

Nell carried on battering. Then she stopped and heaved a sigh. It wasn't the shirt's fault and no amount of wishful thinking would turn it into Jemima, stretched prone and helpless across the ironing-board to be steamed flat.

'Work.'

Miriam suppressed a smile.

'You mean the man you work for, presumably. What's happened . . . lovers' tiff?'

Nell stared at her. Miriam really was the limit.

'I hate it when you do that. How,' she demanded, 'could you possibly *know*?'

Miriam's fingers hovered over the box on her lap. 'Eeny meeny miney mo. Lovely, Turkish delight.' Swooping down, the fingers seized their prey. 'Really, darling, why should you be the only cleverclogs around here? Where do you suppose you inherited your talents from, anyway?'

'Hmm,' said Nell, not believing her mother for a second. Miriam might have the gift of the gab but she was about as psychic as a sink plunger. More than likely she had spotted Nell rushing home last week for a mid-morning change of clothes, put two and two together and hazarded a lucky guess.

'It's all right,' Miriam chuckled. 'I'm not interested in the sordid details. So what's he done to upset you? Come along now, tell Mother.'

All in a rush, the story spilled out. Miriam, listening patiently, carried on munching chocolates and allowed Nell to get everything out of her system.

'So it isn't Marcus who upset you,' she said finally. 'It's that sister of his.'

'No . . . yes.' Nell, who had given up on the ironing, bundled up the half-done shirt and lobbed it back into the basket. Glancing at her watch, she realized she had less than twenty minutes in which to get herself ready and out of the house. She gestured impatiently in the direction of the castle. 'I don't know. Timmy Struther started the whole thing off, Jemima spread the news and Marcus believed it. God, talk about being ganged up on.' She paused, then shook her head. Jemima's shrill, venomous attack was replaying itself over and over again like a video she couldn't switch off. 'Oh, but you should have heard her, Mum. She called me a common jumped-up cow. She said I'd been giving myself airs and graces. As far as Jemima's concerned I'm a member of some subterranean underclass, not fit to *speak* to people like her. She is such an unbelievable snob—'

Nell's diatribe was interrupted by the shrill of the phone. Miriam, reaching across to answer it, told soothing lies to whichever of Derry's girlfriends was on the other end. Derry was working late, he wouldn't be home from Bath until midnight at the very earliest, she explained. Derry, who had, in fact, sloped off to Sherringham to see a pretty divorcee called Margo, and who was supposed to be sorting out his complicated love life, wasn't making a marvellous job of it. The more he tried to ease away from them, the more clinging and panicky his myriad women got.

'You know what would really cheer me up?' said Nell suddenly, when Miriam had hung up the phone.

'No.' Her mother grinned. 'And *don't* say a baby.'

'What would really cheer me up would be to hear you tell me that the old Earl was Derry's father.'

Silence. Miriam gazed at her, unblinking.

Nell held her breath. It was something she had occasionally wondered about over the years. If Miriam's affair had begun before it was generally assumed to have begun, then it wouldn't have been beyond the realms of possibility. And how brilliant it would be, Nell thought now with renewed longing, if Derry could indeed turn out to have aristocratic blood coursing through his wayward young veins. Wouldn't *that* be a blissful one in the eye for class-conscious, ultra-prejudiced, vicious-tongued Lady Jemima?

Her hopes were dashed within seconds. Miriam gave an apologetic shrug.

'Sorry, darling. If it were true, I'd tell you. But it isn't. The Earl wasn't Derry's father.'

Damn. Nell wished she hadn't said it now. Bang went that fantasy.

'Mind you,' Miriam added casually, 'he wasn't Jemima's father either.'

Chapter 36

The next day, Saturday, was the hottest of the year so far. It was the first week in June, half-term for schools, and the castle grounds swarmed with children from morning till night. Most were lovely; some were little monsters. Nell was called to sort out a couple of cheeky eleven-year-olds, barracking one of the pottery workers over in the south stable block. The poor, heckled potter, a timid girl called Gudrun who had been attempting to demonstrate her art to a group of equally polite Japanese visitors, was at a complete loss as to how to deal with the two boys. She was close to tears and her poorly thrown pot had gone wobbly.

Nell, alerted by one of the painters from an adjacent workshop, marched across the outer courtyard in time to hear the skinnier of the two boys shouting, 'Give us a go on yer wheel, missis. Gordon Bennett, wot a mess . . . come on, I'll show 'em 'ow it's meant to be done. Give us a go, missis—'

'Right.' Seizing each boy by a tuft of hair at the back of his head, Nell propelled them briskly past the cluster of astonished Japanese tourists. 'This is how it's meant to be done. You two get out of here and you don't come back. OK? Got it? Shift.'

'Ow!' screeched the plump boy, struggling unsuccessfully to free Nell's painful grip on his hair. 'Get off us . . . we'll tell the police on you.'

The shifty sidelong glance of the other boy clinched it for Nell. That was the giveaway. Releasing the hair, she dived instead into the pockets of their track suit tops.

'Eight bars of Kilburton chocolate fudge, three silver photograph frames and six Kilburton Castle key rings. Goodness me,' she mocked, '*now* who's going to call the police?'

Click went the camera of one of the Japanese tourists. He bowed at Nell, his expression hopeful. 'Madam, you make . . . citizen-harrest?'

The two boys were rubbing the backs of their heads and looking scared. In the shaft of sunlight streaming in through the stable doors behind them, Nell could see bits of yanked-out hair floating lazily to the ground. The prospect of being arrested herself and charged with child abuse floated through her mind.

'Just this once,' she said severely, 'I'll let you off. But I never want to see you here again. Are you listening to me?'

The boys shuffled awkwardly from one foot to the other. The Japanese visitor with the camera took a couple more pictures for good measure. Over at the wheel, Gudrun threw another pot and managed this time to get it centred. Flushed with relief, she smiled shyly at the watching tourists and prepared to start the demonstration all over again.

'Nell, quick!' shrieked Hetty, who had rushed across the cobbled courtyard almost killing herself in her high heels. 'In the restaurant . . . you have to come now!'

It was lunch-time and the restaurant was packed.

'Well for heaven's sake, you can't do that in here.' Nell grinned down at the woman causing all the trouble. 'You'll put these people right off their food. Come on, we'll help you up. Let's get you across to the castle and find you somewhere comfortable to wait.' She glanced at Hetty, preparing to help support the woman on the other side. 'Someone has already phoned for an ambulance, I suppose?'

'Oh help,' wailed Hetty. 'I didn't think. Quick, somebody . . . dial 999.'

The visitor, who was black and very beautiful, was obviously in extreme pain. She gritted her teeth as Nell and Hetty, between them, helped her to her feet.

'I don't want to alarm you,' gasped the woman, panting for breath, 'but that ambulance had better get a move on. Last time I did this, I had the baby in twenty minutes flat.'

Having managed to get her up the grand staircase Nell steered the woman, whose name was Dora, into the first available bedroom. Over four hundred years earlier, Lady Jane Grey had stayed at Kilburton Castle in this oak-panelled boudoir. Now, unceremoniously turfing out a dozen or so goggle-eyed French tourists and bolting the door shut behind them, Nell and Hetty managed between them to lift Dora on to the crimson-and-gold, velvet-canopied bed.

'I'm sure this wasn't in my job description.' Nell, who knew nothing at all about midwifery, looked stern and said, 'Just wait until the ambulance gets here. Breathe slowly and don't push. No, Dora . . . I said don't push.'

But Dora was pushing anyway, gripping Nell's hand and letting out a sustained yell before running out of breath and collapsing back against the lace-edged pillows.

'Told you I'd be quick,' she panted between contractions,

her shining face breaking into a huge smile during the brief moment of respite.

'As long as you know what you're doing.' Nell flexed her fingers, which had been squeezed numb. 'Are we supposed to be boiling water or something? How many children have you got, anyway?'

'Four.' Dora wiped the perspiration from her forehead with a corner of fragile, five-hundred-year-old Flemish lace. 'My husband took them for a walk in the park, to see the deer. I wasn't feeling great; that's why I stayed behind in the restaurant. When he gets back he's going to wonder what's happened to— Aaarghh, here we go again . . . oh my word, this could be it . . . YEEEAARGHH!'

Hetty couldn't help marvelling at the sheer speed and power of the delivery. Her own experience of labour had been a seemingly endless twenty-three-hour nightmare, spent mostly with a horrid rubber mask clamped over her face. Exhaustion had sapped her of all strength and her bones had turned to marshmallow. In the final stages she had begged the nurses to let her go home.

Yet here was this woman, exchanging jokes with Nell, in charge of her own body, calmly and efficiently getting on with the job. Taking her lead from Dora, quite forgetting her own squeamishness, Hetty moved to the foot of the bed.

'I can see the baby's head,' she exclaimed as Dora took a deep breath and braced herself for the next contraction. 'Oh, you're right, it's almost here. Quick, hold my hand . . . one more push . . . my God, this is *amazing* . . .'

It was a good job Marcus wasn't here, thought Nell,

surveying the drenched sheets. Dora's waters had broken at the last minute, gushing all over the ivory bedspread reputed to have been embroidered by Lady Jane Grey herself.

'Here we go,' gasped Dora, every muscle straining with the effort of the final push. 'Aah, aah, AAARGH!'

'Catch it,' shrieked Nell as Hetty reached forward, hands cupped like a scrum-half around the emerging head. 'Don't drop it, whatever you do.'

'Open the door,' ordered Marcus. Having arrived back from Sherringham earlier than expected, he had met up with Alistair Munro – called from Swan Cottage by a quick-thinking Hilda Garnet – at the foot of the staircase. 'Nell, Dr Munro's here to see the patient. For God's sake unlock the door.'

Dora groaned. The baby slithered out in a whoosh. Hetty gasped and caught it, and felt her eyes fill with tears.

'It's a boy,' cried Nell, and Dora broke into a grin, pushing herself up on her elbows to see her new son.

'He's beautiful,' Hetty whispered as the baby coughed and cleared his lungs before opening his mouth to bawl. Placing him reverently in Dora's arms, smiling at the expression on her face, she said, 'I'm sorry, but I'm way too squeamish to cut the cord. We're going to have to let the expert deal with that bit.'

'Nell!' Marcus roared. 'Open the damn door. *Now*.'

Giddy with exhilaration and relief, Nell unlocked it.

'All done,' she told Marcus, as in the far distance the wail of an ambulance siren made itself heard. 'Mother and baby doing fine. Dora, this is Dr Munro. And this is the Earl of Kilburton. Don't worry, I won't let him send you any dry-cleaning bills.'

'He's good-looking, isn't he?' Dora was too elated by the birth to bother keeping her voice down. Whilst Alistair busied himself cutting the cord and checking out the baby, she squeezed Nell's hand and said, 'And this whole castle belongs to him?'

'Don't you go chatting him up now,' Nell warned. 'Your husband'll be here any minute.'

Dora laughed and hugged her son. 'I'm thinking he had good luck on his side. Looks, money, great big house . . . that's it, I'm going to name my boy after him.' Her gaze swung round to Marcus and she gave him a questioning glance. 'If it's OK with you, sir. As long as you don't mind.'

'Mind?' Looking as absurdly pleased with himself as if he had delivered the baby single-handed, Marcus grinned down at his wailing, wriggling namesake. 'I'm flattered. Excellent choice. It means warrior, you know. Hello there, Marcus.'

Dora, momentarily taken aback, shook her head in dismay.

'Oh no, you've got it wrong. Not Marcus. I'm going to call him Earl.'

'Well done,' said Alistair Munro, when Dora had been carried off to the waiting ambulance with her proud husband and numerous children in tow. Nell had stripped Lady Jane Grey's drenched bed and disappeared with Marcus to discuss the plans for some forthcoming rock concert to be held in the park. Hetty's hormones, having witnessed the miracle of birth, were all of a flutter. She had a sudden terrible urge to rush out and start breeding again. Hopefully it wouldn't last long enough to risk leading to anything . . .

Even if it did, she thought, it definitely wouldn't lead to anything involving Alistair Munro. Well done indeed, thought Hetty, scornfully. Patronizing git.

'What?' Alistair protested, intercepting the brief flickering glance she gave him as they descended the stairs. Determined to win her around he said, 'Actually, I've been meaning to get in touch. A grateful patient gave me a couple of theatre tickets for next Saturday. Some Willie Russell play at the Theatre Royal in Bath . . . it's supposed to be pretty good. Would you be free for that?'

Hetty was free for everything. She had never been freer in her whole life. Next Saturday night yawned emptily ahead of her like Moby Dick's gaping jaw, as did every other night of the damn week, month, year . . .

'Sorry, I'm not free.' She said it quickly, whilst the resolve was still strong. Once a snubber, always a snubber, Hetty decided. Alistair Munro was the kind of man it was best not to tangle with in the first place. It was just a shame, she thought, that not getting involved left you with such acres of free time in which to become lonely and depressed.

As a doctor, however, Alistair was used to the glib lies of patients assuring him they never smoked more than five cigarettes a day or drank more than two glasses of wine a week.

'Oh come on.' He looked amused; Hetty was definitely lying. 'Say you'll come with me. I'm trying to think of the name of this play.'

Hetty had seen it publicized. It was *Shirley Valentine*, appropriately enough. Another gullible woman with lousy taste in men. No sooner had she managed to run away from one than she fell dopily into the arms of the next. It helped, of course, that he was Tom Conti in disguise, but the film version had still managed to reduce her to tears of self-pity. Another good reason, she thought, not to go with Alistair to see the play.

'I really can't.'

'Won't,' Alistair corrected, to let her know she wasn't fooling him for a second. Since he wasn't about to let her think he cared, either, he smiled and paused to allow Hetty through the door ahead of him. 'Maybe I'll take Clemency instead.'

'She's going out with Rachel next Saturday, to a youth club disco in Sherringham.'

This time Hetty returned his smile, those big Bambi eyes of hers doing a poor job of concealing her satisfaction with the riposte.

'I see. Two rejections.' Alistair nodded and looked thoughtful. 'What's the problem? Am I too . . . old?'

Someone else having a sly dig, thought Hetty. She found it extraordinary that other people could even imagine she and Derry O'Driscoll were having a fling.

She looked deliberately vague.

'You aren't too anything, Alistair.' The words sounded vaguely insulting.

'Well, that is a comfort,' said Alistair. 'Thanks a lot.'

'Right, let's get this straight,' Marcus said flatly when he and Nell were alone in his office. 'I believe you. If you say you didn't sleep with Timmy Struther, that's good enough for me. Sod what Jemima thinks.' He paused, sitting back in his chair and surveying Nell through narrowed eyes. 'I still think it would be simpler, anyway, to tell her about us.'

'There's no point.' Nell was busy tearing open a family-size packet of crisps. Midwifery had given her an appetite, and the safe arrival of baby Earl had cheered her up no end. Learning the truth about Marcus's mother and discovering that Jemima wasn't quite as aristocratic as she liked to think had been better still.

'But don't you see what you're doing?' Marcus pushed back his blond hair with an impatient sweep of the arm. 'You're pandering to her prejudices. You're saying exactly what she's saying . . . that people of a different class shouldn't mix.'

'I'm not saying they *shouldn't* mix. It's just simpler all round if they don't.' Nell flashed him a brilliant smile. 'It's definitely simpler if we don't. How do we know this isn't a flash in the pan, anyway? We could go off each other tomorrow, hate each other's guts by next week. Imagine the hassle if everyone else was watching it all happen. They'd have a field day . . .'

God, she was stubborn.

'This isn't a flash in the pan,' said Marcus. 'And you know it isn't.'

'We don't know anything.' Nell was teasing him now. 'We O'Driscolls are a fickle bunch, working class and flighty to boot. Dear me, how risky can you get?'

Something had certainly happened to improve her mood. Marcus didn't know what it was but he wished it was as easy to change her ludicrous attitude to this class thing.

'You don't like it when Jemima has a go about your family,' he declared. 'Yet you're doing exactly the same.'

Nell looked thoughtful for a moment.

'It's like if I was bald, I suppose. It's OK for me to joke about wearing a wig but it wouldn't be so funny if other people started pointing it out.'

Marcus blinked. 'You don't, do you?'

'Might, might not. Anyway, that isn't important.' Unable to resist it, Nell broke into a grin. 'I'm just saying Jemima has to hope her hair doesn't suddenly drop out. Because if she isn't careful, she'll wake up one morning to find herself gone bald.'

Chapter 37

Summer had finally, properly arrived. The temperature rocketed into the eighties and Minnie Hardwick sold out of ice lollies. When Clemency phoned Rachel on Sunday morning to invite her over to Swan Cottage so they could revise together for their impending exams she added persuasively, 'We have Loseley strawberry ice-cream, Häagen Dazs caramel cone explosion and frozen Snickers. All you need to bring is your mouth.'

When Rachel arrived at midday she found Clemency stretched out on a pink-and-white striped sun lounger in the back garden. Clemency was pink and white too, her fair complexion not lending itself to a tan. Ever hopeful, however, that this could be the year she cracked it, she was slathered in sun cream and bursting out of a too-small, white, cotton bikini.

'Oh come on, you can't sit in this heat wearing jeans,' Clemency protested. 'I'll lend you a bikini. You can borrow my Ambre Solaire, it's factor ten. Go on, don't be daft; you'll boil in those clothes.'

Rachel wasn't happy about taking them off. As far as she was concerned, Clemency looked like an overfed piglet. But she hadn't bargained for the sun beating down quite this fiercely. Her black INXS T-shirt was already drenched in perspiration and droplets of sweat threatened to drip from her eyebrows. She was going to be uncomfortable if she didn't remove at least something.

'Go on.' Clemency took a great slurp of Coke and wiped her mouth on the back of her hand. 'Dad's out for the afternoon. Who's going to see you?'

'Hi,' said Derry, appearing round the side of the cottage half an hour later. 'I've been knocking at the front door but you obviously couldn't hear me. I guessed you'd be out here. I'm not interrupting, am I?'

As far as Rachel was concerned, it was hard to bear. At Clemency's insistence she had changed into an old and droopy orange nylon bikini studded with gold plastic stars. Her skin was even whiter than Clemency's and she had scraped her horrible red hair away from her face with one of the laces from her trainers.

Derry's eyes were hidden behind dark glasses and his long black hair was slicked back. He was, of course, conker brown. In his loose, daffodil-yellow shirt and white trousers he looked both cool and effortlessly glamorous. He was also carrying something behind his back.

Clemency, unashamed of her own rolls of fat, threw aside her geography books and hauled herself into a sitting position.

'How lovely to see you again,' she exclaimed with delight. 'What is it, does Lottie need someone to babysit again?'

'Probably, but that isn't why I'm here.' Derry took off his glasses and grinned down at Clemency. From behind his back he withdrew a box of Milk Tray. 'These are for you, just to say thanks for saving my life the other night. You were brilliant.'

'You're kidding!' Clemency's eyes widened and she flushed with pleasure. 'You didn't have to buy me chocolates! Gosh, I hardly did anything at all.'

Lottie and Tom's home hadn't been quite the safe-house Derry had imagined when he had taken refuge there earlier in the week. Within fifteen minutes of his arrival, the peace had been shattered by the outraged ex-girlfriend hammering on the front door. Derry, in the living-room, had listened with admiration to the cool, confident way Clemency had answered the door, lied through her teeth, told the girl off for waking the baby and despatched her efficiently into the night.

'Well, I still think you were fantastic,' Derry told her now. 'The thing is, you don't look the kind of person who *would* lie. You seem far too nice.' He grinned. 'It's the perfect cover.'

'I hope you don't think he fancies you,' Rachel muttered when Derry had left. Clemency had told her the babysitting saga a hundred times already; she knew every detail of their brief encounter and was completely sick of it.

Derry O'Driscoll's way of looking at girls – and grown women – was the reason he got himself so hopelessly entangled in the first place. Since he had barely glanced at Rachel at all, she'd had plenty of opportunity to watch him in action. To see him chatting to Clemency, Rachel decided, you wouldn't think for a moment she was plain, dumpy and about as exotic as Coal Tar soap. He treated her as if she were out of this world.

'I know, I know.' Sighing, Clemency unwrapped the box of chocolates and offered them across. 'That would be too much to hope for. That ex of his – the one who came to the house –

she was beautiful, like some kind of film star. Gosh, imagine actually being his girlfriend. I wonder what it'd be like to *sleep* with him . . .'

Rachel's irritation with Clemency rose another couple of notches. Here she was trying to lose weight and being sabotaged at every turn by Clemency, who couldn't give a stuff about diets. She weighed a good ten pounds less than Clemency too, yet Derry all but ignored her. All his attention had been lavished upon bloody Clemency. It was as if he didn't even care how much she weighed. It was bloody unfair.

'Still, at least we can be good friends,' Clemency babbled chirpily between chocolates. 'Sometimes it's better that way. And I'm only fifteen. Give me a few more years and I may blossom. You never know, one day he might come to his senses and suddenly realize what he's been missing.'

These pathetic fantasies were what pissed Rachel off most of all.

'Don't hold your breath,' she snapped. 'He goes for older women nowadays. Women old enough to be his mother.'

Clemency was instantly enthralled.

'Who?' she demanded excitedly, sensing revelation.

Rachel closed her eyes. 'My mother.'

The castle and grounds swarmed with visitors. By one o'clock the restaurant was bursting at the seams and the parkland was dotted with picnickers. Nell, closeted in her office doing the books, stopped for a rest and gazed out over the park. The lake glittered like diamanté in the sunlight. Several dogs had jumped into the water and were swimming for sticks. Those picnickers in search of shade had settled beneath the chestnut trees whilst others congregated around the lake. A group of children were playing an energetic game of rounders, another smaller group were hurling frisbees at each other and two small boys were locked in a desperate struggle with a red-and-white striped kite.

Nell's attention was diverted abruptly away from the park. Much closer to hand, in the courtyard below, someone was waving to her. When she met his gaze he blew her an extravagant kiss.

She was out of the office and clattering down the tower's stone steps in a trice, intercepting Timmy Struther at the main entrance and steering him briskly across the Great Hall.

'How exciting.' Timmy removed his sunglasses as Nell led him through the door marked 'Private'. 'I'm being kidnapped. One of my favourite fantasies come to life.'

Nell kicked the door shut behind them. Now, at least, they were in the private wing and couldn't be overheard.

'You're even more of a prat than I thought you were,' she told him. 'And that's saying something. Whatever makes you think you have the right to go around spreading vile rumours about me? How *dare* you make me look stupid? I swear, I could knock your teeth right down your throat—'

'Oh come on,' Timmy protested, laughing. 'It was a joke. Something to annoy jittery Lady Jemima. I thought you of all people would see the funny side.'

'Of everyone thinking I'd leapt into bed with you? Terrific.' Nell's eyes glittered. 'That's about as funny as one of Hilda Garnet's jokes.'

313

'Dear me,' said Timmy. 'I had no idea you'd take it this much to heart. I'm sorry, darling.'

'Never mind sorry. Just make sure you tell Jemima it didn't happen.'

Goodness, she really was cross.

'Of course I will.' Flashing the famous lazy grin, Timmy shook his head in mock disbelief. 'Though I must say, I'm intrigued. So concerned all of a sudden about what other people might think. What's brought it on, I wonder, this unexpected morals-attack?'

'Of course I'm concerned,' Nell snapped back. 'Like I said, you're a prat.'

The drawing-room door was pulled open. Jemima, who had been waiting impatiently for Timmy to turn up, appeared in the doorway looking even crosser than Nell.

'What's going on?' Jemima demanded. 'What are you doing talking to her?'

'Go on.' Nell glared at Timmy. 'Say it.'

'All this fuss,' he drawled, 'over a harmless bit of fun.'

'Not that kind of harmless fun,' Nell put in, as Jemima's lips pressed together.

'Look, I didn't sleep with her.' Timmy turned to look at Jemima. 'Not that it's anything to do with you, but it's clearly been bothering Nell. So there we are.' He shrugged, unconcerned. 'It didn't happen. Nell O'Driscoll has no carnal knowledge of my splendid body. Personally, I feel sorry for her. She doesn't know what she's missing . . . eh, Jem?'

* * *

The trouble with Jemima, Timmy decided three hours later, was she never knew when to leave well alone.

The lunch party in Bath to which they had been invited had been a jolly affair hosted by distant cousins of his, but the afternoon had been all but ruined by Jemima going on and bloody on at him like some obsessed fishwife. To relieve the boredom of having to listen to it Timmy had retreated to one of the bathrooms and buoyed himself up with a couple of toots of cocaine. Then he did another for luck, because Jemima could nag for England. He deserved a reward for putting up with it. If he'd known she was going to spend the day whining like this he would never have brought her along.

The Pimm's had been flowing pretty freely too. Timmy, who had let Jemima take the wheel on the way back to Kilburton in order to let him have a doze and sober up, was further irritated when her continued droning meant he couldn't even get to sleep. By the time they reached Kilburton High Street he'd had enough.

'You just don't realize how stupid you've made me look,' Jemima ranted on beside him. 'It's humiliating, Timmy! And who will Marcus be furious with when he finds out? Me, that's who. I'm the one he'll blame—'

'Right,' Timmy howled, 'that's it, that's fucking enough. I've had it up to here with your mouth. You don't own me, you definitely don't have the right to lecture me, and nobody tells me what I can and cannot do. Stop the fucking car and get out. *Now*.'

Stunned by the ferocity of the outburst, Jemima automatically braked. They were halfway down the High Street, a couple of hundred yards from the castle entrance. Two small children who evidently lived at the gatehouse were playing with plastic swords on the worn patch of lawn in front of their home. At the sound of screeching brakes, they stopped trying to kill each other and turned to see what was going on.

'Out!' Timmy didn't give a stuff if he was being watched. Reaching across, he snatched the key from the ignition and opened the driver's door.

Jemima stayed rigid in her seat.

'Timmy, you can't.' Appalled, she tried to take the key back. His driving was reckless enough when he was sober.

'Watch me.'

'But you were going to stay!' Jemima wailed. 'You were going to stay the night and tomorrow we were driving up to Ascot. We can't not go ... the Markham-Denfields are expecting us.'

'Sod them. The Markham-Denfields,' drawled Timmy, 'are about as boring as you are. Now are you getting out of my car or do I have to push you out?'

Jemima's day was going from bad to worse. If Timmy stormed off now, her whole week would be spoiled. Biting her lip, she prepared to tough it out.

'There's no need to be cross. Look, why don't we—?'

'Right, I'll take that as a no.' Wrenching open the passenger door, Timmy staggered out of the Maserati and stormed round to the driver's side. When Jemima cringed he grabbed her arm and dragged her out. The more she resisted, the more it annoyed him. When she let out a squeak of pain and tried to wriggle away, he flung her violently to the ground.

'Nobody tells me what to do,' Timmy hissed. Jemima, lying face down on the hot tarmac with her pink dress rucked up around her hips, looked ridiculous.

'P-please . . .' Gasping for breath, realizing to her horror that her mouth was full of blood, she tried to raise herself up. This was a complete nightmare. Timmy had to be out of his mind.

'Maybe this will teach you a lesson.' He climbed into the driver's seat and stuck the key back in the ignition. 'And don't say I didn't warn you either. You brought it on yourself,' Timmy snarled, 'when you pissed me off.'

He wasn't bluffing. As Jemima struggled unsteadily to her feet she was almost blasted off them again by the roar of the engine. Then Timmy stuck his foot right down, released the clutch and scorched up the road in a cloud of exhaust fumes and dust, leaving her standing there like a scarecrow with grazed knees, a cut lip and bits of melted tar stuck to the front of her pink dress.

Chapter 38

'Blimey, love, you all right?'

Turning, Jemima came face to face with a buxom, dark-haired girl a few years older than herself, wearing a black T-shirt and fluorescent green leggings. Since she had appeared from nowhere, Jemima could only conclude she lived in one of the estate cottages lining the High Street.

'What a bastard!' The girl gestured indignantly towards the dust cloud that had been Timmy. 'One of my blokes tried punching me once. I hit him into next week. D'you want to come in for a minute and clean yourself up?'

Nosy, interfering bitch. Jemima, struggling to hold back tears, shook her head. 'No thank you. I'm absolutely fine. Slight m-misunderstanding, that's all. Absolutely f-fine . . .'

To prove it, she turned away and began walking stiffly towards the castle gates. It could have been worse. Apart from those two goggle-eyed brats and the girl in the frightful leggings there was nobody else around.

Trish O'Driscoll, put out by the snub, sniffed loudly and said, 'Suit yourself.' Then, with a shrug, she made her own way back up the path to The Pink House. It made you wonder, she thought crossly, why you even bothered to try and help.

There might not have been anyone else around to witness the actual incident but there were plenty in the castle grounds.

Tourists milled around everywhere. Jemima, keeping her head down and trying desperately not to attract attention, knew she was failing. With her blood-spotted dress and tear-stained face she was horribly conspicuous. All she could do when asked if she needed help was shake her head and walk faster. She prayed too, over and over again, that the visitors to Kilburton Castle hadn't recognized her. She would die if this story ever got out.

'My lady! Whatever's happened? Oh, my poor girl, come and lie down. Shall I call for an ambulance?'

It was such a comfort to be swept into Hilda Garnet's sturdy embrace. Wilting, Jemima allowed herself to be led into her own bedroom. She felt sick and miserable and of all the people in the world she knew Hilda would be on her side. Better still, she was well-trained enough not to ask awkward questions.

'I tripped, getting out of Timmy's car.' The words came out sounding cotton-woolly. Her lower lip, hugely swollen where a tooth had gone through it, was hurting like mad. The hideous taste of blood still clung to her tongue.

If Hilda Garnet wondered why Timmy hadn't stayed to help Jemima up to her room she didn't say so. Her loyalty to the Kilburtons was absolute.

'Come along, my girl.' Gently, she helped Jemima into bed. With warm water she sponged the poor wounded mouth and grazed knees. The legs were going to look pretty unsightly for the next couple of weeks but the grazing was only surface damage.

'I don't know about the dress.' Hilda, having eased it off her, looked doubtfully at the ripped hem and speckled tar stains. 'We may be able to rescue it.'

'Don't bother.' Jemima never wanted to see the dress again. 'Bin the sodding thing.'

It came out as 'thodding'. Her lip, puffed up like something belonging to the Elephant Man, had given her a painful lisp. At the sound of it Jemima burst into noisy sobs.

'Shock,' Hilda murmured in soothing tones. 'What you need is a nice cup of tea.'

'It'll hurt too much,' wailed Jemima. 'It'll thting.'

'There now, be a brave girl and wait here for a minute.' Hilda rose to leave. 'I'm going to phone the doctor.'

'Dr Carling? That doddering old fool! He'th not giving me thtitcheth.' Jemima's eyes widened in alarm.

'Dr Carling's retired. Dr Munro's the new man. He's charming, my lady.' Hilda, who had been charmed only last week when she'd confided in him about her bladder, gave Jemima an encouraging smile. 'Young, too. Not a bit like Dr Carling. Dr Munro's hands don't shake at all.'

Alistair's annoyance at being called out practically the moment he arrived home was soon dispelled when he realized who he was being asked to see. It was his first encounter with the Kilburton family, in fact his first encounter with any flesh-and-blood member of the aristocracy. Shaming though it was for a grown man to admit, the prospect of meeting Lady Jemima was a heady one. Now, would the turquoise sweater and green checked shirt be too casual or should he go for the hound's-tooth jacket and yellow Paisley cravat . . .

* * *

320

'No need for stitches? Are you sure?'

Having concluded his examination of the lip, Alistair met Jemima's apprehensive gaze and smiled.

'Quite sure.'

'Oh, thank goodness!' Heaving a monumental sigh of relief, Jemima sank back against the pillows. With her straight blond hair and pale-green eyes, and with that ethereal sea-green silk robe trailing across the bed, she looked to Alistair like a poor battered mermaid. From the moment he had been shown into her room he had been smitten, captivated by her vulnerability and air of sadness. It had never happened to him like this before. It was almost embarrassing. But all he could think of was how desperately in need she looked of a bit of cherishing. Stupid word, but it wouldn't go away. I want to cherish you, thought Alistair helplessly. You're unhappy. You need to be cherished. And I could do it, I could help . . .

'You must think I'm a complete wimp.' Exhausted from crying, Jemima lay back and let her pulse be taken. It was so soothing, having one's wrist held in that firm-but-gentle way. This Dr Munro was definitely nicer than that miserable sod Carling. And he had wonderfully steady hands.

'Of course I don't think you're a wimp. Mouths are sensitive. It must be painful.' Alistair paused for a second, then decided to risk it. 'But I'd like to know what really happened. I'm afraid I don't believe this tripping-up story.'

He was a doctor, he would be discreet, thought Jemima. That confidentiality thing meant she could tell him. And he seemed so genuinely concerned, too.

'Bit of a misunderstanding,' she confessed, gingerly touching the swollen lower lip, 'with my boyfriend. He'd had quite a lot to drink and lost his temper. I still can't believe he did it.'

Alistair couldn't believe anyone would want to do it. Not to Jemima. Who was this bullying oaf of a so-called boyfriend anyway?

'Has he ever hit you before?'

'No.' Jemima thought for a moment. 'But I've heard some rumours about his father. He used to beat his wife fairly regularly, I believe, with a riding crop. But the duke's a ghastly man. Timmy doesn't take after him at all.'

'Or he didn't,' said Alistair quietly, 'until now.'

'You think I shouldn't see him again.' Her eyes filled with fresh tears. 'Oh hell, I *know* what you're thinking. But I love him. I hate what he did to me but I still love Timmy . . .'

'I have to say, it's extremely likely to happen again. Once this kind of behaviour rears its ugly head, it has a habit of recurring. You deserve better than that.' Alistair spoke with urgency. If Timmy-whose-father-was-a-duke were to appear in the bedroom doorway now, he would happily flatten him. He felt his own pulse quicken with indignation on Jemima's behalf. 'He certainly doesn't deserve you.'

He was so nice, Jemima thought an hour and a half later. He really seemed to care. And to think people moaned about the NHS. Well, Alistair Munro couldn't have been nicer. Heaps nicer than bloody Timmy, anyway, with his sarcasm and short temper and that horrid way he had of turning away when he was bored by whatever she was trying to say to him. Alistair, in contrast, gazed at her as if what she had to say was completely riveting. And for an older man, Jemima decided, he was actually rather attractive. It would be so lovely to spend the whole rest of the evening like this, all cosy and relaxed, just chatting . . .

It wasn't until a woman waiting at a zebra crossing gave her an odd look that Nell realized she was smiling to herself. She couldn't help it; every time the thought resurfaced in her mind she broke into an uncontrollable grin. It made the journey to Oxford pass more quickly, too.

But it was just so brilliant, so perfect, thought Nell for the fiftieth time, her memory flashing back to the moment when Miriam had finally dropped the delicious bombshell. Good old Mum, breaking the promise she had made to Marcus's father never to breathe a word to a living soul about Marcus's mother's moment of madness.

Sarah, Countess of Kilburton, had been known, evidently, as the Ice Countess. Cool, composed and beautiful in a remote, somewhat intimidating way, she had led a blamelessly conventional life. Having provided her husband with a healthy baby boy, the necessary son and heir, she had considered her duties in that department complete. Their sex life had dwindled to next to nothing. By the time Marcus was four, it had petered out altogether. The Earl, who hadn't yet met Miriam O'Driscoll, formed a discreet relationship with an elegant London divorcee, and his wife turned the traditional blind eye. Sex had never been her forte anyway. Sarah preferred croquet.

That is, until she met Harry Warner as she walked in the castle grounds one warm spring morning and for the first and only time in her life fell head over heels in love.

It was, according to the Earl when he later confided in Miriam, simply one of those uncontrollable passions. The fact that it was so completely out of character was the reason nobody else had ever imagined what might be going on up at the castle between Sarah and Harry Warner. It would never have occurred to anyone that anything *could* be going on. Not between the Ice Countess and the village milkman . . .

Harry was, by all accounts, a charming, thoroughly nice man, as taken aback by the situation in which he found himself as the Earl had been when he discovered what was going on under his own roof. At thirty-one, a year younger than Sarah, he lived in one of the council houses on the outskirts of the village with his elderly parents. Simply educated, good-looking but a natural loner, he had delivered milk since leaving school fifteen years earlier. As far as his relationship with Sarah was concerned, logic didn't enter into it. The two of them couldn't have been more different.

But passion had overwhelmed the Countess of Kilburton and made her careless. When her husband came home unexpectedly one day and caught them together in her south tower bedroom, Sarah was unrepentant.

'You have your comforts in London.' She spoke with an air of recklessness whilst poor Harry cringed behind her. 'You can hardly blame me for doing the same. Don't worry, darling, there won't be a scandal. We aren't planning to run away.'

Ever the gentleman, the Earl had nodded in acknowledgement. As long as they were discreet, he felt he couldn't object. And the situation might have continued for far longer if Sarah hadn't fallen pregnant a couple of months after that. Harry, unable to accept the fact that Sarah had no intention of leaving her husband, was distraught. She was expecting his child and apparently had every intention of passing it off as her husband's.

'But I love you!' he had shouted at Sarah.

She had simply shrugged.

'Darling, I love you too. But you can't seriously imagine I'd come to live with you in some kind of workman's cottage. I mean, really. Making sacrifices is all very well but you can't expect me to give up *everything* . . .'

Distraught, Harry Warner had chucked in his job and moved away less than six weeks later. He had gone to live in Southern Ireland, apparently, had married a cheerful dark-haired girl from Dublin Bay and proceeded to have five children in quick succession. Following the death of his parents eight years ago there had no longer been any reason for Harry to visit Kilburton. He hadn't been seen there since and there was no reason to suppose now that he would ever return.

Meanwhile, Jemima had been born and raised a Kilburton and nobody had ever guessed, they had never thought for so much as a moment that she might not be who she was assumed to be. It was simple, thought Nell admiringly; and it was brilliant because it was about as likely as a love-child being conceived between Anne Robinson and Billy Bragg. What a heavenly, *heavenly* secret to be in on.

Chapter 39

'You're late,' said Ben.

Nell, who was early but didn't want to get into an argument about it, bent over the wheelchair and dropped a kiss on his forehead.

'Sorry. Hassle at work.'

It was easier, too, not to mention the incident with Timmy. Ben, with his suspicious mind, wouldn't automatically believe in her innocence. Fibbing, she said, 'One of our tour guides tripped and fell down the spiral staircase in the east tower. No bones broken but she was pretty shaken up—'

'*Our* tour guide?' Ben raised his eyebrows. Clearly in a pernickety mood, he said, 'As in "our" castle, perhaps? You and Lord Kilburton getting on well together, are you?'

'Don't be stupid.' Nell got on with unpacking the food she had brought him. She dumped the box of Fortnum and Mason champagne truffles in Ben's lap. If they didn't cheer him up, nothing would.

'Smaller box than usual,' he observed waspishly, then caught the look in her eyes and heaved a sigh. 'Sorry. I get jealous. You're out there. I'm stuck here. I can't help *thinking* things . . .'

'It's just work.' Nell, who knew how much it bothered him, stroked his thin, pale cheek. Hampered by his uncontrollable tremor and general lack of coordination, Ben had spilled orange juice down the front of his white shirt. 'Do you want to change into something else?'

This time the expression on his face was one of almost unbearable sorrow. Taking a deep breath in an effort to speak more clearly he said, 'I want to change into someone else. Someone who can walk and talk and get out of this bloody place. I want us to be together, like we were before.'

Nell's eyes filled with tears. Her throat ached.

'Oh Ben. You're getting better, it just takes time. When you're well again—'

'You won't leave me.' He squeezed her hand. 'You won't, will you? Promise?'

'Of course not.' It wasn't a lie, thought Nell, justifying the deception to herself. She would never abandon Ben, but she had to have her own life.

The old Ben, she knew, would have understood.

This Ben, the one he was now, let go of her hand and managed a lopsided smile.

'Over there on top of the TV. Can you get that box for me?'

'Not more cuff links.' Nell picked up the small leather box. Ben's obsession with cuff links – which he was forever either losing or asking for help with – was the bane of the nursing staff's life.

'Open it. See what you think.'

Nell thought she felt sick. There, nestling amid folds of royal-blue satin, lay a heart-shaped diamond ring. The box, upon closer inspection, bore the name of the smartest jeweller in Oxford. The square-cut diamond glittered like nobody's business, flashing iridescent sparks of light at her as she turned the ring this way and that.

'Put it on.' He sounded impatient. 'I bought it for you.'

'Oh Ben.' So this was why he had needed so much money. Nell realized she was digging herself deeper into a hole of her own making, but what else could she possibly do? The situation was hopeless.

'Third finger, left hand.' Ben watched intently as the ring fitted into place. Then, shakily, he kissed her hand. 'Now we're engaged. Do you like the ring?'

He must have contacted the jeweller and had a selection brought to him from which to make his choice.

'It's beautiful. I love it.'

'Just as well.' Ben looked proud. 'It cost me an absolute fortune. Oh, and speaking of money . . .'

Hetty was on her way up to bed when the doorbell rang. It was Wednesday night, gone eleven. Rachel was already asleep.

Thinking it was Tony, who had phoned several times begging her to change her mind about not seeing him any more, she didn't bother to put on the safety chain before opening the door. As a result, Derry O'Driscoll all but cannoned into her unsuspecting arms.

'Oh Hetty, I'm so glad you're here. Is this OK? Is it OK if I come in? He isn't here, is he? I'm sorry about this but I had to come and see you . . .'

He was amazingly drunk. Having ricocheted off Hetty, he staggered towards the sitting-room then reeled around once more and made a grab for her.

'You come too. He isn't in there, is he? Have I had too much to drink, d'you think? Do I smell of whisky?'

Derry absolutely reeked of whisky. His baggy white Gap T-shirt was marked on one shoulder with what looked suspiciously like mascara. His long dark hair was tangled as if some poor girl had been clutching at it in a frenzy of desperation. Hetty was mystified to realize she could smell the remnants of both Obsession and Miss Dior.

'No, Tony isn't here.' She followed Derry's unsteady progress into the sitting-room. 'And yes to everything else. Why don't you sit down and let me make you a nice cup of black coffee?'

He looked appalled. 'What an awful thought. Only a sober person could suggest something so horrible. Don't you have any Scotch?'

Hetty made him an incredibly weak one, ninety-five per cent tap water, and threw in tons of ice. Having half-expected him to be out cold by the time she returned from the kitchen, she was unprepared for the strong brown arm curling around her waist, pulling her down on to the sofa next to him.

'Oh Hetty, Hetty . . .'

'Come on, sit up and drink it slowly.' She passed him the glass, made sure her cream satin dressing-gown was properly secured at the waist and tucked her bare feet up beneath her. Derry clearly needed to get something off his chest and she was happy to listen, even if she was unlikely to be of much help. It was girlfriend trouble, of course; the question was, which girlfriend and what particular kind of trouble?

Derry took a mouthful of his drink and pulled a face. 'Is this a joke? Hetty, you forgot to take the cap off the bottle. This is worse than the dodgy measures they serve at the Hen and Chicken.'

'Never mind that. Tell me what's been happening. Now,' said Hetty sympathetically, 'have you finished with one of your girls or has one of them finished with you?'

'Me. I did it. God, it was awful, but I had to do it.' He shook his head and looked sorrowful, then raised his dark eyebrows and shrugged. 'And now I've done it.'

'Which one?' Hetty couldn't help it; she was already feeling sorry for the poor creature, whoever she turned out to be.

'All of them.'

'*All* of them?'

Derry nodded. He gazed long and hard at the mountain of ice-cubes in his glass. Then he tilted his head back against the sofa and shot a brief, sidelong glance at Hetty.

She frowned. 'But why?'

'I had to, to prove I was serious. You look . . .' he struggled to find the word, 'perplexed. Hetty. You are perplexed, aren't you? You don't have the least idea about all this. Listen, I made up my mind earlier this evening. Since then, I've been in a taxi visiting each of them in turn. I told them it was all over, I can't do it any more . . . because now I've found someone better than any of them and I want to be faithful. For the very first time in my life. Don't you see? I want to be completely . . . properly . . . *faithful*.'

Oh dear, no wonder the T-shirt was blotched with mascara. Talk about tactful. Hetty tried hard not to smile.

'Well, I suppose they'll get over it. But you have to admit, it's a bit of a bolt from the blue. It *must* be love. So who's the lucky girl then? Tell me all about her. She must be amazing . . . has Nell met her yet?'

For a second Derry looked almost as if he wanted to hit her. Then he shook his head in despair.

'You really don't get it, do you? OK, *yes*, Nell's met her. Yes, she's amazing. And yes, I'm in love with her, actually. Since you ask.'

'And?' prompted Hetty, faintly exasperated. It was almost midnight after all. She couldn't stay up playing guessing games all damn night. 'Does she have a name?'

'Oh Hetty, you don't make things easy, do you?' The glass toppled sideways out of Derry's hand, spilling ice-cubes down the back of the sofa. 'You're her. Didn't you realize? The lucky girl is you.'

It was turning into one of the weirdest nights of Hetty's life. The situation, both ludicrous and absurdly flattering, had caught her so much by surprise that she hardly knew how to react.

But at least Derry was drunk, which helped. A dramatic declaration of love if he had been stone-cold sober would have been even trickier to handle.

'You don't mean it.' Hetty spoke in soothing, matter-of-fact tones. If she sounded enough like a schoolmistress maybe Derry would be put off.

'I do, I do.'

'You can't possibly mean it! I'm old, I'm fat, I can't even tell jokes without getting the punchline wrong.'

'I think you're brilliant.' Derry hauled himself upright as a melting ice-cube, slithering down the back of his jeans, made its presence felt.

'I'm a wimp.'

'How can you be a wimp? You sorted Vanessa out, gave Tony the elbow . . . and what about that picture of you in the paper? You should be proud of what you've done. *I'm* proud of you.'

'Have another drink,' said Hetty brightly. Maybe if he got completely plastered he would wake up tomorrow morning with total amnesia. 'More Scotch?'

But Derry was looking desolate. 'I don't want another drink. I want to kiss you. I just can't believe you don't want to kiss me.'

All the girls adored Derry O'Driscoll. He was outrageously attractive. Hetty knew perfectly well that if she'd been twenty years younger, she would have leapt at the chance – and probably have made a fool of herself into the bargain.

But she was almost forty, old enough to be Derry's mother. And although it was flattering it was also so out of the question that she wasn't even remotely tempted. Some relationships, thought Hetty with a rueful smile, were simply too unlikely for words. They were never meant to be. Besides, it wasn't as if Derry really meant it anyway. Not seriously. It was only goodness-knows-how-much whisky talking.

This time when she returned from the kitchen with another one for Derry and a stiff gin for herself, she found him fast asleep, draped across the sofa with his head propped on his hand, the open palm resting against his tanned cheek.

He was out for the count. Hetty stood watching him for a minute whilst she sipped her gin. Then, bending down and smoothing his glossy dark hair out of his eyes, she kissed him very lightly on the forehead.

Going upstairs to bed, she felt more attractive than she had done for many, many years.

Rachel awoke with a start as her bedroom door creaked open. A glance across at the alarm clock told her that it was two-thirty. Whatever was her mother doing up at this time of night?

But by the time she had struggled into a sitting position, Rachel realized it wasn't Hetty at all. A hand was fumbling for the light switch where no light switch hung. As her eyes grew accustomed to the greyish darkness, she recognized her night-time visitor.

Derry O'Driscoll, on the other hand, clearly hadn't recognized her.

'Oh Hetty,' he whispered, advancing unsteadily towards her. 'I love you so much. Please let me come into bed with you.'

His white T-shirt seemed almost luminous in the dark. As if hypnotized, Rachel watched him move closer. She could smell whisky mingled with perfume. The next moment the bed juddered as Derry crashed unsuspectingly against it, stubbing his toe on the base.

'Ow . . . ow, that *hurts*. Hetty, I've broken my leg. I can't walk. Now you have to let me into bed.'

Rachel gulped. What an offer. What a heavenly prospect. Her toes curled in helpless ecstasy just thinking of it.

But she didn't have the nerve to carry it through. Besides, Derry might be as drunk as a skunk now but he would wake up sober.

'No.' Firmly, to show she meant it, Rachel lay back down and turned on to her side, facing away from him. 'Go away, I don't want you here. Leave me alone.'

As far as Hetty was concerned, Rachel had slept through the whole thing. Tiptoeing past her daughter's bedroom door the next morning, she had slipped downstairs and found Derry stretched out on the sofa exactly where she'd left him the night before.

'Oh, thanks.' Looking subdued, Derry pushed his hands through his rumpled hair before taking the mug of tea Hetty held towards him. Into his other hand she dropped two Panadols.

'It's seven-thirty. I thought you'd probably want to get home earlyish.' Hetty smiled. 'Although knowing the kind of hours you keep, I suppose midday's more your idea of earlyish.'

'Doesn't matter.' Swallowing the tablets, he pulled a face. 'I've made a complete prat of myself, haven't I? I'm so sorry, Hetty. Will you ever want to speak to me again?'

'You haven't made a prat of yourself.' Hetty had perched on the arm of the sofa. As she sipped her own tea, she pleated the satiny folds of her dressing-gown where it fell across her knee. 'You boosted my ego no end. It was the most flattering thing I've ever had happen to me.'

A glint of hope appeared in Derry's eyes. 'I meant it, you know.'

Hetty nodded. 'I know. And thanks, but . . .'

'But no thanks.' He sighed, then grinned. 'It's OK, I won't beg. One favour, though. Can you absolutely promise me one thing?'

'Of course. What?'

'Don't tell anyone in my family.' Derry shuddered at the awful prospect of being teased unmercifully until he was eighty. 'Especially not Nell.'

Chapter 40

It was interesting, thought Nell, how women differed. Some, like Hetty and even Kiki Ross-Armitage, were attractive yet lacking in self-confidence.

Then there was the other kind, the Vanessa Dexter kind, who weren't actually that attractive at all but who were somehow convinced they were.

And now here was another one like Vanessa, brimming with the kind of confidence that almost had you wondering if you were the one in the wrong, if maybe you were just too stupid to recognize her extraordinary beauty and appeal to the opposite sex.

But it was a huge con trick and Nell wasn't falling for it. Constance Carruthers was forty, married, a mother of three boys. She had mousy, old-fashioned hair held back with an Alice band, hideous dress sense and a leathered, out-doorsy complexion. Her eyes were small, and her mouth large. Gawky, verging on scrawny, she walked like a chicken. She looked, as far as Nell was concerned, like everyone's idea of a spinster librarian. And she flirted like Mae West.

She did it forcefully too. If her husband Bertie could have flings, so could she. It made marriage bearable, Constance loudly maintained, and life more interesting in general. Some people collected stamps, after all. Where was the harm?

Marcus, finding himself on the receiving end of Constance's greedy attentions, could have told her. Now deeply regretting his decision to allow this charity opera gala of hers to be held at the castle, he wrote RESCUE ME on a slip of paper and slid it into Nell's hand when she dropped into the office to check the bookings diary.

'What super timing.' Constance, whose chair had been pulled up next to Marcus's, pressed her thin legs against his and glanced up at Nell. 'Two coffees, dear. Nice and strong, no sugar for me. So Marcus, about these seating arrangements . . .'

'Actually, I'm a bit pushed for time.' Having glanced at the note, Nell gave Constance an innocent smile. 'But I'm sure Marcus could make you a coffee.'

Constance looked disapproving. Marcus seized his chance. 'Of course I will. Back in two minutes, Constance. You just wait here.'

'Don't worry.' She wriggled provocatively in her seat and beamed up at him. 'I'm not going anywhere. Here to stay, that's me.'

'Help,' murmured Marcus, when they reached the kitchen. 'She's out to get me. Maybe you should run downstairs and get that chastity belt out of the display cabinet. I'd feel safer wearing it.'

He had his arms around Nell. As he backed her towards the kitchen table, she reached out and flicked the switch on the kettle.

'Just tell her you don't want an affair with an oversexed chicken.'

'I've already tried.' Marcus kissed her lingeringly on the mouth. 'She's pushy. Pushier than Kiki, which is saying something. The trouble is, she thinks I'm single.'

'You are single.'

'Available, then. It means she isn't going to give up. This bloody charity gala's getting to me already.' He sighed. 'I really wish I hadn't let her talk me into it.'

Constance was arranging the entire event herself. Severio Guerrero, the renowned Spanish tenor, was flying in especially for the occasion, which was being billed as a Midsummer Night's Extravaganza, and the whole thing was to be held outdoors amid the romantically floodlit Tudor gardens. It sounded wonderful. Marcus only hoped she was as efficient at organizing this kind of venue as she clearly thought she was. There were so many opportunities for error yet Constance dismissed each in turn with an airy flick of the wrist, refusing to believe for so much as a second that anything could possibly go wrong.

'It's for charity, darling,' she had trilled when he dared ask whether she should be relying on a team of new, previously untried caterers. 'Of course they won't let me down. They'll be fine!'

'Kettle's boiled.' Nell, slithering from his grasp as footsteps sounded in the corridor outside, mouthed 'Hilda Garnet' and began busily spooning coffee into cups.

'This is ridiculous,' said Marcus when the danger had passed. Having caught sight of Nell in the kitchen, Hilda had stalked past with her nose in the air and her arms full of freshly laundered sheets. 'We shouldn't have to sneak around like fifteen-year-olds. There's no *need* for us to hide.'

He meant it. He was tired of the subterfuge and the ludicrous limits it imposed on their relationship. Sod what other people thought, Marcus decided irritably. As far as he was concerned, going public solved far more problems than it raised. An added attraction, too, would be getting that old crone Constance off his case.

'Speaking of ridiculous.' Nell looked amused. Reaching up, she attempted to rub away the smear of rose-pink lipstick at the corner of his mouth.

The stain, however, proved to be stubborn. Unzipping the inside pocket of her white jacket, she pulled out a cotton handkerchief to use instead.

'What's that?' Marcus reached for the ring as it clattered to the floor. Picking it up, he let out a low whistle. 'Where did you get this?'

Nell watched him admire it. She had forgotten to take the ring off last night following her visit to Ben. Only as she had been on her way into work this morning had its glitter caught her eye. Taking it off, she had zipped it into her jacket pocket for safe-keeping.

She thought quickly. 'Impressed?'

'Very impressed.' Trying not to look too interested, Marcus handed the ring back to her. 'Is this yours?'

'No, I mugged one of the tourists, a rich Australian woman. It's OK, she can afford it.' Nell grinned. 'Yes, it's mine. And so much for you being impressed. It isn't real.'

'No?' Eyebrows raised, Marcus took a second look.

'Well, real gold,' Nell put in hastily as he glanced at the hallmark. 'But not real diamonds. It's those cubic zirconiwhatsits. They're as cheap as anything. Good, aren't they?'

'Amazing.' Passing it back for the second time and smiling slightly, Marcus said, 'You had me wondering there for a moment. I had visions of some secret fiancé. So why aren't you wearing it? What's it doing stashed away in a pocket?'

'I brought it in to show Hetty,' said Nell. 'And of course I'm not going to wear it at work.' She pulled a face. 'Yuk, just imagine. People might think I'm engaged.'

By Friday afternoon, Marcus had had enough. The idea which had been formulating itself in his mind all week became something he could no longer delay carrying out. Constance, her clawing fingers and her apparently unshakeable conviction that it was only a matter of days if not hours before he succumbed to her charms, was the final, back-breaking straw.

At four-thirty, he made the necessary phone call.

At five o'clock he tracked Nell down to the dungeon tower, where the gift shop was situated. Nell and Suzanne, one of the sales assistants, were bagging up the day's takings, even higher than usual thanks to an ecstatic married couple from Denver, Colorado, who had fallen in love with Kilburton, and to prove it had bought up the entire season's stock of tapestry-print silk ties for their friends back home.

Marcus drew Nell to one side.

'Go home, pack an overnight bag, be back here by six.' His voice was tantalizingly low. Suzanne, still counting fifty-pence pieces into plastic bags, did her damnedest to eavesdrop but still couldn't make out what his lordship had just said.

'Why?' Nell couldn't help marvelling at the way her body coped. Quite unable to control the spasm of desire zapping up and down her spine, she nevertheless knew she hid it well. We look like two fellow workers discussing a business problem, she thought, her pleasure only heightened by the clandestine nature of the affair. Looking at us now, whoever would guess the truth?

'Never mind why,' murmured Marcus. 'I think you know why.'

'He's so handsome,' sighed Suzanne when he had left. Daringly she added, 'You must fancy him, don't you? Isn't it frustrating working with someone like that? Don't you ever wish . . . ?'

Her courage failed her. Nell was giving her a quizzical look, as if she'd suggested Mother Teresa might secretly hanker after the Pope.

'Funnily enough, no.' Nell broke into a grin. 'But I caught the Richard and Judy show the other day.' With a flourish, she counted out the last of the money and slammed the till shut with her hip. 'According to some expert, the better looking the man, the smaller the willy. So maybe it's just as well.'

Thank goodness it wasn't true, thought Nell later that night, her legs comfortably entwined with Marcus's as they lay together in bed.

He had brought her to the Manor House in Castle Combe, booking for the sake of discretion one of the deliciously picturesque doll-sized cottages which stood apart from the hotel itself. It had been a blissful evening, particularly for Nell, since

Marcus, for once, hadn't so much as mentioned his irritation with her passion for secrecy. Instead they had a fabulous candlelit dinner in the cottage, bitched pleasurably about Constance and Mrs Garnet, demolished over the course of the evening two and a half bottles of St Emilion and made love both before and after the meal. Escaping from Kilburton had done them both good, Nell realized. The hours she had been putting in both at the castle and with Ben in Oxford, not to mention the extra evenings she now spent fortune-telling, were beginning to take their combined toll. A holiday was what she needed, a proper get-away-from-it-all break in the sun. Marcus had been talking about St Lucia, where friends of his owned a house on the beach, but that couldn't happen until early October, when the castle was closed for the season, and they would still run the risk of being recognized together.

'I'm not asleep.' As Marcus murmured the words against Nell's bare shoulder, his hand slid along the curve of her thigh. 'Just in case you were wondering if you'd left it too late to go for the hat-trick.'

In the semi-darkness, she smiled. 'That's an overdose.'

'I call it making the most of the occasion.'

'Hmm.' Afterwards, Nell stretched pleasurably, replete in every sense. 'I could get used to this.'

I'm counting on it, thought Marcus.

Chapter 41

Sunday, sunny and bright, was another record-breaking day for visitors, thanks to the success of Nell's kite-flying fiesta in the park and enough accompanying wind to keep the event airborne.

The atmosphere of cheerful, good-natured rivalry, however, didn't extend to the castle's private wing.

Jemima, her whole chin a mass of ugly greenish-yellow bruising, had spent most of the past week closeted in her room, mourning her disfigurement and the departure of Timmy Struther from her life.

The arrival of Kiki at lunch-time did nothing to improve her mood. Kiki, offended by the lack of welcome when she had come down to Gloucestershire solely to cheer Jemima up, stalked off and tried out a few chat-up lines on Marcus instead. Marcus, on the phone discussing details of a photographic fashion shoot to be held in the castle itself, could have done without the distractions of Kiki shoving gin and tonics into his hand and Constance bursting into the office at ten minute intervals mouthing 'OK to use the fax?'

Giving up when it became apparent she was getting seriously on Marcus's nerves, Kiki wandered outside and made her way across to the park instead.

'I don't know who's worse,' she grumbled, upon finding Nell down at the lakeside with a photographer from the local paper.

'Mmm?' Nell's attention was on one of the more spectacular kites which had just triple-salkoed into the water. Around them, onlookers screamed with delight.

'Bloody Jemima and bloody Marcus.' Kiki gazed in disgust at a blob of strawberry ice-cream melting into the suede toe of one of her all-time favourite shoes. They were the pale-blue Ferragamos, the ones that matched her Porsche. 'What a complete waste of a journey. This is no fun.' She glanced not very hopefully at Nell. 'I suppose you're too busy to come out for lunch?'

'Sorry.' Experiencing a rare pang of sympathy for Jemima, who did look frightful, Nell said, 'But I'm sure Jemima's glad you're here really. She's been so down this week. Not that she's said anything to me, of course, but the split with Timmy does seem to have hit her for six.'

Kiki suspected it was Timmy himself who had hit her for six, but Jemima was sticking stubbornly to the tripped-and-fell story. She thought for a moment of all the times in the past when Nell had helped her.

'You're right, she does need cheering up.'

A gust of wind at that moment sent Kiki's white organza skirt billowing up to her thighs. Clamping it down, she glared at the young photographer, silently daring him to try it. She'd fallen victim to the paparazzi coming out of San Lorenzo last week when the bastards had caught her chewing a breadstick. The resulting picture had made her look like a hippo in mid-yawn.

'Take her to lunch.' Nell touched her arm. 'Go on, she'll feel better once she's out.'

But Kiki shook her head. 'She won't go, and Mrs Garnet's cooking something anyway.' She glanced up at Nell. 'Look, I know Jemima's been horrid to you but would you be prepared to do a reading for her? I just think it would give her something to look forward to. And take her mind off Timmy.'

Nell stopped feeling sorry for Jemima.

'She wouldn't do it,' she said flatly. 'All she'd do is sneer. Besides, her future might not *be* something to look forward to.'

'Let me ask her.' Kiki, who sensed that Jemima was ripe for conversion, persisted. 'Oh please, Nell. It's what she needs at the moment. It wouldn't take long. You could really cheer her up.'

Kiki was so nice, thought Nell. Whatever had Jemima done to deserve a friend like her?

'I'm only doing this because Kiki won't stop nagging until I do.' Jemima scowled to show she meant it.

'Same here,' said Nell, scowling back.

'This fortune-telling business is all codswallop, you know. Don't expect me to believe a word you say.'

Nell sat down on the edge of the bed. Jemima, huddled bad-temperedly in the middle, was wearing a yellow-and-green silk-printed dressing-gown which matched her bruised chin.

'I won't, but we may as well get on with it. Give me an item of jewellery or your watch, something you wear all the time. Come on,' Nell added with a sigh when Jemima shot her a suspicious look. 'I won't steal it. The sooner we get this over with, the sooner I can get back to work.'

* * *

'Well?' Kiki demanded, bursting into the bedroom twenty minutes later. Ash from her cigarette showered on to the ivory counterpane as she collapsed heavily on the bed.

'Load of crap.' Irritably, Jemima shook the ash on to the floor. 'As expected. Ouch, you're sitting on my foot.'

'You,' howled Kiki, 'are a stroppy, ungrateful cow. And I paid good money for that reading so the least you can bloody do is tell me what Nell said.'

'You mean Gypsy Petronella?' Jemima mocked. 'OK, if it makes me happy. There's a man not far away who's mad about me, but I'll refuse his advances because he's just not my type. I'm going to be visiting Australia within the next year and I must double-pack because one of my cases will end up in Alaska, of all God-forsaken dumps.' Rolling her eyes in disgust, Jemima continued ticking statements off on her fingers. 'Then we had a load of garbage about putting bad relationships behind me and looking to the future, where it seems the initial P is going to become all-important. My significant colour is dark blue, and butterflies are going to mean a great deal to me. Butterflies . . . I ask you! Ah, and the *pièce de résistance*, within three months I'm going to be swept off my feet by a man who'll make me happy beyond my wildest dreams. He'll be titled, fabulously wealthy and foreign.'

'Handsome?' Kiki's eyes were like saucers. 'Will he be handsome?'

'Oh, pull yourself together,' Jemima snapped. 'What do you think? When did any fortune-teller tell anyone they'd be swept off their feet by someone broke, bald and ugly?'

* * *

Alistair Munro felt like a schoolboy. He had spent practically the entire week feeling like a schoolboy. Every time he allowed himself to think of Lady Jemima Kilburton his stomach started to churn in true adolescent fashion. Adrenalin surged, druglike, through his veins. Meeting Jemima had sparked his weary soul back to life, Alistair decided in uncharacteristically poetic fashion. Like jump-leads.

Now, waiting in the Grand Hall while one of the tour guides went to tell Hilda Garnet he was here, he took deep breaths and tried to look casual though his new fawn corduroys were a good inch too tight at the waist.

The heavy oak door leading to the private wing finally swung open.

'Dr Munro, do come through.' Hilda Garnet, his number one fan, ushered him inside. 'How kind of you to call. Lady Jemima will be delighted to see you again, I'm sure. Poor lamb, she's been so down this past week.'

Alistair was even more delighted to see Jemima again. His heart crashed joyously against his ribs as Jemima, from her bed, greeted him with a fragile smile.

'I look a fright.' She touched her chin as if in apology. 'I've spent the whole week in hiding, like Quasimodo.'

'A few more days and you'll be as good as new.' Anxious to remind her that she wasn't his patient, Alistair said, 'Did you see your own doctor?'

Jemima shook her head, her straight, shiny blond hair swinging around her face.

'No. I must admit, I wasn't expecting to see you again either.'

'I wanted to make sure you were on the mend.' Changing

the subject, working towards the true reason for his visit, Alistair nodded in the direction of the window. 'I've been hearing from Mrs Garnet about this opera festival. Sounds impressive. Are you a music lover yourself . . . um, Jemima?'

Music, as far as tone-deaf Jemima was concerned, was a largely pointless invention. It came in handy sometimes as background noise at parties, she granted it that much, but how some people could actually sit down and listen to the stuff for hours on end was beyond her.

Somehow, though, it seemed rude to say so. Alistair Munro looked as if he might take it personally.

'Music? Oh, I adore it,' lied Jemima, casting around for the name of that pianist fellow with the nice blue eyes. Ah yes, that was it. 'Especially Richard Clayderman.'

Her reply barely registered. 'I'm a bit of an opera buff myself.' Alistair tried not to sound too eager. His hand, inside his jacket pocket, curled around the ruinously expensive tickets he had bought for *Die Fledermaus* to be performed by Kiri Te Kanawa at the Royal Opera House in eight days' time. 'Light opera, you know, mainly. Nothing too gloomy.' He cleared his throat. 'As a matter of fact, I was wondering if—'

'Oh *drat* it.' As her phone began to ring, Jemima rummaged energetically beneath the bedclothes. 'Where on earth has the damn thing got to? Don't you just hate it when this happens?'

Locating the mobile at last, buried behind the mountain of plumped-up pillows, she said briskly, 'Yes?'

Then her tone changed. Alistair observed her tightening grip on the phone, and the way her eyes darted almost guiltily in his direction before fastening upon the rumpled bedspread.

He was even more certain who was on the other end of the line when Jemima murmured, 'Hang on a sec,' before turning to him with her cheeks flushed and her eyes almost feverishly bright.

'Sorry, Alistair, would you be a dear and excuse me for just a few minutes?'

'Yes, Alistair. Piss off, whoever you are,' drawled Timmy. 'There's a good fellow. OK, has he gone? Who is he anyway, some new young lover? Some gorgeous rampant stud?'

Just the sound of his voice sent shivers of pleasure down Jemima's spine. Her stomach was a seething mass of butterflies. She had spent the whole week missing him and now here he was, teasing her in that irresistible, laid-back way of his, as if nothing had ever happened.

'Of course not. He's the doctor who came out to see me last Sunday.' Determined not to make things easy for him, she added, 'I almost needed plastic surgery, Timmy.'

'OK, OK. Have your apology if that's what you're waiting for.' In Northampton, Timmy rolled his eyes. 'But you have to admit, sweetheart, you weren't entirely blameless. All that nagging just about did my head in.'

'Sorry.' Jemima's voice was small. She didn't want him ringing off. And it wasn't as if he had punched her in the face; all he'd done was pull her out of the car. She was the one who had stumbled and fallen over.

'Forgiven.' Timmy grinned. 'There we are, all sorted. And I suffered too, you know. Only pranged the car on the way home, didn't I? Smashed into a bloody phone box.'

Jemima's heart leapt into her throat.

'Were you hurt?'

'No, but the Maserati's a write-off.' He sighed. 'So you're still on, then, for the Fitzwilliams' party at Henley?'

'Oh yes! Super . . .' She may have missed out on Ascot but at least she wouldn't miss Henley too. Overjoyed, Jemima blurted the words out, then faltered. 'But it's only three days away. My bruises won't have cleared completely. I'll look a fright.'

'I don't mind,' Timmy assured her. 'Cover the worst of it with make-up and tell everyone you fell off a horse. Look, you don't mind driving, do you? It's easier if you come and pick me up. Be here by ten, sweetheart. Don't be late. And whatever you do, don't turn up in that God-awful white dress with the sailor collar. Wear something halfway decent, OK?'

When Alistair finally knocked on the door it was clear she had forgotten he'd been waiting like a lemon outside. The bedclothes were flung back. Jemima, standing barefoot before the open doors of the wardrobe, was holding dresses up against herself and flinging the no-hopers into a heap on the floor behind her.

'Oh hi. Sorry.' She smiled abstractedly over her shoulder. 'Which do you think looks better, this pink one or the blue-and-white striped?'

Anger and disappointment spurred Alistair on. Ignoring the dresses she held towards him he said curtly, 'That was him, wasn't it? I can't believe you're doing this. Look, he's hit you once, he'll hit you again. You can't—'

'You don't understand.' Vigorously, Jemima shook her head. 'He didn't hit me. It was an accident. He loves me.' Timmy had never admitted it as such, but she knew he did, deep down. 'We love each other,' she went on, chucking both dresses on to the floor and reaching for her favourite Bruce Oldfield, cinnamon-yellow voile splashed with crimson poppies. 'And it doesn't appear to have occurred to you, but this isn't actually any of your business.'

Alistair had spent days planning this. Now it was all going wrong. In desperation he pulled the two tickets from his pocket.

'Please. All you need is something to take your mind off him! Dame Kiri's appearing in *Die Fledermaus* next week . . . please say you'll come with me. It's the most marvellous production; you'd love it, I know you would.'

'Is this a joke? Are you seriously telling me the NHS provides tickets to the opera these days, to cheer people up?'

Jemima stared at him. Then, at the expression on Alistair's face, she began to laugh. 'Oh. *Oh.* So that's why you came here this afternoon. To invite me to the opera anyway. Am I right?'

It was all going disastrously wrong. Sickened by the realization that he had made an almighty fool of himself, Alistair nodded, unable to speak.

'You mean like a date, an honest-to-goodness *date*?' The look Jemima now gave him was almost pitying. 'Oh dear, you really don't understand, do you? I'm afraid that isn't how we operate. Can you imagine how my friends would react if all of a sudden I was seen in public with . . . well, no offence, but someone like you? I mean, whatever next? A trip to the cinema with the postman, maybe? A day-trip to Blackpool illuminations with one of the local farm hands?'

Anger flooded through Alistair.

'But you're happy to be seen in public with a violent, bullying thug?'

Jemima's clear blue eyes narrowed in displeasure. He really didn't understand at all.

'Timmy isn't a thug, he's a viscount. And when his father dies,' she added with an air of chilly finality, 'he'll be a duke.'

Chapter 42

Nell's world fell in at eight-thirty on Monday morning when Hetty, clutching a copy of the *Daily Mail*, hammered on the front door of The Pink House.

'I don't think you're going to like this.'

Nell, who was eating honey on toast and doing her make-up in the mirror above the fireplace, pulled a face.

'Don't tell me, more rubbish from Constance about the gala. I told her she was asking for trouble, dropping all those hints about Pavarotti making a surprise appearance. She'll end up getting the pants sued off her if she isn't careful.'

Hetty waited until Nell had finished her eyeliner. She didn't want to see it go wonky.

'It isn't about Constance, it's about you.' She glanced at Miriam, who had been frying mushrooms in the kitchen and singing along to 'Tie a Yellow Ribbon' on the radio. 'And Marcus.'

Nell turned slowly around, crimson lipstick poised in mid-air.

'Me and Marcus? What about me and Marcus?'

'You'd better read it yourself.' Hetty sat down at the dining table and gratefully accepted the cup of tea Miriam poured her. 'And I'd better warn you, it's already round the village. I only popped into the shop for a pint of milk. Minnie Hardwick couldn't wait to share the news with me. I'm amazed she hasn't come bursting round here herself.'

The ensuing silence was broken only by Hetty accidentally slurping her hot tea. Nell, folded newspaper in one hand and half-finished toast in the other, perched on the arm of the sofa in order to read the relevant piece, which took up most of the gossip column.

It was headlined oh-so-wittily 'Marcus's Happy Medium' and the source of the story, apparently, was Marcus himself. With rising disbelief, Nell learned that she was the girl he'd been waiting for, that her humble background didn't bother him a jot and that this was his way of proving it.

It got worse. Nell's palms grew damp as she read on.

'Sultry Petronella hasn't only inherited stunning good looks from her gypsy ancestors,' crooned the article. 'As clairvoyant to the rich and famous, she numbers royalty, politicians and stars of stage and screen among her many devoted clients. Believing absolutely in her mystic powers, they regularly return for advice concerning matters both financial and emotional. Discretion, needless to say, is Petronella's watchword; she is known to her loyal clientele as the keeper of secrets. Well, thanks to Marcus, here's one secret that's been let out of the bag. My congratulations go to the two of them and *I* predict a glittering wedding before the year is out!'

'I don't *believe* this.' Nell flung the paper across the room.

'Um, I think the mushrooms are burning,' said Hetty tentatively as clouds of smoke began billowing out of the kitchen.

Unperturbed, Miriam sauntered out to rescue them.

'Oh dear,' she called cheerfully over her shoulder. '*I* predict little bits of Marcus Kilburton being strewn across the castle grounds.'

'How could he do it?' Nell seethed. Her dark eyes glittered with fury.

'More to the point,' wailed Hetty, who still didn't understand why Nell should be so upset, 'how could *you* do it, without telling *me*?'

Hetty wasn't the only one who didn't understand.

'Just calm down,' said Marcus when Nell exploded into his office twenty minutes later. This was exactly why he hadn't warned her in advance, why it had been necessary instead to present her with a *fait accompli*. 'Calm down, sit down and take deep breaths. Now, think it through and tell me honestly whether what I've done is the most terrible thing in the world or the most sensible. It's done. Out in the open. Big deal. This bee in the bonnet of yours about the difference in our backgrounds is too ridiculous for words. Apart from anything else,' he added forcefully, 'if we're happy with each other, who gives a stuff what anyone else thinks?'

But Nell showed no sign of either sitting down or calming down. He had never seen her so angry.

'Look,' Marcus went on, hazarding a guess why, 'I'm sorry about the fortune-telling bit; I know you wanted that kept quiet. It didn't come from me, I swear. One of the girls who works for the paper knew all about you. As soon as she heard your name she put two and two together. I really am sorry, sweetheart, but you have to admit it's a miracle that the story hasn't come out before now.'

'It still wouldn't have come out,' Nell said bitterly, 'if you hadn't broken your promise to me. You don't know what you've done, Marcus.' She closed her eyes for a moment, struggling for control. Then, pushing back her hair with a despairing gesture she shouted, 'You have absolutely no idea how much trouble you've caused! You had no *right* to go to the papers . . .'

She was shaking. This, Marcus realized, was more than a mere preference for keeping out of the limelight.

'Go on,' he said evenly. 'Exactly what kind of trouble have I caused? I think you'd better tell me.'

'His name's Ben.' Nell sat down at last. Having adjusted the fraying cuff of her black shirt, she removed a black thread from her short white skirt. 'Ben Torrance.'

'And he is?' Remembering the supposedly fake diamond ring and feeling sick, Marcus said, 'Boyfriend? Fiancé? Husband?'

Nell shook her head.

'What, then?' That was a relief but he still didn't have an answer. Then another thought struck him. 'Is he your son?'

'He isn't my son.' Nell sighed, because the existence of some hitherto unsuspected love child would have been so much easier to explain.

Then she told him about Ben.

Nell relayed the story simply, in a matter-of-fact manner. When she had finished, she looked for the first time at Marcus. Sunlight, streaming through the leaded windows, turned his blond hair blonder still. His green, darkly lashed eyes were serious.

'Look,' he said finally, a pen twirling between his fingers as he tilted back his chair, 'I'm sorry. It's a terrible thing to have happened. Don't think I don't sympathize. But, Nell, you can't seriously sacrifice your whole life, your own happiness, just because you don't want to hurt this guy's feelings! I mean, if you were married to him . . . well, that would be different. But you weren't. You weren't even seeing each other when the accident happened. You aren't responsible for him.' He looked exasperated. 'You certainly don't have to feel guilty about building a new life for yourself.'

Nell's stomach contracted. He didn't understand.

'It isn't a question of guilt; I just think he's suffered enough. I don't know how he'd cope if I let him down now.' She glanced at the red light flashing on the answering machine, like an ominous warning signal. 'And as far as Ben's concerned, we never did stop seeing each other. The amnesia wiped all that from his mind.'

'You still weren't married,' Marcus said bluntly.

Nell's pulse began to race as annoyance gave way to anger. Perspiration prickled along her spine. He was being vile.

'So you're saying you wouldn't feel any responsibility towards someone until the moment you signed on the dotted line,' she retorted. 'If you met a wonderful, beautiful girl and fell in love with her, bought the ring, booked the church, planned to spend the rest of your lives together being blissfully happy and having children . . . you're telling me that if this beloved fiancée of yours was critically injured in a car crash on the way to the church, you'd go: Phew, lucky escape! You'd think it was OK, she wasn't your responsibility because the two of you weren't actually *married*?'

'Don't twist my words.' Marcus glared back at her. 'And that isn't a fair analogy either.'

'Isn't it?' Nell raised her eyebrows. 'OK, let's call it a for-instance. Say it did happen to you. What *would* you do with a hypothetical, head-injured fiancée?'

'Everything in my power to help her,' Marcus replied evenly. 'I'd make sure she had the best standards of care, the best treatment available . . . everything she needed.'

'How amazingly generous,' Nell mocked. 'How thoughtful, how loving, how kind. But the moment she regains conscious-ness you tell her what? That it's no good, the wedding's off, you can't marry her because she's brain-damaged . . . oh and by the way, you're seeing someone else now; you'll probably end up marrying her instead?'

'OK, that's enough.' Marcus shot her a warning look. The desperate futility of the situation infuriated him. It was sad and hopeless, and if he were to find himself in such a situation he didn't know how he would react. Nell, having sprung the news of Ben's existence on him, was expecting him to come up with answers to questions he had never considered before in his life. Anyone could say blithely, yes of course they'd stay with a partner who was severely brain-damaged, but actually facing the situation and making that sacrifice was another matter.

Marcus had to admire Nell, even whilst he despaired of the effect it was threatening to have on his own life. In all honesty, he didn't know if he could behave with such bravery and selflessness.

In the meantime, Nell was looking as if she wanted very much to knock him senseless.

'I'm sorry.' He nodded slightly, acknowledging her fury. 'It's a lot to take in. I'm sorry, too, about putting the story in the papers, though it might have been sensible,' he pointed out, 'to mention Ben before now.'

'It's no concern of anyone else's.' Ben had been deserted by his family and friends. Nell was still unable to forgive them for that. She had certainly never felt the need to tout the tale of Ben's tragic life around with her, to satisfy the morbid curiosity of people who had never even known him.

'It concerns me.' Marcus stood up and moved towards her. 'You concern me. Look, I have to say this. If Ben lives to be ninety, what happens to you? Are you planning never to marry, never to have children, never to have any kind of normal family life of your own?'

It was only twenty past nine and Nell was already exhausted. When he took her in his arms she leaned against him, grateful for the physical contact.

'He isn't likely to reach ninety. His doctor told me that people like Ben generally don't live to a great age. Maybe fifty or sixty. And I'm not some saint, either.' She pulled momentarily away, gazing up at Marcus and managing a brief smile. 'I decided a couple of years ago that if the right man came along, I'd marry him. As long as Ben didn't know, I figured it was OK to do it. Don't ask me how I was planning to handle the pregnancy bit. I suppose I thought

I'd find some way to deal with that when it happened.'

'What if I'm your right man?' Marcus demanded. His grip on her tightened and Nell saw the pulse beating in his throat.

'You can't be.' She shook her head, meaning it. 'My plan only works if I marry someone anonymous, someone who's never going to be photographed or written about in the press. You're about as anonymous as . . . as Ewan McGregor.'

'Who?'

'You're hopeless.' Nell's mouth twitched. 'And you know perfectly well what I mean. You're newsworthy. Ben spends his life reading the newspapers. That puts you off-limits.'

'Not only me,' Marcus drawled, glad to see her mood improving. 'As far as I can see, your choice is horribly limited. No Jimmy Hill, no Trevor McDonald, no Roy Hattersley. No Jack Duckworth, no Al Pacino, no—'

'Interesting,' Nell mused, 'the things you discover about people you thought you already knew.'

'What?'

'You said Jack Duckworth.' Her dark eyes widened in gleeful accusation. 'And you told me you'd never watched *Coronation Street* in your life.'

Chapter 43

Jemima, alerted by an apoplectic Hilda Garnet, barged into the office less than five minutes later.

'What is this bullshit?' she shrieked, jabbing at the paper and almost tripping over the hem of her dressing-grown. 'Marcus, tell me it's somebody's idea of a bad joke . . . tell me you haven't gone completely mental . . .'

'It's true, actually.' Marcus watched her flinch, as if he'd whacked her across the face with a wet herring. Unable to resist it, he added, 'Oh dear, I thought you'd be pleased.'

Jemima glared at Nell. 'This is all your doing. It's deliberate, isn't it? You want to ruin us. Well, let me tell you, you're nothing but a common, conniving bitch and you won't get away with it. I won't *let* you get away with it . . .'

Never in her life had Nell been more tempted. Snobbish, supercilious Jemima almost seemed to be asking for it. And she, Nell, could give it to her. For a second she imagined breaking her promise to Miriam and spilling out the horrid, humiliating news that Jemima had about as much right to her precious title as Abel Trippick's dog.

Jemima, meanwhile, her perfect complexion all purple and blotchy, was shouting, 'What have you done? You slut, if you've got yourself pregnant—'

Nell, opening her mouth to retaliate and praying she wouldn't say what she so badly wanted to say, was stopped by Marcus.

'If you knew how ridiculous you sounded,' he said icily. 'My God, sometimes I'm ashamed to have you as a sister.'

At his side, sensing another golden opportunity to speak out, Nell opened her mouth once more.

'And no, she isn't pregnant,' Marcus went on. 'There isn't going to be any wedding either. Nell doesn't want to marry me.'

'Oh what *is* this?' howled Jemima, almost hopping up and down with rage. 'Marcus, are you on drugs?'

The phone in Nell's handbag began to shrill. Since it was easier to answer it than leave it ringing, she took the call.

'What is this?' shrieked Meg Tarrant on the other end of the line. 'How could you *do* this to me? My editor's just hurled the paper at my head and demanded to know why I didn't get the story first. Nell, I thought we were friends. You could have given me an exclusive!'

An awful lot of papers appeared to be getting hurled around this morning. Nell, who had been leaning against the edge of the desk, glanced over her shoulder as behind her a fax began chuntering out of the machine.

Kiki's outlandish scrawl was instantly recognizable:

Tell Jemima to switch on her phone, the note demanded. *I can't believe what I've just read*. IS IT *TRUE*???

'Is it true?'

Oscar's forehead creased in concern. He was on Nell's side

but he was also aware of the nightmarish implications. As a result of Nell's frantic phone call earlier he had managed to intercept the delivery of Ben's papers and remove the relevant one. It was only a temporary measure but it had given Nell time to reach Oxford and deal with the situation herself.

'Kind of.' She could admit that much because if there was anyone in whom she had absolute trust, it was Oscar. 'But as far as I was concerned, we had a discreet arrangement. I wasn't expecting anything like this.'

Outside on the striped, emerald lawn, other residents of Rowan House sat in their chairs enjoying the perfect weather. Ben, once the original sun worshipper, nowadays remained incarcerated in his room, stubbornly refusing to venture out.

'How are you going to explain it?' Oscar's shirt strained across his massive chest as he reached for Ben's medical notes. His brown eyes flickered across the last few entries. 'He isn't going to be happy, whichever way you do it. Maybe I should give Dr Webster a call.'

Nell knew only too well how Ben would react. To abandon him now would be like inflicting a death sentence.

'It's OK, I'll sort this out,' she told Oscar. 'I know I can't let him down.'

'Come on, Ben, you know what these journalists are like.' Briskly, Nell gestured at the lurid headlines adorning several of the other papers strewn across his bed. There was currently huge speculation about a possible royal re-marriage. 'They'll make anything up if they think it'll sell a few more copies. This thing about me and Marcus isn't true and that's all there is to it.'

'Doesn't look made up to me.' Ben's face was like thunder. 'Doesn't *sound* made up. Where would they get this from if it wasn't true?'

It was frighteningly easy to lie.

'Right.' Nell began ticking the sequence of events off on her fingers. 'Marcus doesn't like Timmy Struther. He stopped Jemima seeing him. Timmy, who doesn't like me *or* Marcus, vowed to get his own back and he knew something like this would really muck things up between Kiki and Marcus. Timmy, I guess, phoned the paper pretending to be Marcus . . . and it's had exactly the effect he wanted because Kiki is hopping mad, Marcus is furious and, thanks to Timmy, there's every chance I'll lose my job.'

'Good.' Ben, whose mood swings were erratic, tried to wipe his face as tears rolled helplessly down his cheeks. 'Best thing for it. You're engaged to me, don't forget. When I get out of here and start working again, you won't need their stinking job anyway. May as well get out now.' He sniffed loudly. 'Tell them to stuff it. Bastards.'

'I'm taking a holiday,' said Nell. She had made the decision during the drive into Oxford. 'I need the break. By the time I get back, it'll all have been forgotten.'

'Not by me.' Ben was still suspicious. 'And what's this crap about happy mediums, anyway?'

'You see? That's something else they've got wrong . . . I told a few fortunes, that's all. It started as a joke. Mediums talk to dead people,' Nell exclaimed with an impatient gesture. 'All I did was read tea-leaves for fun.'

'You and Marcus Kilburton.' Ben clung desperately to her,

his expression bleak. 'Promise me there's nothing going on between you.'

'Promise.' Nell smiled. 'Nothing going on at all.'

She heard his sigh of relief. Thank goodness he believed her.

'So will Marcus Kilburton let the papers know the truth,' said Ben, 'or shall I?'

'You can't go.'

Marcus, turning up at The Pink House, found Nell chucking clothes into a battered suitcase.

'I can't stay.' The strap of Nell's thin, cotton camisole slipped off her shoulder as she bundled summer shoes into a Sainsbury's carrier bag and crammed it into the left-hand corner of the case. 'Even I can't handle this much gossip. The whole village is aghast. Your lovely sister may never recover from the shock. And poor Hetty will certainly never forgive me . . .'

She had her back to him. In those white shorts and flat gold sandals her legs seemed endless. And she was taking herself off for a bloody fortnight. This wasn't what he'd planned at all.

'Where are you going?' Marcus demanded, since he clearly hadn't a hope in hell of stopping her.

'Don't know.' Nell shrugged. 'I haven't thought.'

'Some fortune-teller you are.'

She turned and smiled. 'Sometimes not knowing's more fun. I'll send you a postcard when I get there.'

Miriam, who had earlier beaten an uncharacteristically diplomatic retreat upstairs, appeared in the living-room doorway.

'There's a man with a zoom lens lurking outside, talking to Elsie Cutler.'

'Go on.' Nell looked at Marcus. 'You'd better leave. Use the back door.'

'This is ridiculous,' he said wearily. 'Why does it need to be so complicated? Why did this have to happen to me?'

'Serve you right for taking advantage of my innocent daughter.' Miriam burst out laughing at the expression on Marcus's face. 'Oh my, you aren't quite used to us yet, are you? Joke, dear boy. Joke.'

'Thanks for coming.'

'My pleasure,' lied Marcus. It wasn't a pleasure at all but at least now he understood Nell's dilemma.

Coming face to face with Ben Torrance, however, still came as something of a shock.

Nell had, if anything, played down the extent of Ben's handicap. Here, closeted in the room from which he so seldom emerged, was where he spent his time obsessively reading magazines and newspapers. His skinny frame, folded into the wheelchair by the diamond-leaded window, was expensively clothed but the overall effect was somehow bizarre.

He had clearly been an extraordinarily good-looking boy. Vestiges of it remained, but Ben could no longer be called handsome. It wasn't just the crooked mouth and uncombed dark hair, thought Marcus; he didn't look normal. And the smell in the room, of antiseptic and urine not quite disguised by liberal applications of men's cologne, was unsettling.

Not nearly as unsettling, though, as Ben's voice. Slow,

slurred and hard to comprehend, he took – as Nell had earlier remarked – a lot of getting used to. She had had years in which to get accustomed to it. Marcus, receiving Ben's phone call that afternoon, had been hard pushed to understand more than two or three words at a time.

'I wanted to meet you,' Ben said slowly, 'to make sure Nell wasn't lying.'

A silvery dribble of saliva ran from the corner of his mouth with the effort of forming a whole sentence. Marcus glanced at the box of tissues resting on the window-sill and wondered if he should offer to help.

'She isn't lying.'

Ben nodded. 'I've been ill, you see. But we are engaged. As soon as I leave this place, Nell and I will be married.'

The diamond ring she had dismissed as fake hadn't been fake at all. In a strange way, Marcus realized, finding out about Ben had unlocked a great many doors. So much about Nell had clicked into place; so much that had puzzled him had now been explained.

'She's told me that.' Luckily she had also related to him the fabricated story of how the piece had got into the paper. Marcus, who had no compunction about using Timmy Struther as a scapegoat, said, 'Look, we both know who was behind this so-called announcement. I'm really sorry it had to happen and it's all my fault. Nell had nothing to do with any of this.'

'Tell the Press.' Ben pointed a shaky finger towards the crumpled paper in his lap. 'Make them retract.'

Easier said than done, thought Marcus, particularly when you had spoken in person to the columnist himself.

'I could.' He nodded and looked thoughtful. 'But in my experience that just rouses their curiosity. The Press love a reaction, I'm afraid. Far better to say nothing and let the story die down of its own accord. The less you give them, the sooner they'll lose interest.' Like Nell, Marcus was finding it increasingly easy to lie. 'And since there isn't going to be anything *to* give them,' he concluded, 'it'll be forgotten by the end of the week.'

Ben seemed reassured. For the first time, his mouth twisted into a half-smile.

'Maybe you're right. OK, we'll leave it. Now tell me what you make of this fortune-telling business of hers . . . load of old cobblers or what?'

Just for a second, Marcus caught a flash of the old Ben.

'I couldn't agree more.' He broke into a grin. 'An absolute load of cobblers. What a relief to know someone else thinks so too.'

Chapter 44

Constance wasn't only a pain in the neck, Jemima decided. She was a scrawny vulture, beady-eyed and intent on seizing her prey.

Practically moving into the castle and making the most outrageous passes at Marcus hadn't only irritated Marcus. Jemima, on edge anyway because Timmy was still giving her the run-around, couldn't abide Constance's foghorn voice and nauseatingly playful manner. It would serve her right if this opera bash of hers was an out and out major-league disaster. What would really be fun, Jemima had confided to Kiki, would be a torrential thunderstorm on the night, hailstones the size of golf balls, the caterers serving up salmonella-infested food and the opera stars going out on strike.

So far, however, and completely bloody unfairly as far as Jemima was concerned, the evening was going like a dream.

'It looks like heaven,' sighed Kiki, leaning out of Jemima's south tower bedroom window and gazing down at the floodlit outer courtyard below. There was no doubt about it; crumbling battlements and centuries-old, ivy-strewn walls provided an unbeatable backdrop. The July night air, undisturbed by so much as a breath of wind and deliciously warm, lent an almost Mediterranean feel to the occasion. It meant, too, that maximum flesh could be exposed without fear of goosebumps. The men, in black ties, looked so much more handsome than in everyday life and the women, in multicoloured strapless gowns, dazzled in the semi-darkness like jewels.

Even Kiki, who had been everywhere and done everything, was impressed. Stubbing out her half-smoked cigarette, turning to Jemima sprawled on her stomach across the bed, she heaved an irritated sigh.

'Come on, if he didn't answer two minutes ago he's hardly likely to answer now.'

But Jemima carried on punching out the number anyway. Timmy had promised he'd be here and she couldn't believe he simply wasn't going to turn up. She would never have stayed down here for this crappy opera thing if he hadn't sounded so keen on it himself.

By ten o'clock, the event was well under way and continuing to run like clockwork. Everyone was saying how marvellous it was; how magical the music, how stupendous the food, how inspired the medieval setting. Even the champagne was excellent, in terms of quality several notches above the kind of thing they had grown used to drinking at charity galas of this type.

Jemima, her stomach wrapped up in a half-fearful, half-furious knot because Timmy hadn't turned up in the end after all, was bored rigid by the stupid music. As far as she was concerned, opera was the pits. How people could rave about the genius of the Spanish tenor currently bellowing out some gloomy-sounding number when he wasn't even doing it in English was beyond her. How the orchestra knew which bit of the music he was up to, furthermore, was one of the great mysteries of the world. They couldn't all be fluent in French or Italian or whatever language it was being sung in.

'I think maybe this kind of music is not your cup of coffee,' murmured a voice in Jemima's ear. It was an extremely sexy male voice, Italian-accented but not too off-puttingly hard to understand. Jemima had nothing against Italians as long as they spoke English.

'No, tea. I mean tea,' the owner of the voice corrected himself as she turned to look at him. 'I make a mistake. Many apologies. Always I get it wrong, this tea. Now you will think me stupid.'

Hazily, Jemima shook her head. She was having trouble thinking anything at all, apart from the fact that this Italian stranger looked even better than he sounded. At a guess, he was a year or two older than herself. And extraordinarily handsome, with those luminous dark eyes and that amazing bone structure. Tall, deeply tanned and with his dinner jacket slung casually over his shoulder, he leaned against the gnarled trunk of the mulberry tree, almost-but-not-quite smiling at her as he nodded towards the stage.

'Was I right, you have heard enough for the minute?'

When Jemima nodded back, still unable to speak, he smiled once more before diffidently offering her his arm.

'I hope not to be impolite, but would you enjoy a walk with me? I introduce myself . . . I am Pierangelo di Cappelini, Conte d'Atene . . . but to whisper is hard, and the others here prefer to listen to the music. If we move away we can talk more . . . happily. Is this, you think, a good idea?'

'A very good idea.' Jemima, relieved to find she could still speak, and charmed by the tentative way he waited for her to say yes before taking her arm in his, caught her breath as the first physical contact was made. Pierangelo, what a heavenly name. What a heavenly body too, long-limbed, elegant and athletic looking. That was one thing about the Italians, they certainly knew how to wear clothes. You could tell he had class just by looking at him.

Unable to resist showing him off to Kiki, who had been so vile about Timmy earlier, Jemima made sure they passed her on the way. Kiki, looking like a giant meringue in a cream-and-white lace-encrusted number by Versace, was standing next to Marcus at the edge of the floodlit lawn.

'Pierangelo di Cappelini, Conte d'Atene.' Proudly, Jemima introduced him to them both.

'Ah, we met in Deauville a couple of years ago.' Marcus nodded, smiling in recognition. To Jemima he added, 'I was at university with his elder brother, Giorgio. Giorgio once lost fifty grand in one night at the casino in Monte Carlo. On the roulette table. Completely mad.'

Pierangelo responded with a good-natured shrug. 'Is only money. Not that I gamble myself. I prefer to invest in property than chance my luck in casinos. If you are ever visiting Italy,' he urged Marcus, 'you must, of course, stay with us. The *palazzo* I acquire last year is now renovated. If I may boast a moment, it is superb . . .'

Kiki was gazing as if mesmerized at Pierangelo's chiselled, aristocratic profile. When he turned to speak to Marcus once more she signalled frantically at Jemima, mouthing: 'He's the one.'

Puzzled, Jemima mouthed back: 'One what?'

'You remember.' Kiki leaned closer. This was too complicated to lip-read. 'It's what Nell talked about,' she murmured excitedly. 'Tall, dark, foreign . . . his name even begins with a P, just like she said. Jem, this is *it* . . .'

A strange, unfurling sensation spread through the pit of Jemima's stomach as the implication of what Kiki was saying sank in. Having sneered at Nell's so-called predictions – and at Kiki for being stupid enough to believe in them – the realization that what Kiki was now saying to her might be true after all was positively creepy.

Oh God, thought Jemima, racking her brains in desperation. What else did Nell say? Damn, I should have written it down . . .

It was turning into one of those magical nights.

The sky was alive with stars. The heady scent of honeysuckle hung in the superheated night air. Crickets chirped under cover of darkness and in the dim distance the acclaimed Spanish tenor, sweeping the orchestra and enraptured audience along with him, approached the triumphant climax to the show.

In the secluded walled garden, in the summer house, Jemima sat with her bare feet resting across Pierangelo di Cappelini, Conte d'Atene's lap. Her satin shoes lay upturned on the bleached wooden floorboards next to his discarded jacket. An empty bottle of Taittinger rested on its side.

'I should stop.' Pierangelo, idly stroking the soles of her feet, gave her a reproachful smile. 'I talk too much of myself, telling you my hopes and dreams. You must be more bored by me than by the opera. You should tell me to shut up.'

His accent was mesmerizing. Jemima could have listened to him all night. He was so gentle, so sensual, she thought dreamily. He had such charm.

'I'm not bored.' She trembled as his warm hands moved to her ankles, massaging slowly and moving subtly upwards. She was dying to be kissed. At this rate it would be another three hours before he even reached her kneecaps.

'I'm glad.' Pierangelo gave her big toe a playful pinch. When he smiled, an irresistible dimple appeared from nowhere. 'I want to tell you everything about me, as I wish to know everything about you. This is a special night for me, I feel.' He hesitated, pleating the honey-coloured satin of Jemima's frock between slender, agile fingers. 'I hope you feel something special too.'

In the distance the tenor's voice soared. For the first time in her life Jemima realized how stunningly beautiful the music actually was, and in that moment she knew this particular piece would always remind her of tonight.

'I do.' She nodded, closing her eyes for a moment as the music dipped and soared again. 'What are they playing, do you know?'

'Puccini.' The way Pierangelo pronounced the name, in a seductive murmur, was enough to turn Jemima's legs to jelly. '*Madam Butterfly*. You like?'

Jemima's eyes filled with tears of joy. Now there really couldn't be any doubt at all. Nell had talked about butterflies. She had *known* they would be significant.

'Oh . . .'

Concerned, he touched her arm.

'You are upset? What is it?'

'No, not upset.' Jemima smiled through her tears. 'Happy. And I can't tell you why; it would sound too extraordinary for words.'

A moment later she jumped as a massive explosion heralded the beginning of the firework display. Within seconds the sky was filled with brilliant light, each gigantic chrysanthemum a burst of pure colour accompanied by a roar of appreciation from the delighted crowd.

'I think this is a night for extraordinary things to happen,' Pierangelo whispered. He drew her towards him until their faces were almost touching and she could feel his warm breath on her cheek. 'Look at you, with your golden hair and perfect skin. You are a goddess. May I kiss you, Jemima? Is it permitted, to kiss a goddess?'

It was more than permitted. As far as Jemima was concerned it was long overdue. She moved a fraction of an inch closer, remembering just in time not to pucker her lips. Timmy had once said she snogged like a sink plunger; she didn't want to blow her chances now.

But Pierangelo, skilled Latin lover that he was, appeared to have other ideas. Closing her eyes and shuddering with helpless longing, Jemima surrendered to sheer pleasure as his warm mouth and warmer tongue explored the base of her throat. As his hand had earlier moved oh-so-slowly up her leg, so his lips now began a teasing, lingering journey along her neck, on their way to her own eager mouth.

'Blimey, you're a right cosy armful and no mistake,' murmured a strange voice in Jemima's ear. ' 'ow d'ya fancy a roll in the 'ay, m'lady, reckon you could go for a bit o' that, do ya?'

Jemima sprang backwards like an electrocuted cat. Going hot and cold all over, so stunned she could barely think straight, she panted for breath.

'*What?*'

'Oh dear.' Struggling to keep a straight face, he shook his head in sorrowful fashion. 'Don't say you've gone off me so soon, just because I don't really talk like a Cornetto salesman.' He broke into a dazzling grin. 'Come on now, don't be cross. I may not be titled and I may not be rich but I'm still a nice person underneath.'

'You *bastard*.' Jemima felt almost faint with disgust. She was confused, too. The sexy, refined Italian accent had gone, and now so had the repulsive yokel's burr which had so brutally broken the spell. This impostor, whoever he was, spoke without any discernible accent at all, neither upper nor lower. Just sort of . . . middling.

Which was unhelpful, since it gave Jemima no clues at all. But he had lied to her, deliberately made a fool of her, so she hissed 'Bastard' again, took a wild swing and slapped his handsome, lying face as hard as she knew how. Then she slapped the other side of his face harder still.

'Ouch,' said Derry, but it was hardly the first time in his life he had found himself on the receiving end of a stinging slap from a distraught female. He'd had heaps of practice.

'I'll have you arrested for this,' shouted Jemima, so angry she didn't even know she was crying. It was like that horrid common gamekeeper in *Lady Chatterley's Lover* . . . ugh.

'You'll be put away, you . . . you *animal*. And you may as well tell me now who you are before I call the police because they'll find out anyway—'

'Calm down.' Derry waved his hands in a placatory manner. With undisguised amusement he said, 'I'm Nell's brother. Derry O'Driscoll. A bit common, I'm afraid. Not very posh. But I meant what I said earlier,' he added kindly. 'I wasn't lying when I said you were beautiful. And your skin is definitely perfect.'

Nell's brother. Nothing but a village boy, and a filthy gypsy at that. Through her tears, Jemima lunged at him again. This time Derry effortlessly fended her off.

'Look, I'm sorry.' He tried to look sorry. 'But think of it this way; in years to come you'll be able to look back and laugh at tonight. It is quite funny, you know, when you stop to think about it.'

Jemima didn't think it funny at all, but then she was barely listening.

'Marcus,' she seethed, her teeth clenching together at the hideous realization that he too must have been involved in the deception. 'Marcus was in on this! He deliberately lied about knowing you. How could he have stood by and let it happen?'

'Stood by?' Derry O'Driscoll's eyebrows shot up. Earnestly he shook his head. 'Oh no, you've got it all wrong. You see, it was Marcus's idea.'

Chapter 45

Alistair Munro, just out of the shower following a particularly long and tedious evening surgery, answered the front door in a frayed towelling dressing-gown that had once been pale yellow but had acquired an unflattering pink tinge in the wash. It wasn't until he pulled the door open, at the same time rubbing his wet hair with a sage-green towel, that he realized the weather had finally changed. Weeks of unbroken sunshine had come to an end. The skies were charcoal grey and rain bucketed noisily down, battering the poor parched garden like machine-gun fire.

Rachel stood like a drowned rat on the doorstep, her red hair plastered around her white face. Her funereal black clothes, hanging limply from her hunched shoulders, looked as dejected as she did.

'I've come to see Clemency.'

'She isn't here.' Alistair frowned. 'Didn't she tell you? That new boyfriend of hers, Martin, has taken her to meet his parents. I think they're going out to dinner in Sherringham. She told me not to expect her home before eleven.'

Clemency hadn't even mentioned going out, let alone being introduced to Martin's parents.

For Rachel, it was the last straw. Tears sprang up from nowhere. Before she could stop herself, she was sobbing noisily on the doorstep. Her nose began to stream in sympathy. No handkerchief meant she had to wipe it on her sleeve.

One good thing, though, about Clemency's dad being a doctor was the way he was neither alarmed nor disgusted by the spectacle.

'Oh dear, come along.' Matter-of-factly, Alistair took her arm and drew her inside. 'You can't go home in this state. I think you'd better tell me what the problem is. Look, why don't you stick the kettle on and make some tea while I get dressed?' He smiled slightly. 'I listen better with clothes on.'

As far as Rachel was concerned, her life was hopelessly out of control. First she had lost her father, who might still be living here in Kilburton but who wasn't where she wanted him to be, at home with her and her mother. Instead, he was acting young and shacked up with Vanessa, who went on about sex all the time, which made Rachel feel sick.

Then she had lost Hetty, who had changed out of all recognition and pinched from under her nose the only boy she'd ever truly fancied in her life.

Derry, she'd lost Derry because he preferred her mother.

And now, clearly, she was losing Clemency too.

It isn't fair, Rachel thought miserably. I never even wanted her as a friend when she first turned up. She *forced* herself on me. She can't change her mind just like that and swan off with spotty Martin.

'Everything's going wrong,' she hiccuped, wiping her eyes on the remains of the soggy tissue she had been shredding between her fingers. 'It's all my fault. I can't get anything right, *ever*.'

'Nobody gets it right all the time.' Lighting a cigarette, Alistair took the first pleasurable drag of the evening. 'Saying that,' he added, 'I'm not sure what you think you've done wrong. You certainly aren't to blame for your parents' divorce.'

'I'm too fat,' Rachel blurted out. 'People didn't like me because I was too big. I tried dieting but that didn't work, so I decided to get anorexia.' She hung her head, hiding her white face from his gaze. 'I knew that if I was anorexic people would fuss over me, look after me, *help* me . . . But I've tried and I can't even do that. I can't even have anorexia properly,' Rachel mourned, her voice desolate. 'You see? That's how much of a failure I really am.'

'. . . still, I imagine it did her some good to get it out of her system.'

Alistair had taken the decision to phone Hetty and let her know – in no uncertain terms – what kind of a mess her daughter was in. Since Rachel wasn't registered with the Kilburton practice he felt justified in doing so.

'I can't b-believe this,' stammered Hetty. She sounded dazed. With a stab of irritation, Alistair wondered if Derry was there with her. His own voice sharpened.

'Believe it, it's true. I don't know if you realize how fortunate you are, but your daughter has had an extremely lucky escape. Anorexia nervosa is no laughing matter. If it takes a grip it can be fatal.'

The fact that Hetty wasn't his patient either entitled him to be brutal. Her gasp of horror told Alistair he'd hit home.

'But . . . but this is terrible! I'll speak to Rachel . . . I had absolutely no idea.' Then Hetty's voice changed. Though still shaken, she spoke with growing suspicion. 'You sound as if you're blaming me. Are you? Is this *my* fault?'

'Look, I'm divorced too.' Alistair's tone of voice was rigid with disapproval. 'I know it isn't easy, but I think you should take a good look at yourself. This . . . relationship with the O'Driscoll boy. I mean, really. It's hardly the most sensible thing you've ever done, is it? Has it even occurred to you how Rachel feels about this? Have you any idea how deeply affected young teenagers can be by the actions of irresponsible parents?'

Hetty, stunned by the attack, said, '*What?*'

'I don't suppose you even noticed. Your daughter has a tearing crush on your boyfriend.' Alistair placed the emphasis deliberately on the word 'boy'. Coldly he added, 'No wonder she's confused.'

She isn't the only one, thought Hetty.

Not even giving herself time to think things through, desperate not to waste another moment, Hetty raced upstairs and hammered on the bathroom door.

'I'm in the bath.'

'Quick, open the door.'

'Why?' Rachel sounded outraged by the intrusion. Her bath-times were sacrosanct. 'Use the downstairs loo if you're that desperate.'

'Either you open this door or I break it down,' Hetty shouted, startling even herself. 'Right, I'll count to six. One, two . . .'

The sound of much splashing ensued. A moment later, swathed from neck to knees in a bath towel, Rachel unlocked the door.

'Why six?'

Hetty looked bemused. 'What?'

'You either count to three, five or ten. Or a hundred for hide and seek.' Rachel shook her wet head. 'Never six. Six is completely stupid.'

'Oh well, so am I. Maybe that's why I chose it.' Nodding towards the foaming bath, Hetty said, 'I just wanted a chat. You can get back in.'

Rachel hesitated, then shook her head again. 'No, it's OK.'

'Please.' Hetty couldn't bear it; her beloved only daughter was ashamed to reveal her body to her own mother. Quickly, still not giving herself time to think, she began pulling off her own clothes. Up and over her head went the Wedgwood-blue cotton top. Down came the white drawstring trousers.

'Mum? Are you all right?'

Hetty's bra and pants landed on top of the other things. Nobly taking the tap end, she lowered herself into the bath and gave Rachel an encouraging nod.

'Now you can get back in too.'

'What, both of us together?' Rachel looked appalled. 'In the same *bath*?'

'When you were a little girl, sharing a bath was a huge treat.' Hetty smiled slightly at the memory. She was trying hard not to cry. 'The thing is, you still are my little girl. I love you so much, darling. More than I've loved anyone else or ever *will* love anyone else. Come on now, we need to talk. Climb in.'

Eventually, Rachel did so. It was a big bath, with plenty of room for the two of them. Mountains of Badedas bubbles at least meant their naked bodies weren't on full view.

'That was Alistair Munro on the phone,' said Hetty.

'Huh. I guessed that much.'

'Sweetheart, we definitely have some talking to do.'

'Guessed that much, too.' Unable to meet her mother's gaze, Rachel swirled a drift of foam up against the side of the bath. In a low voice she said, 'He shouldn't have told you. It was private. It's OK, anyway, I'm not going to diet any more.'

'Good.' Wondering if she could possibly trust her, because that was what those teenage anorexics always seemed to be promising in TV documentaries, Hetty said cautiously, 'It might not be that easy, though. Maybe we should see an expert . . . it may help . . .'

'Mum, it's OK.' With a sigh, Rachel waved the suggestion away. 'Like I told Clemency's dad, I tried to be anorexic and I couldn't do it. I've decided, anyway, that it's all a waste of time. Why should I slog my guts out trying to lose weight and make people like me? It doesn't bloody work,' she declared crossly. 'They still prefer fat people. Look at Clemency, she's much bigger than me yet *everyone* likes her. And it's the same with—'

Only the abrupt halt gave it away. Hetty, so amazed she almost laughed aloud, raised her eyebrows and pointed to her own chest.

'Me? Were you really going to say *me*? Oh Rachel, what an extraordinary idea . . .'

'Why?' Rachel looked defensive. 'It's true. You are fat . . . well, fattish. It doesn't seem to bother some men though, does it? Like Derry O'Driscoll . . .'

Hot water lapped around Hetty's shoulders. Badedas bubbles slid slowly down into the valley of her cleavage.

'This is something else we have to talk about.'

'It's OK.' Rachel spoke rapidly, the colour rising in her cheeks. 'I already know.'

Hetty shook her head. 'You mean you know I've been seeing someone on the quiet. Sweetheart, it isn't Derry. I'm twenty years too old for Derry!'

'He said he loved you,' Rachel mumbled defiantly. 'He came into my room by mistake one night and said he loved you.'

'It was just some kind of silly crush.' Hetty couldn't help smiling at the extraordinary memory of that evening. 'You mean the night he drank two bottles of Scotch? Well, it was flattering but it would have been more flattering if he could have remembered a single word of it the next morning.'

Rachel heaved an inward sigh of relief. The fact that Derry hadn't seemed to know where Hetty's bedroom was had been puzzling her for weeks.

'So who is it?' Curiosity compelled her to ask, but the fact that they were sharing a bath made it that much easier to do so. She couldn't for the life of her imagine who it might be, either.

'Who was it.' Hetty, looking oddly embarrassed, swished her toes around in the water. 'Past tense. I'm not seeing him any more.'

'If you don't tell me soon, I'll think it's the vicar.' For the first time, Rachel's mouth turned up at the corners. 'Or else Abel Trippick.'

'Not quite.' Hetty giggled.

'But he is married, right?'

'Well, he was.' This time, even more intriguingly, Hetty went bright pink. 'To me, actually.'

'You mean . . .?' For a moment Rachel was confused. '*Daddy*? You've been seeing *Daddy*?'

It sounded ludicrous. Still blushing, Hetty nodded.

'But that's fantastic!' Rachel sat bolt upright. Water slopped over the side of the bath. 'That is so *brilliant*.'

'We aren't getting back together,' Hetty put in hurriedly, afraid she had raised her daughter's hopes.

'It's OK, I know you won't get back together.' Rachel didn't care. That wasn't what was most important right now. Her eyes bright, she said, 'Go on.'

'I didn't do it because I loved him either.' If she was going to be honest, she may as well go the whole hog. Hetty looked shamefaced. 'I did it out of spite, because I was so sick of bloody Vanessa.'

Overjoyed, Rachel let out a whoop of delight. Clumsily leaning forward in the bath she threw her arms around her mother.

'You mean Vanessa's spent the last six months swanning round, promoting her stupid book, running you down and telling everyone how happy Dad is now he's with her instead of you . . . and all this time you two have been secretly seeing each other?'

'Um, well . . . yes. Aargh, don't drown me . . .'

Her mother's low self-esteem and general air of helplessness when Tony had walked out had at the time filled Rachel with impotent rage. It had seemed almost as if Hetty had hung a placard round her neck saying 'It's OK, I deserved it'. Now, hugging her mother tighter still and resting her cheek against Hetty's wet shoulder, Rachel said joyfully, 'This is so perfect.'

Then, leaning back, she gazed at her mother with new respect and more love than she'd even known she possessed.

'That's that little misunderstanding sorted out then.' Hetty grinned and looked relieved.

'One more question.' It was weird; for the first time in her life Rachel felt she could ask her mother anything. 'Just out of interest, why did you stop seeing Dad?'

Hetty's eyes sparkled. 'Oh dear, don't laugh. I felt sorry for Vanessa.'

Chapter 46

Nell O'Driscoll, having returned from her timely jaunt abroad, was back at work, but Vanessa had made sure her appointment was with Marcus Kilburton. Nell made her uneasy and her close friendship with Hetty was another good reason, Vanessa felt, to steer clear. She could handle Hetty, but Nell was in an altogether different league. Vanessa had often had the uncomfortable feeling that Nell was inwardly laughing at her.

Besides, what hot-blooded female wouldn't prefer to discuss business with the Earl of Kilburton himself? Marcus really was divine, Vanessa thought, admiring the way that stray lock of sun-bleached, gold-blond hair fell across his tanned forehead. And what about the seductive slant of those amazing, thickly lashed green eyes? If the riveting gossip concerning Nell and him turned out to be true . . . well, one could hardly blame Nell for grabbing the opportunity. It was just a shame, she decided with a twinge of regret, he couldn't have chosen someone with a bit more class . . . someone more accustomed to being in the public eye . . . someone, perhaps, whose bestselling novels sold in their multi-millions in twenty-seven different languages around the world . . .

But there it was; he hadn't. Doesn't know what he's missing, Vanessa thought huffily. She pouted and licked her lips as Marcus, finishing his calculations, glanced up at her.

'Right. This is my estimate.' With his pen, he indicated the figure at the bottom of the page. 'For a wedding reception with three hundred guests. That's all-inclusive.'

Goodness. For a second, even Vanessa blanched. But the castle was making a spectacular name for itself nowadays; she had known it wouldn't be cheap.

'Sounds fine.' Tapping scarlet fingernails against the clutch bag on her lap, she said casually, 'Ten per cent discount, maybe? In view of the tremendous publicity it would bring you . . . ?'

'Sorry.' Unfazed, Marcus shrugged and smiled. 'You see, once we start discounting, everyone will expect it.'

'Fine, fine.' Vanessa wished she hadn't said anything now. Hurriedly, she rose to her feet. 'Well, Tony and I shall discuss this and reach a decision within the week. We'll be in touch.'

Marcus shook her hand. Through the open window filtered the sounds of children playing outside.

'And thank you for sparing the time to see me when you're so busy.' Daringly, Vanessa added, 'You must be glad to have Nell back.'

'Of course.' His mouth twitching, Marcus showed her to the door. 'She's a great help, particularly when it comes to dealing with difficult customers. Can you find your own way back out?'

Now that she was here, Vanessa decided she may as well stay for lunch. Sadly, despite lingering over an excellent chicken and walnut salad followed by two black coffees at a table right at the centre of the busy restaurant, nobody asked for her autograph or even seemed to recognize her.

Hetty didn't appear to be working today either, which was a shame. Tony had become decidedly twitchy at the prospect of telling her about the wedding and Vanessa had decided it would be far simpler to inform Hetty herself.

At that moment, brightening, she became aware of a couple three tables away, watching her and leaning sideways in order to whisper earnestly in each other's ears.

Vanessa's back straightened; her diamonds flashed. She adored the attention.

Then, as the couple rose to leave, the woman raised her voice. 'I'm sure it's that one from *EastEnders*. You know, common as muck and done up like a dog's dinner. She's got to be an actress, Malcolm – I mean, who else would wear that much make-up during the day?'

'. . . and everything's so much better now. Rachel's a different person. I really think she's going to be fine. The only bad news is that I have Clemency's smug, moralizing, holier-than-thou father to thank for it all. Honestly, it makes me shudder to think poor darling Rachel was going through such hell and I hadn't even realized . . .'

Hetty, who was working the afternoon shift, had bumped into Nell in the courtyard and steered her into the cloakroom for a quick de-briefing. Since she wasn't due in the restaurant for another ten minutes and they had the cloakroom to themselves, she perched on the edge of the marbled vanity unit, rummaged in her bag and dug out a lipstick and comb.

'Well, you know now. And I think you've handled it brilliantly,' said Nell. Grinning, she added, 'Nearly as well as you handled Tony. Is he still pestering you or did the message finally get through?'

Hetty looked shamefaced. Meeting Nell's gaze in the mirror, she pursed her mouth and ran the nearly used-up lipstick round in a quick circle. 'I was rotten. He rang again last night and I made Rachel answer it. She told him to get his act together and stop cheating on poor Vanessa . . . oh, you should have heard her! Do you think this lipstick suits me or should I go for something more orangey?'

'I hope you also let him know that despite all the extra practice with Vanessa, self-styled sex goddess, he's still a lousy lay! No, the pink's fine. Damn, and I must get back.' Regretfully Nell glanced at her watch. 'Urgent meeting with some rock promoter. Fingers crossed, Tom Jones may be doing a concert here. Hetty, are you wearing Obsession?'

Hetty shook her head. Nell, eyebrows raised, pointed to the last toilet cubicle on the left, from which no sound had emanated since their arrival. Upon closer inspection, however, the door was definitely locked and not just pushed to.

On the other side of the locked door, Vanessa shrank away as high heels clicked across the stone floor. She winced as the rat-tat-tat of authoritative knuckles sounded against the wooden door.

'Hello?' Nell's voice was brisk. 'Can you hear me? Is there someone in there?'

Vanessa closed her eyes and prayed they would just go away.

'Oh help,' Hetty wailed, 'what if someone's died in there?'

'Hang on.' Nell sounded less alarmed. 'It may be kids

playing tricks, locking the door from the inside then climbing out over the top. Although I'm sure I can smell Obsession. Come on, I'd better take a look. Give me a leg up.'

But the door was already opening to reveal – horror of horrors -- Vanessa. With a gulp, Hetty wondered whether she was going to be screeched at or get her face slapped.

But Vanessa wasn't yelling, she was trembling all over.

After a long and hideous silence Nell said, 'Oops.'

'Oh Vanessa, I'm so sorry,' Hetty gasped, her eyes like saucers. 'I didn't mean it, we were just messing around . . . I mean, it isn't true . . . nothing happened.'

'Don't be silly,' chided Nell. Resting her hand beneath Vanessa's elbow she guided her towards a cushioned rattan chair. 'Of course it's true, she's just heard us saying so. You'd better sit down, you look wobbly.'

Vanessa sat like a marionette, with her knees together and her feet splayed. Finally, jerkily she said, 'So how long has it been going on? Weeks? Months?'

'Months? No!' Mortified, Hetty shook her head. 'Not even weeks. Just once or twice, you know, and almost by accident . . . oh no, *definitely* not months!'

'Yes.' Nell interrupted quietly but with great firmness. 'Months. But it is all over. He's all yours from now on. Thanks to Hetty, you've got him back.'

The immediate effect of the shattering discovery may have been to knock the stuffing out of Vanessa but by the time Tony arrived home from work at seven-thirty, shock had given way to outrage.

Tony's own first impression upon realizing that no evening meal had been prepared was to think hooray, instead of some tedious, calorie-counted salad they were going out somewhere smart for dinner.

He was shrugging off his grey suit jacket when Vanessa appeared at the top of the stairs. He only just managed to duck in time as a Georgian silver photograph frame hurtled past his left ear.

'You cheating bastard!' Vanessa grabbed a handy candlestick and flung it wildly, like a boomerang, down the stairs.

'What? What?'

'You see? Even now you're lying! I *know*, Tony . . . I know you've been carrying on with Hetty behind my back. How *could* you?' Tears of rage began to slide down her carefully powdered cheeks as she flew down the stairs at him. Her clenched fists pummelled his chest. Tony tried not to wince, but some of those rings of hers were sharp.

'Ouch! Who told you?'

'She did! Hetty and that bloody friend of hers, Nell. For God's sake, whatever possessed you to do it, with her of all people? Have you any idea how stupid this is going to make me look if it ever gets out? And I wouldn't put it past Nell O'Driscoll to leak it to the Press,' Vanessa added hysterically. 'I mean, what have I ever done to her? Nothing, that's what, but she still seems to have it in for me. Can you imagine the effect something like this could have on my *career*?'

Tony's jaw tightened. Grabbing Vanessa's flailing fists he pushed them away from his chest. Icily he said, 'Is that what's bothering you, the threat of bad publicity?'

'Ow.' Vanessa made a great show of rubbing her wrists. 'It's humiliating, Tony! Don't you *see* how humiliating this is? People are going to wonder what's wrong with me . . .'

She was starting to screech again. Tony shook her. 'And you aren't listening,' he said bitterly. 'I asked you if that was all you were bothered about, your precious public image. Don't you even care that our relationship could be over?'

'You stupid ignorant bastard, of course I care,' shrieked Vanessa, blond hair flying as she shook her head and took another wild swing at his ribcage. 'I overheard Nell and Hetty talking up at the castle, didn't I? I was there booking our wedding . . . it was supposed to be a wonderful surprise . . .'

'Ah.' Tony nodded. 'I see. And instead, you got a less-than-wonderful surprise of your own.'

'I love you,' Vanessa sobbed. Bright-pink lipstick smeared across her chin as she wiped her wet face with the satin sleeve of her white Arabella Pollen sweater. 'I want to marry you. I thought we were so happy, and all this time you've been screwing your fat ex-wife.'

He looked furious. 'That's uncalled for.'

'Well she is.' Misery had made Vanessa bitter. The fact that even now he seemed to be sticking up for Hetty was even more unbearable. 'Tell me why you had to go and bloody do it, Tony. For God's sake, I still don't understand why!'

'OK. Maybe because she is fat.'

'*What?*'

'Plump,' he corrected. 'Comfortably rounded, like me. Hetty was fun to go to bed with, if you really want to know. And we were comfortable together. I didn't have to perform to Olympic standards and remember to hold my stomach in at the same time.'

'You left her because you were bored with your marriage,' Vanessa wailed. 'I was *exciting*.'

Tony's patience snapped.

'Maybe too much excitement isn't all it's cracked up to be,' he retaliated with a cruel shrug. 'Maybe now I'm bored with that. Not to mention wholewheat spaghetti, fifty-seven varieties of designer lettuce and bloody mung beans.'

There was a long, dreadful silence.

Vanessa finally spoke.

'Don't leave me,' she whispered. Her eyes, bleak with fear, had lost all trace of anger. 'You can eat whatever you like. You don't need to hold your stomach in during sex, either . . . just *please* don't leave me.' As she buried her face against Tony's chest she let out a sob. 'I don't know what I'd do without you.'

Once the August Bank Holiday had been successfully navigated, Marcus packed his cases for a week in the States. This entailed endless plane-hopping from city to city in order to keep up with a gruelling schedule of guest appearances on TV and radio chat shows across the country, in order to publicize and promote the joys of Kilburton Castle to the great American public.

'This is going to be like two hundred hours in the dentist's chair,' he grumbled to Nell, whose bright idea it had been in the first place.

'You're British, you're titled and you sound like something out of *Brideshead Revisited*.' Nell kissed him and swooned.

'You're also better looking than Anthony Andrews and Jeremy Irons rolled together . . .'

'What a libellous idea.'

'. . . and your audience will fall in love with you! By next spring we'll be bracing ourselves, ready to be inundated by thousands of besotted Americans, most of them female, all desperate to meet in person that dishy earl they saw on TV last fall . . .'

Marcus grinned. 'I wish you were coming with me.'

'Someone has to stay and look after the shop. Don't worry,' Nell blithely assured him, 'any problems and I know I'll be able to rely on the lovely Hilda. Jemima isn't likely to come down this weekend, is she?'

She kept a straight face. Since the night of the opera, Jemima had remained firmly ensconced in London. As far as Nell was concerned, she just wished they could have dreamt up such an effective plan months ago.

'About as much likelihood as there is of her joining an Outward Bound course in Snowdonia.' Marcus checked his watch; he had to leave in five minutes. 'Now are you sure you're going to be OK?'

Nell shrugged. 'What can go wrong?' She looked innocent. 'Apart from the castle burning down, your plane being hijacked and me eloping with Ewan McGregor?'

'You keep on about this McGregor guy.' Marcus frowned. 'And I still don't know who he is.'

Chapter 47

Nell knew something was very wrong the moment she saw Oscar waiting for her at the entrance to Rowan House. He stood in the doorway, almost filling it with his vast bulk, his black face creased in concern.

Feeling sick, Nell climbed out of the car.

'What is it?'

'His chest, I'm afraid. He's in a pretty poor condition.'

Oscar stepped back to allow her through the door. With a sorrowful shake of his head he said, 'It started yesterday evening but he took a turn for the worse this afternoon. It looks as if we may have to transfer him to hospital.'

Ben's room, with the heavy curtains drawn, was in semi-darkness. When Nell moved towards the light switch, he croaked, 'Don't. Leave it.'

Ben didn't look well at all. In fact, Nell realized with a lurch of fear, he looked dreadful. The chest infection, which had escalated at such a rate because his natural defences were so weakened, had ravaged his thin body. His once-beautiful face was greyish white, the skin stretched like cling film across the prominent cheekbones, the bruised-looking eyelids so heavy he seemed barely able to keep his eyes open.

'Nell, do something. Bloody Oscar won't let me have my cigarettes.'

'You're too ill to smoke.' She squeezed his arm. 'Give your lungs a rest and you'll be better in no time.'

Ben coughed feebly, gasping for breath. Beads of perspiration appeared on his forehead and he closed his eyes.

'Oh, who cares. I'm bloody bored with waiting to get better. Fed up with it.' Wearily, he raised his hand and gestured around the room. 'It never bloody happens anyway. I'm still stuck here in this dump.'

Nell blinked hard, determined not to let him see her cry. She had never heard him like this before, so desperately depressed.

'You only feel like this because you're ill,' she began, but Ben shook his head. His dark curls, once so glossy, lay limply across the pillow.

'No, I'm just tired of it all. I'm never going to get out of here . . . we're never going to get married . . . I've had enough, Nell. Just about bloody enough.'

Nell phoned Hetty and – to Hetty's absolute horror – placed her in charge of Kilburton.

'Just take messages, tell everyone I'll ring them back,' she said briefly, before Hetty could fly into a complete panic. 'All the keys you need are in the left-hand kitchen drawer at The Pink House. Hilda Garnet will show you which is which.'

Trying to be brave, though the mere thought of having to cope with that nerve-racking fax machine was enough to send shudders through her, Hetty said, 'When will you be back?'

'When Ben's better. They're admitting him to the Radcliffe. I don't know,' Nell faltered. 'He's in a bad way. I can't leave him when he's like this.'

'OK. Well, you don't have to worry about us.' Hetty made an effort to sound brave. 'We'll be fine.'

Nell was so exhausted it took her a while, upon waking, to work out how long she had been there at Ben's bedside.

Forty-eight hours, she figured eventually, and forty-five of them without sleep. The nursing staff must have pulled the curtains around his bed and left the two of them in peace when she'd dozed off in the chair after lunch. Now, massaging her cricked neck and gazing foggily at her watch, she pulled herself upright. It came as a shock to realize Ben was lying on his side watching her.

'What?' Nell bent across the bed and took his hand. 'Sorry, I must have dozed off. Is there something you want?'

Ben's dark eyes were bright rather than cloudy. His mouth, curved up at the corners, seemed almost to be smiling. He looked better. With a rush of hope, Nell wondered if he was finally on the mend.

But Ben, his fingers tangled with hers on the crumpled bedspread, shook his head.

'Lots, but none of it's going to happen.' His voice, no more than a husky croak, was barely audible. 'I don't care. Soon be over now. Sorry, sweetheart.'

He lifted her hand, clumsily turning the ring on Nell's finger.

Swallowing, Nell said, 'Sorry about what?'

'Everything. Us not getting married. It's not that I don't love you, Nell. I'm just so tired of it all, so bloody *tired* . . .'

* * *

Ben died two and a half hours later. It was as if he had already made up his mind. His heart simply stopped beating and refused to be re-started. Behind the closed cubicle curtains, sitting with him whilst his soul departed to heaven, Nell wept all the hot, desperate tears she had forcibly forbidden herself to release during the last two terrible days.

Marcus, back from his USA trip, heard the news of Ben's death from Hetty and drove directly to The Pink House where Nell had spent the last few days closeted in virtual isolation.

'Look, of course it's tragic,' he said finally, shocked by the extent of her grief, 'but maybe in a way it's also a release. Ben all but said so himself, didn't he? He didn't *want* to spend the next forty or fifty years living half a life.'

Marcus's attempt to reassure her earned him a thunderous whack on the arm.

'You don't know,' Nell shouted, beside herself with rage. 'You didn't know him! And you're only saying that, anyway – as far as you're concerned he couldn't have timed it better. Ben was nothing to you but a damn nuisance,' she went on, her dark eyes glittering with accusation. 'I bet you're glad he's dead.'

It was partly true, of course, though he would have preferred to call it relieved rather than glad. Still, at least Marcus was able to admit that much to himself.

'When's the funeral?' he asked quietly. 'I'd like to go.'

'Well you bloody can't.' Nell wiped her eyes with the back of her hand. It was a continuing source of amazement to her that she was still able to carry on producing tears. 'You didn't even like him. You can't go.'

'You're being irrational.'

'Shut up.'

'Nell, listen to me.'

'No. Piss off.'

Marcus wondered how long it would take Nell to come to terms with the realization that her grief was compounded by guilt, and that she too was experiencing a tidal wave of wicked, shameful relief.

Chapter 48

'Nell, is that you?'

'Of course it is.' Nell smiled slightly. 'This is my phone, isn't it? Hi, Kiki.'

'Oh thank goodness,' Kiki sighed. 'You sound normal! I heard on the grapevine that you'd left the castle in a frightful state. Gossip is absolutely rife. How are you really? More to the point, *where* are you?'

It was October the fifteenth, a Thursday. Midday. Summer was over and Nell was lying in bed. Not her own bed, either, but the one she had occupied for the past month, ever since her abrupt departure from Kilburton.

'I'm fine,' she said, only semi-truthfully. 'And I'm staying in London for a while. Why, where are you?'

'Venice. Can't you hear the gondoliers wolf-whistling?' Kiki giggled, then seemed to remember why she had called. 'I'm glad you're in London, though. I rather hoped you'd be there. Now listen, talking of frightful states, I've just had Jemima on the phone, gibbering with rage and hell-bent on revenge. Naughty of me really, I suppose, I should have told her before now, but she's just found out Timmy Struther's getting married this afternoon. Nell, she isn't taking it at all well.'

'Hooray.'

'No, I mean it.' Kiki hesitated. 'She really is in a complete tizz; she's just told me she's planning to turn up at the church and throw a wobbly. Can you *imagine* it? She'll make a *complete* fool of herself . . .'

Leaning across the massive bed, Nell drew back one of the cobalt-blue damask curtains. Outside, rain pelted diagonally from a leaden sky. The poor battered chestnut trees at the far end of the garden were being cruelly stripped. As leaves whirled crazily past the double-glazed window, she let the curtain fall back and wriggled down beneath the duvet once more.

'No,' said Nell. 'Absolutely not. Even if it wasn't tipping down with rain.'

'Is it really?' Kiki was momentarily diverted. 'How ghastly, it's as sunny as anything here.' Then, trying to sound severe, she said, 'And you're changing the subject.'

'The answer's still no. I can't believe you're even asking me to get involved,' Nell protested. 'Why should I be bothered by what Jemima does in her spare time? She can rip off all her clothes and swim naked in the font, for all I care.'

'The thing is,' drawled Kiki, 'you aren't nearly as mean as you like to make out.'

'Oh yes I am.'

'Anyway, the wedding's being held at St Olaf's in Islington. Two-thirty kick-off.' On her sun-drenched veranda overlooking the Grand Canal, Kiki sipped coffee and smiled to herself. 'You'll recognize Jemima. She'll be the one not wearing the long white dress.'

'You hope,' said Nell.

* * *

The journey from Meg's house in Notting Hill, where Nell had been staying, to the imposing church in Islington took her longer than she had imagined. By the time Nell found somewhere to park, the ceremony was already under way.

The ushers at the door, doing bouncer-service in their morning coats, looked momentarily doubtful when, with a dazzling smile, she slipped past them. Luckily, her decidedly unweddingy black sweatshirt with holes in both elbows and the even more ancient jeans were hidden beneath one of Meg's floor-length trench coats.

Nell paused at the back of the church, gazing at a sea of glamorous hats and wondering which of them was being worn by Jemima. The musty, churchy smell was overlaid with the scent of the ornately arranged flowers with which even the pews had been decorated. The flowers, in turn, vied with a hundred different designer perfumes all battling to make themselves known. The effect was positively nostril-numbing.

And there, way up ahead of her, stood Timmy and his bride. The vicar, facing them, had just launched into 'Dearly beloved'. Nell shoved her icy hands deep into the pockets of the borrowed trench coat and began studying each row of the congregation in turn.

Moments later, incredibly, she heard a nervous, throat-clearing cough several pews away and recognized it. Nell stood on tiptoe and craned her neck past the gaggle of photographers waiting in the draughty doorway.

There was Jemima, fifteen or so feet away, gazing fixedly at the ceremony in progress ahead of them. Her blond hair was piled up beneath a smart, black, straw hat trimmed with silk poppies. Her shoulders were back, her spine rigid.

Nell silently cursed Kiki for phoning her and interrupting a perfectly good day in bed. OK, she was here. What the hell was she supposed to do now?

But Nell had been paying attention to Jemima and not the vicar. At that moment he intoned sombrely, '. . . does anybody here present know of any reason why this man and this woman should not be joined together in Holy Matrimony?'

A breathless silence ensued. In their sconces, the beeswax candles flickered. Nell realized with a dreadful sinking sensation what was about to happen.

As if in slow motion, Jemima rose to her feet.

Nell closed her eyes.

'Actually, I do.' Jemima's clear, high-pitched voice echoed up to the dusty, elevated rafters. 'He's a no-good, two-timing pig, physically incapable of being faithful to anyone, so this whole ceremony's pretty pointless. If you ask me, Timmy Struther should have his—'

The excitement in the air was palpable. Everyone had turned in their seats to gawp. Jemima, blurting the words out, ended with a muffled 'wwherrff mffhh' as Nell, moving like lightning in order to beat the riveted press, peeled off her trench coat, raced across the aisle and threw it over Jemima's outraged head.

Nell just had time to glimpse Timmy's appalled expression before bundling Jemima, still with her head covered, out past the frantically snapping photographers. They could take as many photographs as they liked but they wouldn't get Jemima's face.

Jemima didn't even know who was hijacking her until they reached the sanctuary of the car.

'Oh no, this is too much,' she wailed when Nell finally shovelled her, kicking and cursing, into the passenger seat and removed the coat. 'Don't tell me, bloody Kiki's behind this. Just as I was getting my own back.'

'Just as you were making a serious idiot of yourself.' Now that she'd got her, Nell hadn't the faintest idea what to do with her. 'Congratulations, by the way. It was a brave thing to do.'

Jemima was silent for several seconds. While Nell drove, she appeared to be considering her actions. Finally, sounding almost surprised, she said, 'I suppose it was. All I know is that I was hell-bent on wrecking the ceremony, ballsing it up for that bastard Timmy.'

Nell had noted at the time Jemima's use of the epithet 'pig' rather than bastard, because she had been in church. Still not knowing where they were going, she carried on retracing her earlier journey.

'Well, you did that.'

'Marcus will go wild when he hears about this.' Jemima bit a perfectly manicured thumb nail. 'At least there aren't any pictures of me. Oh God, do I have to actually thank you for chucking that coat over my head?'

'Don't worry,' Nell assured her, 'I won't hold my breath.' Smiling, she added, 'It was worth it, anyway, to see Timmy's face when you opened your mouth. I hate to say this, and please don't tell Marcus, but for a bizarre moment I actually admired you.'

They had reached Meg's house. Peering through the misted-up windscreen, Jemima looked deeply suspicious.

'Where on earth are we?'

'Notting Hill. This is where I've been staying.' Nell nodded at the Victorian terraced house with the scarlet front door. 'It belongs to a friend of mine. Don't worry, she's away this week.' Her mouth twitched once more at the thought of Meg, wide-eyed and slavering at the prospect of another delicious scoop. 'I wouldn't be inviting you in if she was here.'

'Charming,' sniffed Jemima.

'She's a journalist.'

'Oh.'

It took several hours and as many glasses of rather good red wine to relax Jemima and smooth the prickly manner to which Nell had grown so accustomed over the past months. Disrupting Timmy's wedding had been a spur-of-the-moment decision but it had hopefully exorcised the ghost of their ill-fated relationship and so done her some good.

'I still can't believe how he used me.' Fretfully, Jemima twiddled her wineglass by its stem and gazed into the flickering flames of Meg's Wonderfire. 'And he kept *on* using me . . . bloody hell, only last week he had me driving up to Northampton at two o'clock in the morning, just because he fancied a quickie. And this girl he's marrying – she's nothing! Her father, evidently, is a geography teacher and her mother's a nurse. The girl's pregnant, of course, which explains how the wedding came to be arranged in three weeks flat. Poor cow, she thinks she's struck gold. Just you wait, as soon as the honeymoon's over she won't see her precious husband for dust.'

Nell sat back and let her get the whole lot out of her system. Jemima carried on ranting and raving through a second bottle of wine, then announced, 'Ah well, once a rotter, always a rotter. Timmy had his chance and he blew it. He didn't deserve me anyway.'

Nell said, 'Good,' and nodded to show she meant it. She hadn't been lying, either, when she'd said she admired Jemima for having made her extremely public stand. It had taken a lot of guts, and it was all true, too, which made her doubly glad she hadn't stopped Jemima saying it. For the first time, Nell realized, she was close to actually *liking* Marcus's spoilt younger sister.

'OK, enough about me.' Timmy had been dealt with, taken care of. Emptying yet another glass, Jemima said briskly, 'Marcus has been a complete pain since you left, and none of us even knows why you did. What the bloody hell's going on?'

'Gosh.' Nell realized she was using a Hetty-word. Mildly, she said, 'Does that mean you've missed me?'

'I wouldn't go that far.' For a second, Jemima looked embarrassed. 'It's just . . . well, you do know, I suppose, who's taken your place.'

'You mean Constance? I know she's working there, helping Marcus out until the end of the season.' Nell raised her eyebrows. 'Or does "taking my place" involve more than just work?'

This time Jemima burst out laughing. 'Well, you can't say she hasn't tried! Poor Marcus is having a terrible time. He's probably being advanced upon at this very moment. Much longer and he's going to have to start beating her off with a stick.'

Constance, Nell mused, would probably regard it as an exotic form of foreplay. Following her own retreat to London, Marcus had been forced to find a temporary replacement and Constance had volunteered herself so forcefully he'd had little choice. She had managed to organize the opera gala, after all, and against the odds it had gone off without a hitch. Too late, Marcus had discovered that whilst the event itself had been a huge success, Constance had got her sums very wrong indeed. Each of the six charities set to benefit from the proceeds had received a cheque from Constance for twenty-five pounds and eighty pence.

'I needed some time away, to think things through,' Nell told Jemima. She wasn't going to elaborate. Jemima, who didn't understand so many things, would certainly not have understood about Ben.

'And you've been here all along.' Jemima gazed around at Meg's comfortable, cluttered home. 'I thought you'd probably be staying with relatives in some painted caravan somewhere.' She hesitated and twirled a strand of hair around her middle finger. Trying to sound ultra-casual she said, 'Speaking of relatives, how is your brother these days? Derry, isn't it?'

Nell had been wondering when that particular subject might crop up. If she was honest, the Derry thing was what had finally propelled her out of bed earlier and taken her along to the church. She might not have come up with the plan to teach Jemima a lesson but she had been more than happy to collaborate with it. And although Jemima *had* deserved it, that twinge of guilt had stubbornly remained.

'Derry's fine. It really was Marcus's idea, you know.'

'I know.' Jemima carried on twiddling her fine, blond hair. With a look of resignation she said, 'Marcus took great delight in telling me what a snobbish, bigoted, jumped-up little cow I was. He said I deserved to be humiliated and it was about time I learned to accept people for what they were. If he expects me to turn overnight into Mother Teresa,' she added crossly, 'he's got another bloody think coming.'

Intensely curious, Nell leaned forward to refill their glasses. They were going to have to eat something soon, before they both passed out on the floor.

'But did it make you think? Could you see the point Marcus was trying to make?'

'I'm starving,' Jemima announced abruptly. Her frantically twiddled-with hair stuck out at right angles from her head. 'Is there any food in this house or shall we find a restaurant?'

'*Did* you see it?' Nell persisted. 'The point of the exercise?'

Jemima, having risen to her feet, was making her way fairly unsteadily towards the kitchen.

'Of course I bloody did.' She said it with her head in the fridge, as if admitting it this way didn't count. 'I'm not completely thick, you know. And I *did* like him . . . Pierangelo . . . I mean, you know, Derry. I've just asked you how he is, haven't I?'

'He's very well.' Nell smiled. 'Actually, he liked you too.'

In the kitchen, Jemima flushed suddenly scarlet. Luckily her head was still hidden in the fridge.

'There's nothing to eat in here. We'll have to go out,' she declared when the awful redness had died down. Maybe over

409

dinner she could subtly pump Nell for more details of Derry O'Driscoll.

As Nell stood up, her head began to spin. 'Well, we can't drive, but there's a brilliant Caribbean restaurant just round the corner.'

Jemima peered at her watch. Incredibly, it was almost eight o'clock.

'I'm going to need to book into an hotel somewhere, too.'

'You can stay here,' offered Nell. Jemima really seemed to be making progress. If she could get this class fixation out of her system once and for all, she might actually end up human.

Jemima hesitated. She bit her lip. Finally, as if the decision had been momentous, she smiled and nodded.

'OK, thanks.'

'Good.'

'Just so long as you don't spread it around,' warned Jemima, 'that I spent the night at a house in Notting Hill.'

Chapter 49

When a long hard look at the finances of the Kilburton estate had brought it home to Marcus that in order to survive he needed to open the castle and grounds to the general public, he had aimed, with what his legal advisers had regarded as hopeless optimism, for 100,000 visitors a year.

The final figure at the end of their first season had been a staggering 165,000 visitors and that excluded the various special events such as October's hugely successful open-air rock concert in the park, with further concerts planned in the new year. And whilst the castle and grounds were closed to the public for the winter, hiring the facilities in a private capacity for wedding receptions, corporate entertaining, fashion and film shoots was on the increase. Barely had Kilburton recovered from the shock of playing host to a clutch of supermodels being photographed against the backdrop of the castle for Italian *Vogue*, than it had found itself inundated by an American film crew shooting scenes for a mega-budget movie.

For the villagers, the past year had definitely brought change into their lives. Grateful for their wholehearted support and the hard work everyone had put in to ensure the success of such an initially daunting project, Marcus had organized a party to be held seven days before Christmas. It was his way of thanking everyone and celebrating that success.

On the afternoon of the party, temperatures outside plummeted. At three o'clock, slowly at first then with gathering speed, snow began to fall. By dusk, the floodlit castle grounds were covered in a good two inches of snow. It was all very Christmas-cardy and picturesque but with seven hundred guests arriving from all over the country Marcus only hoped it wasn't planning to get out of hand. Seven hundred people, finding themselves unexpectedly snowed in, was no laughing matter.

At least the vast marquee was warm, thanks to the dozen powerful gas burners working overtime to blast superheated air at unsuspecting ankles. The castle could have held that number of guests at a pinch, but Marcus knew his army of domestic staff, who lovingly polished the ancient oak panels and dusted the precious, fraying Oudenaarde tapestries, would never have been able to relax and enjoy themselves at their own party for fear of spilled drinks and carelessly handled cigarettes. A marquee it had to be, and a rather smart one it was too. The floor was parquet. There were chandeliers. In the very centre of the marquee at its highest point, a gloriously decorated Christmas tree rose up, twenty-two feet tall.

The first of the villagers, beginning to trickle in at seven-thirty, gazed in wonder at the un-tentlike tent, in no way resembling the grubby, creaky, greyish contraption that went up on the village green each summer to house the fruit and vegetable show.

They were even more profoundly impressed when they reached the bar and realized they didn't have to pay for their drinks.

*　*　*

'I'm sorry, my lord, I know this isn't the best time to tell you, but I felt it only right to let you know as soon as possible.'

Hilda Garnet, in a bulky, steel-grey wool suit to match her hair, and with an alarmingly festive crimson and silver brooch pinned to her flat bosom, spoke firmly but with regret.

'Oh dear.' Behind his back, Marcus crossed his fingers. 'Not bad news, I hope?'

'My sister Henrietta lives in Tenerife. She's alone and in need of companionship.' Hilda took a deep breath. 'She has begged me to move in with her, my lord, and I haven't the heart to refuse. I'm afraid I have to hand in my notice, although I shall of course remain here until a suitable replacement can be found. This isn't my decision, you understand. It's Henrietta, she put such pressure on me . . .'

To Marcus's alarm, Hilda's eyes were beginning to glisten. Her grey, unplucked eyebrows creased with the effort of maintaining control. She had been with the family for almost thirty years.

'Of course I understand. Your sister needs you more than we do.' He smiled. 'You'll be a hard act to follow, Hilda, but somehow or other we'll manage. And think of it, retiring to Tenerife. You'll have the time of your life.'

'I'm not much of a one for sunbathing and sitting out by the pool. Oh dear.' Hilda sniffed and wiped her nose with an immaculately laundered lace handkerchief. 'I'm going to miss Kilburton so much.'

Clutching schooners of sweet sherry, Minnie Hardwick and Elsie Cutler nudged each other frantically in the ribs.

'Look at that, I don't believe it,' Minnie gasped.

'Hilda the Hatchet, crying,' Elsie marvelled. 'What d'you reckon then?'

'I reckon 'is lordship's just told 'er Nell O'Driscoll's comin' back.'

By nine o'clock the marquee was heaving. Villagers in their smart party outfits mingled with actors, musicians, photographers and members of the film crew who had spent the last month shooting in and around the castle. Nolan Ferguson, whose silver jewellery had sold so well this summer from his workshop in the old stable block, beamed from ear to ear as he danced with the most glamorous of the young actresses, a sweet girl who hadn't the heart to turn him down. Despite the snow outside, Nolan was wearing pea-green socks and leather sandals. As he flung his poor partner around the crowded dance floor, Hetty overheard him shouting, '. . . take raw spinach, for example, practically a meal in itself – *and* rumoured to be an aphrodisiac . . .'

Hetty smiled and decided it was just as well she didn't like spinach. As Nell had promised, she had met a lot of new men. It had, all in all, been an adventurous year. But since rebuffing dear Derry and returning not-so-dear Tony to his rightful owner, she had found herself landed back at square one. Not right back, since she had definitely gained in self-confidence, but still without a man.

If she'd known this dismal state of affairs was going to stretch itself out for quite so long, Hetty thought now, she would never have been so horrid to Alistair Munro. Although he had asked her out several times, she had snubbed him until

414

evidently he could take no more. Finally and quite sensibly, he had stopped.

And Hetty, too late, had found herself thinking, Damn . . .

At a table away from the dance floor, her view of it partially obscured by the huge Christmas tree, Vanessa's bright, plastered-on smile belied her own inwardly rising panic. As the music stopped, then started again, her stomach screwed itself into a tighter, even more inextricable knot. Tony was on to his third dance with the same woman, a drippy looking blonde. Her name, Vanessa knew, was Gudrun and she worked as a potter in one of the studio workshops. For her birthday last month, Tony had given her a three-foot-tall, beige, semi-glazed pot about as exciting as Gudrun herself. Vanessa had dutifully pretended to love it. And this, it seemed, was her bloody reward. Whilst she sat here alone, rattling ice-cubes around her empty glass, Tony flirted publicly with a washed-out girl wearing what looked like a jumble-sale floral-print dress with holes in it.

'Look at 'er over there,' hissed Elsie Cutler, as Vanessa gazed fixedly at the band playing up on the stage. 'Reckon Hetty Brewster's old man's givin' that 'un the runaround. See the mouth on 'er.'

And there was Hetty, Vanessa observed, dancing gaily past with a member of the film crew, one of the cameramen. Unlike Gudrun, she had to concede, Hetty looked quite good tonight in an off-the-shoulder black velvet dress that flared flatteringly over her generous hips. Despite what Hetty had said that terrible afternoon in the castle cloakroom four months ago, Vanessa still regarded her as a threat. She would never trust her again, just as she now knew she could never trust Tony.

But there were ways of dealing with situations, ways of minimizing the risks. Desperate now to hang on to her man, Vanessa knew she had to sell up and move out. As soon as Christmas was over she was putting The Old Schoolhouse on the market. There was too much temptation for Tony here in Kilburton. She would choose their next home with extreme care.

'Look at your mum,' Clemency said admiringly, 'dancing with that cameraman . . . Adam, isn't it? I say, lovely bum he's got.'

Rachel smiled slightly as Hetty and Adam danced past Tony and Gudrun. For a split second, she saw her parents' eyes meet.

'You think everyone's got a lovely bum.'

Clemency looked smug. 'James Harrington thinks you have. He told me at the club last Saturday. He said the rest of you wasn't bad either.'

Rachel tried, without much success, to look as if she received such compliments on a daily basis. Clemency was still seeing Martin, whom she had met at the church youth club in Sherringham, but she had dragged Rachel along with her several times now. James Harrington, sixteen years old and one of Martin's best friends, was thin and shy with rumpled dark hair, a discreet dental brace and gold-rimmed glasses. But at least he didn't have spots, and behind the glasses his eyes were dark and surprisingly sexy. Rachel had at first told herself she was imagining the way he looked at her. Now she knew she wasn't. James might not have the film-star looks and breathtaking charisma of Derry O'Driscoll but he was somehow more real. She could definitely go for him.

'You sly old thing,' Clemency crowed in delight. 'You fancy James and you never even told me! I know, we'll get Martin to fix you up with him for the disco on Tuesday . . . Charlotte Crewe reckons he's a brilliant kisser. She says that brace thing doesn't get in the way at all.'

Alistair Munro, trudging across the snow-covered lawns, approached the huge marquee from one direction just as Jemima and Kiki Ross-Armitage teetered in their high heels along the gravelled path leading from the castle itself. He paused at the entrance, watching the clouds of condensation puffing from their mouths as they hurried, heads bent, to escape the icy night air. When Kiki murmured something, Jemima laughed. Alistair dug his cold hands deep into the pockets of his overcoat and experienced a spasm of helpless regret.

For a second, having waited for them to catch up, he thought Jemima wasn't going to recognize him. At the last moment she looked up.

'Oh. Hello, Dr . . . Munro.'

She had remembered his name, just. He supposed he should be grateful for that much. Drily, he replied, 'Good evening, Lady . . . Jemima.'

She hesitated. 'Jolly cold, isn't it?'

'Jolly cold,' Kiki agreed, blowing on her hands and wondering why the doctor was just standing there gazing at Jemima like that.

Abel Trippick, for whom forty minutes of socializing was more than enough, whistled for his beloved dog Albert. It was nine-thirty and he was on his way home to bed.

'Brass monkey weather and no mistake,' he muttered as he squeezed past the trio blocking his way. Then, beneath the dark-blue hood of her cape, he recognized Jemima. 'Sorry, m'lady, but it is.'

'Hi,' murmured a voice in Kiki's ear twenty minutes later. 'I wanted to come and say hello but I thought I'd better test the ground first. What are the chances of me being thrown across three tables and kicked into next week?'

Kiki giggled. Nell's extraordinarily handsome younger brother, smiling and hovering behind her out of Jemima's field of vision, was breathing minty-warm breath into her ear. The sensation was ridiculously erotic.

'I don't know, but you're about to find out. Come on, sit down next to me.' She patted the chair. 'Look as if you know judo or something.'

Jemima had been speaking to a tearful Hilda Garnet, reassuring her that they would be able to manage without her and saying – with rather more honesty than Marcus – how much she would be missed. Poor Hilda, who had buoyed herself up with two port and lemons in order to break the tragic news to her beloved Jemima, had developed an almost instantaneous hangover and made her unsteady way back to the castle for aspirin and a hot drink.

'Don't hit me,' said Derry when Jemima reached their table.

Kiki, clutching his arm and almost setting fire to his sleeve with her cigarette, vigorously shook her head. 'No, don't hit him.'

'It wasn't my fault—' Derry, who had been about to protest that he hadn't been the organ-grinder, only the monkey, caught himself just in time. What an embarrassing thing to nearly say. He shut his mouth instead and exchanged a sideways glance with Kiki who promptly collapsed in fits of giggles again. This time her cigarette landed in his wineglass, sizzled for a moment and then died. She really was amazingly clumsy, Derry thought, but goodness, she had a brilliant laugh.

'It wasn't his fault,' Kiki loyally supplied, when she was able to speak again.

'What are you, his pet parrot?' Jemima smiled slightly as she tucked her dark-blue ruffled taffeta skirt beneath her and sat down. She had no intention of hitting Derry O'Driscoll; he was the sole reason she was here tonight. It was weird, not to mention embarrassing, but try as she might she hadn't been able to put him out of her mind.

'I must say, you're looking amazing tonight.' Derry gazed in admiration at the blue taffeta dress, its whaleboned bodice accentuating Jemima's narrow waist. Then he turned to Kiki, deliciously voluptuous in a crocus-yellow creation plunging almost to her waist. 'You both are.'

'Flatterer,' sighed Kiki as his dark eyes glittered and that irresistible dimple came and went in his cheek.

'Only when it's the truth. Look at that.' Derry nodded in the direction of the dance floor as Constance Carruthers, her mousy hair done up in a beehive, swept past on the arm of her long-suffering husband. 'Some people are just unflatterable. I mean, did you ever see *Jurassic Park*?'

Constance did indeed resemble the velociraptor, that chicken-like creature with turkey-sized legs. Jemima, entranced by Derry's observation and eager to show him she could be witty too, said, 'And what about those dreadful girls over there, the ones doing the cancan?' Gleefully she pointed them out. 'What *do* they look like? If they have to flash their knickers they could at least make sure they match their skirts.'

As the music came to an end, the two girls completed their party piece with wild yells and the splits. Around them, their appreciative audience whistled and applauded.

'That's Lottie and Trish. They're my sisters,' said Derry.

Chapter 50

'I'm having a lovely time.' Dreamily, Kiki rested her head against Marcus's chest as they danced to 'White Christmas'. Through the plastic windows in the sides of the marquee, the floodlighting outside illuminated the snowy landscape. She could never have relaxed like this had she still been caught up in the clutches of her towering crush on Marcus. The passing of it had come as such a tremendous relief.

'I don't think Jemima's having a lovely time,' said Marcus.

'But she's dancing with Derry.'

Marcus shook his head and smiled slightly. Having done his duty with Jemima, Derry was now dancing with Hetty Brewster. Jemima, not looking at all cheerful, was in turn being lugged around the floor by the bearded veggie-bore himself, Nolan Ferguson. She was probably at this moment being given a blow-by-blow account of how to make turnip and apple quiche.

'Oh dear.' Having followed his gaze, Kiki tried not to laugh. Then she said, 'And what about you? I thought Nell was going to be here tonight.'

She wasn't the only one. Marcus, who felt he'd been doing a good job of appearing unconcerned, felt the muscles in his jaw involuntarily tighten. Nell's self-imposed exile, which she had justified as a means of testing the strength of their feelings for each other – and which Marcus regarded as totally unnecessary, since he already knew exactly how he felt about Nell – had been due to end tonight. She was coming back, she had told Marcus only yesterday evening. She had made up her mind. She just hoped he wouldn't live to regret it.

But it was now eleven o'clock and Nell hadn't bloody turned up. He must have looked at his watch a million times, almost as often as he caught himself glancing across at the covered entrance to the marquee. Still no Nell, and no reply, either, when he had twice rung her on the mobile. Turning up three hours late for her own romantic reunion was permissible, but only just . . . and only if there was a damn good reason for the delay. Marcus only hoped she hadn't changed her mind altogether and buggered off to Australia instead.

'Mind if I join you?'

Hetty, swivelling round in her seat, gazed up at Alistair Munro. The girls had just gone off to the bar and she was temporarily alone at the table. Since her own wineglass was empty and he was holding a bottle of burgundy, she nodded and moved her velvet evening-bag out of the way.

'Do. Sit down. Oh thanks . . . just half a glass, please.'

Since he couldn't trust Clemency and Rachel not to come belting back before he had time to say his piece, Alistair came straight to the point.

'Look, I know we haven't exactly hit it off,' he began, then hesitated. 'Well . . . maybe that isn't an accurate way of putting it. Let's say we've had more than our fair share of false starts.'

Hetty, clearly not intending to make things easier for him – apparently she hadn't yet forgiven him for bawling her out on the phone about her wild, non-existent fling with Derry O'Driscoll – gave him that innocent, doe-eyed look of hers.

'Have we?'

Alistair lit a cigarette and took a long, measured drag. Only two weeks to go; Clemency had bullied him into making that most dreaded of New Year's resolutions and this time he was going to use nicotine patches. Not that anything could possibly be more of an incentive than his endlessly nagging daughter's digs and jibes . . .

'You know we have. And I think we need to put it behind us now.' He hoped he sounded suitably authoritative and in control. 'Hetty, I hear you and Rachel will be spending Christmas Day on your own. So will we be. It seems ridiculous, when the girls are such good friends, not to . . . um, well . . . pool our resources.'

Alistair was looking so smart in his dinner jacket and bow tie, thought Hetty. He was, without question, an attractive man. If it weren't for the single white shirt button sewn on to his white shirt-front with bright green thread he might not even have looked like a divorced man in need of a new wife.

'It does seem ridiculous, I suppose.' She nodded, then frowned, seemingly puzzled. 'What resources would we be pooling, then?'

'Ah, well. I'd be happy to buy the turkey if you'd like to cook it.' It had been Rachel's fault, for having boasted about her mother's brilliant home-made stuffings and perfect roast potatoes. Then, once the idea had come to him, the prospect of Hetty's cheerful company had become more inviting still. All of a sudden it had mattered terribly to Alistair that she should say yes. Christmas with Hetty and the girls would be fun.

'Actually, I'm sick of spending the whole of Christmas Day cooking and washing up whilst everyone else enjoys themselves.' Hetty's smile was apologetic. 'It's really kind of you to offer, but I'd sort of promised myself a day off this year.'

'How about an hotel?' Eagerly, Alistair stubbed out his cigarette. The idea had come to him in a flash. 'We could book a table for lunch. Somewhere really special, my treat. How about that?'

'It sounds perfect.' Hetty nodded, overjoyed. This was much more like it.

'That's settled then.' Unaccountably, Alistair felt as if he'd just won the pools. He had an overwhelming urge to touch Hetty's creamy, freckled shoulders and possibly to kiss each delicious pale freckle in turn. 'The girls will be thrilled. Now, how about a dance to celebrate?'

'How about another drink first?' said Hetty.

Much as Vanessa had done earlier, Jemima now sat alone and watched everyone else enjoying themselves. There was Nell's friend, Hetty Whatsername, laughing with Alistair Munro. There was the pretty blonde girl who worked in the castle gift shop, dancing happily with one of the actors who had been filming here the other week. From the back he looked quite like Timmy. Since she no longer allowed herself to even think of Timmy, Jemima looked determinedly away.

And there they were, Kiki and Derry, still bloody dancing
– no not dancing, *smooching* – and looking for all the world
as if they'd been superglued together all the way from neck to
knee.

It was too unfair, thought Jemima, hot tears of outrage
pricking the backs of her eyes. She'd learned her lesson, hadn't
she? Taken her punishment like a man? And now, just as she'd
decided to overlook the fact that Derry was the original nobody
from nowhere and fancy him anyway, he was snatched from
under her very nose by that shameless sex-starved rich-bitch,
Kiki Ross-Armitage. It was *bloody* unfair.

Derry was happy to have been snatched. He was enjoying himself immensely. Kiki was wonderful, a fabulous
combination of everything he liked in a girl; with those big
brown eyes of hers and those luscious scented curves she
reminded him of Hetty. At twenty-three, she was a perfect
two years older than himself. She had a sense of humour, the
glossiest hair ever and a terrific laugh. Not to mention a
helicopter . . .

'What are you doing for Christmas?' Kiki whispered as his
hands momentarily tightened around her waist. 'Come with
me to Zermatt. Our chalet's empty for the next fortnight.'

Derry looked regretful.

'I don't ski.'

Beneath the straight blond fringe, Kiki's eyes shone with
new resolve. She moved closer still.

'Who said anything about skiing?'

* * *

425

'Hi there!'

Startled out of her solitary gloom, Jemima gazed up as Nolan Ferguson materialized once more like a genie out of a bottle before her. His ruddy face was damp with perspiration from all his energetic dancing. Droplets of sweat glistened in his beard and the tails of his hand-dyed ivy-green cotton shirt had escaped from his crumpled beige trousers.

'Oh.' Jemima forced a smile. 'Hi.'

'Tell me to go away if I'm being a pain,' said Nolan, all in a rush, 'but I so enjoyed that dance with you earlier, I just wondered if you'd like to do it again? Sorry if I stepped on your toes before,' he added, blushing like a teenager, 'but I'll really try not to again, and you're such a jolly good dancer . . . well, oh dear . . . no, I don't suppose you'd be interested . . .' As he faltered, the blush deepened further still. Jemima realized that from a distance several of Nolan's friends were watching, nudging each other and waiting for him to publicly lose face.

Poor Nolan, he might be a bit dull, droning on and on as he did about his beloved green issues, and he certainly wasn't her type, but he was a kind man, thought Jemima. A nice man who, she knew, spent much of his spare time raising money for charity.

'I'd love another dance.' Rising from the table, Jemima held out her hand. The look of unalloyed delight on Nolan's face made her feel better at once.

Nolan led her shyly but with immense pride on to the dance floor. 'You must tell me as soon as you've had enough. Please don't feel obliged to keep going on my account . . . oh I say,' his eyes lit up as the music changed, 'how marvellous, my all-time favourite song. Unless you don't . . . ?' His eyes anxiously searched Jemima's face.

In reply, she smiled and gave his hand a reassuring squeeze. 'Mine too.'

Chapter 51

The last guests finally staggered into the night at two o'clock. Nell hadn't turned up and there had been no word from her. Feeling badly let down, exhausted with the effort of smiling all evening and pretending nothing was wrong, Marcus went straight to his room.

She was there in bed.

'I'm s-sorry,' said Nell, through chattering teeth. 'It's been a hell of a night. I just got here t-ten minutes ago . . .'

She was shivering. As he pulled back the sheets Marcus realized she was wearing at least five of his sweaters and three pairs of socks.

'M-me and my glamorous n-night clothes.' Nell half-smiled before tugging the blankets over her once more. 'I'll be OK in a b-bit when I've warmed up. If you could just pass me that mug of c-cocoa.'

Her nose and cheeks were still bright pink with the cold. When he passed her the steaming mug, he realized her hands were frozen. But she was here. She had come back. She hadn't bolted to Australia after all, though Marcus guessed the prospect of doing so would at this moment be a tempting one.

'What happened?'

'My car broke d-down on the M bloody 4.' Nell sighed, sipped her cocoa and lay back against the massed pillows. 'Not the best time for it, either. From the sound of it I was the AA's millionth caller of the night. Anyway, about three hours later the chap came to have a look. After half an hour of fiddling about, he managed to fix it. I got back into the car, belted on down here and forgot to stop for petrol at Membury Services.' She pulled a face. 'So you can guess what happened after that. Four miles outside Sherringham I ran out of sodding petrol.'

The narrow road which ran between Sherringham and Kilburton was long and lonely.

'You mean you walked here,' said Marcus flatly, glancing down at the sodden shoes lying on the floor beside the bed. At a rough guess she had covered five miles through the snow in those ludicrously flimsy high heels. 'Why the hell didn't you phone?'

At least Nell's teeth had stopped chattering. She looked shamefaced. 'The batteries went dead in the mobile. The phone box at the Combe Lane crossroads was out of order. Like I said, it was just one of those nights.'

Marcus looked at her.

'You're here now.'

She smiled. 'Not quite the romantic reunion I'd planned.'

'I told you, you're a hopeless fraud.' Marcus shook his head. 'You'll never believe what's been going on here tonight – and how much of it did you predict? Nothing.'

'Don't be cruel,' Nell protested. 'I'm too cold to make predictions. I'm definitely too cold to be made fun of.'

She was back. He was so very glad she was back.

'In that case, I'd better warm you up.'

'Mmm, nice,' sighed Nell when he had removed his clothes,

climbed into bed and taken her in his arms. Even through the five sweaters she could feel the heat of his body against hers. She squirmed with pleasure as one hand snaked its way between the fifth sweater and her own shivering ribcage.

'I can do much better than that.' Marcus kissed her, slowly and thoroughly. He had waited far too long for this to want to hurry things along now.

'I think I'm beginning to warm up,' Nell gasped, minutes later. Wriggling into a sitting position she peeled off a couple of layers. 'Can you check under the bed?'

Marcus raised an eyebrow. 'For what?'

'Meg Tarrant.' Nell grinned. 'I only just managed to stop her chaperoning me down here tonight. She's determined not to miss out on any more scoops.'

'Well she definitely isn't getting this one.'

'All the same,' Nell's voice grew muffled as he moved on top of her, 'better check.'

Nell was the first to wake the next morning, stirred into consciousness by bright sunlight streaming through the open curtains and by the overwhelming realization that her life was on the brink of changing for good. Although changing, she thought dazedly, was hardly the word for it. Transformed beyond all recognition, more like.

Marcus lay asleep next to her, his arms flung out and the sheets tangled around his waist. With those broad brown shoulders and that wonderfully flat stomach he looked irresistible. Nell smiled to herself, recalling her first less-than-favourable impressions of him all those years ago when he had been a cocky sixteen-year-old, too spoiled by half and too self-assured for his own good.

She had made the right decision, Nell knew that, but she knew too she had been right to make that retreat to London. An almost seamless transition from Ben to Marcus would have felt wrong. It wasn't like flicking an electric switch or buying a new budgie when the old one dies. She had desperately needed the break, and enough time to grieve for the loss of her first love and to come to terms with her new life.

Marcus half-opened his eyes. His bare foot moved against Nell's ankle.

'You're wearing socks,' he groaned. 'We made passionate love and all the time you kept your socks on. I thought only men did that.'

'Actually, they're your socks.' Happily, Nell removed them and waved them in the air like flags. 'Hmm, cashmere and silk,' she teased. 'So this is how the other half keep their feet warm.'

'Speaking of the other half,' Marcus drawled, 'there's something I forgot to ask you last night.'

He hadn't forgotten at all.

Hot cocoa, good sex and physical exhaustion had simply got to Nell before he had had a chance to broach the subject. Within seconds she had fallen asleep in his arms.

'Oh God.' Nell pulled a face. 'You don't want to know if I was a virgin.'

Marcus grinned, rolled sideways and propped himself up, his head resting on his cupped hand.

'I'm talking about marriage. We are getting married, aren't

we? I mean, when you said you were coming back I kind of assumed the answer was yes . . .'

'If that's a proposal,' Nell declared, 'it stinks. You're supposed to go down on bended knee, not up on one elbow.'

'And have you take the mick out of me?' Marcus looked amused. 'Do you seriously think I'd take that kind of risk? Say yes first, *then* maybe I'll ask nicely.'

Nell thought for a moment. She would become Nell, Countess of Kilburton. Lady Nell sounded ludicrous, but then so did Lady Petronella. She really should have been christened something more suitable like Anne or Jane. Or Daphne.

'Well?' Marcus demanded.

'Oh.' Nell looked surprised. 'Yes.'

'About bloody time too.'

She kissed him. 'Mrs Garnet isn't going to like it.'

'And if you could really tell people's fortunes, you'd have known she was eloping to Spain with an onion seller called Pedro.'

Nell giggled. 'I knew that.'

'Look, this whole fortune-telling thing.' Marcus felt he had to say it. 'It's harmless, I know. It's a bit of fun, and I really don't mind you carrying on with it . . . as long as you don't expect me to believe in any of your silly predictions . . .'

'Gosh, thanks.' Nell gazed at him, her dark eyes wide. 'But? Do I foresee a but?'

He sighed. 'But don't do it for money after we're married, OK? Do it for nothing by all means, but please don't charge people money.'

Now that Ben was dead, Nell no longer needed the money anyway. 'But I can't do it for nothing.' She shook her head. 'People wouldn't believe what I told them . . . they only take notice if they've paid to hear it.'

'Donate what they give you to charity, then. The NSPCC or something.'

'I'll donate half of it,' Nell said firmly. 'To Rowan House. The other half I'll keep, because it's my job and I'm good at it. Don't be so stuffy, Marcus. Fortune-telling is what I *do*.'

He sighed. In one way she was right; a little interior design business would have been perfectly socially acceptable. It was just that as far as he was concerned, fortune-telling was out and out . . .

'Crap?' Nell smiled, tilting her head to one side. 'OK, get dressed. You're coming with me.'

'Where?'

'Don't ask questions, just do it.' She wrenched the blankets off the bed. 'There's something I want you to see.'

When they were halfway down the drive, Nell glanced back at the castle. Its ancient battlements were iced with snow. With the sun blazing down out of a cornflower-blue sky, the weather owed more to Austria than Gloucestershire. The snow, blue-white and glistening, clung to every branch of the low hanging, leafless chestnut trees above their heads. She shivered with pleasure as Marcus slid his arm around her waist and dropped a kiss on her forehead.

'You're freezing. And whatever will the neighbours say?' he mocked as they approached the gatehouse. The High Street, with its higgledy-piggledy Cotswold stone cottages and tiny, carefully tended front gardens, stretched ahead of them. Nell, wearing what she had driven down in last night for the party, was pretty much exposed to the elements in a black velvet jacket, short, peacock-blue sequinned dress, sheer black stockings and the still-soggy, high-heeled shoes in which she had trudged through almost five miles of snow.

'The neighbours can say what they like.' She smiled and took his arm. They would walk down the sunny, snow covered High Street together. There was no longer any need to hide.

'Where are you taking me anyway?'

'We've been to your place,' Nell said cheerfully. 'Now we're going to mine.'

Marcus groaned. 'Do I have to ask your mother's permission to marry you?'

'It's OK, she's away. Remember Archie Halifax, the chap who tried to pick up the fifty-pence piece?' She grinned. 'The one you might have ended up marrying if I hadn't come along and taken his place?'

'I remember,' said Marcus. As if he could ever forget.

'Well, his back's better now.' Pushing open the gate, Nell led the way up to the front door of The Pink House. 'And he's developed a bit of a crush on Mum. She rang on Wednesday to tell me he was whisking her off to Rome.'

Good Lord. Archie Halifax. The power of the O'Driscoll women, Marcus decided, was almost uncanny.

Inside, the house was warm.

'*Now* where are we going?' Marcus demanded as Nell ran two at a time up the stairs. Following her at a more leisurely pace, he saw her open a cupboard, take out a stepladder and place it beneath the hatch leading up into the loft.

Before he could even begin to imagine what she was up to, Nell was balancing on the top step, pushing the hatch open. She was still wearing those ridiculously impractical high heels. Her long legs, though, in their sheer dark stockings, looked wonderful. Marcus smiled. To think he'd be marrying those legs.

Nell lifted herself up into the loft. As her feet disappeared she shouted, 'Come on, you too.'

At that moment Marcus heard a scuffling sound coming from one of the bedrooms further along the landing.

'Who's up there?' It was Derry's voice. 'If that's Father Christmas trying to climb down the chimney, bugger off, you silly old fool. You're a week early.'

'Ho ho ho,' said Marcus, as the bedroom door opened. Derry, his long hair tousled, his nakedness semi-concealed by an emerald-green bath towel, appeared in the doorway rubbing his eyes.

'Oh hi, it's you.' He grinned when he saw Marcus, then looked at the stepladder. 'What's going on?'

'Your sister.' Marcus shrugged. 'Don't ask.'

'Who is it?' Kiki, peering round Derry's shoulder, put her hand over her mouth when she saw Marcus. Slightly more formally dressed than Derry, she was wearing a blue-and-white striped duvet, a fair amount of jewellery and the remains of last night's make-up. The hand, however, couldn't conceal the blissful expression on her face.

Derry said, 'Santa. Go on, tell him what you'd most like for Christmas.'

The smug grin widened. Kiki pinched his thin brown arm.

'I've already had my present, thanks. Well, the first instalment anyway.'

Nell's voice drifted down from the roof space.

'Marcus, where are you?'

He winked at Kiki.

'Better get back to bed.'

She looked puzzled. 'I'm glad Nell's back, but whatever is she doing up in the loft?'

Marcus sighed. 'I suppose I'd better go and find out.'

Nell was waiting impatiently for him. Her sequinned dress glittered like the sea in the dim light and there was a long grey cobweb in her hair. Dust had settled in a thick layer over the haphazard piles of junk that had been stored up here out of the way. From the look of it, no one had ventured up into the loft for years.

Marcus wasn't surprised. Boxes of ancient magazines jostled with laundry baskets, bundles of blankets, tatty lampshades, children's toys and an open suitcase stuffed with shoes.

Beside him, Nell touched his arm.

'That trunk over there, behind those picture frames. How much dust do you suppose it's covered in?'

Marcus decided to humour her; she had clearly gone mad.

'About a hundred years' worth?'

She nodded, satisfied. 'Well, ten years. At least you can see it's been left undisturbed.'

Completely mad, he amended.

'Right.'

'So go on, open it.' Nell smiled at the expression on his face as at that moment a great hairy spider scuttled across the lid of the trunk. Marcus waited until it had disappeared from sight, before bending down. He turned the key and lifted the lid.

There, nestling amid piles of old school books, lay the crimson velvet scarf he remembered so well, and which he had last seen tied around the aerial of his very first car, the infamous Mini. Nell had liberated it and punished him with a pint of milk tipped over the back seat, unaware that by then the car no longer belonged to him anyway.

The scarf looked dreadful – tatty and frayed at the edges and with its sequins dulled with age – but Marcus remembered how precious it had been to Nell, handed down to her as it had been by her beloved grandmother.

'Don't worry, it wasn't really an heirloom.' Her dark eyes glowed with mischief. 'I bought it in a jumble sale. It isn't why you're up here, either.'

Marcus removed the terrifying cobweb from Nell's hair. He didn't want its former owner to track it down and resume residence.

'OK, get to the point.'

But Nell was already rummaging through the books, searching for the one she needed to prove her point. Finally she found it.

'Your diary?'

'This is when I was fifteen. Look.' She pointed to the Easter holidays. 'That was when you tried to run me over. Now July . . . and here's when you met me at the bus stop on the last day of term.'

'Marcus Kilburton thinks he's so great,' Marcus read aloud, his mouth curling with amusement at the impatient way her handwriting splashed across the page. 'What a cretin he is – I so wanted to whack him round the head with my satchel. He thinks he owns the world and I hate him.'

He broke into a grin. 'Ah well, anyone can make a mistake.'

'Now turn the page,' said Nell.

'Something terrible happened this morning,' he read. 'Had one of those dreams, a really strong one, that I'm going to end up marrying Marcus Kilburton. Yuk, definitely don't want this one to come true.'

'There you are,' Nell said lightly, 'proof at last.'

Marcus shook his head. He was impressed. Maybe there really was something in this business after all.

'It was a premonition.' He shivered slightly at the thought of it. She had actually experienced a genuine premonition. 'This is amazing – we've got to show this diary to someone . . .'

Nell shook her head. As she leaned forward and pressed her lips to his, she took the diary from his hands and dropped it back into the trunk.

'You're impressed. That's all that matters to me. Come on, we'll leave it up here. It's more romantic this way.'

'I still can't get over it,' said Marcus. 'You knew. You really *knew*.'

Nell smiled, said nothing and thanked her lucky stars he hadn't turned to the next page. She couldn't remember word for word what she had written, but it went something like: 'Another dream, and much better news this time. Forget Marcus Kilburton (hooray!) – I'm going to marry Tom Cruise instead.'

Staying at Daisy's

Jill Mansell

Daisy MacLean runs the country house hotel owned by her flamboyant father, Hector. When she hears who's about to get married there, she isn't worried at all – her friend Tara absolutely promises there won't be any trouble between her and ex-boyfriend Dominic, whom she hasn't seen for years. But Daisy *should* have been worried. Dominic has other ideas. And seeing Tara again sets in motion a chaotic train of events with far-reaching consequences for all concerned.

While Daisy spends the ensuing months doing battle with Dev Tyzack (Dominic's so-called best man), Tara battles with her conscience. Meanwhile, Hector's getting up to all sorts with . . . well, that's the village's best kept secret. And then Barney turns up, with a little something belonging to the husband Daisy's been doing her best to forget.

That's the thing about hotels, you never know who you're going to meet. Or whether they're going to stay . . .

Acclaim for Jill Mansell's novels:

'A jaunty summer read' *Daily Mail*

'An exciting read about love, friendship and sweet revenge – fabulously fun' *Home & Life*

'Slick, sexy, funny stories' *Daily Telegraph*

0 7472 6487 2

headline

Perfect Timing

Jill Mansell

Poppy Dunbar is out on her hen night when she meets Tom Kennedy. With his dark eyes and quirky smile, he could lure any girl off the straight and narrow, but what really draws Poppy to him is the feeling that she's known him all her life. She can't go through with the meeting they arrange – but she can't go through with her wedding either.

Suddenly notorious as 'The Girl Who Jilted Rob McBride', Poppy moves to London. Soon she's installed in the bohemian household of Caspar French, a ravishingly good-looking young artist with a reputation for breaking hearts. But even in her colourful new home, Poppy can't get Tom off her mind. Until she's tracked him down, she'll never know if their meeting was destiny – or if the future holds something entirely different for her . . .

Praise for Jill Mansell:

'Fabulous fun . . . to read it is to devour it' *Company*

'A riotous romp' *Prime*

'A jaunty summer read' *Daily Mail*

'Sexy and mischievous' *Today*

'Frothy fun' *Bella*

0 7472 5444 3

headline

Now you can buy any of these other bestselling books by **Jill Mansell** from your bookshop or *direct from her publisher*.

FREE P&P AND UK DELIVERY
(Overseas and Ireland £3.50 per book)

Solo	£5.99
Staying at Daisy's	£5.99
Fast Friends	£6.99
Millie's Fling	£5.99
Sheer Mischief	£6.99
Good At Games	£6.99
Miranda's Big Mistake	£6.99
Head Over Heels	£6.99
Mixed Doubles	£6.99
Perfect Timing	£6.99

TO ORDER SIMPLY CALL THIS NUMBER

01235 400 414

or visit our website: www.madaboutbooks.com

Prices and availability subject to change without notice.